ASCENSION
OF THE
PHOENIX

ALSO BY JESSICA PIRO

ASCENSION
OF THE
PHOENIX

Book One in The Phoenix Trilogy

JESSICA PIRO

ASCENSION OF THE PHOENIX
Copyright © 2020 by Jessica Piro

www.jessicapiro.com

Cover Designer: Faera Lane

ISBN: 979-8677291982

For Ms. Sandy Lowintritt,
who has always asked about when this book would come
out.
Well, here it is.

Like the mighty phoenix,
Once again I rise from the flames set to destroy me & take
flight.
I am
Stronger
Glorious
Powerful
Victorious.
-Kirsti A. Dyer-

I.

Even though this murderer had butchered two families, he wasn't the sadistic Bryan Foster.

Metal trash cans crashed to the ground, scattering their contents as the suspect barreled through. Leila Wells smirked at the obstacle—his fourth attempt at slowing her and David Neal, Jr., her partner, down. The two detectives vaulted over the garbage cans and continued their pursuit.

Since he bolted at the sight of them at his apartment, the chase had spanned two blocks, snaking through alleyways—alleyways she knew like the back of her hand. David, behind her, enjoyed the chase like a hound after a scared rabbit.

His adrenaline, Leila thought.

Up ahead, the alleyway branched into two separate paths. Leila ran over the map in her head—eventually, both pathways crossed again. Knowing David would likely guess at her plan, she turned down the right one.

"Move!" she ordered the two men standing in the middle of the alley. They flattened against the walls of the lane. She charged through and kept running.

She kept track of her location relative to the others'. On the map in her head, two red dots traveled down paths, and both lights raced toward the crossroads. Since the suspect and David would be close to reaching it, Leila pumped her arms harder.

Near the intersection of their alleys, pounding footfalls and panting grew louder. By the sounds of his running, the suspect neared her exit. She lunged.

Within seconds, Leila collided with the running man—knocking him off his feet—and sent them both to the ground.

Only stunned for a second, the criminal scrambled back to his feet. It was enough. Leila quickly jumped up and kicked the man across his face, sending him cartwheeling.

Leila landed into the Tiger stance of her Five-Animals Kung Fu, ready for his next attempt to evade capture. Cradling his nose, the man rolled in pain, moaning. Not many could take a kick to the face and keep going, so maybe she should've dealt a lesser blow.

David slowed to a jog as he met them. "I had him," he said, breathless.

She straightened and walked over to the downed man. "Sure, you did." She threw handcuffs on the man's wrists as she Mirandized him.

"And now you won't let me arrest him?"

Leila smiled. "I got him; he's my collar." She led him back the way they came to their unmarked car. David sighed behind her but followed.

THE STATION'S LOCKER ROOM WITH its drab navy blue and gray color scheme and metal lockers dating back to the eighties wasn't aesthetically pleasing, but it did provide Leila some isolation. David dealt with the apprehended criminal—who, courtesy of her boot, sported a broken nose—so she had time to herself.

After redoing her black hair into a smoother ponytail, she waited a moment to see if anyone would come in, then she pulled a thin notebook out from under a folded NYPD hoodie.

Her private case notes. Flipping it to the middle page, the written numbers one to twelve were marked through while thirteen was untouched... until tomorrow began. She heaved as her hazel eyes traveled up to the number at the top: 14.

Thirteen days since 12 became 14. Almost two weeks since Bryan Foster killed Detectives Penny Uehl and Jamie Washington, and no hint of that killer resurfacing.

Paper crinkled as Leila's hands clenched. She shut her eyes against the memory, but the images, sounds, and smells came anyway.

Burnt flesh. Vacant eyes staring at the equally dead clocks Foster hung around the room, each frozen on either the time of her kidnapping or her time of death. Uehl's mouth agape in a scream. A sudden gunshot; Washington's body thudding onto the tile floor. Fresh, dark blood pooling around his head. Gunpowder, body odor, the sickeningly sweet smell of Washington's brain matter...

Leila took in a sharp breath to prevent from getting sick again. She had visited many murder scenes, but the smell that accompanied headshots was the worst.

Like most times, her frustration and disgust turned into anger, which became stored by internal heat. Leila looked into the mirror, seeing the darkness broiling within. Her face remained calm only because those emotions were now muted. That dark side emerged whenever she needed it—absorbing the horrors of her job and powering her through—putting her rage in reserve.

Saving it to release on Foster.

That man. With the way he left his horrendous killings, it remained a mystery how he continued to elude capture. Foster played on psychology. No one escaped him; no one survived. The victims were chosen because of how their deaths would affect others.

It wasn't how he killed his victims, where he put them, or how many he murdered, but the way he got under the skin. Every kill he made personal. He'd snatch a cop, a cop's family, or someone well-known in the community, and then he'd lead Leila and her squad on a goose-chase as he tortured his victim—or victims. He'd make the pursuers think they were almost there—they'd have rescue right at their fingertips—only to find another trail, or if they bored him, a body.

All the people he had killed or families and communities he had ruined had been despicable but killing Penny Uehl and causing Jamie Washington's suicide will be his downfall. For it involved Leila.

She'd show him what a mistake it was involving her. She would catch Bryan Foster—the most-wanted person in the States. It would be known nationwide—perhaps internationally—that no criminal could escape Leila Wells.

"What was that today?"

Leila jumped, not hearing the door open. She stashed her notebook back under the hoodie and shut her locker. If someone discovered her private notes, she'd be taken off any future Foster cases. She smiled innocently at David leaning against the doorway. "What was what?"

"Tackling my criminal."

"That's part of my job—stopping felons. Besides, you were too slow."

The brown-eyed, brown-haired man walked in and grabbed her around the waist. "I would've gotten him."

"In thirty minutes, if I hadn't taken that shortcut," Leila said.

Leila wouldn't be one of the 'Super Cops' or share the record of only one lost criminal—Bryan Foster—if not for her partner, David Neal, Jr. With a fierce drive and constant optimism, he was the most logical and levelheaded of the duo.

Well… mostly. He never hesitated in throwing himself toward danger to save an innocent, but he'd still be cautious.

When their partnership began turning romantic five years ago, and they proved to the captain that they could continue working together, he allowed them to date and keep their positions.

"About that." He poked her in the head as he spoke. "I wish you would let me into that head of yours sometimes."

She scowled. "You wouldn't like what you found, but why? You figured out what I was doing."

"I *guessed*," he corrected.

"You've been around me too long to be surprised at anything I do."

"That other side of you *is* a surprise; sometimes I can't tell what you're going to do," he said.

"I'm not stressed out or—" she began.

"Pissed off," he added.

Leila rolled her eyes. Three weeks ago in her apartment, he mentioned her temper wasn't healthy for her, and she lost it. His backing away empowered her dark side. "I'm in control now."

"Making sure. I don't want to see you change like that again. If we were in the kitchen, you might've stuck a knife in me. That *Psycho* killing-music probably would've played in the background."

"I scared you?"

"You *worried* me," David corrected. He nipped her ear. "You can't intimidate me."

She squirmed out of his arms and cut her eyes at him. "I can't?" she challenged.

He grinned with that crooked, charming smile. "Nope. I'm bulletproof. I pretend I'm worried to guilt trip you and pull out your nurturing side."

Leila smiled—she could always rely on his snarky attitude to lighten her spirits. "You're terrible."

"But you're smiling."

She matched his snark. "Only because you expected me to, and I pity you."

He pretended to wince. "Ouch. I guess I haven't restrained that temper enough. You still burn me."

Leila hit him in the stomach—not hard. He recoiled, and she smiled. "You can't restrain fire."

Heath Fonda, the third of their squad, poked his head in. He stood slightly taller than her and David with short-cropped blond hair. His love of bench pressing gave his big frame enormous arms and chest. "Hey, lovebirds, stop hitting each other, and come on. The captain has called all of us."

That didn't bode well.

She followed Heath out of the locker room, David behind her.

The precinct buzzed like a beehive in constant movement and noise. Phones rang, the sound lost among the noise of officers speaking to victims, answering calls, and other personnel. People snaked through the narrow aisles between the desks, loaded with papers or coffee cups in hand. Other officers escorted criminals to and from the interrogation room. If the hive ever grew silent, David would be the first of the bees to die from lack of busyness.

In a somber but eager line—since this kind of meeting only occurred when something major happened—each stepped into his office. The black decal on the door reading **Captain Colin Sullivan** wasn't needed. Because of the 5th Precinct's nearly flawless incarceration record, all in New York City knew the name of the police captain. Once they were in, David shut the door behind him.

DeMarcus Dixon—the fourth of their squad—with skin as dark as tar and the shortest of the four, sat before the captain's heavy desk. Fast and stout as an NFL Running Back, he could plow a criminal over—he shared their cockiness, too.

Completely bald, Captain Sullivan carried a little extra weight around his middle. He looked older than a man in his early forties. Only ten years separated him from Leila, and she was thirty-two.

DeMarcus turned to greet them with a smile. "So, how long did it take the Super Cops to catch our butcher?"

"Nine minutes and fifty-two seconds," David boasted.

"Ha!" DeMarcus turned on Heath. "My guess was closer! You owe me five bucks."

David looked at the blond man. "What did you guess?"

"About fifteen minutes. D said ten," Heath said.

"Such faith you have in us."

Leila got straight to business. "What's happened, Captain?"

Captain Sullivan had a smile on his lips as the men joked around as usual, but now the smile dropped and his eyes hardened, becoming serious—all humor gone. "Bryan Foster is back."

She jolted still like electricity had shot down her spine. Silence enveloped the room. Because she had just been thinking about Foster, fate *must* be on her side. This was Leila's chance to finally get him.

David grabbing her hand pulled her back to the present, out of her dreams of catching Foster and the praise she would receive.

"Where?" Heath asked.

The captain shook his head. "He's only just been sighted. When we get an exact location, you four will be the first ones notified."

His blue eyes encompassed Leila and David both. "But we won't lose our heads over this, right? Do not make this case a personal vendetta."

David saluted to smooth over the tension. "Sir, yes, sir! Keep our heads attached at all times!"

He shook his head ruefully. "Until then, business carries on like usual," the captain concluded. "Lei. David. I need to speak with you."

"Busted," DeMarcus whispered as he and Heath headed out of the room.

After they left, the captain ran a hand down his face as he sighed—a habit of his. His blue eyes were strained from a sleepless night.

"I know getting Foster means more to you two than Heath or D… which is why I'm ordering you to take the rest of the evening and tomorrow off."

Leila frowned. The captain revealed that Foster roamed the streets again—the opportunity she'd been waiting weeks for—and he now forced a break? And he refrained from looking at her or David.

David picked up on it too. "Something's bothering you…"

A quick smile ghosted his lips. "Damn cops, I can't keep anything from you."

"We *are* the best for a reason," Leila said.

"I know." The captain sighed heavily and ran a hand down his face again. "Things aren't getting any better from here on out. I don't know what or how, but it starts next week. Call it detective's instinct."

She needed an elaboration, but David speaking took her chance. "Freedom for an evening and two days… What do I do with it?"

"Something that keeps you away from here. I'll see you two Monday. Enjoy your weekend."

To satisfy him, they hurried out of his office to do as he said. Leila tried to pay attention to David's suggestions for their weekend, but her mind lay elsewhere.

No matter what reason lay behind the captain's order, Bryan Foster was close, and she wouldn't let him escape this time.

II.

Softly lit and not reeking of cigarettes or beer, *Mosely's* was more of a lounge than a bar, with recessed lights above the bar and seating a few men. Antique light fixtures—advertising past and present alcoholic drinks—hung over the four pool tables. A raspy voice sang out of the antique jukebox near the pool tables. Small tables sat to the right of the bar; Leila and David spotted their unoccupied table and headed for it.

The ballerina waitress saw their entrance and glided toward them, acknowledging them by name. After writing down their usual order, she danced back to the bar and later to the kitchen, handing the chef their order.

David began, "So, I assume you're going to Hyun's gym tomorrow..."

"Of course," she stated. "Since I can't take my anger out on Foster, dummies and punching bags will get it."

He nodded in approval. "Safer for everyone that you do. Then what?"

"Might stay at Hyun's all day."

He shook his head. "You're as bad as an exercise junkie."

"Am not. They work out to stay in shape; I work out because it's relaxing."

The waitress returned with two long necks. "Your Name Night is Wednesday, David."

Leila smiled. "Sounds like we'll be back."

He turned to the waitress. "That's also my birthday. Could I get two deals?"

She laughed. "I think we can arrange it."

"Next week it is, then."

"I'll be looking." She sashayed to a table that had just become occupied by a couple.

Leila reached for her cold Budweiser. "Have any ideas on what you'll do?"

David took a long drink from his. "No, but your idea of hitting the gym sounds pretty good. I'll go about ten, though."

"You and your sleep."

He smiled. "At least it's not like you and me."

"It would be if I wasn't in the picture."

"You're always in the picture. I can't get away from you; you're even in my dreams."

She would've thrown a utensil at him for the cheesy statement if it wasn't so sweet he had said so.

"I also need to go to keep up with you," he said.

"Keep up with me?"

He nodded as he took a drink. "You're a better fighter than me and that's embarrassing."

"You're good in your own way."

"Oh, please! You and Hyun probably laugh at me."

"We do not." She couldn't keep a straight face, recalling times when she suggested Hyun spar with David, and he wouldn't for not wanting to hurt him.

David caught it. "Ha! See? You two make fun of me because I don't use a great martial arts technique."

"That's not it."

"What is it, then?"

Her lips twisted, but she gave in. "Hyun doesn't want to hurt you."

"Hurt me? He's the one that had his femur broken and couldn't hold a kick on it for a year and a half!"

JESSICA PIRO

She kept her eyes down on her finger rubbing the perspiration on her beer bottle, embarrassed about the rest of her confession. "And I'm jealous of you, and you know that's dangerous."

Her honesty threw him. He took a moment to regain his voice. "Of... me? How? You're the Five-Animals Kung Fu master and I... fight."

"I only have one set of techniques to rely on, you have your own style; you can change if things get too pressured. I have nothing else to fall back on."

David didn't reply for the longest, stunned at her confession. He reached across the table and took her hands, tugging them to make her look at him. "You don't need a safety net; you have so much confidence in yourself. I'm a coward reverting to different methods to win."

"I see that as being arrogant and weak."

"That other side sees it as strength. There's a constant dueling inside you, and when you find balance by losing yourself in your techniques and fight not with anger, you become so powerful nothing can get to you. I wish you could see that."

"But that anger can distract me," Leila stated.

"No, not you; it gets to your dark side, and when you give it too much reign, only then will you lose focus.

"I admire you, Lei: your strength, serenity, and control in fighting. And you apply that to your daily life, which if you hadn't motivated me all these years to follow you, we—along with the precinct—would've cracked already. You don't realize how much influence you have on everyone you meet. No one can turn away from your fire."

His words were comforting, but Leila couldn't believe him unless someone who didn't know her said the same. "How did you become a fortune cookie?"

David collapsed into laughter, almost coming to tears. "Are you saying I've been eating too much Chinese?"

"If that's the reason."

The return of the waitress with their medium-rare steaks and loaded baked potatoes quieted his laughter to pockets of chuckles. Conversation stopped as they savored their meal.

Once finished, the detectives lounged in the peaceful atmosphere of the bar. The silence felt odd instead of the usual clamor of the police station. Leila appreciated it, but David couldn't stand the stillness.

"Let's play a game or two." He pulled Leila up, and they headed to one of the vacant pool tables.

After setting the table and playing Rock, Paper, Scissors to see who would break, Leila sent the cue ball speeding off down the green velvet to strike the multicolored balls, sending them in different directions; two striped balls dropped into opposite pockets.

Leila moved to another spot and sighted. "I wish the captain would have explained his feeling he has about next week. Now he's making me paranoid. Something *must* happen now," she said as she sent another striped ball down into a pocket.

"Don't worry about it. You've never had a conscience—"

She turned on him. "I don't have a conscience?"

He raised his hands in defense. "—that made you worry about the danger you know we'll be in. And the captain worries about everything we do."

Appeased at him finishing his statement, she sighted down the cue ball. "But that's what bothers me: he's never told us before; he's always kept his worry from us." The ball she shot stopped short of the pocket.

"There's nothing to worry about." He sent a solid ball into a pocket. Walking around to a new position, David sighted and shot another into a pocket. "No need in worrying about your future; it will happen whether or not you like it. You can't change your fate."

Leila stared at him. He shot again but missed. "Your go, Lei." David looked up when she didn't move. "What?"

"Nothing," she answered as she walked around the pool table. "You've been talking deeply lately, and it's more than just getting too many fortune cookies. I'm wondering what's brought on this change..." She eyed him.

"I guess you've worn off on me these last five years."

"About time."

Leila leaned down on the table and aimed. As she pulled the stick back to hit the cue ball, David tapped it and sent it hitting the ball at an angle. The cue ball missed its target. She scoffed in disbelief as she straightened to face him. "You cheat!"

He skirted around her just in case she swung the pool stick. "You're wiping the floor with me; I have to preserve my dignity somehow."

When he leaned down to aim, he watched her, expecting retaliation. She leaned against her pool stick and waved him on. His gaze lingered on her rueful grin—full of mistrust—but David *was* on the opposite end, so she couldn't reach him. He looked down to hit the billiards.

As his stick hit the cue ball, Leila bumped into the table, making the balls shift. Even though the white ball hit its desired target, it bounced off the corner guarding the pocket. Now he frowned at her.

"You started it."

David laid his pool stick on the table as he headed to her. "No, no. You deserved it; I only returned the favor," she said as his advancement had her backing away. Leila pulled the pool stick up to defend herself. "You back up."

Stumbling back into another pool table, David seized the moment of her defenses falling to pin her to the table, laughing. "I did it because you need to let me catch up. You did it because you don't like losing."

"I have good sportsmanship; I don't mind losing. What do you call what you're doing?"

He grinned. "Winning."

"I call it cheating."

He suddenly bent closer to her, lips brushing against hers, his breath heating her face. But he never kissed her, even pulling back when she lifted to catch his lips. They instead moved to her neck, kissing his way down.

She caught on. "Is this bribery?"

"Only if it works," he whispered into her ear. His lips trailed back down her neck.

With immense effort, she pushed him off. Her denial surprised him. She got off the table and supported herself with the pool stick to hide how weak he had made her legs. "That's not fair."

David smirked. "Will it work?"

"Nope; you'll have to do better." She returned to their table to make her shot.

He scoffed. "I *can*."

Pulling her around, David's lips attached to hers with no teasing or laughing this time. His lips curved into a smile against hers—a kiss of victory. He pulled away with that crooked grin, knowing he had won.

"Cheater," she said, breathlessly.

David chuckled. "How about we call that game a tie and start a new one?"

"No more cheating."

A smile lightened his voice, "Let me win." He gave her a quick kiss before pulling away. "I'm breaking."

III.

Even though she planned to release her frustration at Foster *still* eluding justice, Leila looked forward to seeing her lifelong friend. She parked at the brick building with large windows allowing a view into the lobby. The sign above the door had a man wearing a Taekwondo uniform in a kick with the name, **Hyun's Gym**.

Upon entering, trophies and pictures of Hyun winning at tournaments and students as winners with their mentor proud beside them filled trophy cases or adorned shelves. Bamboo grew in pots in every corner of the room, and shoji doors separated the lobby from the actual gym. Hyun had taken her advice on sprucing up the place.

Gentle music flowed from a guan and she followed it to the secretary behind the desk, playing the reed flute. The Chinese immigrant knew English well, so Leila pushed her friend to hire her. Hyun and Nuan confirmed their chemistry by going to movies or restaurants; now, they were a couple.

Leila watched her play the small instrument, wishing she had musical talent. "Nuan," she said when the song faded.

The music halted as she looked up, startled. Surprise smoothed her face.

"Leila! What a treat!" She came around and hugged her. Nuan Hataye was a foreign jewel: a lovely woman inches shorter than Leila, and her midnight hair cut in a bob with pieces sticking out everywhere—a beautiful mess. Nothing like her shy and quiet personality.

She stepped back, holding the woman by the arms. "Where's Hyun?"

Nuan nodded toward the shoji doors. "He's setting everything up for his students."

With a final hug, Leila walked over to the doors, slid one open, and slipped into the large gym.

More shoji doors blocked off the area to her right—where she'd head as soon as she found Hyun. The Taekwondo practice area with Tatami flooring for protection took up the left side, and bleachers placed against the wall closest to her were for the parents who came to watch their children.

A man kneeling at the end of the floor arranged Taekwondo equipment and padding: wearing a white dobok, and a black belt tied around his waist. Red padding wrapped around bare feet, and his black hair pulled back into a ponytail as usual.

"I like what you've done with the place; it's actually inviting now," Leila said.

His head rose in recognition. "I haven't heard that voice in a while." Looking over his shoulder, a warm smile broke out on his face. The smile was one that spread, impossible for another not to share in the warmth.

Hyun-Ki Myung was a handsome man; the Korean genetics showed in narrow eyes, dark hair, and golden-beige skin. An excellent practitioner of martial arts, he now taught children since his last championship fight broke his leg so severely that it left him with a limp. They treated each other as siblings; friendly rivalry pushed each to advance their martial arts and found comfort in each other not found anywhere else.

He rose to his six-foot-two height and moved toward her, the limp disrupting his smooth walk. "Your return date has long expired. I thought you had moved on to bigger things."

"You know time isn't a luxury," she said.

"I'm not worth your time anymore?"

"Be happy I'm here." She ducked into his chest for a long hug. "The captain forced a mandatory break, and I thought about you."

"I'm touched." He truly meant it. "But, 'forced'?"

Leila didn't want to explain Foster was back. "Hard case," she lied.

"Oh." Hyun gave her a comforting squeeze. "You came for release, then."

They broke off the hug. "Yes, but seeing you again is a bonus, Hyun."

Hyun smiled. "Not all the time, I think."

She chuckled. His psychological lessons could get tedious and irritating. "This time it is."

"Seeing you in person—not just in the paper or on the news—is a bonus, as well." He walked her over to the shielded area. "Unless you want to show your Five-Animals Kung Fu, you best stay hidden when the students come."

"I'll show them if it doesn't affect your lessons."

"I might take you up on your offer." Hyun slid one of the paper doors aside. "Don't put my dummies out of commission yet—I still need them." He closed the door to let her practice alone.

Multiple punching bags and body opponent dummies waited near the far wall, next to a new contraption. With cross-wires dangling sandbags on ropes, it had to be the Sui Sau Jong Hyun told her about weeks ago. This bigger version would let her dodge and strike the moving bags.

Changing and coming out of the locker room, the sound of children talking and laughing came from beyond the secluded area. Any noise would draw their attention away from the lesson, so Leila would try to stay quiet.

She went to the middle of the padded floor and loosened her muscles through a series of stretches. After loosening up, Leila breathed out, emptying herself of her environment as she slid into the Panther stance. Unlike in an actual fight, she slowly transitioned from one stance to the next. It wasn't hard becoming lost in the smooth, calm movements.

Fully relaxed, she headed over to a body opponent bag and dropped into Tiger. She remained still before her hand shot out like swatting with a paw.

The dummy shuddered. It transformed into the green-eyed Bryan Foster, and she unleashed herself. After mutilating his image with kicks and hits, next brought her to the wooden dummy—the Muk Yan Jong with three arms and a leg. It became another ghost of the serial killer.

Her hand shot out to hit off one arm like a deflection and it spun. She jumped out of the way as the wooden arms spun around—it usually didn't move.

He's modified it. She jumped back in, attacking the wooden dummy and relishing the challenge. With a final spin kick over the arms, Leila headed toward the Sui Sau Jong.

There were two clocks: one to give her time to set and run into position, and the other to set how long she wanted to practice. Leila set a few seconds for her to get in place and its duration then pressed the green button. She hurried to the center of the sandbags and waited.

The whirring began. She quickly stepped into Crane as the mechanics set to work, and the sandbags pulled away. A *whoosh* sounded behind her, and she hit the bag out of the way. Another came at her, and she knocked it away as she spun to dodge another. Each one was Bryan Foster. She deflected a punch. Slipped under a kick. Threw a punch into his stomach.

For ten minutes, she ducked, dodged, hit, and kicked at the sandbags until the whirring died off, and the sandbags slowed to a stop.

"Loose yet?" David asked from where he leaned against the shoji door.

"I think so," she panted.

"Do I have permission to approach, or will you beat me up thinking I'm an opponent?"

Leila cut her eyes at him. "Get over here."

"Bossy—sign you need more loosening up." He walked over anyway and kissed her.

"Enjoy your extra hours of sleep?"

"It would've been better if *someone* could've woken beside me..." His hand drifted down her back.

"Hmm," she sounded against his lips. "I'm bossy, and you're horny. Sounds like we need to beat that out of our system."

David jerked back with mock horror on his face. "Lei, watch your mouth!" He looked over his shoulder. "The students have already heard you playing over here—they'd surely hear *that*." He turned back with a wicked grin. "You aren't quiet."

Leila popped him in the stomach. "I think you're louder."

"I probably am. Anyway, they asked Hyun who it was. So now, you've got to show them what you know."

"You say it like it's a bad thing. I told Hyun I would do it."

He headed toward the locker room. "It is a bad thing for me."

"Why?"

He walked backward as he answered, "Because I'm your dummy."

Leila laughed as he disappeared into the locker room. She went to the shoji doors, slid one aside, and found Hyun frozen in a stance with seven young kids copying him—all in their white doboks and yellow belts. She watched them go from stance to kick, then back to the stance with a battle cry. The smallest one yelled the loudest but stumbled as he returned to the beginning stance.

"You may scare your opponent before you strike them, little Ty," Hyun encouraged, causing the boy to puff out his chest from being praised. The instructor spotted Leila and smiled in greeting. "Our expert on Animal Kung Fu has joined us."

The children turned around and stared.

"You may call me Leila. Now, I'm just waiting for my practice dummy."

"I'm here," David said behind her, and the children giggled. He looked at her as he walked past. "Don't push it."

"I love you," she whispered as he walked over to stand beside Hyun.

Leila stepped closer to the waiting children. "Like your master told you, I fight using Five-Animals Kung Fu, but I am different; unlike others who use only one or two of the techniques, I use all five."

She stepped back from them and eased her breathing. Then she flowed out like a bird landing, her right arm lower than her left and her left leg lifted. "Crane." She crouched like a cat ready to pounce, bringing her hands out before her like claws, palms facing the children. "Tiger." She slinked lower, leaving her left hand in front and the other at her side, both hands still curved. "Panther." Leila widened her stance as if she had grown, bringing her hands out in front of her with her fingers touching, looking like jaws. "Dragon." She moved a final time to create a snake, with her arm being the body and her hand pointed as the head; her left arm bent for a platform the snake danced upon. "Snake.

"Those are the basics of Five-Animals Kung Fu, but I also use Phoenix." She stepped to the side while bringing her left leg and both arms up, held at shoulder's length—the proud bird ready for flight.

"That one's pretty," the little boy named Ty said.

Leila brought her arms and leg back down. "It is, and it is powerful." She looked at the two men watching. "I think it's time I showed you some moves."

The children's faces lit up. David smiled as he walked to the middle of the matted floor. "Time to get beat up, I suppose."

"The dummy doesn't talk," she chided as Hyun herded his students to the side.

David pointed at himself. "This dummy does."

Leila chuckled, bowed, then took her beginning stance; David mimicked her, then took his own stance. They stood still until David lunged. Leila sidestepped him as she moved into Crane and slammed her arm—held like a folded wing—into his back. She froze as she touched him, not to inflict injury.

She looked at the children. "The Crane's Wing."

Leila retracted her arm but stayed in Crane. David waited until she had moved back before throwing fists. Holding the stance, she danced back like the bird as she blocked his punches. During another punch, Leila dropped down to Panther. When his hand passed over her, she dove for him, knocking him down as she flipped over to her feet. She spun on the balls of her feet, looking like a panther ready to spring.

"The Panther Pounce."

David scowled as he returned to his feet, and Leila pulled her right hand up before her for Tiger.

He shot forward, and she continued to deflect his attacks until she spun with her leg out to trip him. As he landed on his back, Leila looked at the students.

"Tiger's Tail."

"Love it," he groaned.

"Dummies don't complain," she said.

David laughed, then spun his legs around to trip her, but she jumped and landed into Dragon. He jumped up and reached for her; she blocked him and threw both hands into his chest, shoving him back. When he stumbled, she rotated her arms to drive them into his stomach and sent him sprawling.

"Dragon's Roar."

"I like that one; it looked cool," one boy said.

"And it hurt," David mumbled as he rose.

"I'm not hurting you, am I?" she asked as she slipped down to Snake. Hyun chuckled.

"I know this one too well." David ran at her but slipped to his left to trick her as she struck out at him. Missing, Leila slipped away from his grab and transitioned into the Phoenix's light step. She spun, bringing up her back leg to kick him softly in his stomach.

"The Phoenix Illusion."

Leila didn't wait before moving back into Snake. With her first step, she lashed out her right hand, striking him in the shoulder with a sharp hand. Moving farther into him, she lashed out her left to hit him in the other shoulder. With another step, she circled both arms to strike him in the stomach and sent him falling back.

"The Angry Viper," Leila finished. After a release of breath pulling her out of the fighting-mindset, she helped David rise.

"I think you enjoy beating me up," he mumbled.

"Trust me, if I had, you wouldn't be standing."

David made a face at her.

"That was superb; you've greatly improved." Hyun bowed, with the students mimicking him, and they all spoke their appreciations. "We appreciate both of you taking the time to show us what you know."

David waved it off. "No problem."

Ty stepped closer to Leila. "Will you come back to teach us more moves, Miss Leila?"

"Of course we will—whenever we have time off work."

"Where do you work?"

David answered, "We're detectives with the police department."

His eyes widened, and some children behind him wore the same look of shock. "You use martial arts as a police officer?"

They both nodded. "Yes, using martial arts is an excellent defense against criminals."

"Wow," Ty whispered in awe.

"Alright, Ty," Hyun called. "We need to get back to practice. We can't keep Leila and David forever."

"Bye, Miss Leila and Mr. David." He hurried back to the group of students bowing in farewell. Leila and David copied them, and with a final wave, they headed back to the enclosed area.

"I'm going to be a police officer, so I can use Taekwondo to protect people," Ty said behind them.

"Well, I still want to be a dog," another said.

"Why a dog?"

"Because people pet you, feed you, and you get to sleep all day."

David laughed. "That one's got it figured out."

FOR THE REST OF THE day, they stayed at the gym, practicing and spending time with one another as they fought. Hyun joined them whenever free of his students, and the three of them along with Nuan went out to enjoy lunch.

"I need a shower," David complained as they finished their third round of the modified Sui Sau Jong.

Leila looked him over. "You're covered in sweat."

David grinned, eyes twinkling in mischief; she recognized trouble too late. He grabbed her, rubbing his sweaty head over her as she begged him to let her go and struggled to get away.

"Thanks," she complained when he released her.

He laughed as she tried to smooth her hair back out.

"You two are the most disgusting couple," Hyun said from the entrance.

"That's quite a compliment," David said.

Hyun shook his head. "I don't see how you put up with this man."

"I love him; that's the only reason I have," Leila said.

David turned to her. "Have or need?"

"Both."

"Sweat doesn't have an influence?"

"Well, when you keep it to yourself, it doesn't matter."

"It matters to me. Go get a shower before you stink up my gym," Hyun said as he turned for the lobby.

IV.

Leila stayed the night with David wrapped around her, but she couldn't share his enjoyment in sleeping late—she never could sleep in. He was the night-owl; she the morning-bird. So, she slipped out of his hold to make breakfast as he flipped back over.

The strong aroma of sizzling peppers, eggs, and a hint of onions pulled David out of bed by his nose to stumble into the kitchen. He loved food more than sleep, so she had cooked two omelets.

"You need to turn off that internal alarm clock; it's messing up my affair with sleep," David complained as they ate.

"The only affair you should have is with me," she said.

He skewered her with doubt. "I'm not allowed to get some rest?"

"Do I tire you out that much?"

His chocolate eyes swirled with laughter. "Just a little. Work delivers the knockout blow."

Finished with breakfast, David pushed his plate aside and reached across the island for her hands. "Alright, give me the percentage of what I can have."

It took her a second to think of an order. "2% to sleep; 3% to food; 45% to work; and the rest belong to me."

He blanched in disbelief. "Just 2%?" With a groan, he laid his head down and mumbled against the countertop. "My relationship with sleep is ruined."

She rubbed his hand in comfort. "We can give or take some on certain days."

His head lifted. "Like today?"

"Sure, today I get 80%."

David groaned again as his head dropped, beat down by her laughter.

THEY SPENT THE SUNDAY ROAMING the city. David's presence alone helped keep Leila's mind off searching for news on Foster. Being detectives gave them purpose but being with each other kept them wanting nothing more.

Leila and David waited until the sun began to yawn before visiting Central Park—the place they claimed wasn't as peaceful until paired with her favorite time of the day.

Working their way deep into the park, their isolated tree had no onlookers. Being in early October, the trees were still clothed but colored with an array of dying embers: gold, brown, slight touches of red, and yellow.

Their shade-tree waited just below the crest of a small hill, and they threw themselves down underneath it. Its yellow-brown leaves waved in greeting.

Other than a dog barking at something upsetting him somewhere in the distance, it was serene. No angry car horns, no screaming sirens, and no sweet promises between lovers, just the whispering wind dancing above the rippling waters of the lake. Eventually, the dog quieted once appeased of his discomfort, and the detectives became lost in their world within a world of chaos.

David let out a sigh after the last dog bark disappeared. "Can we do this every day?"

Leila chuckled but kept her eyes glued to the fiery colors of dusk. "I thought you enjoyed the adrenaline of our work too much?"

"I do, it's just this is so peaceful and relaxing. Lying here sounds better than work."

"You should try it while being at a lake or the ocean. It's much better."

"I bet doing this in the snow is great too," he added. "The feeling of the cold snowflakes melting on your face."

"We also need to try it in the rain."

They fell quiet underneath the tree. The bright blue of the day exploded in blazing reds, warm pinks, and splotches of yellows and oranges. Some darker blues and purples bled onto the lighter colors, making way for night to blanket the city. Leila was more enchanted by the changing sky with her favorite colors than any of man-made fireworks.

She remained entranced until David shifted. "What do you think of our future?"

Leila rolled her head over to look at him. "I thought you said not to worry about your future..."

"You know what I mean."

She smiled. "We're going to keep what we're doing until we retire or get hurt badly enough where we can't work anymore."

He chuckled in agreement but then became serious. "What about children?"

She suddenly forgot words for a moment. "I haven't thought much about it since we started dating but, yes, I would love to have some."

David smiled. "We need a little girl."

"Really? I expected you to want a boy."

"A boy would be a mini-me; nobody needs that." He paused. "A girl would look like you—beautiful—and melt hearts too."

Her heart tugged at his words of children and of becoming a mother. "No, we need a boy who will be just as stubborn as you, crave adrenaline, and capture a girl's heart the way you did mine."

"You're more stubborn than me," he stated.

"A trait we share."

"Your stubbornness is your only fault, but I wouldn't even change that—it lets you bang your head against mine."

Leila smiled. "That's why we're meant for each other."

"Well, then there's your temper..."

She rolled over to lie on his chest. "You've helped tone it down. That's something."

"But it keeps coming back, fierier than before."

"So? You'll always cool me down."

David kissed the top of her head. "Yes, I will." His fingers combed through her hair.

The repetitive gentle tugging should've eased her into sleep like the soothing action did to David beneath her, but Leila's musings from two nights ago crept in. David had been right; she knew they faced possible death every day at work—walking in the wrong neighborhood didn't improve odds—but she couldn't shake off the premonition that something was coming.

Even with David's slow breathing and usually calming musk, Leila felt uneasy about the coming week. The dark approached with stars, but it only brought foreboding darkness to her.

V.

"I'm moving to Siberia and living with the wolves; I'm gonna be a wolf-man."

His absurd statement brought Leila out of her stupor. Stopped two steps below on the station's inner stairs, David scowled at her. "What?"

"Really? That's what you heard? Not the whole 'I'm-leaving-you-because-you-smell-weird' rant?"

"What are you talking about?"

"I've been trying to get your attention since we got here."

Embarrassment turned her away. "Sorry, I wasn't paying attention."

"I had no idea."

Leila turned back to face him. "What *were* you talking about?"

"Nothing important." He ascended to her. "What's got your mind?"

"Something you think I shouldn't waste time on."

"This again? You're making this worry grow a bigger shadow over you." He grabbed her hands. "Look, I know it's hard but let it go. There's no need worrying if it won't change anything. Just believe me that everything will be alright."

"I need your optimism."

"What you need is to stop frowning. Seeing you smile makes me feel that I can do anything."

She looked at him. "I mean that much to you?"

He kissed her jaw. "More than I can say. But not until I see that" —he poked her cheek, causing her to laugh and swat his hand away— "smile."

Leila went into the squad room with a smile on her face but not in her heart. They entered the main hive buzzing with activity, as usual. David fell into the synchronization, but she disturbed the order: bumping into people, bringing a shade cloud, blocking everyone basking in the sunlight.

Instead of going to their desks, David and Leila headed straight for the captain's closed doors. The blinds weren't shut, meaning he wasn't in a conference with someone or seeking privacy. He sat at his desk, busy with paperwork.

"What's on the agenda for today?" David asked as he opened the door.

He didn't look up or stop writing. "Sometimes your eagerness worries me, David."

"I've built it up from having two days off."

Combined with the captain's, Leila's sunlight-preventing-cloud-of-foreboding grew. "What is it?"

Did Foster do something over the weekend that the media didn't report? Surely, she didn't have to add another number to his death total in her notebook...

"A robbery ending with murder—or the other way around. The call came in a few minutes ago. Thought about sending Heath and D on it if you two didn't show—"

"We're on it!" David cut him off, got directions, and practically dragged Leila out.

THE WOMAN HAD FOUGHT VALIANTLY against her attacker, but fists were a poor defense against a blade. Pictures had been dislodged under their struggle, and a desk lay on its side. It appeared the burglar got caught in the act by the woman coming home, killed his only witness, finished his job, and fled. She lay in a pool of blood in her living room, jugular sliced and eyes staring lifelessly.

It took a quick check of the room for Leila to determine that it was a robbery gone wrong. No evidence of a rape, and no extreme show of violence hinted at a crime of passion or revenge. David questioning a crime scene investigator of details became background noise. A cut-and-dried case, but David trying to make more of it tested her patience.

"If it isn't the 'Glory Hogs' from Precinct Five. Come to steal my case?"

She tensed at the scratchy voice from years of smoking, patronizing as usual. Already picturing the ugly sneer on his greasy face, Leila turned to meet Detective Marv Stipe. He— along with the rest of the 25th Precinct—hated her and David, thinking they were just pretty faces the media gobbled up with simple and easy tasks.

On the contrary, Stipe reminded her of a weasel, slithering in to accept praise but otherwise refusing to offer aid. He encouraged the stereotype by being the overweight, greasy, rude, and doughnut-eating cop. His patrols consisted of riding around his precinct, yelling orders through his intercom for pedestrians to move, and eating. A mall cop had more use than him.

"Stipe, never a pleasure seeing you," she said.

His beady eyes narrowed even more into slits. "Believe me, the feeling is mutual."

"I wondered what produced that smell—too revolting to be the dead woman yet," David greeted as he came to stand beside Leila.

He offered no reply to David. "So, why are you here?"

"Homicides are kind of what we're known for," David said.

Stipe's gaze slid over to him. "Burglaries aren't."

She folded her arms—Leila couldn't stand being around him. His presence oozed, and she needed another bath. "A dead witness isn't beneficial to building a burglary case."

"Not really degrading either when I already have a suspect."

"How so?"

"We've dealt with a string of robberies these past two weeks while—"

Anger flared up within her, cutting off his comment. "You had a suspect in sights!"

Her outburst bringing his intolerance into light pressured him into stepping back. "He hasn't killed before."

"So that means he wouldn't!"

He stepped back up to portray dominance. "He's never shown violence! He gets in, takes what he wants, and gets out!"

"No one has stepped in on him, have they!" He didn't try to disagree.

Stipe tried to talk back. "I wouldn't push her," David warned.

Leila gestured back at the dead woman, now covered with a white sheet. "Her death is on your hands!"

"The suspect is in my precinct! This is my case!"

"You dropped a body on our doorstep! We don't pick and choose cases like you!"

"You just came to get your name in the papers!"

Leila advanced on the round man with a pointed finger. "No, that's all *you* care about! You don't care about the crime as long as your ugly mug is seen! You're probably glad this robbery turned violent for it makes a bigger story!"

David's arm shot out to hold her back when she bore down on Stipe. "That's enough heat, Lei. Don't want to mess his face up for his picture when we arrest the murderer."

She calmed down immediately. "You know what, I don't care. I don't care, Stipe. Go and arrest your criminal and get praise you actually deserve. I just want you out of my sight."

Leila brushed past him. The gathered officers attending the yelling match stepped out of her way. Behind her, David told Stipe good luck then hurried after his partner.

THEY SAT IN DAVID'S UNMARKED cruiser, watching Stipe attempt to arrange his men before they went up the suspect's stoop to arrest him while Leila's anger simmered down.

"I'm surprised I pulled you back quickly this time," David began.

"You've been the only one ever able to."

"He almost pushed you too far this time."

Stipe puffed up in authority and wobbled his way up the steps to the door, glancing at Leila and David monitoring from afar. She let out the last of her anger trapped in her lungs. "He's an idiot, I know that, but he needs his eyes opened to how he is; they've been crusted for too long."

"Your temper is getting harder to control, and that other side of you gets out more easily. I still think you need to get rid of it."

"It's a part of me; you know I try, but I can't."

David grunted. "I just can't see how something that intense and unpredictable doesn't scare you."

She turned on him. "Are you trying to say I enjoy letting it out?"

"On Stipe, probably, because he deserves it." He faced her. "But no, that's not what I'm saying. It doesn't only show up when you're angry or stressed but to protect you. So, what do you need protection from?"

Leila faced back front. "I don't know."

A young man answered the call, stepped out when asked, and was arrested—no hassle. Someone handcuffed him then Stipe butted in to lead the criminal down the stairs, taking credit.

"Are we done here?" she asked.

David cranked the car. "I think we are."

TUESDAY TOOK THEM TO A dead drug dealer in Washington Heights. Eyewitnesses claimed a couple—previous workers for the drug dealer—did it. As David drove to Tyronne's apartment, Leila discussed their plan on getting him first, then Oshana, with the captain on the phone. Since nothing matched Foster's MO, she relaxed some.

"Watch after you two, Lei; something's waiting for us this week," he warned under his breath, like he feared the premonition would hear and strike earlier.

She built up the courage to ask Captain Sullivan to explain, but David had parked and stepped out of the car. Leila agreed, ended the call, and followed suit—her easygoing mood back on edge.

UP THE STAIRWAY OF ROTTING carpet, they stopped before a door with years outlining where the number two and one once sat with the three barely hanging on, marking room 213. "I have a feeling this isn't going to be easy," Leila whispered as David raised his hand to knock.

She had been stiff, eyes jumping to every shadow since arriving at the rundown apartment building. Her uneasiness only grew stronger with each step down the tight hallway; whatever waiting to happen would be coming soon. Feeling the apprehension thick in the air didn't come off as anxiety for David—he was instead wide-eyed and eager for it.

He grinned at her. "But that's the fun of it."

His knuckles rapped on the door. It creaked open, and they peered in. Leila saw a gangly man with dark brown skin sprawled out on a torn couch watching TV.

"Who is it?" he demanded, eyes never leaving the screen.

David glanced at Leila before answering, "Oshana sent us."

His lip came up in a sneer; he waved them in. "What does she want now?" He turned at their approach, and eyes widened at the two detectives.

Quicker than the blink of an eye, Tyronne jumped over the arm of the couch and shot out the window.

"Alley, David!" Leila ordered as she barged into the disgusting room and crawled out the small window to a shaking fire escape. The stairs wobbled as the man hurried down.

"Stop! Police!" she yelled as she descended. Rust flakes broke loose under their feet.

Tyronne landed down in the alley and glanced up. He took off as she twisted around the side of the fire escape and jumped, ignoring the drop of eight feet. Leila gave chase after him, yelling at him to stop.

Following him around the corner, Leila met Tyronne now facing her with a gun aimed. She dove to the side—right into some trash—as he fired. Before he turned the gun on her again, David slammed into him, knocking him into the brick wall, and the gun flew out of his hand. Tyronne fought the detective, but David quickly subdued him by throwing him on the ground and handcuffing him.

She climbed out of the smelling garbage. Holding back a gag, she peeled a sticky noodle from some Chinese takeout off her shirt.

"Man, I didn't do nothing!" the man yelled as David droned on about his Miranda Rights.

"And the innocent *always* run." David looked over at her. "That was fun."

Leila holstered her gun. "Your adrenaline cravings." She headed over to the discarded gun. With a pencil from her pocket, she picked it up. "How much do you bet this is the murder weapon, David?"

"I'm all in. I also want to bet there're some *illegal* drugs in Tyronne's apartment, so" —he picked up the handcuffed man and handed him over to Leila— "you can babysit our suspect in the car while I call Narcotics and watch his apartment until they get here. Maybe your stink will teach him not to shoot at people, especially cops."

She rolled her eyes as she pulled Tyronne down the alleyway for David's car; her partner chuckled behind her.

VI.

An officer opened the cell, and David threw Tyronne and Oshana—none too gently—inside. Based on their threats in the car, they would kill the other if put in the same lockup.

"Now, please shut up! I've had enough!'"

Tyronne pushed his face against the bars as he walked off. "Hey, cop! Aren't you forgetting something?"

"Knocking you out? Thanks for reminding me!" He moved to do just that.

Leila stopped him. "David, let them go."

He turned around—clearly displeased at her interruption—and headed toward his desk, ignoring Tyronne's outbursts about being uncuffed.

"Usually, it's *your* temper they get to," David said as he plopped down into his chair.

"They weren't worth letting it out on, but they tested me."

The forty-minute drive back was revealing and annoying. Tyronne and Oshana in the back seat confessed to the murder of their previous boss while blaming the other for ruining their plans for taking over his drug-dealing business in their verbal battle. Even though it wasn't needed now because their confession was caught on tape, evidence of the gun just made the case stronger. Smelling like rotten trash and them constantly yelling almost made Leila turn off the camera and shut them up for good.

She left to change shirts at her locker as David rummaged through his desk for some aspirin; she took her own painkillers with some water before leaving. When she came back feeling better in a clean shirt, he had his head against the table.

"I see and hear that you got both of them," the captain said when he walked up.

Leila looked over, him avoiding eye contact. The chase after Tyronne wasn't the premonition he had warned her about like she hoped. It still waited for them.

She swallowed to steady her voice. "This will be a cut-and-dried case: they've already confessed."

He looked over at the resting man. "You alright, David?"

"Just a splitting headache and regret for bringing the mouths here." He lifted his head. "You need something?"

"No. You two take the night off; you look like you need it."

"Does it show that much, Captain?" David asked, his voice muffled by him laying his head back down.

"Just slightly." He laid a hand on Leila's shoulder. "Go. Relax and get some rest."

"Captain—" she began, but he cut her off.

"Go. I don't want to see you tomorrow." His hand slipped off her shoulder as he turned away, but she grabbed it to stop him.

"What is going on? You've been tiptoeing around because you're scared of something happening. What is it that you're afraid of? You can tell me."

A tremor went through him; as it passed, it left his hand cold as ice. He stayed facing away from her. "I dreamed that my station becomes... disillusioned, dysfunctional, and where you and David sit is nothing but gaping holes. I don't know what it's supposed to be, but it involves you and David, and it's not good."

That omen passed over her like a shadow, icing her own skin. She shook it off the best she could. "We're coming in tomorrow; we can't have a dream scaring us off."

Captain Sullivan finally faced her. His eyes shook just as bad as his hands like he could see a ghost. "Why don't you run when someone tells you to?"

She hugged him, hoping that reassuring heat in her would pass into him. "I tell others to run from danger. I can't run too."

He smiled, caressed her face like he did with his daughters, and then turned away for his office.

Leila watched him, wondering why she seemed so solid now when earlier she was just as shaky in faith as him. David not including himself in the conversation surprised her—being asleep on his desk said why. She touched him, and he jolted awake.

Seeing her, his head ducked back into his arms folded on the desk. "Bunking at my house tonight, Lei?"

"You don't look up to having company."

He mumbled against the table, "I'm asking you to take care of me, please." He sounded pitiful.

She chuckled. "You always need someone to take care of you." He mumbled unintelligibly—some sarcastic response. Leila pulled him up and helped him stumble out, his optimism finally seeping into her.

LEILA SHOT UP IN BED, her whole body shaking and covered with sweat, breathing hard, and hands clutching the sheets. Her eyes darted around the dark room, David's drawers and closet highlighted by the outside light on the street. The curtains didn't help by throwing large shadows over everything, making objects grow in the darkness.

On his chest, David faced her, his hand lying on the bed where it had been draped over her. The comforter sat halfway down his bare back.

It was a wonder she hadn't woken him—he was a light sleeper.

Well... not really. That migraine he had received thanks to Tyronne and Oshana wore him out; combined with medicine, he became a heavy sleeper for tonight.

She placed a hand against her pounding heart and tried to remember the nightmare. It lingered out of reach—she could almost bring the memory back. But she was lost in a fog, feeling the dream's presence but dissipating as she neared it. A dream hadn't frightened her into uncontrollable shaking since childhood.

Leila kept trying to remember the dream as she threw off the warm sheets on her side, waited a few seconds to adjust to the cold exposure, then eased out of bed and walked to the small kitchen for water from the refrigerator. Hearing about the captain's dream likely inspired her own. She nearly drained the bottle as she walked back to bed and softly groaned at the time.

4:30 a.m.—an hour earlier than when she usually woke for work.

She got back in bed, scooted closer to David, and kissed him on the forehead. "Happy Birthday," she whispered. He mumbled in his sleep—either barely hearing her or feeling her touch—and turned the other way.

Chuckling to herself, Leila lay down and closed her eyes— she bet she wouldn't be able to sleep, but it couldn't hurt to try. Unwanted, her mind focused on remembering the dream. The same chill she had felt earlier when the captain repeated his dream raced up and down her spine again. She caught some of her emotions in it and if her dream resembled Captain Sullivan's, she understood why he was afraid: pain, numbness, emptiness, loneliness.

A long, warm shower would soothe her trembling nerves. Trying not to disturb David again, Leila eased out of bed.

As she walked to the bathroom, something pulled her back. *Did David make a noise?*

He hadn't moved from his sleeping position—on his chest with him facing away from her.

Her eyes roamed for anything out of place, and the streetlight highlighted a picture of her and David. Instead of both of them, it only had her—her face distraught and wet from tears.

Leila quickly flicked the bathroom light on, and the picture returned to normal. Even though the shaking of her body had calmed from before, it iced again as if water poured down her back, almost making her fall under weakened legs, too shaky to support her.

She stepped into the bathroom and shut the door, hoping to shut out the intuition barreling into her: the omen the captain feared would wreck her and David today.

VII.

D avid sighed and set his head against the headrest. "Hopefully, we can rest now."

"Still feeling the effects of yesterday?"

Eyes closed, he just nodded.

Leila watched Heath and DeMarcus drive off with the suspect of the murder they investigated this morning. She hoped the cases would continue being easy. "Call it in and ask the captain."

He reached for the car radio. "Super Cops to HQ."

"Skipper here." Background noise nearly overran the captain.

"Suspect headed your way."

"Good. You two take the evening off; after all, it is your birthday."

Leila knew it wasn't only a gift—maybe it would prevent his dream from coming true. She may have been more grateful than David.

"Thanks for the present. What's that noise behind you?"

He huffed. "A water main has burst, and that's the workers fixing it. Now, go celebrate your birthday, David."

"Ten-four." He placed the radio back down and changed gears of the car.

Anticipation of a relaxing evening eased her into her seat. "Where do you want to go? *Mosely's?*"

"Well…" He looked at the clock on the dashboard. "It's already six, and we're not dressed for something nice so… *Mosely's* will do. Good for you?"

"Of course. It wouldn't bother me if you chose *Burger King*; it's your birthday, and as long as you're happy, I am."

"Good because I need a drink."

"So do I." Perhaps a drink would chase off that lingering dread.

THEY WALKED INTO *MOSELY'S* AND went straight to their table. Even though busier than normal, the waitress still spotted them, smiled, and bounced over.

"Happy birthday, David." She leaned down close to them. "I sweet-talked the manager and got a double discount for you. But don't tell anybody."

David smiled. "My lips are sealed."

"So, two Buds and medium-rare steaks?"

"That would be it."

The petite waitress wrote the order down. "It'll be right out."

As soon as she disappeared, David grabbed Leila's hands across the table. "I don't think we could've made a better choice." The crowd wasn't a loud and obnoxious bunch. They could still hear the twang of the country song on the jukebox.

"We'll do something more extravagant this weekend."

"Like a birthday cake?" The kid was coming out of him.

She laughed. "Yes, a birthday cake… and balloons. But you get your present tonight." Leila let go of his hands and reached down into her purse, hiding his gift. She whipped out a small black box. "Happy Birthday."

David grinned. "You shouldn't have." He took the box and opened it. Brown eyebrows shot up at the gift. "Rolex?"

"Now you won't be late for work," she said as he wound the hands to the correct time and slipped the designer silver and black watch on his wrist.

He stopped admiring the watch and looked up at her, his brown eyes now soft like melted chocolate—her favorite for that warmth enveloped her. "Thank you, Lei." He leaned over the table and kissed her, holding it for a while before drawing back.

"You're welcome, David, and happy birthday."

The waitress came back and placed their drinks on the table. "There you go. Your steaks should be——" A whining from the radios on their hips cut her off; everyone in the lounge turned at the shrill call.

The detectives jumped up. "Sorry, but forget the steaks," David said.

She nodded. "Of course."

David already held his radio at his mouth as they ran out to the car.

"What's the situation?"

"Ten-ten at Citizen's First Bank, Midtown Manhattan," the dispatcher reported. "Suspect identified as Bryan Foster."

They stared at each other. Foster had somehow slipped her mind, with everything else going on. Determination flared in Leila's heart; the same reflected in David's eyes. "We're on it."

David clipped the radio back on his hip as he ran around to the driver's side, and Leila jumped into the passenger, already speaking with the dispatcher about more details on her own radio. He cranked the car, flicked the lights and siren on, and sped off down the street.

"What about the night security?"

"Eight are present. No reply since first report."

That was an omen. "Have multiple buses en route."

"Ten-four."

Leila looked over at David. "Sorry about this ruining your birthday."

David dismissed it with a wave of his hand. "No need apologizing; when we catch Foster, it'll be the best birthday."

"Better than a birthday cake?"

"I think so."

Even though Foster had finally shown himself, the scenario didn't seem right. "Why go to a bank, knowing there'd be security?" Leila asked.

David shrugged. "No idea; we'll ask him later."

"David? Lei?" Heath's voice came over the radio. "D and I are ten minutes out with the S.W.A.T. team, so save some fun for us."

"No promises." Brakes squealed as they arrived at the scene. "Ten-eighty-four. Keep you updated." Leila pulled out her gun as she jumped out of the parked car and looked for lights in the tall glass building as they approached. Finding none, she refocused ahead to burst through the revolving doors into the spacious lobby.

The dim night lights made it difficult to spot a difference in the clumps of darkness. David leaned over the reception desk and flicked the lights on; the security stationed there for the night littered the floor. Seeing seven bodies stalled her for a moment—premonition urged her to flee.

Ignoring it, she joined David in checking for pulses although each man lay in a puddle of blood. The one she checked had no heartbeat; she looked up to find David shaking his head. Leila radioed Heath as her partner continued checking the others—she hoped Foster left a survivor for once.

Eight security officers were listed as being here, and one was missing. According to Foster's MO, he held that one hostage somewhere, torturing them.

"Lei?"

"We found the security stationed here for the night," she paused as David stood but shook his head. "One is missing; the others are deceased."

Heath's end remained silent for a moment. "Any sign of Foster?"

"No—" A clang echoed down the stairs, and the two detectives whipped around, aiming their guns at the marble stairs.

"Lei?"

Leila kept her eyes on the stairs as she raised the radio. "We heard a noise upstairs; it might be him with a hostage."

"Are you waiting for backup?"

Leila and David caught each other's gaze; he shrugged and looked back at the stairs. The hairs on the back of her neck prickled in warning of the foretold omen.

She made the decision: they would catch him—restoring their reputation of always retrieving criminals—and save the hostage. "No. We're going to chance it. If not, we could lose him."

"Then you two be careful and keep me updated. We're almost there."

"Ten-four." She clipped the radio back onto her belt and nodded to David. Making their way to the stairs, they pointed their guns straight up. No lights revealed any shadows as the stairs twisted up into obscurity.

The detectives proceeded up the stairs, stepping lightly to keep their approach quiet. At the second floor, they stopped at a door; David grabbed the doorknob, and Leila flattened against the wall. With a nod from her, he quickly pulled the door open, and she peered down the long hallway.

She nodded for him to go; David poked his head in then retreated for precaution. Since he didn't see anyone, he stepped into the hallway, gun held level and steady out before him. Leila copied his form, looking down the vacant hallway of empty offices—none of the doors stood open, nor were any of the lights on.

David jerked his head back at the stairwell, and they proceeded to the third floor. Nothing there, they continued up to the fourth where they halted, eyes glued to the open door and lit room.

A flicker of caution along with apprehension passed through her as they stepped up to the floor silently, both guns aimed at the door. Leila flattened against the wall to see the large room occupied by cubicles and sleeping computers—an informational room. Glass windows created a panorama of the city at night. Papers were strewn across the floor, and some computers had been knocked off their stands like someone trashed the place looking for a paper trail. A body sat propped against a cubicle, dressed in the security's uniform. She glanced at David and nodded—they had found Foster.

Heart pounding, she watched David take the handle and pull the door open wider. He stuck his head in quickly and retreated, trying to catch sight of the criminal. Motioning it safe, they both stepped in, eyes and guns seeking Bryan Foster. The room remained eerily silent as the detectives entered, backs to each other, facing opposite directions. Stopping before the aisle running between the cubicles, she rose on tiptoes to see if the criminal hid as David checked the man's pulse.

"He's dead," David said.

Dropping back down, Leila huffed angrily: they missed him.

The air stilled in warning as someone approached from behind. Her hand shot out to warn David, but a leather pant leg kicked him in the back, sending him into a cubicle wall, collapsing under his weight. Her gun came around to fire, but an arm knocked it out of her hand. Completing the rotation, she came face to face with Bryan Foster. With buzzed head and dressed as usual in all-black motorcycle getup, signature snakeskin boots, and a black strap holding some gun on his back, his sharp green eyes, cold and piercing in their cruelty, remained the only detail to linger in the mind.

He smirked in greeting before his legs shot up in his kick-boxing technique. Deflecting them, she advanced with her Five-Animals Kung Fu, then knocked him into a cubicle wall. As he fought for balance, David appeared and tackled him to the ground. Leila brought her radio up and turned to find her fallen gun.

"Ten-thir—" Foster's leg shot out and tripped her, making Leila drop the radio as she fell. She turned onto her back to fire at him, but he had managed to throw David off, knocked the gun away again and pounced.

Her legs caught and flipped him off. Seeing her gun over by the dented wall alongside her radio, she scrambled to her feet; Foster rose with her, and they exchanged punches and kicks. She grabbed a fake-potted plant and threw it at him, hoping the distraction would give her an opening. It backfired; he ducked, and a fist to the stomach knocked the breath out of her. When Leila doubled over, he grabbed her and threw her into a desk.

Landing on her left arm, a knife of pain cut through bone, breaking her elbow and forearm. She screamed and reached for her useless arm as the collapsing desk rolled her off. Continuous grunts and hard impacts of fists behind her lessened her cries of agony to focus on the calls of her name through a radio. It took her a moment to locate it; someone's body jarred the floor when she grabbed it and forced herself up with the gun held by her broken arm.

"Ten-thirteen! Engaged with Foster! Get here now!"

"Lei! What's happening?" Heath cried.

Her finger pressed the side button to speak, but the words died, frozen at the situation before her: David shakily returning to his feet as Bryan Foster straightened with an MP5 pistol submachine gun. Time slowed to a crawl.

"DAVID!" Her gun painfully rose as Foster pulled the trigger, unleashing rounds into her partner. Deafening blasts filled the room, and David jerked violently as bullets pierced his body.

Her delayed response finally emptied the cartridge, making Foster yank the gun away from shooting David to Leila. David fell backward as sharp pain exploded—she jerked and tried to escape from the bullets. The gunfire halted abruptly but not the pain, feeling like constant knives stabbing her. When one stabbed and withdrew from her arms, another repeated in her torso, followed by another in her legs. Buckling beneath her weight, she dropped to her knees. Even though she could feel the blood seeping out, her body had become numb and gaping like a black hole. Ringing filled her ears.

David's immobile form lay far away before the world tilted, and Leila ended up on her side. A thought couldn't solidify in the fog her mind transformed into; she couldn't focus. Her vision flickered between blurring and clarity. Blood pooled before her chest, and air came in painful gasps until she couldn't breathe from drowning. Someone endlessly cried out her name through static before it devoured the voice.

Something heavy thudded the floor as it drew closer, matching the slowing beats of her heart. Her eyes focused on the snakeskin boot before traveling up to the grimacing face of Bryan Foster. One hand held the gun while the other pressed against his shoulder, blood seeping through his fingers. Another dark spot oozed at his waist.

His green eyes briefly held hers—no emotion passing through—before he walked away. She could feel the deep thuds of his boots on the floor until they stopped. The lights flickered on and off like an S.O.S. signal to the rescuers; Leila closed her eyes against the painful strobe lights. The lights finally stopped—remaining on—and Foster's heavy footsteps faded away.

A steady beat, loud and heavy—sounding like blades cutting wind—rumbled, overpowering sirens and loud voices. Eventually, all sounds faded, as if someone slowly turned the volume down. Her vision blurred and darkened but didn't clear this time. She wanted to sleep but something kept tugging at her to stay awake. The warm beckoning of rest won and pulled her eyelids down.

VIII.

Blackness. Not a dull black where shapes could be out-lined if focused on. More an inky blackness. No cor-ners or indentations, just smooth like the endless space but without stars. She forced her arms up, at first resisting her commands as if asleep and not wanting to be awakened. Leila's searching hands brushed against nothing as she turned. Empty darkness surrounded her.

What is this? Where am I? Leila crouched to feel around her; finding the floor solid, she walked with her hands out before her. She blindly walked through the darkness for what seemed like forever since nothing changed. No difference in tempera-ture or light; everything remained dark and silent.

After a while, she stopped. There was no ringing in her ears, no sound of her breathing, no noise. Nothing.

She should be afraid. The normal blackness of night had the comfort of knowing something existed nearby. Leila couldn't see anything and didn't know where she stood. Even with the endless darkness and no light radiating warmth, she wasn't cold. Instead of fear, she felt content with the loneliness. She was completely alone—not even sure if she herself existed; she seemed incomplete and wavering in solidity. Although adrift in a black sea, she wanted to remain.

"Lei." The voice disrupted the silence but blended with the darkness, cool and collected. It didn't echo and drift off into the silence—it belonged there. Curious, she turned.

David stood in a lit area, not causing her to squint and shield her eyes. She stared at it with awe and longed to be in the warm glow with him. The longer she stared, the more she saw. At first, it was just white, then flecks of gold and silver shimmered throughout, then all colors blended, happily belonging together. Now with the light present, she felt cold and isolated in the darkness, distant and far away.

Her eyes went back to David, seeming transparent and shimmering with the light. He considered her a moment before approaching; the light stayed in place, but a dim radiance lingered around him. The light didn't cast a shadow over his face—David remained vivid and glowing like he absorbed it.

"David." Her voice sounded loud and echoed endlessly into the darkness. "Where are we?"

He smiled faintly. "You are in The Between; I have passed on."

"The Between?"

"Between here" —he gestured behind him— "and there." He motioned behind her, and she turned.

A hazy picture had materialized, seeming to never end as it stretched left to right, but she couldn't make out the blurred image. The background stayed white, not the beautiful and inviting white and gold glow behind David, but duller and boring. Things moved chaotically as different colors appeared: peach, white, black, brown, and blue, before swirling together.

She watched it, not understanding. "What is that?"

"That is where you belong," David said.

Leila turned and stared at his emotionless face. "What? I don't belong here?"

"Not yet. You belong back in your present home, not your future one."

"Why not?"

"Look at me, then down at yourself."

53

Leila took in his form, peaceful and still with the soft glow cradling him. He didn't wear regular clothes, impossible to make out but she could tell he wore something white—a beautiful, pure white that hurt her eyes, unlike the surrounding glow. Then she looked down at herself.

She wore her usual outfit: jeans, black boots, and a shirt, but torn with holes and splotched with red. Dark blood ran down her right arm in a meandering thick river before it dripped into the darkness. Her left arm was twisted grotesquely at the elbow, and another hole bled in her upper arm. By the looks of her bloody body, she should be enveloped with pain, curled on the floor unable to move, much less breathe. It could be no more than a gruesome makeup job from not feeling the pain it marketed.

"What happened to me?"

"You were shot, and so was I."

"Shot—" Images flashed before her eyes. Stairs appeared, followed by an open door and a room with cubicles. David thrown into a wall, and she faced a man with cruel green eyes. They fought, he threw her onto a desk, and pain stabbed her left elbow. When David collapsed, the other man turned to her; pain, pain, sharp, biting pains dug into her until she fell. When she choked for air, everything darkened.

Leila could see David before her again, waiting. "I was... You were shot... You, you..." Her heart fell.

"I died."

His words hit her with a cavernous void sucking away her breath. Lightheaded, she started to sway; he placed his hands on her shoulders to steady her. Reaching for him, she was struck another blow when her hand passed through him—he could touch her, but she couldn't feel him.

"You survived, Lei. You're fighting to stay alive right now." He nodded toward the picture behind her.

"I don't want to. I don't want to go back. I want to stay here with you."

"No, Lei, a part of you is dragging you to survive; quit fighting it and submit. You are going to live on until your true day brings you here."

Tears streamed down her face. "David, how can I live on without you? You're all I know." Her left arm suddenly jerked on its own accord, and she screamed at the agony. The pain her body displayed crashed in on her like waves, not giving her time to catch her breath before rushing back over her.

His hands grabbing her face took her focus off the re-breaking of her arm. "No, I'm not. You have Heath, Captain Sullivan, DeMarcus, the entire squad, Hyun, Nuan, my parents, and so many others you don't know yet you must return to. If you don't go back, some will go before their time and won't come to the place where they belong. Others will remain adrift, forever lost unless you pull them out of their sea."

A tugging made her look at the scene behind her. Heath's distraught face drenched in tears showed before it faded. With every intake stabbing her chest, she moaned and panted.

"I would leave all of that so I'm not away from you. You know I'll di—"

He cut her off. "No, don't say you'll die for me. Only half of you is willing."

If she couldn't believe David was truly dead and not really talking to her, she didn't doubt her love for him. "I love you; you know I do."

His face tightened and a hand ran down her jaw. "You did."

Her knees buckled under his statement. "I can't let go of you."

"Yes, you can. Know that I will be within your grasp if you ever need me, but one day, you will find someone and won't need me."

Pain bit her and it became harder to breathe—the air thickened. "I can't live without you. I can't forget you."

He lifted her face. "Yes, you can. You can live on without me because you are destined for much more, and for another. I was not. He is waiting, and you must find him. I'm not saying you will forget me completely; you just have to let me go."

A powerful shock pierced her chest, burning and rippling her body in spasms. Leila couldn't recover her breath before another followed. The jolts left her exposed, but the pain came roaring back, consuming her entirely. She didn't realize she had fallen until David held her up in his arms, her head in the crook of his elbow.

"Please… don't let me suffer."

Remorse contorted his face. "Fate has played its part."

She opened her mouth to plead again, but a little cry came forth. He placed his fingers over her mouth to stop her from trying.

"No, don't speak; you don't have much time. You're making your way back, and you will be immersed in new pains and emotions you've never dealt with before." He leaned in closer as her eyes focused in and out. "Now promise me this, Lei: you'll find the will to survive, find your way back in life, and you will look for the one who desperately needs you in his life. He is hurting just as much and needs you to heal him. Will you do that for me?"

She focused on his molten chocolate eyes. Pain's grip wouldn't let her nod, so she closed her eyes and opened them for affirmation.

David smiled. "Thank you." He kissed her on her jaw. "Survive and love another the way you loved me."

As the darkness swallowed her, his kiss lingered.

IX.

A beep repeated over and over in a slow, droning manner. Listening past the continuous beeping, it was deathly silent. Only a slight whoosh—compressing, then decompressing—made a sound other than the annoying beep. Air forced its way in at the same rise and fall of her aching lungs, smelling fresh, sharp, and sterile.

Like a hospital.

One finger outlined itself with extra weight added; she tried lifting it but couldn't—too weak. Abandoning her idea of moving, she took inventory of her body. There wasn't one place that didn't throb. She would have accepted pain in her left arm if it reassured her that it remained attached. Instead, a hole replaced where she should've felt it; when she focused hard enough, a tingling numbness answered her. Moving the muscles in her left arm shot pain up her neck, starting at the elbow. The beeping increased as she tried to catch her breath flittering away.

Now fully awakened, her pain receptors sounded off, reflecting her body back to her like a sonar. Lying down and slightly propped up, with her left arm bent over her stomach. Moving her right hand gingerly—the only part responding to her commands—she felt crisp sheets tucked around her body. A textured pillow cushioned her heavy head. She strained against the resistance of her eyelids to open; they flickered until adjusting to the dimmed lights of the hospital room.

Mint colored the walls, and white bordering frosted the top. One blinded window cut into the smooth wall, and a closed door stood far from the foot of her bed. Two lavender-colored recliners sat to the right of her bed and a couch to her left, all with sheets balled on top.

Her arms lay lifeless on top of the white sheets. A tube had been attached to her hand with a blood pressure monitor on the finger she had tried to lift; her left arm was bandaged heavily, mainly around her elbow. She followed the tube up to an I.V. and different monitors keeping track of her heart rate and blood pressure, beeping smoothly. The oxygen machine contin-ued to inhale and exhale as its tube weaved to her face and un-der her nose.

Where's David? Her mind reared back at the pictures of the bank: finding the security dead, checking floor after floor for Foster, fighting Foster in the large room, watching him shoot David.

The heart monitor beeped faster as her heart trembled. *Where was he? Is he okay? David...*

Her room's door opened. A nurse with soft brown curls pulled back in a ponytail hurried in followed by— Her heart-beat rose higher, then flatlined for a moment at the sight of Heath. His face creased with worry vanished into relief.

"Lei!" he cried as he ran into the room.

At seeing the moisture threatening to overflow in his, she averted her eyes to the nurse.

"Are you in pain?" the nurse asked, eyes also brightening at finding her awake.

"I don't feel anything right now." Leila found it a strain to speak.

She checked the monitors' readings and nodded approv-ingly. "Do you feel okay enough to be raised?" Leila nodded— the nurse pushed a button, and the bed slowly curved her to a straighter position. "I'll leave you two alone," she began, eyes shifting between the two detectives. "Call if you need anything." After hesitating, she retreated out of the room and pulled the door closed.

Leila took a painful, steadying breath as Heath pulled a recliner closer to her bed. He looked terrible, with dark circles underneath his eyes from lack of sleep, a deep sorrow glazing them, and his hair in a matted mess. His clothes were wrinkled from being stuffed into a duffel bag and sleeping on the couch or recliners. With a heavy sigh, Heath placed a hand on hers.

"Lei... I'm so relieved to see you awake again."

"How long have I been here?"

He licked his lips. "Three days." Moisture appeared again in his eyes, and his voice trembled, "We thought you weren't going to make it."

She took another steadying breath. "You've stayed with me?" she asked, glancing over to the couch.

Heath nodded. "With the captain and D taking turns."

Leila feared the hesitation in his eyes—he kept something from her. "Heath," she began, and he met her eyes. "Where's David?"

Joy in his eyes darkened, and he looked away from her. He didn't answer for the longest, his jaw working as he tried to speak over emotions wracking his face and wanting to leak out. "He... he didn't make it, Lei."

The heart monitor flatlined again. His words knocking her heart out of its place and leaving a gaping hole. He gave that chilling apprehension a reason for hanging over her. She looked down at her sheets. *He's dead.*

The Between. It was real.

Tears now fell down his face. "I'm so sorry. We were too late. Both of you had been shot multiple times. You lost so much blood, but he…" He swallowed back a hiccup. "He was already gone. A bullet had… gone through his head."

Leila cringed at the picture of his body jerking from the bullets flying into him. And when she shot Foster, his arm went up first, making David jolt rigid before falling as his gun turned on her. *I caused him to die thinking I was saving him… I killed him.*

"Lei…" She looked back at Heath, not feeling the hot tears carving paths down her face. Her chest hurt—each breath stabbed.

"I killed him, Heath," she gasped. Heath began to deny it. "No, I did. I decided to find Foster. I ignored the warning in my gut and the dreams the captain and I both had." The breath hitching in her throat halted the rest of her confession about how David really died.

"You can't think like that. Foster killed David. It was his gun; his bullets. Not you. David could've disagreed about going after Foster alone, but he didn't." His hand cupped her face, holding her face steady with his. "Even if David hadn't been shot in the head, he wouldn't have survived. He had been shot too many times in the chest." He shuddered, probably from the images of one comrade suffering and the other already dead.

But she understood his words: David had been shot in the heart. *I should be dead with him.* She choked from releasing emotions. Heath carefully pulled her into him to let her cry into his chest. Her shoulder dampened with his tears.

She couldn't tell Heath that she was at fault for David's death. Wanting glory, Leila ignored her intuition, and the cost ended up being David's life. He'd think of her as scum and never look at her with admiration again. Even though the bullet belonged to Foster, she caused him to raise his arm, helping him deliver the death blow. Guilt increased her sobs.

Leila remained held to his chest until she calmed down. Only then did Heath release her, his shirt wrinkled from her clutching him and damp from her tears.

Now, an emptiness resided where a sun used to be; that nothingness had swallowed her happiness—no trace of it could be found. She was adrift in that sea from The Between. And she thanked the numbing waters, protecting her from everything breaking inside.

"You need to rest, Lei. It'll be hard, but you have to try."

Leila nodded the best she could. "How many times was I shot?"

Heath grimaced. "Six times."

Her body shuddered from the ghosts of the bullets entering her body again. Heath reached out in alarm. "I'm fine," she replied as she rested back against the pillow.

"Lei, if you're in a lot of pain I'll call Ashley."

"No. How's the captain?"

Heath opened his mouth but closed it. With a sigh, he answered, "He's extremely worried about you and is beating himself up. He's not here right now because he's dealing with... something."

"The media?"

Frowning, he nodded.

"When he's free, I'd like to see him. Put him at ease... or at least, ease about me."

"Are you sure?"

Leila closed her eyes. "Yes. And tell D to come too."

Heath hesitated. "As long as you are up to visitors."

"Only them. No one else."

After a long silence, he stood from his chair to go. "I'll call and let them know that you're awake but to wait before seeing you."

His footsteps headed for the door. "Heath." She opened her eyes to see him turn. "When's the funeral?"

He stood still, debating internally. "In two days."

She swallowed back a cry—the admittance of a funeral finalized David's death being real. "I'm going."

Heath took a step toward her. "Lei, you can't. Your injuries are too severe."

"I have to go." She turned away from another objection. Heath grew silent, and once he realized her set mind wouldn't change, the door clicked behind him.

Immense loneliness suddenly pressed down on her, forcing out her breath and squeezing out more tears. Her soul was broken. She turned into a pillow and let exhaustion overtake her.

X.

The woman in the mirror was unfamiliar. Her right side leaned heavily against a crutch, relieving weight off her injured leg. She wore a dress uniform: coat and pants in midnight blue, with yellow piping down the sides of the pants and on her collar and shoulders. A black sling cradled the broken left arm.

A black belt strapped her fitted shirt to the shrunken form of a body and a matching shoulder strap held a pistol. The black strap of mourning tainted the brilliant gold of her badge. White gloves covered her hands, and a dark service cap sat on her head. Once proud, the golden eagle on the hat now looked sad and defeated.

Her hazel eyes held a cold indifference. They reflected nothing—no grief or sorrow. She looked extremely tired—even with the makeup Ashley applied—and dark circles rimmed her eyes. Spending five days in the hospital with her hauntings had her losing an extensive amount of weight, leaving her thin and pale. Leila turned from the mirror, not able to stand the emotionless depths of her eyes for long.

Ashley had helped her bathe and dress and now moved used towels to a laundry basket. The young nurse hurried to and fro as she tidied up the wash area, moving to prevent nerves from kicking in.

"Lei." She turned and found Heath similarly dressed, holding onto a wheelchair. His somber eyes kept her looking at the chair. "It's to get you down to the car; I'll help you in the cemetery."

The crutch helped Leila limp toward the chair. Her torso made her want to scream at the twists, but she ground her teeth at the pain, keeping her mouth clamped tight—any whimper and Heath would demand that she stayed. Ashley walked beside her to the wheelchair and helped her turn to sit.

Seeing her struggling, Heath pushed the wheelchair around behind her. The nurse helped Leila sit, then pulled out the footrests. Her head had dampened with the perspiration of her efforts to move; Ashley dabbed the beads of sweat away with a tissue.

She nodded to the nurse, thanking her for her consideration. Ashley smiled, then looked up at the man behind the wheelchair. "Ready to go."

Heath took a deep breath before pushing out to the hallway with the nurse beside them. Nurses and patients stepped aside for them to pass but not without gawking at Leila and whispering.

"She's alive?"

"She survived!"

"I can't believe it. She lived through all of that?"

"Where are they going? Is she strong enough?"

"Poor girl, losing her partner and lover."

After they passed the last patient, Heath placed a comforting hand on her shoulder. She didn't register his gesture or what had been said—that emptiness numbed her where she didn't feel.

Leila closed her eyes at the blinding sun when Heath wheeled her out toward his car. Keeping them shut, she raised her face to let the warmth kiss her cold face. It felt like she had been living in the emptiness of her soul forever. She breathed in deeply—ignoring the pain in her lungs—to taste the fresh air, not chemical sterility.

They stopped beside Heath's navy-blue car. Ashley pulled open the rear door, and Heath laid Leila's crutch against the car. "I'm thinking about just picking you up and sitting you in the back seat. Is that alright with you, Lei?"

She nodded. He placed a hand on her back and underneath her legs, apologizing in advance if he hurt her. He gingerly lifted her out of the wheelchair and cradled her to his chest. Her unintentional whimper brought out an endless string of apologies as he sat her in the back seat.

Leila fell back against the cushioned headrest.

"I'm sorry, Lei. I didn't mean to cause you pain," he continued.

"You didn't," she replied in a quick breath.

After they looked her over, Ashley asked where she should sit. The passenger door opened and shut, and the door closed beside her. Once the trunk had opened and shut, Heath got in. She felt his gaze land on her, but Leila kept her eyes closed, concentrating on blocking out the pain.

The car purred to life; Heath backed out and drove out of the lot. Leila opened her eyes to watch cars happily speeding past, oblivious to the darkness of the day. After a while, the landscape changed from metallic skyscrapers and buildings to gently rolling hills and snug homes resting among pine trees.

Turning off the highway, they drove through the iron gate of **Woodlawn Cemetery**. Silent tombstones and solemn trees passed by as they fell behind a procession of cars. Their car finally pulled to a stop at the edge of a curb; a gentle hill ascended to a gravesite under a large willow tree.

Many had gathered; those not huddled together and talking were in a steady progression up the hill. Few people were already seated among the rows of white chairs. Most belonged to the police squad—all matching Leila and Heath. Hyun and Nu-an stood beside Captain Sullivan and DeMarcus. Past the gathered people, a large tent waited. Underneath, among numerous wreaths, lay an American-flag-draped-casket.

Leila couldn't take her eyes off the casket, even when Heath blocked her view to open the door. "Let's get going," he whispered.

He helped her pivot by pulling her legs around until her feet touched the ground, then held underneath her arms to lift her. Leila balanced on her left leg and held tight to the car as Ashley came around with her crutch.

She propped the crutch under Leila's good arm. "I'll stay back here." Ashley shrank close to the car, eyes flickering up to the burial site.

With a look at Leila, Heath supported her in their slow ascent. While they made their approach, a black wind blew away noise as everyone caught sight of her. She couldn't tell whether their looks were through pity, concern, or bereavement, for her focus was before her, gaze frozen to the casket. Captain Sullivan appeared next to her with DeMarcus. They walked with her before she halted, seeing a man and woman with hair matching David's.

They sat in the front with one chair empty between them. Gray streaked through their brown hair, but the sun reflected the red tint in the mother's. Someone spoke to them; they turned, and Leila's heart stopped at the disbelief and sadness in the brown eyes of David's father.

David Sr. stood and helped his wife up. Shock had turned his brown mustache nearly gray as he walked down the aisle of chairs and stopped before Leila. His eyes strained to remain composed, but there wasn't a single ounce of blame directed toward her.

"Mr. David—" A hand rose to stop her.

"No, Leila. You do not have to apologize." He blinked a few times to refocus before wrapping his arms around her in a gentle hug. His body absorbed her heartache like a sponge. He continued, "Don't blame yourself, Lei. He went down in honor, that's how he would've wanted to go."

Tears sprung out of her careful restraint on emotions. *But I am to blame.*

Leila bit her lip to prevent the truth from escaping. If he knew, he would shove her away in disgust, and she longed for his comfort. She took a shaky breath to steady herself and stopped the tears threatening to showcase her guilt. Just as she did with Heath, she tucked the truth away—nobody would know.

He joined in as they resumed walking, Leila's eyes now on the ground. They stopped at the front, and her eyes lifted past the array of flowers to the covered casket. She could only stare, too many thoughts and emotions swirling within. But she caught and held onto the one thought that gave her comfort of David resting peacefully within.

Staring the longest at his coffin, Leila tore her eyes away when they began to ache to meet his mother, Julianne. Her reddened eyes held the same disbelief and sorrow reflected in her husband's, only intensified. Tears had already left paths down her face, but new ones refilled the dried riverbeds when their gazes locked.

"Leila." That whimper yanked her forward, and she threw her arms around Leila like she became a saving lifeline. "At least we still have you."

Leila sucked in painfully at the words. Sharp needles pricked her skin, opening holes that warmth seeped through. Like David's father, Julianne wasn't angry that Leila lived while her son died—she remained just as much as a daughter. Words dissolved at her searching for a response as the older woman hugged her; Leila felt colder when she pulled away.

David's mother smiled as she wiped away a tear escaping down Leila's thin face. Julianne motioned toward the empty seat between her and her husband. "We saved it for you, Leila."

She couldn't hold back her tears anymore. The sight of hers brought more to Julianne's face; she dammed the flow with an already damp tissue, chiding her softly about ruining her mascara. Leila chuckled at her attempt to lift her mood; once the tears halted, she limped to the reserved seat with Heath's aid.

David's parents took their seats on both sides—Julianne immediately grabbing a hand and David Sr. laying a hand on her knee. Heath seated to the left of David Sr. with the captain and DeMarcus; Hyun touched her shoulder in comfort from his and Nuan's seat directly behind.

Brother Thomas, the preacher from David's family church, appeared after everyone had taken a seat to stand underneath the tent. He faced the congregation of mourners.

"Isaiah 57: 1-2: The righteous perish, and no one ponders it in his heart; devout men are taken away, and no one understands that the righteous are taken away to be spared from evil. Those who walk uprightly enter into peace; they find rest as they lie in death."

He glanced back at the casket. "There is nothing that could've prepared anybody for David Neal, Jr.'s death. But let us not dwell on his passing; instead, let us share treasured memories and celebrate his life." He looked to the parents seated in the front row before heading to his seat.

David Sr. looked to his wife. Julianne squeezed Leila's hand for courage before standing and, hand in hand, headed for their son's casket. They faced their audience, both with eyes down and Julianne clinging to her husband. Not a sound came from them for the longest, searching for the strength to talk and hold it together.

David Sr. finally released his breath and looked up. "I can say words to describe David to you, simple words, and I'm sure all of you would agree with me because that's who he was, a simple man. But those words wouldn't describe what he meant to us; they couldn't express our pride or love of him. He was our son; our flesh and blood."

Julianne took a shaking breath as she dabbed under her eyes with a napkin. "No parent could've asked for a better child. David was brave. He didn't have a selfish bone in his body; he thought of nothing but helping others, and he dedicated that thinking to his job. He was a special man with a love of life."

Her husband chuckled. "Like father like son, he became a cop, even though his mother wished for a more... subdued job because of his reckless nature. But he answered his calling, and he became a much better detective than I ever dreamed of becoming."

"Our grief is expected—as any parents would have at losing their child." Julianne actually looked at her audience. "We are proud of what he stood for, and who he died for." Her eyes landed on Leila at the end; Leila averted her gaze to maintain her composure, but the dam cracked.

So focused on keeping calm, Leila jolted when they touched her in comfort, not knowing they had reseated. Her gaze remaining at her feet or them covering her shaking hands told them she wasn't ready.

A deep inhale and release followed by the creaking of a chair from a heavy frame standing brought her head up to the captain making his way to the front.

His hands slid into his pockets. He released another sigh to begin, but his shoulders remained slumped as if weights continuously pressed down on him.

"I was unsure about David when he joined the squad; he was too ambitious for my tastes, but we needed his energy—his drive to succeed far beyond what his job required inspired the whole force to do the same. So, David Neal, Jr., became one of my best detectives and a crucial part of my best team. Even though I wanted to bang his head at the danger he and Lei inserted themselves into" —he gave Leila a small grin as some of the audience chuckled in agreement— "I was always proud of the outcome.

"Every man and woman in and outside the force would agree that the city is better because of his actions... because he lived. His passing will be hard, but David would not want us to stay in mourning; he'd want us to keep doing what he did best by saving and protecting those in need, and those that don't ask for help." He turned to the casket. The captain remained still for a while before patting David's casket in farewell, then he walked back to his seat.

The cemetery grew dense in expectation; Leila would never be ready to say her final goodbyes, but neither could she hold it off any longer. She lightly squeezed Julianne's hand so she would release her hold, and David Sr. followed suit by removing his hand from her knee. He reached for her crutch, but Heath already grabbed it. Along with the aid of David Sr., she stood. Heath gave her the crutch, and the two of them headed to the canopy.

It was hard standing near him, but she kept reminding herself of him being at peace. The thought helped, but guilt kept her posture defeated. She wanted to fall beside his casket and beg to be buried with him. Heath stepped to the side when she turned to face a sea of sad faces to resist doing just that.

"I don't know how I can tell you what David meant to me. More than just my partner, he became that partner in life everyone searches for. He was *my* guardian angel, easing the captain's frustration when we persistently injured ourselves in saving someone's life. But he couldn't protect us from getting in trouble." She heard a few chuckles among the gathered. "He would always call me an idiot for doing something reckless or putting myself in harm's way, and I would say the same back to him."

She sighed. "But that's not all. He—" Her breath hitched, and the intake of air stabbed her ribs. She clutched at them but waved off Heath's concern. It took her a moment to steady her breathing, but the pain continued to throb in a sense of unease against what she wanted to say. So, she changed from saying what he had meant to her, and the pain slackened but remained present.

"I loved him; I saw myself marrying him. I saw us having children and retiring together. We were going to do everything together because he'd be by my side." Her throat trembled, so she took a few breaths to calm back down.

"We never questioned our actions of throwing caution to the wind. Saving a life only mattered. So, it wasn't unusual for us to go into that bank without backup; we were determined to put a dangerous man away for good." She paused. She told the truth, but not all of it—confessing her selfishness of getting Foster would not be received well. "He and I knew the risks and were unafraid to face them. David always said that risking our lives to save another's was a reward far greater than the cost."

His voice repeating those words followed by his crooked grin broke the dam; Leila turned to hide the tears and her quivering under the pressure of emotions. She couldn't face the crowd and say any more. Once her body quit trembling, Leila moved over and leaned down to David's casket.

"I gave you my promise, and I will hold it as long as I breathe," she whispered, then kissed the casket, imagining the kiss melting down to him so he could know he still had her

JESSICA PIRO

love. She wrenched herself away, and Heath helped her back to her seat.

Heath, DeMarcus, Hyun, and others expressed memories of David, but they drifted before her like noiseless ghosts—lips moved and eyes watered, but with no sound, like a silent movie. She had said her goodbye; she had nothing left. Julianne still held her hand, and David Sr. patted her knee periodically, but she couldn't feel the warmth within the gestures.

Everything after passed without emotion from her: of officers marching to the casket, lifting the flag, and folding it in precise order into a tight triangle; the Firing Party forming a line and firing blank cartridges for the three-volley salute.

But when the trumpet player prepared to play Taps, and all personnel saluted, Leila woke. With the aid of David Sr.'s hand on her back, she balanced on one leg to salute.

The final note of the mournful song would forever linger in their souls as it dispersed through the trees of the cemetery. Saddened even more now by the desolate song, the gathered watched as the officers performed Order Arms and then saluted the flag as it was carried to David's parents.

"It is my high privilege to present you this flag. Let it be a symbol of the greatest appreciation this nation feels for the distinguished service rendered to our country and our flag by your loved one." Julianne's hand shook as she reached for it. David Sr.'s steadied hers as she pulled it to her chest; the officer turned and marched away with the others.

An officer kneeled to turn the lowering device on; the dark casket slowly descended into the grave and disappeared from everyone's view.

When his casket slipped underground, Leila collapsed. Someone caught her before she hit the ground, but even if they hadn't, she wouldn't have felt it. Now completely empty, she couldn't hear anything again. Whoever caught her now laid her down, and all crowded around with movements of concern and

72

alarm, but nothing registered. At this angle, she could see where David's casket used to be past someone's folded legs. She couldn't remove her gaze from the now-gaping hole. He was truly gone.

The constant throbbing pain suddenly receded and left her feeling nothing. Past the waves storing up in intensity, she glimpsed a lighthouse in the distance—warm light beckoning her in. Leila swam toward it, needing that security it promised, but the waves crashed into her. She didn't try to fight and allowed the undertow to take her.

XI.

Attending the funeral left her weaker and bedridden for three days. Leila couldn't find the strength to force herself up; she just wanted to lie there. But a dream one night—taking the place of her nightmares of David's death—awoke her to her senses again.

Darkness surrounded her. Leila thought she had returned to The Between—lying in the exact position she had fallen when Foster shot her and bleeding just as profusely. She fought to breathe as the sting of the bullets bit into her... but she was losing.

As the pain almost won, that tugging reappeared, but this time, she sensed a presence approaching. She opened her eyes and struggled to focus on the apparition before her: she could hardly make out the outline of a human engulfed in bright gold and red flames.

Straining against her body as it screamed in protest, Leila pushed herself up to meet the figure. It stopped before her, then a limb of light reached out from the body, urging her to rise.

She shook her head. "I can't. Not without help."

The limb of fire merged back into the body before it bent down and entered Leila, fusing with her body, her soul. A blazing tornado of fire whipped away her pain and replaced it with heat, warming and awakening her cold muscles. The flame burned endlessly within her, empowering and strengthening her to stand.

Waking from the dream, the heat still burned as warm embers, fueling her new strength—she couldn't accomplish her promise to David if she gave up living.

Two weeks later, Leila rested on the edge of her bed after completing her daily walk with Ashley through the hospital. Her sudden improvement and determination to recover astounded the doctors.

Every wound healed with remarkable speed, and even the shattered elbow and broken forearm were re-fusing cleanly. She would always bear the scars of that night's injuries, but one looked the ugliest: the bullet that had almost pierced her heart. That wound never warmed. Always frozen, it held the reminder of David's pierced heart.

She massaged it as her eyes roamed around the room. Cards of encouragement, condolences, and best wishes she would get well soon sat on the small retractable table, and a variety of flowers and gifts crowded her windowsill.

Her visitors ranged from officers of the police force to even the waitress from *Mosely's*. David's parents, the captain, Heath, and DeMarcus were the most overjoyed to find her returning to her feet. She appreciated their support and encouragement to return to the world, but it became overpowering, so she asked to be left alone for a few days. Leila hadn't seen anybody—other than the nurses and doctors—for five days.

She needed space to think. Leila couldn't just return to being a detective and normalcy—pretending her life hadn't shattered. Neither could she let the tragedy haunt her like a dejected dog. If she remained stuck in pity, she'd never recover.

David's death plagued her anyway. Every time she fell asleep; when she kept her eyes closed for an extended time. As she sat still, thinking.

The S.O.S. signal with the lights bothered her, though. Foster did that intentionally, directing Heath, D, and the paramedics where to find her before she bled out. He wanted her to live. Him abruptly jerking his gun away proved it, too, but he had almost gone too far.

Why?

A soft tap on the door pulled her out of her jumbled mess of thoughts. Ashley.

"Yes?"

The nurse poked her head in. "Leila, you have a visitor. Is it okay to let him in?"

Leila thought of Heath not being able to stay away—he had become too watchful, and it irked her. Refusing his visit would make him worse, so she sighed in defeat. "Sure."

Ashley turned and nodded the visitor in. It surprised and delighted Leila to see Hyun.

"Lei." He sat beside her on the bed, then wrapped an arm around her, bringing her in for a soft hug. She leaned further into him and rested her head on his shoulder, embellishing in his warmth and familiar scent—grateful for his long-standing friendship.

They remained silent for a while as he held her. "I must apologize for not coming sooner or as frequently."

"You don't need to. I wanted privacy for a while. Everyone was becoming too much."

"Does that apply to me?"

She chuckled against his shoulder. "No, you're a welcome sight."

The muscles in his neck shifted as he turned to her. "Nuan and I figured you wanted some time alone after the funeral…"

"You don't have to give me an excuse, Hyun."

His chest rumbled with a chuckle. "Just makes me feel better that you know."

Silence fell over them again until Hyun hugged her tighter in comfort. "I know you've heard this over and over again, but I'm sorry for your loss, Lei."

"It wasn't only my loss and to his parents but a loss to this city." She pulled herself off his shoulder to look at him. "It doesn't matter how many times it's repeated, it's comforting."

Leila changed the subject away from David—if only she could do the same, "So, where's Nuan?"

"She thought it would be better if only I came since we've stuck onto each other like mud over the years."

"Sorry that you can't rid yourself of me."

"I don't want to."

His reliable friendship touched her. "She would've been welcomed too."

"I'll tell her." Hyun looked down at his hands; she followed his gaze to a single blue flower. He turned to her with it raised. "This is for you. I know it's not astounding in a bouquet." He eyed the surplus of flowers. "But it has a special meaning."

He handed Leila the flower, and she looked it over, admiring the slight purple staining the petals. "What is it?"

"It's a Morning Glory."

"What does it mean?"

Hyun paused. "In Romaji, it means willful promises."

She stopped admiring the flower to look at him. "What?"

He placed a hand around the one holding the flower. "Heath told me that at the funeral you promised David something. This flower will help you keep your promise through whatever you are to do."

Leila understood the question he left unspoken. "I promised him I would keep living," she said quietly.

Hyun's eyes became soft. "The best promise. How?"

Through loving another. Her thought drew tears, and she ducked her head away to spare Hyun. But an arm pulled her back, and the other held her head as she wept into him.

XII.

A month passed before the doctors released Leila. Even though she had recovered quickly, she remained pale, thin, and relied on her crutch to get around. The doctors suggested she get a ride home, not to push herself. Because of the caution reflecting in their eyes, they weren't worried about strain—her withdrawal from everybody troubled them. She bet their imaginations flew with the possibilities of her shattered soul behind the wheel of a car. So, Heath drove her home.

The lock clicked as Heath unlocked the door and held it open. Leila took a breath, then stepped inside her apartment.

It had been tidied up for her return, looking better than ever. The wood floors shined from a long-needed mop and polish. Picture frames, little trinkets, and a small supply of genres had been shifted since they were found guilty of dust and cleaned—under the sharp eyes of Julianne Neal.

She stood in her bedroom, spotting differences and returning items to their original positions, when Heath came in carrying her duffel bag from her stay.

"What do you plan on doing now?" Heath asked while placing the duffel bag in a chair.

Satisfied with fixing her valuables, she sat on the edge of her bed; her sheets weren't ignored—they smelled of fresh and clean linen. "I'm going to stay and enjoy being out of the hospital."

His hands slipped into his pockets. "You sure?"

Leila smoothed out a pretend wrinkle in her sheets. "I'm sure."

His weight shifted, uneasy with the silence. "Well, call if you need anything."

"I will. Thanks, Heath."

Heath hesitated to leave. He placed a hand on her shoulder, and after she didn't respond, the hand slipped, and he walked out of the room. The door opened in the distance and snicked closed.

Leila stayed on the bed, looking around. Her gaze stopped at the picture frames on her dresser. Most of the pictures consisted of her and David, but others were of her and David with members of the force or at a New Year's party. One of her favorites was them with his parents at their spotless home, causing her eyes to drift over to the picture of her deceased parents.

Focusing on the picture of her parents replayed her reaction to their deaths. The day had been quiet—much to David's disappointment—and they had gathered to discuss a case when her phone rang; she answered it to the coroner's office.

"Detective Wells? This is Coroner John Hall. I have some bad news concerning your parents… They were involved in a severe car wreck. They didn't survive, and I am sorry."

After discussing the details of the wreck to find that her parents were killed on impact and setting a time when she would go claim them, Leila hung up.

"Lei, is everything okay?" David asked.

"My parents are dead."

She didn't feel anything that her parents were gone, just surprise. Her world hadn't been shattered like now.

Forcing her eyes off the pictures, they drifted to the nightstand and her favorite picture: she on David's back and them laughing in Central Park, both helping immune the other to the horrors of their job. Leila glanced back around her room until something foreign caught her attention near the closet doors—a plain Tupperware box sealed with a blue lid.

Using her crutch to stand, she limped over to the box. Leila nudged it with a foot to test its weight and found it quite full. She wouldn't be able to lift and carry the box to her bed, so she eased herself down to her good knee, then used the crutch to sit.

Laying the crutch beside her, she grabbed the top, popped up one corner, and lifted the rest. Immediately, David's scent struck her—his cologne, matching aftershave, and his natural musk. She leaned over the box to inhale and relive memories of being with him in his apartment.

Once the trapped scents dispersed into her room, Leila opened her eyes and found a loose-leaf piece of paper folded on top of the stacks of picture frames, clothes, and other objects she recognized as belonging to David and things she had left in his apartment. The top flap fluttered because of her bedroom fan.

She grabbed it, but apprehension made her hesitate before opening it. Straight off, she recognized Julianne's florid handwriting:

Welcome back, Leila! I debated whether to leave this as a house-warming gift or to give it to you later, but I thought you would like to have it now. I'm sure you know that we already had to clean out David's apartment, and this box is what we thought you would want. Let us know if you need anything, ever.

With our heart,
David Sr. and Julianne

Leila glanced back at her keys on the nightstand; the spare key to David's apartment was missing. She had noticed the difference when she handed her keys to Heath and even when Julianne tried to discreetly take them to return to the landowner by using her husband as cover back in the hospital.

She set the letter aside and hesitated again before fishing into the box for memorabilia. Picture after picture of her and David came out, followed by her favorite sweatshirt of his—the one always lent her—and other small objects they collected.

Lifting the last folded sweater revealed his calendar with a date circled repetitively in blue ink. *"This is the night"*, *"For sure"*, and more encouraging writings surrounded October 7th. At first, she couldn't think of the significance of that date—five days after his birthday—but then remembered it became his funeral.

That realization dulled her contentment of reminiscing the days with him. But her intrigue kept her from turning away, desiring to find out but also frightened to do so.

She picked up the calendar folded at October to reveal a crème envelope trying to obscure a small black box. Leila stared at the envelope with *"For my Lei"* being the only ink visible, clearly in David's handwriting. She set aside the calendar—unable to take her eyes off the envelope—and reached out a shaking hand.

Leila picked up the slightly bulging envelope and brought the black box into full view; she froze: a ring box.

"Dear God... please, don't let it be so." Her breathy prayer went unanswered.

It took a moment to thaw and tear her aching eyes off the box to the trembling envelope in her hand. Her other hand steadied the envelope as it turned over; she untucked the flap and pulled out a blank white card. No writings or graphics kept her interest, so she opened the card to find two notes: one David's handwriting again and the other not.

Love you, Lei, but your gift's not in here, it's in the little box. But read the other note first. David.

She flipped to the other note:

The Phoenix's Eye is one of the rarest jewels in the world. Resembling a fire opal, it is stronger than a diamond; it will never scratch, chip, fade with time, or be destroyed under pressure. Like with the Phoenix, its beauty can only be seen after flames and ashes.

Dread seized her, numbing and icing her fingers to where the envelope and notes slipped back into the box, now leaving her only point of focus being the ring box.

"Dear God, please... please, no," she pleaded again, water welling in her eyes. Like being controlled by an invisible puppeteer, her hand drifted toward the box; it covered the case and pulled it up. Unresponsive to her silent will not to open it, her other hand reached up, grabbed the lid, and opened it.

No sound broke through Leila's throat as tears exploded. Her eyes clamped shut, but she couldn't erase the beautiful red gemstone with the colors of yellow, orange, and gold sparkling fiercely on the silver band of an engagement ring.

Her hand pulled the ring box to her chest as she lay on the floor, curled in the best she could, and continued her silent mourning of lost love, all the while hating herself for having to know.

XIII.

November, December, and January passed painfully through physical therapy before Leila returned to work. Even though glad to see her again, Captain Sullivan watched her constantly in worry. Heath's mouth fell open when she walked into the squad room. He became insensible when she refused to do anything else than be back in the field, so the captain placed her with Heath, and DeMarcus stayed at his desk.

On her second day back, she made sure no one saw her slip into the locker room and retrieve the thin red notebook holding her private case notes about Bryan Foster. After work, Leila drove to an abandoned building—known for housing the homeless. The residents eyed her as she headed toward one of the rusted fire barrels. She didn't hesitate in tossing in the used notebook—her being driven to arrest Foster for selfish glory caused David to die. Not able to let him go.

Watching the flames devour curled-up black pages, she now had no reason to hold on to the killer.

For an entire month, Leila worked with an overprotective Heath, catching minor criminals, or just providing security around New York City. She grew irritated that the captain gave them easy jobs—and with Heath being too careful with what they did. But whenever Leila thought she saw David waiting for her at the cruiser or mistook Heath as David, she appreciated the simple tasks.

"Lei, can I speak with you?" Captain Sullivan began after she and Heath returned from a routine patrol.

Her body locked up at the regret lacing his voice and how he wouldn't make eye contact.

"Sure," she finally answered, and the captain headed toward the hallway containing the interrogation rooms. She left her partners without a glance, knowing through their silence they knew what awaited her; Leila feared what she would see in their downcast eyes.

When they were alone, the captain released a heavy breath, causing her to tense up. "Trust me that I didn't want to force you, Lei, but according to the law… I have to. Uncomfortable as we all were, Heath, DeMarcus, I, and plenty of others had to talk about David. And it truly *did* help."

Once he reached a closed interrogation room, the captain turned to her. Leila stopped farther back when she realized what waited. "A shrink? Come on, Captain. I'm okay; I know I am."

"I don't doubt your judgments, but the law says I must do this… I'm sorry in advance."

True sorrow wavered in his voice. Leila looked away from his glistening eyes to the door hiding a shrink within. She had hoped to skip talking with the forensic psychiatrist—she didn't want someone to see her fragility—and since the required evaluation took so long, the captain must've had a hand in delaying their appointment. But the captain needed to know he could rely on her—make sure she wouldn't freeze in tense situations and risk lives. And she needed to hear it too.

With dread, Leila gave a short nod.

Captain Sullivan placed a hand on her shoulder. "Thank you, Lei. I know this will be tough, but it's necessary. Talking will help you come to terms with David's death."

I really don't think so. She nodded regardless of her thought, took the door handle with a shaking hand, and slipped inside.

Dr. Wes Moretti looked up from a file and placed on a welcoming smile as he stood and offered a hand. A graying man with black-rimmed square glasses, he always wore 'casual psychiatrist' attire—khakis, blue button-up, gray shirt underneath, and brown loafers. She hadn't seen him since Detectives Uehl and Washington's deaths, and she didn't want to see him now. "Hello, Leila. Please have a seat."

After accepting his hand, she seated herself in front of him, and he retook his seat. A yellow notepad obscured the file he had been reading with writings already halfway down the page. Two cups half-full of water sat on the table; Dr. Moretti pushed one to her. "In case you want some."

She thanked him and immediately took a sip, her throat dry at the thought of speaking about her feelings.

"I am deeply sorry for your loss," he began. "David was a good man."

Leila didn't reply, only nodding, and silence ensued.

Dr. Moretti laced his fingers atop the notepad—time to get on topic. "Now, Leila, I know this will be hard, but you must try to cooperate. No one likes admitting their feelings—openly or inwardly—but it is something that needs to be done for your health. When traumatic events occur and you keep those feelings to yourself, they fester inside and become a danger to others if they are released and had not been properly confronted."

Again, she didn't react, just kept her eyes down on the cup in her hands.

"How would you like to begin?"

She shrugged. "However you like."

"This is not my life we are discussing; it is yours. Start wherever you are comfortable." When she still didn't give an answer, he gave a nudge. "How about we start with David? How did you two meet?"

A small smile brushed across her lips at the memory of their first meeting. Arriving late one day, David had to sit in the front, right in front of her. Hurrying to his seat, he literally braked at the sight of her. She greeted him politely, but him blocking the PowerPoint slide annoyed her. He stuttered a one-word reply, then his crooked grin appeared. Leila couldn't look away until the instructor called them out for disrupting the class.

His tardiness never improved since then, which was why she gifted him the Rolex for his birthday.

"We met at the Police Academy, seven days in. We advanced quickly, graduated early, and became homicide detectives here."

"Do you remember your first case together?"

"Yes: a murder of a young college student."

"Who killed her?"

"A jealous ex-boyfriend. She was pregnant with her current boyfriend's baby. The ex found out, confronted her, and in his rage, he killed her."

"Sounds like an easy beginning."

"At first, we thought we arrested the wrong guy because of it being so easy. The following cases became tougher."

Dr. Moretti glanced at the file underneath the notepad. "Can you tell me about the case where you and David were hurt for the first time?"

Leila chuckled. "A lead on a murder directed us to a known criminal from Hungary. Mr. Gyure was a big man and didn't want to talk. He shoved David out of his apartment, but I ducked under his grab to strike him in the throat; he barely flinched. Grabbing my arm, and without any effort, he snapped it like a twig. David returned, knocked him down, and wrapped his arms around his neck for a sleeper hold. During his rampage through his apartment trying to buck David off, he slammed him against a wall, dislocating a shoulder. I shot him in the kneecaps and even though he fell, he still fought. So, David knocked him unconscious with the butt of his gun; we called backup to get him to the station."

Leila found a smile on Dr. Moretti's lips as his hand flew across the notepad. "Sounds exciting."

"That began David's obsession with adrenaline." The statement slipped out of her mouth and brought Leila's mood back down.

His sharp eyes caught her mood change and now they skewered her. "What did you just think of?"

"Nothing."

"Leila, you have to let me in. I cannot help if you don't."

"Who says I need help?"

Dr. Moretti remained quiet, but his eyes observed her curiously.

"*I* think you do," he answered after a long silence. "May I say what I see in you right now? Can I tell you what I've observed?"

Even though she didn't want to know, she shrugged.

"I see a broken woman sitting before me. A woman who has had her world ripped out from beneath her and is flailing as she falls, trying to grab something to straighten herself again."

The psychiatrist leaned forward. "You're lost, Leila. You don't know what to do, and you don't know where to even begin. The simplest mention of a close memory with David has you withdrawing. You're trying to pick up life where you left it like nothing ever happened, but it's in pieces—it can't be put back the way it was."

She couldn't look at him. "Then what do you suggest I do?"

"Find a drive; find something to keep you going. It must be strong and has to come from within."

"A drive..." Her promise to keep living?

No, something firmer; something so consuming, she couldn't focus on anything else.

He scribbled on the notepad. "That will be enough for today. I leave you with the goal of finding a drive, and next time we meet, you can tell me about your progress. Thank you, Leila."

Leila practically ran out, not wanting to spend another second with a man who pretended to know what she was going through.

Knowing the shrink would inform the captain of her instability, Leila went to his office and tapped on his door before Dr. Moretti could. "Captain, may I speak with you?"

He looked up from a file, surprised she had finished so soon. "Of course."

She closed the door, then hovered at his desk, wanting to sprint out instead of raising the white flag. "Captain, I know I can still do this, it's just... I think I need more time."

Captain Sullivan nodded. "If you need some, take it; I won't stop you. But may I ask what happened with Dr. Moretti?"

"Not something I wanted to be told..." she drifted off then picked up the conversation like she hadn't spoken. "I'll be back. There's no way I could leave this job. It's my life; it makes me who I am."

"Lei, please understand this," he began as he came around his desk and took her hands, "but this life was yours *and* David's. Now you need to ask yourself if you can do this job alone."

Leila averted her gaze before he saw the doubt in her eyes. "Thank you for understanding, Captain."

He led her to the door. "Remember that we're here for you."

Leila hugged him, then retrieved her jacket and purse from her desk. Heath and DeMarcus watched with worry; Heath stood to approach. She raised a hand to stop him from speaking.

"I need some more time, Heath. I'm sorry."

She retreated from the hurt etched on his face.

XIV.

The gas pedal nearly touched the floorboard as Leila tried to escape Dr. Moretti's words caving in on her. What did he expect her to do? Admit she wasn't as independent as she portrayed? Others expected her to be resilient. Her strange dream made her decide not to stay hidden in sorrow; she faced the world again, but with a mask protecting her fragility.

Glancing down at the increasing speedometer, her foot eased up; she blew out the imprisoned breath. So, what kind of drive? A useless hobby? No, something to take her focus off David. She ran through possibilities until a quiet mumble, as soft as a vibration, almost made her lose control of the car.

Foster.

She couldn't. Vengeance wouldn't give her justice, and revenge was never a straight path. It couldn't be the drive Dr. Moretti meant; Leila wouldn't come to terms with David's death by being obsessed with killing his killer. Besides, she gave her oath as a cop not to pursue vendettas.

No. She couldn't consider it for even a moment longer. The thought disappeared at her adamant refusal. Now she focused on maintaining a legal speed, but where did the voice come from?

Arriving at Woodlawn Cemetery quicker than she should have, the black Nissan wound its way through the large cemetery before parking beside the curb at David's grave.

Leila stepped out of the car and ascended to David's grave. A bouquet of red carnations and white roses lay on his grave, placed by Leila four days ago. She stood at the foot of the grave staring at the flowers, trying to ease her racing thoughts.

"You're here every day," a man spoke suddenly. Leila turned to an elderly grave keeper with warm, gentle eyes. Sunspots made his skin wrinkled and splotched, and bruises covered his paper-like skin.

"I've seen that dedication once before, but as time passed, visits became less frequent as they accepted the passing."

"Who was that?"

"Me." He shuffled closer to peer at David's grave. "It took time to realize I could go on without Elaine. I still miss her dearly, but I know she's always with me, so I haven't truly lost her. I just can't physically see or touch her."

"I think that's what makes it so hard."

He nodded. "At this man's funeral, you didn't weep over him like many other cases. Only a few tears escaped your composure, and you spoke so reverently. You wanted not to be seen as a lost woman, but one of strength—one of independence, not weak. Everything you did came from your grief-stricken heart; it showed then, and still shows now."

He looked at her; long years of experiences strengthened his tired eyes. "This is the only place where you can think without others pressing down on you. You don't have to put up a strong front here. 'There is no grief like the grief that does not speak'; Henry Wadsworth Longfellow for you."

She stared at him, speechless. They had never met, but he so easily saw through her.

He considered the grave again until he stretched his back. "Sorry, it's the old man in me rambling on. I should leave you to your time alone." With a palsy-like wave, he sauntered off.

"Sir," Leila called to stop the man. He turned back around, and she took a deep breath. "Thank you. You're the only one who has truly understood, and you barely know me."

"Darling," the man said with a sigh. "Being a grave keeper, you see the true sides of people. I know people better than their closest friends and even their family. When death comes into someone's life, the fake tears wash away façades and reveal their true selves. But you had no mask to wash away; your tears just dried to shield your lamenting soul."

"You still see a soul in me?"

"It's still there. You are broken—shattered even—but the pieces are there to be reassembled, only as a variation of the original picture. Your soul has shrunken in on itself, but I see a flicker of a promise to return, more defined from going through flames." With no more to say, he bowed his balding head and shuffled away.

Leila watched the old grave keeper leave, wishing he would've stayed longer. His words heartened her more than anyone else's—he saw hope for her.

Considering David's grave, she moved to his side and lay down. She watched the long limbs of the willow tree dance above her. The stillness of the cemetery held a mournful air about it, unlike the peaceful atmosphere of Central Park.

"The city is quiet without you, David; there's no life. New York feels... empty. Nothing's here anymore."

A red bird transferred from one branch to another. "Dr. Moretti says I should find a drive, but how can I when nothing takes my mind off you?"

The always cold bullet wound closest to her heart warmed in a comforting heat. The change of sensation stole her breath, and she turned to the mound as if expecting David to be lying beside her, head propped up under an arm and grinning crookedly at her surprise.

She massaged the wound. "You're still there?"

Another warming.

"But how will this help me get past you? Won't I just be pulled closer to you?"

The warming suddenly disappeared, and she was back to feeling the same—he could leave her if needed.

Tears sprung to her eyes with a grim smile. "You'd never abandon me in the sea without a life vest."

The wound warmed like the lifting of his smile. She rolled over to face the mound of dirt, comforted by the realization of his closeness.

XV.

Tearing herself from David's side, Leila arrived back in New York City after the sun had set. As she walked up to her apartment building's front door, she stopped before opening it, feeling that she shouldn't call it a day yet. She turned around and walked down the sidewalk, pulled in the direction of Chinatown.

Bright lights—some flickering to gain attention—blinded Leila as she walked among the bustling crowd of locals and the few tourists who ventured out into the night. The various smells and sounds of frying bread, vendors screaming their merchandise, steaming vegetables, cooking noodles, and sweet spices brought her following her nose to different restaurants and side cafes, but she continued her leisurely walk, not yet hungry.

Neither did she feel a pang of loneliness at seeing the public enjoying life in the company of a loved one; David's presence at the graveyard kept her comforted, if only slightly.

The clamor of the market faded behind her as she neared the close living quarters. Leila stopped, perturbed at the stillness and anticipation in the air. It wasn't a looming dread like the night of David's birthday, just an energy that something would happen. A glimmering hope of the future warmed the air. She waited for the fate to find her, but glancing around and finding nothing in sight, Leila decided she was being too expectant, looking for things that wouldn't happen. So, she turned and headed home, set on grabbing dinner at her favorite takeout.

"Hey! Wait!"

She stopped to look down a wide alley—somewhat lit by the bright neon restaurant lights, highlighting the grouped trashcans and stray trash—to see a black man with his long dreadlocks tied back by a rubber band running toward her.

Just a little taller than her, he wore a dark blue muscle shirt over broad shoulders connecting to long, muscular arms, white basketball shorts, and black basketball shoes. From what she could see of his face shadowed by the lights behind him, his defined features and open eyes made him attractive.

"You're a cop, right?" he asked in a heavy Island accent. His brown eyes glanced down to the badge clipped on her belt.

Leila nodded, eyes and ears straining for trouble. "I am. What's wrong?"

"Well, nothing criminal-like, but I need help." A hand scratched his head nervously. "Can you fight?"

Her brow furrowed. "I can; why?"

"I'm a street fighter; I fight for money to feed my family and keep our home. My partner abandoned me again, and now I either have to fight alone or forfeit and pay them." The man jerked a thumb over his shoulder.

Two Chinese men dressed in Kung Fu pants and white muscle shirts strained to see who the Island native talked to. They were smaller than the black man but both equally broad through their shoulders and arms, and spry looking in their quick movements.

Leila began to decline help—street fighting was illegal—when the wound nearest to her heart flashed hot and a heat flamed up, excited and eager about the fight. *This is the beginning.*

"What are the rules?" she asked.

A wide smile erased anxiety, and he placed a hand on her shoulder. "You don't know how relieved I am, thank you. Anyway, rules: there aren't really any, but you can't use weapons, and once your opponent is down, leave 'em; don't keep going—we only fight until one admits defeat. Plus, this is a Tag fight: two partners, one goes out first, and the other waits until they get tagged in."

"You're first?" They made their way into the alley; the Chinese men eyed her.

"You'll be on deck, if that's alright with you?"

She nodded, then faced their opponents. One of the Chinese men's eyes bulged as he saw her badge and gun.

"She a cop! She has gun! She can't use!" Both backed away, ready to flee.

"She knows. She won't use them," the Islander began to soothe the frantic men.

"Street fighting is illegal, but since I'm helping, I'll look the other way." Leila took off her jacket and laid it against the nearest building's wall, then backed away from the Island native and the Chinese men.

After glancing at each other, one of the Chinese fighters backed away. Leila flexed her fingers, rotated her shoulders, and stretched her legs while keeping her eyes on the two opponents facing off.

The Chinese man brought his feet together, bowed, then took a wide stance. The black man moved into his stance, which never stopped moving—he seemed to be dancing, swiftly and smoothly moving from side to side.

With an odd yell, the Chinese man struck out with a fist at the Islander; he ducked under the outstretched arm. The Chinese man jumped to avoid the sweeping kick the black man performed to trip him and came down with his fist. Bending into a back handspring so the hit missed, the black man stayed in a handstand. He swung his legs around and kicked the Chinese man in the stomach, sending him stumbling backward. The Islander slid out a leg to trip him up. Jumping to his feet, the Islander grabbed his opponent and threw him into the concrete wall. He slid down the wall, shaking his head to clear it but gave up and raised a hand to forfeit.

"Your turn!" the black man said as he ran toward Leila. They passed each other, and Leila changed to the Panther stance while the other Chinese man came out.

Leila waited for her adversary to make the first move. With a yell matching his partner's, he threw a fist which she slipped under and stepped to the side, taunting him to attack again. He did so but followed up his first punch with a second. She dodged again. It soon became one-sided with Leila staying defensive and him struggling to hit her.

A foreign power rose within, angry at her cowardly fighting. Instead of stepping to the side to avoid another of the Chinese's attacks, she dropped her fists down on his feet. When he bent over in pain, she drove a fist into his stomach. Without a chance to recover, her other hand gripped his throat, and she hurled him over her body. He slammed into the pavement, unconscious.

His partner ran over to check on him as the Islander jogged up to Leila. "I think he's out," he said. The Chinese man raised a hand in defeat. "Great hits."

Leila took a breath, lungs screaming in pain from movement and straining her muscles. "Thanks."

She looked down at her palms. Her body ached from the simple movements, but it also pulsated in energy with every beat of her heart. Power surged through her veins. It felt good. *How did I do that?*

The fallen man finally came up into a sitting position. Keeping him steady, his comrade retrieved something from a bag, then approached. "Here, you earned," he said as he handed the black man a roll of hundred-dollar bills. He bowed, then returned to his fallen comrade. Helping him up, they retrieved the bag and made a hurried retreat.

"I can't thank you enough for what you did," the Islander began after the Chinese opponents disappeared. He split the stack of money in half and handed Leila one of the piles.

She pushed the money back. "No, I can't. I don't need it."

"But you deserve it. You're the reason we won."

"You have a family to support and a home to keep, I don't. You keep it all."

His shoulders slumped. "If you won't take your half, how am I to repay you?"

Leila forced a smile to assure him. "You don't have to. Knowing I helped you and your family is enough."

"I have to do something… Have you eaten?"

"You don't have to buy me anything." She pointed back at Chinatown. "I'm grabbing something on my way home."

The man's eyes lit up. "We're having gumbo, and we would love to have you there. Do you agree with that for payment?"

Leila hesitated; she hadn't even learned his name yet. Her wound warming again urged her to go.

"If you're sure…"

"I am."

"And it wouldn't be too much of a problem?" she pressed.

"No, it wouldn't. We'd be happy to have you with us."

A second passed before she answered. "I'd love to."

He smiled with brilliant white teeth. "I'm Jamaal Gordon."

XVI.

On the walk to the Gordons' home, Jamaal kept the time from drifting into awkwardness by going into his life. He married his childhood sweetheart, Jade, then moved from Jamaica to New York where they had two daughters, Zaira and Eve. To provide a steady income since every job he attained he lost when the company experienced budget cuts, he joined the street fighting world by using Capoeira—a Brazilian art form combining elements of martial arts, music, and dance—since he and Jade used to perform Capoeira dances for tourists and in competitions for money.

From the direction they traveled, Jamaal and his family lived in the poorer section of Chinatown, back away from the main tourist attraction. After passing through many alleyways with Leila tensing at each huddled group of men eclipsed by dim lights, they emerged into a square of tenement buildings. Stairs climbed to each of the three floors, and open walkways looked out on the manicured garden in the middle.

Jamaal led Leila up underneath nosy neighbors peering down at his unfamiliar white guest to door 205, muffling little girls' laughter. Jamaal knocked; the laughter quieted as somebody moved to the door. It cracked open, and a cool brown face peeked through the crack.

"I was getting worried, Jamaal," a thick accent—matching her husband's but pitched femininely—came through the crack as the door shut, followed by the click of a chain lock and deadbolts. The opening door revealed a light-skinned Jamaican woman with long hair reaching her waist, shorter than Jamaal. With the perfect hourglass figure, she should've been a model instead of a performer. Light green eyes matching the jade necklace around her neck widened in surprise at Leila.

"Sorry, Jade. Ran into some trouble, and Lei here helped me out."

Jade Gordon's eyes flickered back and forth, defenses rising. "What kind of trouble?"

He lifted his hands to calm his wife before she attacked. "Nothing extreme now; London never showed up to meet the Jeung brothers, so I ran out to the street and found Leila. She fought with me, and we won... for once. She wouldn't take any of the money, so I thought about giving her a meal as reward." He looked at Leila; his eyes saddened as the brashness of inviting a stranger to dinner in his home hit him.

She could understand—it had been pretty hasty for her to accept visiting a stranger's place, but she felt comfortable with Jamaal. He probably had been too caught up in the victory to be rational. "It's the only thing I could think of," he ended.

Distrust disappeared in Jade's eyes, replaced with gratitude, and she smiled. "Sorry for being standoffish." She stepped closer and hugged Leila. "You are welcome here and thank you for what you did."

The sudden gesture surprised her; she couldn't help but stiffen from years of being a detective—and not getting much gestures of kindness anymore. Jade noticed but Leila smiled as she released her to smooth over her own roughness. "I understand and thank you."

Without any hesitation, she motioned them inside the apartment.

As the door closed two little girls—one five and the other seven—hurled themselves at their father. Jamaal caught them up in his arms and kissed them both as he swung them around, bringing forth squeals.

"You're happy, Daddy! Does that mean you won?" one of the girls asked.

"It does!"

The girls kissed him, expressing their happiness.

One noticed her. "Who's your lady friend, Daddy?"

Jamaal turned so both daughters could see. "This is Leila."

"Hi, Miss Leila," the smallest girl greeted.

Her charm was contagious. "Hello, you can call me Lei. What's your name?"

She ducked into her father's chest. "Eve."

"And I'm Zaira," the older sister added in.

"Nice to meet you both."

"Are you gonna stay and eat with us?" Eve asked.

"I am."

Eve wriggled in her father's arm. "We have a guest!" Zaira dropped down to head to the kitchen with her mother.

Jamaal jerked his head toward the kitchen-doubling-as-a-dining room. "In here."

Smells of sausage, rice, spices, and cornbread enveloped the room; she found herself following her nose in. Leila lingered by the table, not sure how to help until, at Jamaal's insistence, she took a seat. Jamaal sat Eve next to him as Jade and Zaira walked around the table: Zaira holding the plate of cornbread while her mother placed bowls of gumbo in front of each. Zaira came back with glasses, and when Jade filled them with tea, they finally took their seats.

After blessing the food, the Gordons and their guest ate. The sweetness of the cornbread balanced the gumbo spices. Eve and Zaira kept awkward silence away by retelling all the details of their day at school, even about how Eve beat Timothy at a game of H.O.R.S.E. to prove he wasn't better than her. As her daughters continued to talk, Jade turned to Leila.

"Sorry about having to listen to this."

Leila shook her head. "No, this is great. I don't have a family of my own and no relatives."

"No family? What kind of job do you have?"

She paused, wondering if she should tell the truth and risk them asking questions about what happened to her and David, but they hadn't recognized her. "I'm a detective."

"Police?" Eve repeated, her interest piqued, immediately pausing her story.

"Yes. I'm with the police force."

"Do you have a badge?"

She nodded, unclipped her badge and handed it to the girl.

Eve's little hands flipped the badge over with wide eyes. Zaira leaned over to see. "Do you carry a gun?" she asked.

"I do."

"Have you ever shot someone?"

"Zaira," her mother said sternly.

Leila raised a hand to signify it was okay. "I have had to, yes."

I wished I killed the last one. Her face grew dark from the memory. She wasn't quick enough throwing up her mask, for Jade gained her daughters' attention.

"Girls, I think it's time for bed; you have school tomorrow."

Eve gave Leila back her badge before Jamaal picked her up.

"I'll take them to bed," he said and grabbed his oldest daughter's hand, but Eve turned in his arms to look back at their guest.

"Miss Lei, are you gonna come back and visit?"

Leila clipped the badge back onto her belt. "If you wish for me to and your parents agree, of course I will."

"Yay!" Her face contorted in a yawn. "Well, goodnight, Miss Lei." Her head dropped on her father's shoulder, and he took his daughters out of sight.

Jade stood to collect the dishes. Leila rose to help, but she stopped her. "Oh no, Leila, let me do this."

"I can help you," Leila persisted.

"But you're our guest. I'm not putting you to work."

"At least let me help take the dishes," she said as she grabbed the glasses and the empty plate of cornbread.

Jade Gordon opened her mouth to deny her offer but closed it. The women took the dishes over to the small sink and Jade began washing.

The girls' departure drained life from the room. Leila had always been fine with silence but not Jade. "What do you do for the police?"

Glancing at her again reassured Leila that Jade was only curious and didn't know her identity. "I'm a homicide detective."

She grimaced. "That must be hard."

"Not when you become used to it. Besides we don't only handle homicides, we help out in any way we can. Someone has to do it."

"Who's we?"

"My squad: Heath, DeMarcus… and me." She caught herself before mentioning David, which could have triggered a recognition pairing his name with hers.

Leila hurried to divert the spotlight off her before Jade inquired about her pause. "So, what made you move up here? New York City has always attracted visitors, but it must've been a big change."

"Jamaal and I always wanted to see New York. We saved up a lot of money from dancing, and we took our chance. We've loved it. Well, I know this isn't much" —she gestured around— "but it's much better than our old home."

"Have you thought about going back to show Zaira and Eve your home?"

"We have. As soon as we raise enough money again, we're going back. To visit or to stay, we're not sure yet."

Silence fell between them as Jade washed away the remnants of dinner. To keep the questions off her, Leila found another topic. "Can you tell me more about this Capoeira Jamaal uses to fight? I've never seen it before."

"It's a warrior's dance passed down through slaves. It usually involves music with the Capoeira participants in a circle; they spar while dancing in Capoeira." She stopped and motioned toward a bookshelf with pictures. "There are pictures of us performing."

Leila walked over. Pictures of large groups of people surrounding two people in the center mingled with others of their daughters and family shots. Jamaal wore green and yellow loose pants and a tight muscle shirt; Jade wore green shorts and a green bikini top with large Samba feathers on her back.

Every picture caught them in a different position as they sparred. Most of the pictures were of Capoeira performances in the streets of Jamaica with a large group of spectators and tourists watching, while a few others on sandy beaches had smaller crowds.

"How did you get into it?" Leila asked as she continued to look at the pictures.

"Capoeira is popular in Brazil and is spreading to Jamaica. We just grew an interest in it and began performing for money."

Jade paused. Leila tensed at the air thick with curiosity, and she waited for the question. "I know this is personal, but are you by yourself? Before, you said you had no relatives and no family of your own… I hope there is someone with your heart. This city is too big to be alone."

There was.

Leila took in a deep breath to answer when she saw their wedding picture on a beach. Her mind flashed back to David's engagement ring and the date he chose to propose. She kept her eyes on the shelf. "No, I don't have anyone I'm seeing right now. Work has been… quite difficult lately." She attempted to chuckle, to brush off her mood-killer, but it fell flat. "Maybe I need to move to a smaller place."

Silence hung between the women; Jade must've known more hid behind her answer, but she let it drop. "I'm sorry, Leila. I'm sure you'll find the right one—whenever you're ready."

Leila didn't reply but turned at Jamaal walking in, bringing back life. "Sorry for leaving, Lei; I always put the girls to sleep."

"Jade showed me some of your pictures from Jamaica. The way you move in fighting is unbelievable."

He shrugged. "Hey, you aren't too bad yourself. You dodged every attack, and before I knew it, you had knocked him unconscious."

Jade turned to Leila. "Really?"

Jamaal jumped in with the story, "Qing kept throwing punches, and she sidestepped him every time. On his last move where he tried to trick her, she ducked under him, slammed her fists on his feet, thrust one in his stomach, then threw him over her."

Jade looked back at her; Leila shrugged. "It wasn't that great."

"Lei, you were incredible. You didn't play around with pretty moves like I did."

"What style of fighting do you use?" Jade asked before Leila could change the subject.

"Five-Animals Kung Fu; it's not much."

105

"Not much?" He chuckled dryly. "It *is* much! Look how powerful you were."

I shouldn't be though because of my injuries and lack of practice.

"I was thinking… Well, if it's not too much to ask of you, that, ummm…" Jamaal struggled.

Jade rolled her eyes. "He's wondering if you will be his fighting partner. London—the man that left him—has always been unreliable, and you're the only one he's talked so much about."

"We don't fight every night; sometimes we'll fight four days a week and others none. It depends on who wants to fight," Jamaal said, close to begging.

The coldest wound near her heart warmed and spread. *I get it, David. I'm needed.*

She nodded.

XVII.

For the next four weeks, Leila practiced at Hyun's gym in the morning, then fought with Jamaal whenever they had an awaiting fight and ate dinner with the Gordons. Jamaal's former partnership must've been unsteady for every match they won to his exhilaration—not used to victory. He put the winnings to good use since the Gordons' apartment improved, and the girls modeled their new clothes for Leila.

They adjusted just fine to Leila's sudden involvement, and she wasn't having trouble doing so either. Just like the Neals, the Gordons became another adoptive family.

After the first week, Leila noticed a difference in her body and mood. Her body didn't ache every time she moved, and she was nimbler than ever, but most importantly, she could feel again. The ghosts of pain still haunted her, but it had dulled. The growing attachment to fighting awoke her senses by returning a sense of control and strength. But as she continued to fight, that desire for power wanted more fuel.

"Fighting is helping, but you need more," Hyun said one morning as Leila practiced in his gym. She turned to find him leaning against one of the paper doors, his eyes admiring her return to stability.

"Like what?" she asked.

He considered her a moment before answering. "A fighting tournament."

A raised eyebrow encouraged him to continue—he had her interest.

Hyun pushed himself off the door and headed for her. "I've heard of a fighting tournament on an island in the middle of the Pacific called Panordom. It's known as the 'all realms' island. This tag tournament determines who are the Rulers of the Realms."

"And you suggest Jamaal and I participate?"

"It is your decision. But I am suggesting that you get away from the stress of your life here, ease your mind in a different world, and relieve yourself of your memories." He placed his hands on her shoulders. "I think this is what you need. You long for something more challenging than just street fighting—you want to prove to yourself that you are powerful and use-ful."

Her eyes shot up to him. A grim smile brushed his lips. "You know you can't hide anything from me. I've seen the doubt in your eyes that you think so. You want to feel accepted again, but you were never cast out.

"Take this opportunity to branch out and find yourself again—if not whole, just start putting pieces back together."

Leila thought about it. "I'll discuss it with Jamaal." Without another word, Hyun's hands slipped from her shoulders, and he left.

"LEI, GUESS WHAT I FOUND out!" Jamaal greeted as she shut the door to the Gordons' apartment.

The two girls hurried to her. "What?" The girls hurled themselves at her; she hugged them and picked up Eve.

Jade turned, halting her preparation of the Chinese food for lunch. "Your fighting has gained the attention of a company that has put together a fighting tournament on some island off the coast of New Zealand, nearly in the middle of the ocean."

"Really?" Leila walked into the kitchen. "Hyun suggested the same thing while I worked out today."

Jamaal looked up from the paper. "So, what do you think?"

"What are the details?"

He waved the paper at her. "It's all right here."

Leila put the little girl down, sat beside the Islander, and looked at the sheet of paper. Jamaal couldn't wait for her to read it herself. "It's a four-week tournament and the rules are the same for our street fighting: no weapons, tag team, and fight to knock down or knock out."

"Have you heard of this island?" she asked as she continued to read.

"No, I haven't. It must be private."

Nor had she heard of the host—a weapons manufacturer known as Xander. Amadeus Xander was a very gracious man indeed for inviting strangers onto his island to fight for four weeks. Something didn't sound quite right.

Jamaal speaking pulled her out of her disconcerting thoughts, "And the prize for winning…"

Leila reached the bottom of the page to read the prize reward of two million dollars. Her eyes stopped at the price; it would be plenty for Jamaal and his family to go back to Jamaica, build a better house for his family and the ones already there, and keep going.

Looking up, Jamaal's eyes were distant and hopeful; his wife wore the same expression. Leila and Jamaal had a good shot at winning, so they could entertain the dream of having that amount of money.

She turned back to the paper; for them to go back home, she must agree to go. Hyun excited her that she could attain what she longed for. Leila should have immediately told Jamaal to get ready, but she hesitated about leaving—going would begin her break from David. Did she want to? Was she strong enough to handle it?

Am I supposed to do this, David? She pressed a hand to the wound and felt nothing. Odd that he wouldn't give her a nudge to go. It made her more anxious.

"Jamaal... I need to talk with someone before I decide."

Confusion swept over his face, but he nodded anyway. Leila stood and looked at Jade. "I'm sorry for running out, Jade."

"It's okay, Leila."

She waved farewell to the girls, then hurried out of the apartment.

LEILA STEPPED OUT OF HER car and stared at the green hump underneath the willow tree. The branches swayed in the wind, assuring her that she came to the right place and beckoning her toward her lover's grave. She folded herself down before the bump, eyes pleading into David's headstone for an answer.

"David... what am I to do? This is the best opportunity for Jamaal and his family to go back to Jamaica."

Her wound icing jolted her like the touch of a cold hand. *"That's not the true reason,"* David's voice whispered.

His voice halted every thought, muscle, and heartbeat. Her eyes flew around the cemetery but didn't find another soul with her. Reason made her doubt it had been him, though no one else could've spoken; her heart knew that it was him.

"David?" her voice wavered, sounding weak and fragile after weeks of strength.

"It's me."

She gasped for air. It took her a moment to find her voice again, "You're able to talk to me now?"

"You need my voice to be your conscience. Do you not want me to?"

"NO! No! No! Please don't. I need you," she cried, frantic he would leave her after providing this spark.

His chuckle nearly killed her by stealing her breath. She missed that rumble in his throat as much as his crooked smile. *"I couldn't do that to you, Lei."*

She sighed heavily at his joking. "Please don't scare me like that again."

"I promise. Helping out as your conscience doesn't mean I'm taking over—there are things you have to figure out yourself."

"Alright."

"Now, admit the true reason why you need to go. You have to tell yourself why; it's not for Jamaal and his family."

Leila stared at his headstone, wishing there wasn't a reason other than going for Jamaal. Her admittance came out quiet and reluctant, "I have to go for me."

"This is the beginning of the future we talked about."

She choked on the breath lumping in her throat. "I will meet... him?"

"What I just say? Geez, Lei." She imagined him rolling his eyes in exasperation. *"You'll learn, but anyway, you may or may not go depending on my answer. A part of you is terrified beyond reason to meet him while the other—and you don't want to admit this—desires to find him, needing to feel love again that he can give you. Fighting has lessened the emptiness, but only he can completely fill it."*

"I don't think I'm ready."

"You will never be ready, but as Hyun said, you need to find yourself again and you won't here."

"David..." Her breath hitched under the pressure of moving on. "I can't do this; it's too soon."

"Yes, you can; you're stronger than you think. It won't be easy, but nothing ever is. This will be one of your greatest tests—not only of your physicality but of your will. You need to see how strong you really are. You must be ready to accept that."

Her eyes watered as she struggled with a decision. She wanted to go to prove that she could come back—to remain the strong one—but then she didn't for fear of realizing that David wasn't everything to her like she had believed.

A gentle breeze blew, moving her hair as if a hand brushed through it to let David whisper in her ear, *"Go."* Her heart swelled up at his poignant desire for her to move on and his reluctance to let her go to another.

Leila remained wrapped up inside, holding onto the warmth his voice provided for a while until she felt someone watching. She opened her eyes and turned to find Jamaal hiding behind a tree. When he saw that she spotted him, he stepped into clear view, embarrassed.

"I swear I wasn't stalking you; I worried that something was wrong, and I followed to make sure. I'm sorry if I—"

Leila stopped him. "Jamaal, it's fine. I just needed to talk to someone."

He shifted uneasily. "Not trying to be nosy but who was he?"

"This is David: he was my boyfriend and partner in the police force."

"When did he go?"

"About five months ago."

He opened his mouth to speak but changed his mind and closed it.

"You wish to know how," she guessed.

"You don't have to tell me."

"No, I will. I should've told you sooner but..." she trailed off. *It was still too early.* She locked gazes with Jamaal. "Come sit by me; it's quite a long story."

He hesitated before walking to her and folding himself down. She slowly began talking about David, which transitioned into their cases and a brief summary of that fateful night. Before she knew it, she told him about The Between and David's connection with her.

After she finished, a heavy silence hung between them. Leila couldn't make herself look away from David's headstone to Jamaal as she waited for his reply.

"How have you kept on this long without David?" Jamaal whispered.

Not what she expected him to say. "He says I'm... stronger than I think."

"You doubt that?"

"How can I not when I've been moping around, lost?"

Jamaal didn't answer for the longest until his hand touched hers, making her look at him. "That's how you think you look; I see a composed, strong, resilient woman who is working her way back to who she was. I had no clue something this devastating happened to you. You've done so well keeping this from sight to avoid pity, huh?"

She couldn't find the words to agree, so she gave a small nod, not looking him in the eye. "How do you know that? Am I easy to see through?"

"No, not at all. I figure someone as stoic as you would hate sympathy. You'd rather deal with a problem by yourself— total opposite from me. You're quiet; you have more going on in your head than you show. You're just a private person."

Could this be what David meant by her being strong? The warming of her wound answered her.

"Can I ask you something?" he began, and with her nod, he went on. "Now that you've let me in a little bit, will you let me try to help? Either by talking something over with me or just venting, and I don't have to reply. I don't want you to be alone anymore."

Leila considered it; with him stating that he knew she was private, he'd understand she would still keep secrets. "I think opening up to someone is what I've needed all along. It's just that thought has always terrified me, letting someone know me inside and out."

"Did you open up fully to David?"

"…Not entirely."

"Then I don't expect any more."

She appreciated his attempt to understand. "There will come nights you probably don't want to hear more of my sob story."

"Don't think that; I'll be there."

Leila let out a lung-emptying sigh, reaching a decision. "Then we will go to Panordom. This chance to get away is too essential to pass up."

Jamaal's face lit up, and he struggled to control his joy. He gave up and wrapped his arms around Leila. She could picture David's crooked grin by the warmth spreading through her body, pleased with her moving on.

XVIII.

The tournament set for the second week of April didn't leave Leila and Jamaal long to prepare themselves. For the rest of March, they abandoned the risk of getting hurt in street battles and practiced under Hyun's watchful eyes in his gym. He noted that they had a great chance of winning, which further improved their morale.

"If either of you had been in the tournaments I participated in, you would be the winners instead of me. You are incredibly powerful." He said it to both, but Hyun's eyes stayed on Leila—he directed the ending statement to her.

Hyun pulled her aside at the end of their last practice. "You're stronger than before, Lei, and I'm not just talking about physically."

A power stirred within her—now even stronger at knowing David hadn't left her completely.

"David said I was, and Jamaal proved it to me," she said.

"David said?"

"A few days ago. He talks to me now; he's acting as my conscience."

Hyun's eyebrows rose in surprise. "The David I remember who had the mindset of a child sometimes? *That* David?"

"*Yes, Hyun. The very same,*" David said. Leila pictured him rolling his eyes. *"Death changes people, don't you know?"*

She chuckled at their comments. "He says he's changed… but how he said it tells me differently."

David snorted. *"I wouldn't be me without sarcasm."*

A wide smile warmed Hyun's face. "That's the best thing to power you." He wrapped her up in his arms. "Things are waiting for you, Lei, but don't let them change who you are. Just let them strengthen you."

Nuan also hugged her. "Be strong but stay soft." Hyun gave his wishes to Jamaal before Leila left with her fighting partner to spend their last night with the Jamaican family.

FROM J.F.K. INTERNATIONAL AIRPORT THEY'D fly to Atlanta then down to Lima, Peru, and board a passenger ferry for Panordom. It only held half of their number; another ferry from Japan would meet them at the island, carrying the rest.

"Bye, Daddy; we'll miss you," Eve said as she hugged her father the following morning in the airport. Jamaal's girls hung onto his neck, reluctant to let him go away for nearly a month. He peeled his daughters off only to be kissed and held onto in almost the same manner by his wife.

"Come here, Leila. You're a part of this family too," Jade said as her family all wrapped around each other in a final group hug.

Leila waved her suggestion away.

"Get over here, Lei," Jamaal ordered.

Eve poked her head over her father's shoulder. "Miss Lei, we want to give you a goodbye hug, too!"

Leila hesitated, but with their persistence, she gave in and went over to their embrace. They enveloped her as well, and she *had* found another family. Letting go of them was hard.

"You take care of yourself and Jamaal for me," Jade said as she cupped the detective's face and gave her a peck on the cheek. Jamaal complained that he would be fine.

"Bye, Miss Lei." The youngest daughter raised her arms to be lifted.

She grabbed her under the arms and spun her around. "Bye, little Eve." Pecking her on the jawbone made the girl squeal in delight. Placing Eve on the ground, she kneeled to hug Zaira.

After the farewells were over, Leila and Jamaal joined the boarding line for their terminal.

"Lei! Leila, wait!"

She turned around, recognizing the voices, hoping it wasn't her imagination. David Sr. and Julianne Neal ran toward them. She didn't tell them about leaving for fear of how they would react.

They waited for Leila to reach them as she made her way back through the boarding line. Only Hyun and Nuan knew about the tournament.

"Who told you?" she asked.

"Hyun," David's mother confessed.

She smiled; she wasn't angry—just nervous. "Should've known."

No anger reflected in his eyes, so she wasn't defensive when David Sr. grabbed her hands. "We're proud you're taking the next step. I know you will never forget David, but this may be the perfect opportunity to ease some of the pain of losing him."

Julianne cupped her face. "We will support you in every way we can. Don't live in the past; move on. It is part of life."

"I'm trying."

Both parents smiled genuinely. "We love you as if you were our own child."

They enveloped her in a hug and kissed her in farewell, but she clung onto them now, afraid of losing them in stepping on the plane.

"Take care, Lei," Julianne said as they broke away from each other.

"And we shall be cheering you on," David Sr. encouraged.

117

She suddenly didn't want to leave, and the Neals saw the fear trembling in her eyes. David Sr. kissed her forehead. "Just breathe and go."

After doing what he said, Leila let them go. A sob would escape if she opened her mouth; she nodded in thanks for their support and turned to join Jamaal in line. She didn't look back as they moved deeper into the terminal, knowing the last sight of David's parents would break her composure.

They found their seats in the first-class section, placed their carry-on bags in the overhead compartment, and seated: Leila by the window; Jamaal on the outside.

Gratefully, Jamaal accepted her withdrawal by assuming who her visitors were. Leaving her in silence, he grabbed a pillow, put in some earphones, and reclined his seat to rest during the flight.

With the increasing speed of the plane taking off, her breathing turned near to hyperventilation; panic consumed her when they were in the air. She almost shook Jamaal awake to call off her decision to go, but the love and support from David's parents pressed down her unease. Wanting to back out infuriated another part of her, needing to prove that she could see it through.

The coldest wound warmed; she massaged it but wondered if she made the wrong choice—this was the first step to leaving David behind for good. Her heart rate increased again at that finality.

David's voice calmed her. *"Staying behind in our past would've been the wrong choice. You have to move on."*

THEY ARRIVED IN ATLANTA, CHANGED flights, and returned to the air in an hour's time. Jamaal couldn't sleep anymore; excitement and nerves hit him as they got closer to South America. The farther they traveled, the more stretched

Leila felt. Everything she knew and loved lay behind in New York City. She chose to come, yes, but it seemed she had been shoved off a cliff into the unknown, falling helplessly until caught and caged into *his* arms.

The plane landed smoothly in Lima, Peru. A taxi took them through the densely populated city to the docks where the large ship waited to ferry sixty contestants over the Pacific.

Out of kindness for the impatient taxi-driver, they retrieved their bags before gawking at the large white ferry—half the size of a cruise ship but just as nice and sleek. As soon as the trunk shut, the taxi sped off back toward the airport, and they hurried onto the docks so the other urgent yellow cabs could drop off their loads. Contestants staked out spots to wait; they did the same, Jamaal drinking in the high anticipation and Leila trying to.

At one on the dot, the ship's horn blew—startling everyone and some roosting seagulls—and the gangplank lowered for passengers to board. Both men and women of the crew stood at the entrance. A man took Leila and Jamaal's names, handed them a key card, and pointed them down the right hallway to find suite 109.

"Nice," Jamaal said as they stood in the doorway, admiring their room: two queen-sized beds, a window facing the city of Lima, two separate closets, a large widescreen TV, a lounging room with couches, and a large bathroom.

Jamaal placed his duffel bags on the bed farthest from the window and checked out the bathroom. Leila claimed the bed by the window and sat on the corner, looking at the thriving South American city.

"We have a Jacuzzi!" Jamaal's voice echoed out of the bathroom. He came back grinning. "I've gotta try it tonight."

"Go ahead."

He fell onto his bed, arms hanging off and facing her.

"You've been quiet, Lei."

She didn't answer right away. "I hope I can go through with this. There have already been times where I almost backed out."

"What kept you?"

"David saying I need this, everyone's belief in me, and you."

He scowled. "You shouldn't have come just because of me. You care more about others than yourself."

"See?" David said, pulling up a smile.

"David's gotten on to me about that, but it's easier to avoid why I had to come."

"Think of it this way: you would've turned back if you truly didn't want to come." She looked over at his quick, encouraging smile. "You would've; if there's something we absolutely don't want to do, we won't. Trust yourself."

The ferry's horn blowing to announce departure ended their conversation. Doors opened, and people moved into the halls, heading for the deck to wave farewell to those watching them leave.

"Want to go?"

Leila shrugged.

They followed the crowds to the wide deck. Quite a few people had gathered to watch the departure of the ship carrying fighting contestants. Relatives waved up at their loved ones along with some locals, wishing them luck.

Leila leaned against the railing as Jamaal waved to the people on the docks. Inhaling the salty sea air, feeling the warm heat from the sun, and listening to the yells of people beside her and below intermingle with the calls of the seagulls cleared her jumbled mind. The blast of the ship's horn caused her to jump along with others, but it mainly blew away her conflicting emotions. She hoped for some escape in the middle of the vast Pacific Ocean.

XIX.

Beautiful chandeliers gently lit the extravagant dining room Leila and Jamaal were ushered into for dinner. The setup of the white-clothed circle tables already supplied with wine glasses, porcelain plates, and intricately wrapped silverware, maroon carpet, and cream-colored walls resembled the elegance of a wedding—too much of a flashy display, or, to a discomforting prod of Leila's intuition, a reminder of the dominance of having wealth.

Contestants quickly filled up the tables—already forming cliques. Jamaal luckily snagged an unoccupied table in the outskirts of the middle, relieving them of choosing an alliance before ample time to size everyone up. He held the chair out for Leila to sit, then sat. Leila tensed when a haughty-looking team entered and glanced at the available slots at their table. She breathed a sigh of relief when they moved to another table.

An odd pairing arrived and after surveying the options, the smaller one—a Chinese man—spotted their table. A merry and innocent air emanated off him, and Leila wasn't dismayed when he pointed out their table to his partner. With a nod from his taller and broader teammate—obvious Irish roots, with red hair and pale skin—they headed over.

"May we join you?" The Irish roots blended with a Brooklyn voice. The Chinese man—looking to be in his young twenties—smiled, which Leila found easy to return.

Jamaal glanced at Leila for approval; she nodded, at ease with the first addition. "Of course."

The two men took a seat. "My name's Shamus Shauns," the red head introduced.

"Luke Zheng," the Chinese man said in strained English.

"Jamaal Gordon."

She took the chance they wouldn't recognize her name. "Leila Wells." But just in case, she turned the spotlight off her. "Brooklyn?"

Their eyes widened. "Yeah. New York City?"

Leila nodded.

Shamus turned to Jamaal. "You have a bit of a New York accent, too. Live there?"

"For the past eight years since moving from Jamaica."

"Wow, Jamaica," Luke began. "Must have special fight style, you do."

"I guess you can say so. I use Capoeira."

The two men turned to Leila; she took the hint. "I don't have anything special, just a style of Kung Fu."

That gained Luke's attention. "Kung Fu kind?"

"Five-Animals Kung Fu with some Phoenix thrown in."

"Hear about technique but never seen. Maybe watch you fight." Leaning over, Shamus whispered 'Heard' to Luke; he waved him off, irritated.

"Perhaps."

Luke beamed. "Bruce Lee trained me!"

Leila and Jamaal stared at him, not knowing how to respond. Shamus saved them.

"He watched his movies and learned Jeet Kune Do from him."

Jamaal turned to him. "What about you?"

"A lot of simple martial arts; I just combine 'em all."

The thudding of someone tapping on a microphone echoed through the room. Everyone turned to a woman in business attire standing at the podium on stage.

She flashed a quick, toothy smile. "Welcome contestants! I am a member of Xander and have this opportunity to escort you to Panordom. We are extremely excited to have you compete in our first tournament. We strive to make this perfect for you, so if you have any questions or suggestions that we can improve on, please don't hesitate to approach any of the staff. With no further ado, enjoy your dinner." With a bow, waiters came out to deliver the food.

They placed the covered dinners before everyone, then with a timed flourish, removed the coverings to reveal grilled steaks, garlic mashed potatoes, and steamed vegetables, then placed a basket of buttered rolls at each table. Water was poured into one of the wine glasses, then the waiters offered to fill the empty ones with any other choice of beverage.

"Tacky speech, but nice food." Shamus pierced his steak with a fork; red juices ran out, and his eyes widened. "Extra Rare!"

"Hate extra rare," Luke complained as he pierced his own steak but only a little juice came out. His forehead creased as he took out his knife and cut the piece of meat. "Medium-well?"

Leila and Jamaal exchanged looks before they cut into their own steaks and found their choice of steak as well.

She looked from the medium-rare steak to the woman from Xander with an overly pleased smile plastered on her face. Leila surveyed the room and found everyone's astonished faces as they discovered about the steaks. Those with allergies and vegetarians required a different choice, and it was before them.

Something's up.

Possibilities of how they would know ran through her head as she took a cautious bite. Everything about the steak:

flavoring, sauce, thickness, and toughness reminded her of the last night she had with David in *Mosely's*. He sat before her in the dimly lit bar as the petite waitress brought their beers to them and promised to bring their steaks soon—the food they would never eat, and that night ending with David's death.

Emotions threatened to overwhelm her, ruining her portrayal of composure. The warming of her coldest wound kept those raw memories from bursting open. She massaged the wound, thanking David for his nearness.

"Lei?" She opened her eyes to Jamaal looking from her face to the hand on her heart, guessing what she thought of.

"It's just memories."

Years of being a detective gave her an idea. "Jamaal, may I try a piece of your steak?"

His forehead creased, but he offered his plate anyway. Thoroughly chewing the well-done piece prompted no other flow of memories.

"You look... disappointed," Jamaal remarked.

"I don't know whether that's good or bad."

He returned to his food. "So, what was that?"

She watched the employee walk off the stage. That foreign heat made her feel exposed and determined to find out what was going on. "An experiment; I'll explain later."

The rest of dinner passed without any more suspicion, and once full, the table discussed their expectations of the tournament and their inklings on who could be challengers by first glances. Other than fantastical suggestions from Luke on beyond ordinary opponents and challenges, the group thought it to be a normal fighting tournament—nothing special, just with a larger reward.

Slightly letdown that no one else joined their group but pleased of their additions—not someone with overbearing competitive spirits—Leila and Jamaal bid goodnight to their newest companions, promising to find them the next day, and left for bed.

With a grin at Leila, Jamaal disappeared into the bathroom to test out the Jacuzzi. She sat on her bed and looked out at the darkened sea reflecting thousands of stars.

Water gushed like a geyser in the bathroom. Jamaal yelled, "Stupid... water... pressure!"

Leila shook her head at the man's predicament as she took off her shoes and curled up under the sheets, but her suspicions on the tournament weren't going to let her rest. The lady employee's wolfish smile, correct food choices, the grandiosity of Xander, and how something just didn't seem right continued to nag at her.

She sat up, reached into her duffel bag, and retrieved the Morning Glory Hyun gave her. The blue flower had begun to wither, but its meaning comforted her as she curled back underneath the covers.

With the flower in her hand, Leila fell asleep, not seeing Jamaal emerge victoriously over his battle with the Jacuzzi.

XX.

Leila criticized her reflection in the foggy mirror after her shower. Circled depressions dented her arms and upper torso from the bullet holes. She inhaled deeply without pain, then released. At one time, she enjoyed her body. Being fit highlighted her muscles and abs, but she was ashamed of it now for what memories the ugly scars held.

Most of the scars would fade over time, but they'd still remain—except for the deep one nearest her heart, close to her sternum. That mark would never lessen in size or depth. Because of it, Leila couldn't dress again without remembering David dying while she lived.

She prevented the onslaught of those memories by throwing on a shirt to hide the scars, dried her hair, and left the bathroom as Jamaal woke.

When his sleepy eyes focused in on her, they shot open. "You're an early riser, Lei."

She moved over to her bed. "Never been one to sleep in."

"I definitely am." He yawned, stretched, then forced himself up and went to the bathroom to get ready.

Leila opened the curtains, only to be blinded by the rising sun. Once her eyes adjusted, she saw the blue sea with nothing else in view.

The expanse of the sea made her feel small, unimportant, and undeserving of all the attention and praise she had received over the past seven years. None of it mattered now. Perhaps she could disappear from her fame on the island and swim through her black waters to find that flashing lighthouse, trying to catch her attention...

Tapping on the door broke her thoughts. She moved to the peephole and found a waiter at their door with a large tray of covered food.

"Good morning! Breakfast!" the waiter greeted cheerfully as he walked in, placed the tray on their coffee table, then retreated out the door with Leila holding the door, dumbfounded.

"Who was that?" Jamaal asked as he came out of the bathroom, groomed and dressed.

"A waiter, I think." She stuck her head out in the hall to catch sight of the man. Leila looked up and down the hallway—he had vanished.

"What he bring?" he asked before removing the covering to reveal an apple, crisp bacon, buttered biscuits, scrambled eggs, a carton of chocolate milk, and orange juice.

"These people keep amazing me!" He raked some eggs, bacon, and a biscuit onto a plate then grabbed the carton of milk. He stopped before ripping open the milk and offered her some.

Leila's brow furrowed. "No. I drink orange juice and eat an apple for breakfast every morning."

"They got your breakfast too," Jamal said before taking a big drink out of the chocolate milk.

"That's what bothers me," she said, grabbing the green apple and orange juice and sitting.

"Why?"

"This isn't just a coincidence. They know this somehow."

"Like they've been watching us? Stalking us?"

"It seems that way," she answered before taking a bite out of her apple.

He frowned. "I don't like the sound of that."

"Me neither."

Realization hit him. "Your experiment last night... You started thinking that."

"This" —she gestured at the breakfast— "makes my suspicion a huge possibility."

"Is there anything we can do?"

Leila replied as the detective, "Just watch around us; make sure nothing more is going on here."

"Then are we going out to investigate today?" Jamaal scooped up the last bit of eggs onto his fork.

"Very discreetly."

"I've always wanted to play cop-for-a-day."

EVEN WITH HER DETECTIVE SKILLS at their disposal, their investigation turned up empty—to their relief or disappointment, Leila wasn't sure. They took note of every room on their walk around the ship: a dance floor, a game room with young men playing video games or trying their luck at backgammon, poker, or pool, and a gym with a boxing arena and various practice mats filled with practicing men and women—rooms for everyone's pleasure.

Luke Zheng caught sight of them and waved them over to the boxing arena where he and Shamus watched two men spar. Both were the same size and muscular, but the blond man had red padding while the bald black man wore blue padding. The white man had a telltale boxing technique, and the black man fought like a kickboxer.

Leila looked away to brace herself against the memory of fighting Bryan Foster and his kickboxing technique. The blue-padded man dealt the final blow to the red-padded man, dropping him to the floor with the cheers of Shamus and Luke.

Smug, the black man offered his wrapped hand down to the white man; they linked arms so he could rise.

"I gave you that one," the white boxer said in a heavy Italian accent.

"Of course you did, you sore loser," the black man replied with his Italian just as thick.

Both men took off their helmets, but the white man left his red gloves on as they walked over to the ropes.

"A little rough around the edges," Shamus commented; both boxers gave him a death stare.

"You don't want to make the mistake of challenging us, Shamus," the black man warned.

"Who're these two?" The white boxer motioned toward Leila and Jamaal—his eyes lingered on her the longest.

"This Leila and Jamaal," Luke said. "Rin, the boxer," he introduced the white man, waving with a gloved hand.

"Actually, Rinieri is the full name."

Shamus turned to him. "Yeah, but Rin is easier to say."

Luke picked up where he left off by turning to the black man, "And Maso, the kickboxer."

"What do you two specialize in?" Maso asked.

"Capoeira," Jamaal answered.

"Five-Animals Kung Fu," Leila added.

"Very varied—Capoeira, dancing warriors and Kung Fu, old martial arts," Rin approved. "You'll be quite a challenge."

Jamaal chuckled. "We hope so."

"How about demonstration, yes?" Luke suggested.

Leila eyed his mischievous smile. "And give away our fighting techniques? I don't think so."

Shamus popped his friend in the back of his head. "Dang you, Luke! You and your smile always ruin our plans!"

Luke's shoulders slumped as he averted his guilty eyes to the ground. Jamaal placed a hand on his shoulder. "Don't worry, Luke; you'll see our techniques in our first fight."

"I hope we're not your first," Maso worried. "I don't want to be eliminated in the first round."

"Or mess up such a pretty face," Rin added with a wink at Leila.

Her defenses shot up, but she kept her tone playful. "I think you should take Maso's worry more seriously."

The edge to her voice made Rin give a surprised, "Oh?"

"I think we've met a player," Maso said.

Leila smiled before touching Jamaal's shoulder for a sign they continue their search for evidence. "We're going to continue our tour of the ship."

The men said their farewells, and the Islander and the New York detective left the gym with them beginning another round.

"I'm thinking of calling home, just to check in on Jade and the girls," Jamaal said after they made a complete circle around the ship—still finding nothing—stopped long enough to grab lunch, and then headed back to their room.

"And to brag about your job title for the day?" Leila asked with a smile.

He looked at her sheepishly. "I wasn't good at it, though."

"Maybe there's nothing to find here; maybe it's all on the island."

"You sure are optimistic."

His words stopped her.

"Did I say something wrong?" Jamaal asked.

She shook her head. "Nothing wrong, you just... David used to be the optimistic one." Leila drifted off, recalling their differences of thinking. He would hope for the best no matter what, and she knew something had to happen for things to change.

Leila snapped back, remembering their conversation. "Anyway, there's a difference in knowing something doesn't want to be found."

"So, a detective's gut?"

"I guess you can call it that."

"That's why I'm not a cop; I just go with the flow."

They went into their room, each grabbed their phone, and Leila made her way out. "I'll walk around the ship. Mine won't be too personal."

As she sauntered through the hallways of the ferry, she dialed Captain Sullivan's personal cell. She prayed he would accept her decision of coming. He answered on the second ring: "Lei?"

"Hey, Captain."

"How are you?"

She headed up to the deck. "Alright, I guess. My break might last longer than I expected."

"What's wrong?" he asked urgently, thousands of thoughts probably running through his head.

"Nothing... bad. I..." She paused, trying to sort out her words, but giving up, told him the truth. She shielded her eyes from the bright sunlight and made her way to the railings. "I'm headed toward a fighting tournament on an island called Panordom. I'm helping a friend by going with him."

The other end remained quiet. "A tag tournament?"

"Yes," she answered cheerfully, hoping to convince him she was happy with her decision.

"Well, who's holding it?"

"A company called Xander. I believe they're a weapons manufacturer."

"Never heard of them. I have one more question: will the tournament be aired?"

His question caught her off guard. "I don't know; guess I need to find out. Odd question coming from you, Captain."

He chuckled. "I know you're good, and I wish to watch... Actually, I have a feeling the whole station will be watching too, so we'll be cheering you on from home."

Leila leaned against a railing. "I'll be sure to listen."

Colin Sullivan cleared his throat. "Well, I'm happy you're doing this because you sound... better."

"I've noticed that, too."

They both remained quiet—her trying not to think of what caused her attitude to falter. He probably did too.

"Oh, Captain! Will you check up on Xander for me? I just want to know more about them." She kept the real reason back, not wanting to worry him.

"Will do." She heard him writing the name down. "Take care, Lei."

"Thanks. I will. Bye, Captain."

He noticed a difference in her voice. Maybe she had taken the best choice.

Her eyes traveled around the deck: men and women sunbathed on the lounging chairs while others meditated or practiced their stances and moves.

She called Hyun. The phone dialed a few times before Hyun's tranquil voice came on asking her to leave a message. Leila thanked him for telling David's parents to catch her and promised to see if the tournament would be aired.

Her phone's wallpaper—a picture of her and David cutting up in a photo booth—caught her eye. Leila thought about calling his parents but hearing their voices might break her composure. Turning the screen off, she remained on the deck, enjoying the warmth on her back, until Leila tensed—someone watched her. Glancing around, she didn't see anyone looking in her direction. The intercom came on announcing dinner, and she gratefully ducked underdeck, uncomfortable with being exposed.

She met up with Jamaal and joined Shamus, Luke, Maso, and Rin—again pleased at the additions to their clique, but she didn't like nor want Rin's stares. Dinner consisted of grilled salmon, steamed rice and vegetables, and buttered rolls. Those who needed different choices received it without being asked again. Leila exchanged a look with Jamaal before eating. The evidence that something wasn't right lay beneath their noses, but they couldn't pin it on anything.

XXI.

Sunday morning began no differently: the waiter delivered breakfast—waffles for Jamaal and a variety of fruits for Leila—and they joined Shamus and Luke in the gym to watch Rin and Maso box again, but they dressed for the gym as well. Knowing not only the men but competitors strained to see their fighting styles, Leila only stretched through her different stances and Jamaal attacked the training dummies in common techniques to keep from revealing any moves.

As they practiced, Shamus watched her, like he tried placing a name with a face. A thought made the Irish man whisper into his partner's ear.

"Leila," Luke called, drawing everyone's attention, "what job you do?"

She hesitated. Since he asked, Shamus wanted confirmation he recognized her.

"Why the question?" Rin said back, taking up for her from noticing her tensing. "It could be personal."

"Shamus thinks—" His partner whacking him on the back of his head stopped him. Luke looked at Shamus, and terse words were exchanged. The Chinese man turned back. "*I* think I know. Maybe job tells me I'm right."

All eyes turned her way, not just the men's.

Leila had hoped to remain anonymous during the tournament, but it might not happen.

She opened her mouth, but the intercom announcing lunch saved her from answering. Because of an 'arriving party' set in the east wing meeting room, they ate quickly to go get ready.

She showered first, then Jamaal followed. He came out in a nice shirt, jeans, and—like a typical Islander—sandals.

"I don't show my true nature enough. They think I'm a city slicker," he answered her questioning gaze.

When they arrived in the large meeting room, most of the contestants were already enjoying themselves with small finger foods, champagne, beer, and various other alcoholic drinks. Leila ordered a long neck, and Jamaal ordered a tropical drink—something native to Jamaica, he said. Shamus spotted them and waved them over to join the group.

"I couldn't see you drinking a fruity drink like Jamaal," Rin said.

The Jamaican stopped mid-sip. "What's that supposed to mean?"

Rin shrugged. "Nothing; just a harder drink fits Leila better."

Leila didn't like the lighting of Shamus' eyes like a puzzle piece finally fell into place. "And why is that?"

"Because cops have characteristics hard to break," Shamus stated, and her breath stopped. "I thought I recognized your face and name."

Maso turned to him. "Why?"

"She's Detective Leila Wells, the best cop in New York City, and one of the... of the Super Cops," he said with pride, but then his boasting air crumbled with realization.

"Who's the other Super Cop?" Rin asked warily.

No answer came from Shamus. His eyes remained on Leila, sympathetic and asking for forgiveness. She didn't react though, just blocked everyone off so nothing could touch her.

"David Neal, Jr., my partner; he was killed."

Her quiet but blunt answer shattered the carefree atmosphere. She read the apologies on their lips and responded with nods of thanks.

The men tried to pick up the conversation before the buzzkill. The block kept Leila from hearing, but it couldn't prevent the pitying and questioning glances. She caught Jamaal's eye, and after understanding her look, he gave her an apologetic smile, and she slipped away from the group.

Exiting through a side door, the strong sea breeze struck her; she descended to the lower deck away from the loud, oblivious party.

Leila threw her drink away as she headed to the starboard side. Clenching the metal railing, she closed her eyes and breathed out, trying to compose herself before her emotions showed. So much for keeping a low profile. She only fooled herself thinking this could be an escape.

She squeezed the railing periodically, transferring her stress out. Alone, Leila cleared her head; it was quiet until heavy thuds of someone approaching sounded. She ignored them, hoping they would pass by.

"You okay?" a deep voice, heavily accented like a Spaniard's, asked.

She turned to a tall man with chin-length, thick and tousled dark brown hair and equally dark stubble surrounding his chin up to his sideburns. At least six-foot-three something in height, his dark, snug-fitting clothing highlighted his broad chest and shoulders. The silver belt buckle identified him as a matador.

His tanned, ripped arms crossed over his chest portrayed a gruff demeanor, and the heat of his brown eyes made him sexy. He had certainly used the power of those sultry eyes before— like he tried to do now—but being full of concern betrayed a softer side.

She mentally shook her head to refocus on his question. "I'm fine. Just needed some fresh air."

"Something is bothering you; the past two days you've looked content." He pulled his hands up in defense when she eyed him sharply. "Not that I've been stalking you, no. I've just seen you around."

"I'm the *only* one you've seen around?" she asked.

"No, but you're the only one I took notice of."

Leila looked away uncomfortably. Declaring his thoughts didn't scare him, and her immediate attraction to him was like a strong, magnetic pull. Waves crashing against the ship kept awkward silence away.

Being rebuffed so quickly seemed to throw him. "Name's Miguel; Miguel Del Toro."

"Leila Wells."

Once again, her walls blocked others when she didn't mean to, and Leila felt bad for pushing him away. "If you want time alone I can—"

She interrupted as she turned, "No, you don't have to go. I just have a lot on my mind, but your presence is… wanted."

Miguel nodded, relief reflecting in his eyes—she wanted him there, and he hadn't lost his smooth touch.

A pause fell between them. "Spain?" she asked.

"*Sí!* Spain it is. What gave me away?" he asked, amusement sparkling in his eyes.

Her smile came easily. "Nothing. Lucky guess."

He leaned against the railing as his eyes narrowed. "I give. I can only tell that you're American."

"New York City."

"What are you coming to fight for? Money?"

"I guess, but not for me, for my partner. And this is a chance to escape."

"I've heard a lot of people are here for escape too. Life chaotic?"

137

Leila looked to the sea. "More… personal reasons."

"Oh." He let it drop and silence came up again.

Leila turned to him. "Why are you here? Money or fame?"

The Spaniard shook his head. "Neither. My reason's personal, too." A dark look slipped into his eyes at some memory.

"I know your pain."

Miguel eyed her, but doubt disappeared at recognizing the same bone-deep pain. "I see that you do."

She looked from him to avoid his intrigue. "I wish those pains wouldn't happen."

"But they reveal who you really are."

Truth rang in his words. Before Leila could dwell on the troubling thought of who she actually was, the ship's horn blasted, causing them both to jump. Knowing what the horn blast represented, Miguel turned back north.

"Land ho."

Leila turned to see the new world of Panordom.

The island was enormous. Sandy beaches stretched from east to west, held at bay by lush foliage going back as far as she could see. Deeper within the island, snowcapped mountains watched the contestants arriving. Seeing it rekindled her hope of a getaway.

So what if the guys knew her identity. She could adjust.

Leila walked toward the bow of the ship and heard Miguel following. As the ferry moved closer, small huts became visible, and a large and fancy dock waited for the ship to anchor. Excited chatter and awe built up in volume behind them as the contestants exited the party onto the stern.

"That looks perfect," Jamaal said beside her. She couldn't respond, hearing him repeat the Xander female employee, and she now viewed the island with suspicion.

Men and women in matching Xander attire waited on the docks while natives dotted the shoreline. More came out of their huts to gawk at the large ship. Another white ship—identical in size—approached from the east.

Jamaal touched her shoulder, suggesting they go pack to disembark; Leila turned to say goodbye to Miguel but found him already gone. They made their way through the throng of people and halls chirping with excitement.

"Hey," he began as they gathered their belongings. She had remained silent, wanting to avoid the following conversation. "I talked with the guys about David. They shouldn't be scared to start a conversation with you now."

Leila started to say he shouldn't have bothered because she shouldn't be running out every time David was mentioned but appreciated Jamaal's friendship. "Thanks, but Rin couldn't start a conversation."

The Islander chuckled as he opened the door onto the noisy hallway. "His eyes are glued to you. By the way, who was that Mexican guy you talked with outside?"

"Spaniard," she corrected. "His name's Miguel, and he showed up after I left."

Jamaal dropped the subject so abruptly she looked at him, knowing he had something to say, but he kept his face forward.

After the ship's final horn, the gangplank lowered. Xander staff greeted the contestants when they descended to the docks. Some directed the contestants to follow guides waiting before a path the lighted Tiki posts outlined.

During the jostling of the moving crowd so the next ship could unload its passengers, Leila looked at the amazed faces of the dark-skinned natives in various skirts of woven long grasses and tree skin. All the men—and some women—had swirling tattoos covering their bodies, marking them as Māori.

On nearing the forest, the ground changed from soft sand to a wide dirt pathway. Tiki posts continued to highlight the way as the ground sloped upward, where it changed from the natural pathway to stone steps. When the hill flattened at the top, they entered a cleared-off area of apartments, extra-curricular courts, a large dining hall, an infirmary, a gym, and an enormous arena. Tiki-torch-lined-pathways branched off into the darkness of the surrounding trees, and black cars waited for use.

The guides paused long enough to point out everything—and filled them in on other resources of the island available—then led them toward the large hotel-type apartment building. Being distant from the other buildings offered seclusion; a lake stretched out behind it to the woods.

A chandelier nearly provided all the light for the large lobby. Numerous couches and widescreen televisions decorated the two lounging rooms. Three clerks behind the reception desks welcomed the contestants with smiles.

One of the guides turned and gained everyone's attention. "If you will all line up for one of the three clerks, you'll be directed to your rooms. Dinner is at six, and orientation is at eight. Hope you enjoy your stay. Thank you."

Everyone shuffled to get in a line before the clerks; Leila and Jamaal came to their turn after about ten minutes of waiting.

"Wells and Gordon," the clerk mumbled as she typed in their names. "Room 308." She handed them their key card and prepared for the next contestants in line.

Jamaal moved toward the elevators, but Leila froze at the mention of the room number. Her memory flew through a burning apartment to save a little girl in room 308. David met her outside, face blackened from soot after running in after her and rescuing a dog, not wanting her heroism to outshine his.

"Lei? Everything all right?"

Jamaal's voice brought her back to the clerk staring in confusion and contestants waiting for her to move. "Yes, everything's fine." She moved out of line and toward the elevators.

"It doesn't look that way."

140

She looked at the genuine concern writ on his face. "*Let someone in*," David whispered.

Leila held up the room key. "Room 308; David and I helped at an apartment fire, and I saved a girl from this same room number. It's frightening how everything reminds me of him."

"But it was a good flashback though, right?" he asked when the elevator doors opened, and everyone crowded inside.

"I guess so."

"Then as long as you remember good memories, it'll ease the pain of the bad one." He nudged her shoulder. "Just keep going."

The elevator stopped at each floor until Leila, Jamaal, and others got off on the third floor. They walked down to 308, inserted the key, and entered.

It had the same layout as the ferry's room, the only differences being the greater space, larger windows, and a balcony with a view of the lake.

"I wonder if there's a Jacuzzi..." Jamaal threw his bags on a bed and ran into the bathroom like an excited kid.

Leila laid her bags on the bed closest to the window, opened the sliding door, and walked out on the balcony.

"Yes, there is! And it's even bigger!" Jamaal yelled from the bathroom.

Brand-new patio furniture awaited use, but Leila leaned against the railing and looked out over the serene landscape. She inhaled deeply, enjoying the crisp pine air and the light breeze. David and her job kept her in New York City when she preferred surroundings like this and Central Park. Isolated. Unhurried. Quiet.

The sliding door opened next door. She looked over to see her neighbor, hoping it wasn't Rin. Miguel appeared.

Delight came over his face. "Leila. Settled in?"

She returned his smile. "Miguel. Not really. I'll wait 'til tonight; Jamaal's in there experimenting with the Jacuzzi."

"Not anymore," Jamaal answered behind her. She turned and tried to hold back laughter at his water-logged form.

"You lost?"

"It's different from the Jacuzzi on the ship." He turned to Miguel's amused face. "Name's Jamaal Gordon."

The Spaniard nodded his greeting. "Miguel Del Toro."

Jamaal turned back to his partner. "I'm going to change before we head out."

"Jamaal." Leila caught him between the open door and the room. "I couldn't help but laugh. You looked pitiful."

The Islander smiled. "Anything to lighten your mood." He disappeared into their room.

Touched by his thoughtfulness, Leila looked over at Miguel. "I should get ready too."

"Perhaps we'll see each other at supper."

"Perhaps."

"Then farewell, Leila."

She said farewell also before disappearing into her room. She hoped they *would* meet again.

XXII.

The dining hall was a cafeteria in its layout of food choices but designed in the mind of a college student union building. Varying tables in height and size with matching chairs were soon occupied. Most contestants stuck to the clique they made aboard the ships and rearranged furniture for larger tables. Others isolated themselves at the higher tables, getting serious by viewing everyone as an opponent.

Leila and Jamaal grabbed a table, and as Jamaal pulled another table to conjoin them for their group, Shamus and Luke appeared. "Where Rin and Maso?" Luke asked as he peered over everyone's heads.

"I don't know. Stand up and call their names, why don't you?" Shamus said after he finished helping Jamaal drag chairs over and had taken his seat. "And it's 'where *are* Rin and Maso'," he corrected.

Surprising Leila and Jamaal, the young Chinese man stood up and yelled their names with his partner desperately trying to pull him down. Other contestants turned and frowned at his disruption.

Shamus placed his face in his hands. "I don't know what to do with this kid."

"Told me to call their names, you did," Luke defended as he dropped back down to sit.

"I didn't think you would seriously do it!"

Luke looked confused. "But you said so."

"Ever heard of sarcasm?"

Jamaal laughed at Luke's face as he struggled to understand.

"Is this seat taken?" a deep Spanish voice asked.

Leila turned to find Miguel smiling in greeting and another Spaniard beside him. She motioned for them to sit. "I guess it is now."

"*Gracias*," he thanked as he and his partner seated. He nudged him and gestured at Leila. "Alvaro, Leila Wells." He pointed back at the man. "Alvaro Munoz."

Big and broad like Miguel, the Spaniard even shared the same dark hair. His bone structure showed no blood relation. The humble and quiet air around him meant he had a subdued personality, unlike his bold fighting partner. "We met in a Matador competition," Miguel said.

"Pleasure to meet you," Alvaro began, struggling more with English than Miguel.

"Same here," she replied.

"About time; I thought you didn't hear Luke," Shamus caught their attention by speaking to the arriving Rin and Maso.

"I think to call you again," Luke said cheerfully, but he gained a dark look from Shamus.

"Had to fight some traffic," Maso explained as he took a seat by Luke. Rin took his as well, but with obvious disappointment at not sitting by Leila.

She hid her discomfort by introducing Miguel and Alvaro. Just as everyone began to converse with the new arrivals, the lights dimmed, except for one shining at the end of the dining hall. A female Xander employee stood in front of the currently vacant lunch lines.

"Welcome contestants to the island of Panordom! Tomorrow, the first round of the Rulers of the Realms Fighting Tag Tournament will begin, and I can't wait to see who will be crowned! In a moment, you will have dinner, then you all will head to the arena for orientation and rules. But for now, please enjoy your dinner, and best of luck for tomorrow!"

Just like the meals on the ferry, waiters brought forth the food only not as quickly—as their number had doubled. As everyone finished their food, the number dwindled in the dining hall as the contestants headed back out. Now serving as gentle ambiance, the Tiki torches laid out the pathway toward the brightly lit domed arena.

A hundred and twenty contestants pushed through the glass doors and ventured toward different entryways into the actual arena. When Leila and Jamaal made it up to the walkway encircling the fighting ring below them, they stopped and took everything in.

The arena could easily seat ten thousand people. Cameras set up everywhere on the ground floor pointed at the stage placed on a raised fighting mat. On the stage and behind the podium, a table showcased the first, second, and third prize champion belts.

Luke gained their attention by yelling from his seat, but Shamus pulled him down to silence him. After showing Miguel and Alvaro the seats, Leila followed her partner up the steps to the row the Brooklynites had claimed. Miguel sat beside Leila before Rin could. Frowning, Rin took the seat beneath Leila with Maso. She stared at the back of his head, not liking the predicament developing with her between Miguel and Rin.

A man walking across the stage toward the podium quieted the arena in expectation. Slim in his black suit and still handsome in his forties, his silver hair hung far down his back. Stopping at the podium, he tapped the microphone for everyone's attention.

"Welcome contestants!" he greeted, charming and smooth. "I am Amadeus Xander."

With the mention of his name, the once-relaxed Miguel sat up stiffly, hard brown eyes boring into the man.

"It is good to have you here—my island will finally see use. You may invite family and friends to join you; I have enough room. But bear in mind that they may bring distractions, or they may help encourage you—it is your preference.

"As I'm sure you have already noticed, my island is not average; it has every biome imaginable—and other scenarios—to test your fighting skills. For example: fighting in the snow or high altitudes of the mountains, calf-deep in a swamp, during a lightning storm, and what tournament would it be without battles in a dojo?

"Since the tournament will be grueling, each Sunday, Tuesday, Thursday, and Saturday are free. This first week, thirty battles per day will take place: fifteen in the morning; fifteen in the afternoon. Each day you chance facing a new opponent, and at the end of the week, the teams with the lowest wins will be eliminated. Advancing on, the fights decrease to fifteen a day, then seven a day. Championship week is different; it will be explained then."

Xander took a breath. "Now, for the rulings—as some of my staff will demonstrate." With a sweep of his arm, four men arranged themselves on the fighting mat with two preparing to spar.

He nodded, and they began. "As in fights you are familiar with, gaining two points gives you the win. In the case of gaining or losing points, as long as you stay in bounds, you keep your point. If not…" One of the men was knocked out of the ring.

"You get a warning. If knocked out of bounds a second time, the point goes to your opponent. The official will raise your colored flag for a point if you knock down your opponent and they do not respond in ten seconds. A knockout would be the quickest victory. The round is immediately over, you receive a point, and your partner gets their turn. In case of a tie, one more fight will determine the winner.

"Tagging your partner." The men demonstrated by one running off to pass his partner. "Simply run in as your partner runs out. I would suggest a sign between you and your partner to avoid disqualification with both of you in bounds.

"To more saddening terms: losing. If you do indeed lose, you are welcomed to stay for the duration of the tournament, but you are not allowed to re-enter. Or you may leave and return to your native home.

"Disqualifications not only forfeit your match but also eliminates you from the tournament. What qualifies as disqualification is what I mentioned before, any type of cheating including muscle enhancers, and fighting outside of a match will not be tolerated. I sincerely hope we do not have these problems."

Amadeus Xander smiled. "Until we meet here tomorrow to announce opponents and locations of arenas, I hope you have a restful sleep and come ready to show the world that you are the best fighters. Thank you." With a bow, the arena applauded.

Xander stayed on the stage as everyone descended from their seats and walked out of the arena. As impossible as it was for him to single her out, Leila swore the eyes of the multi-billionaire followed her out.

XXIII.

According to routine, Leila woke early and showered as Jamaal slept, but she stepped out on the balcony to enjoy the last moment of calm. Even though the Morning Glory twirling in her hands banished some of the butterflies at the tournament starting in a few hours, other pesky butterflies couldn't be swatted away—her worries of what the competition held in wait for her.

Will I be able to do this?

"Yes; have faith in yourself."

Hearing David's belief in her helped slow those butterflies' frantic flutters, but they remained. She watched the sunrise until Jamaal made noise getting ready, and headed back in, ready to see herself through whatever she'd face.

WITH NO MORE DELIVERED MEALS, the contestants reverted to their school days to get breakfast, but they had much more freedom in choices. Leila grabbed her usual breakfast choices and joined Jamaal with his eggs, bacon, biscuit, and chocolate milk at their previous table. As they ate, she looked around the dining hall.

Everyone complemented their partner in attire, and if the mirror-effect meant anything, their techniques were the same. She and Jamaal looked completely different. Leila wore her favorite blue shirt tucked into white pants, knee-high black police boots, and fingerless gloves to protect her hands. Her black gun holster under her arm—without the gun—hinted at her being a cop. Jamaal dressed in his green and yellow Capoeira pants and matching half-shirt.

Many sported Kung Fu attire or plain workout clothes, but some wore clothes of their native lands: Native American designs, feathers, bright colors and face paint, and Hawaiians with their grass skirts. She identified a pair of city thugs with their baggy clothes and overstatement in chunky gold jewelry. A team walked by in some random fantasy clothing. Leila stared at some of the elaborate clothes and averted her eyes at the women with barely any clothing.

"It'll be an interesting fashion show if it's not a good fighting tournament," she whispered to Jamaal, causing him to snort his chocolate milk.

Finished with their meal, they headed toward the arena with the crowds buzzing with nerves and excitement. Instead of going straight to their seats, a Xander employee directed them down the right hallway for live pictures to show in the match line-ups on television; the cameras took a 180-degree rotation, and Leila and Jamaal were shooed off for the next partners in line.

Miguel and Alvaro sat in their seats from the previous night, both dressed in jeans, unbuttoned shirts with black ones underneath, their silver Matador belt buckles, and black cowboy boots.

"*Buenas Dias*," Alvaro greeted.

"Good morning," Miguel translated.

With a slight pop, the speakers turned on. After the song's first chord, everyone in the arena laughed; Miguel leaned over to tell his partner why.

"The song's *Kung Fu Fighting*."

Jamaal began laughing; Leila followed his gaze down to the walkway where Luke Zheng had escaped his partner to sing and act out the lyrics. People around him covered their ears while dodging his arms, but others stopped at a safe distance, entertained by the show.

Shamus finally broke through the crowd and dragged the young man away and up the stairs. Rin and Maso followed them.

"Great show, Luke," Jamaal praised after Shamus forced him to sit.

Dressed in a complete white Kung Fu outfit, he gave a bow in his seat. "Ended too quick, it did." He cut his eyes over at his partner.

"It needed to end earlier." Shamus wore a gray shirt and blue jeans tucked into black motorcycle boots. Rin and Maso dressed in what they practiced in on the ferry, but in boxing custom, they wore individually colored silk robes with their names monogrammed on the back, even though they fought shirtless. Rin's red boxing gloves hung around his neck, but both wore feet and arm wraps.

Amadeus Xander stepped onto the stage, dressed again in his sharp black suit and gradually turned down the volume of the audience as he walked across. Leila snuck a peek at Miguel—his eyes murdered the host.

"Good morning, contestants. This is the day you showcase yourself to the world."

He gestured at the cameras around him. "In an hour, the tournament begins, and these cameras will watch your every move in battle. On the screen above me, you'll see the digital picture you and your partner took along with your opponents and arena. For the morning fights, you are to head there immediately."

Xander smiled again. "I pray with all my heart that no one will be seriously injured in the battles to come. Show sportsmanship in your actions—through victory or defeat—for the entire world will be watching. And so, with no further ado, may the Rulers of the Realms Fighting Tag Tournament begin!"

As everyone applauded, and some whooped and hollered—as in Luke—the lights dimmed and the screens above lit up, showing an overview of Panordom. Fiery letters spelled out '**Rulers of the Realms Fighting Tag Tournament**' on the moving picture. The screen blackened until more chunky red letters appeared spelling: '**Day 1 Opponents: Morning**' and showed the beach with Tiki torches around a fighting arena in the sand. A 3-D replica of two East Asian men appeared on the screen with their names as an announcer came on. Then a blue and red VS sign appeared in the middle of the screen as another 3-D replica appeared, showing two sisters.

The opponents rose from their seats and headed out to the arena as another scene appeared: one of a beaten-down-grass-circle in trees with Tiki torches marking the boundaries. A team of two men showed against a man and woman Tag team.

"Maso Bonucci and Rinieri Anton," the announcer called and showed a replica of the two men before the landscape of a boxing ring.

"Right at home!" Rin and Maso high fived each other. Their opponents were two young men in a fantastical outfit they had designed.

"Good luck," Leila wished.

Rin looked at her and smiled. "You too."

The routine continued with Shamus and Luke versus a man and woman at a helicopter platform with mighty winds.

"Hope the wind doesn't blow you off," Miguel joked at Luke as they began to leave.

"If it do, Shamus catch," the Chinese man defended.

"'Does' not 'do', and you think that," Shamus said.

Luke spun on the red head with shock but then laughed. "Sarcasm, right?"

He grinned. "Sure."

Luke remained unsure whether his partner was joking. Shamus' booming laugh erupted, and he clapped his partner on the back as they headed out of the arena.

With the morning fights done, the screen changed to **'Night'**. "Miguel Del Toro and Alvaro Munoz." The screen showed their pictures alongside a team of tattooed and pierced men in front of a Japanese Dojo.

Leila and Jamaal had the last fight of the day, fighting on an urban rooftop with a subway passing overhead and a bright neon sign lighting the rooftop. Their opponents ended up being the two city thugs Leila saw earlier.

The lights came back on, and contestants filed out, all headed to watch a match. Jamaal turned to his partner and the Spaniards. "Who should we go watch?"

"Shamus and Luke," Leila immediately answered. It would disappoint Rin, but she couldn't take watching Maso fight like Bryan Foster.

The Spaniards agreed, and the four of them headed toward the hangers.

EVEN WITH HER HAIR IN a ponytail, Leila held her hair to keep it from becoming a dangerous whip standing between the Spaniards and Jamaal at the helicopter landing pad. Huge hangers made the backdrop for Shamus and Luke's fight against a married couple.

Up first, Shamus faced the husband. The official waved a blue flag for Shamus and a red for his opponent before dropping them, starting the fight.

The opponent's inexperience compared to Shamus caused an uneven battle. He couldn't keep up with the Brooklynite and Shamus ended the fight with a single powerful punch to the man's stomach to drop him. The official raised a blue flag.

The announcer yelled over the roar of the wind to be heard, "There wasn't much to see, but I *did* see Shamus using some Judo!"

Applause accompanied Luke as he faced the woman in the partnership. Nerves had seized him with his timid approach into the ring and his constant glancing at the cameras. Shamus yelled encouragement as the official began the fight, and the woman moved first. Luke dodged the woman's attempts, then shaking off the eyes watching, he punched quickly to disorientate, then flipped backward, knocking the wife up in the air where her husband caught her out of bounds.

A whistle blew to announce a warning.

"Luke Zheng fights like a young Bruce Lee!"

After checking out his wife, the husband let her go back into the ring. Luke gave Shamus a huge smile, proud of his accomplishment. When the official started the fight again, Luke's shyness had disappeared—he ducked under the woman's attack, rammed his elbow into her stomach, then brought his arm up to smash against her nose. She was knocked down to where she couldn't trade out with her yelling husband.

The countdown expired. "Shamus Shauns and Luke Zheng advance to the next round!" the announcer said. Luke jumped into the Irishman like he just won the tournament.

"Not bad, considering how young he is," Miguel added.

Luke caught sight of them and ran over with Shamus following behind.

"I guess Bruce Lee did train you," Jamaal commented. Luke nodded vigorously, then launched into listing his favorite Bruce Lee movies.

"Didn't he die?" Miguel whispered to Leila.

As they walked to a black SUV to go see another match with Luke gushing about his hero, she explained to the Spaniards.

LUNCH CONSISTED OF A CHOICE of hot meals of pasta, grilled chicken, Chinese, or a constant supply of hamburgers and pizza. Rin and Maso joined them, recapping their victory and promising to see their fight—Leila and Jamaal's, to be precise. Eating their choice, they listened to Luke declare that it was the best day ever. Leila played with the iPad placed at their table and found reruns of the fights they missed; everyone crowded around her.

The opening began with high-energy music and an overview of the island of Panordom. Fiery letters appeared as before spelling '**Rulers of the Realms Fighting Tag Tournament**', then the picture changed to a chunky announcer speaking in front of the arena.

Bob introduced the television audience to the tournament, mentioned the host, and explained how the sixty teams would fight—some in the day, others at night. As he spoke, the screen showed some of the pictures the fighters took.

The main announcer disappeared and showed Amadeus Xander before the awards to wish all the contestants good luck, then it switched back to the announcer where he assured every match would be televised and have a detailed commentary from the attending commentators. With nothing else to say, he enthusiastically began the tournament.

Although she could pick and choose matches, Leila played through them all to appease everyone—and to survey the field of possible future opponents. She tensed at Rin and Maso's fight beginning; up first was a shirtless Maso, revealing his tight abs and tribal tattoos in his blue boxing shorts. The short knee-kicks—typical kickboxing technique—made Leila avert her eyes, reminded of Foster.

She turned back after he won to watch Rin's turn at the other man in his man-made fantasy costume. The boxer's powerful moves compensated for his slow movement. The man stumbled out of bounds and the official whistled a warning. Rin's original opponent couldn't return, so his partner took his place, but the Italian soon subdued him. A red flag lifted.

She replayed Shamus and Luke's fight for them to see how they did. When Luke launched into detailing his emotions during the fight and re-enacted the whole thing, Leila set the iPad down.

"You all did very well," she said.

"Can't wait for your fight tonight, Lei," Rin said with a grin.

"I'm nothing special to watch." She ignored Jamaal's scoffing by turning to get the Spaniards' attention. "Good luck tonight if I don't get to say later."

"*Gracias*," they both replied.

"*Buena Suerte*," Alvaro said.

"Good luck," his partner translated. "Even though you won't need it."

LATER THAT EVENING CAME LEILA and Jamaal's turn to fight. The size of the rooftop allowed no spectators—much to Rin's disappointment—but now she wouldn't have eyes pressing down on her. A black car carried them deeper into the island, through the forests to emerge into a thriving urban city. Skyscrapers, shining apartment buildings, neon lights, and digital billboard signs highlighted the black and silver cars speeding down the highway.

Turning off the main road into a side street, they turned down a more deserted street and parked at a warehouse building. The driver led them through the abandoned building and into an old elevator.

"Excited yet?" Jamaal asked as the floor numbers illuminated one by one.

Leila breathed. "Getting there." A heat stirred within her, eager to be released as it had been the past months of street fighting.

The doors opened and straight off—just like a normal city—a stray newspaper blew in and wrapped around Jamaal's legs.

The solo neon light offered the much-needed light; a subway running above them stirred up even more trash. They looked around their environment, getting accustomed to the bright neon light flickering sporadically, the deafening screech of the moving subway overhead, and another billboard moving its bright pictures. Not to mention the cameras eyeballing every angle of the rooftop, and even one encircling the arena on a track. In a corner, a small command post held various screens and equipment under a tent. A screen, when lowered, hid everything from the cameras filming the fight.

The elevator opened, and their opponents emerged with a dip in their walk as they kept a hand on their baggy pants.

"All we have to do is to trip them up in their pants," Jamaal whispered.

Leila could see it as a quick and humorous way to win the battle. One cameraman gained their attention. "You can watch the other fights before yours." They moved to one of the many screens, and the thugs picked their own.

The opening began just the same as earlier, then changed to the announcer in the arena press box.

"Welcome back to the Rulers of the Realms Fighting Tag Tournament! This morning started off great with fifteen exciting battles!" As Bob spoke, the television showed highlights from the fights that had taken place earlier.

"Now, on to the final fifteen fights of the day!"

The night battles started with teams of all-men fighting on the top floor of a skyscraper with a glass floor, inducing vertigo for those who looked down. Equally matched, both sides traded out multiple times with their partners. But the red team was eventually crowned the victors, and the landscape changed to a moonlit field.

A couple faced down a team of German brothers. The couple put up quite the fight, but the Germans overpowered them in the fighting technique of their military.

"We're up after this next match," the commentator said next to them after the last fight ended. Jamaal breathed out his excitement and warmed up his legs by jumping while Leila stretched to loosen up her muscles.

The grassland switched to inside a Japanese Dojo with Miguel facing a pierced and tattooed skinny man. Just by how he stood screamed Miguel's cockiness. The Spaniard taunted the man for not moving, and once courage finally took hold, he raced toward the big man. Miguel dodged and punched the man hard in the face, laying him out cold.

Everyone watching flinched at the sudden move. Miguel walked off before his smirking picture showed as the winner. When the screen cleared for Alvaro's turn, the unconscious man was gone—he must've been taken to the infirmary. The remaining partner nervously stepped into the arena.

The fight began with Alvaro's tattooed opponent hesitantly moving from foot to foot, fear trembling in his eyes. He didn't move forward. Alvaro made a quick feint toward his opponent, and he jumped back in fear. A whistle warned him of stepping out of bounds.

Alvaro chuckled at the man's skittishness.

"It seems Derek Adams isn't as brave in fighting Alvaro Munoz as he is getting tattooed and pierced," the announcer joked.

He swallowed his embarrassment and stepped back into the ring. The official announced the fight, and with a courageous yell, Adams raced toward the Spaniard. Alvaro ducked under his punch then rose with a shoulder to catch the man, flipping him over and crashing on his back. Expecting more of a fight, Alvaro turned, but Adams couldn't get back up in ten seconds. The blue flag rose.

The commentator chuckled. "The Spaniard looks disappointed." As the last match wrapped up, the cameramen hurried everyone into place with Jamaal facing one of the thugs first.

Red lights blinked on the cameras. Jamaal and the thug bowed to each other, then took their stance: Jamaal's neverending dance, and the thug lifting his hands defensively. The official announced the start of the fight, and the thug tried to keep up with his moving opponent.

Jamaal lunged to the side, twisting as he landed on his hands, and repeatedly kicked the thug in his torso. He stumbled back, clutching his waist. Staying on his hands, Jamaal cartwheeled, bringing his feet across his head, then, like a donkey, he kicked him in the side.

The thug raised a hand in defeat before the official even began the countdown and so raised a blue flag for Jamaal.

"Round One goes to Jamaal Gordon in a fantastic display of Capoeira!"

Jamaal patted Leila on the back as they passed each other. "Enjoy."

Leila bowed respectively, then moved into her Snake stance, with the thug chuckling at her form. The official started the fight, and the thug moved first, but she stopped him by lashing out her left hand, jabbing him in the face, then followed up with her right hand, striking him in his waist.

When he doubled over, she spun on one leg to trip him. Striking his face, the thug lay still as she moved back, holding her Snake stance.

"With a magnificent display of a style of Kung Fu, the battle is over. Round Two goes to Leila Wells! Jamaal Gordon and Leila Wells advance to the next round!"

That energy yearned for more, but Leila breathed it out as she straightened; Jamaal went out to her. "That's how you start it!"

"Does it sound bad that I wanted it to last longer?" she asked.

Jamaal laughed. "No, I did too. We'll get our chance later though."

"At least Rin will be pleased now."

With his partner's urging, the unconscious thug finally stirred. A medic dropped down and checked his vitals. She headed over.

"Are you alright?"

He sat up. "I'm used to being beat."

"Sounds like you don't give up," Jamaal added.

His partner looked up at them. "We usually get a hit in, at least; we're not plowed like that. You're gonna win with those kinds of moves."

"That would be nice," Jamaal said.

"There's no would; you are."

"It's only the first day." Leila tried to keep Jamaal's hope leveled at the praise.

The thug on the ground got up, leaning against his partner. The medic held onto him. "There's something about you two; you're gonna be something if not already."

Jamaal looked at her, but she didn't react. She wasn't anything anymore; perhaps she *could* make a new name for herself here.

XXIV.

"You fight well." A heavy Spanish accent brought them around to the Spaniards walking up as they headed toward the dining hall for supper. Leila couldn't tell if Miguel meant the praise for both of them, for his eyes stayed on her.

She nodded in thanks anyway. "Yours was too sudden to study."

Miguel chuckled as he and Alvaro held the doors open for them. "They weren't an opponent good enough to show moves for."

"It's not like we have moves to show," Alvaro struggled to say.

"True. We don't possess a technique; we just fight."

Surprisingly, the others weren't waiting for them, so they joined the food lines. They snagged the table they had earlier in the day and ate.

Alvaro caught Jamaal as he ate a fry. "How you fight, you're... dancing? What is it?"

Jamaal swallowed the fry. "Oh, my technique?" With a nod from the Spaniard, he continued, "It's called Capoeira."

"Cap-o-ee-ra?"

Jamaal smiled, and the two men tried to speak in terms both would understand. Miguel watched the accent-speaking men communicating with amusement.

"Aren't you going to help?" she asked.

"Not unless they ask; I don't volunteer."

Leila turned back to her food—not jumping to someone's need even without them asking for aid seemed foreign.

"From your disappointment, I guess you do."

She looked back up at him. "I'm not disappointed; it's just that idea doesn't fit me."

"So, you're a... nurse? Paramedic?"

"No, I wouldn't stay calm for what those jobs require." If she gave no hint about David, he wouldn't inquire about him. "I'm a detective."

"The outfit isn't for show, then," Miguel mused, his eyes taking in her empty gun holster and badge at her waist. "You're not calm in gunfire or a hostage situation?"

"That just requires a level head. You have to have some fire, or you won't make a solution. Waiting for one to show up doesn't work."

A pause had them watching Jamaal typing what he tried to say on the iPad for Alvaro to read and understand.

"How'd you two become partners?" Miguel asked with a thumb pointing toward the frustrated Jamaal.

"I helped him in a street fight. Winning, it just went on from there with us fighting to earn money for his family."

"So, you're not..." He looked uneasy. "Together, right? Like he's married to someone?"

Leila was stunned—they weren't affectionate like a couple. She composed herself, but her cheeks flushed at realizing he asked to rule it out. "Oh no; no, we're not together like that. We're just friends."

"Oh." He looked embarrassed at asking, but as he turned away, he sighed in relief.

I won't let anyone here become more than friends, a voice growled within her.

An outburst of quick Spanish from an irritated Alvaro at

not understanding the Jamaican distracted her from discovering where that angry and adamant voice came from.

"Miguel, can you help translate?" Jamaal begged.

He waited for Jamaal to tell him what he wished to say, and Miguel relayed the information in Spanish to his partner; the happier Alvaro responded at understanding, and Miguel translated it for a relieved Jamaal. Leila watched the routine for a while before trying to uncover that voice.

Luke, Shamus, Maso, and Rin looking around for Leila and Jamaal interrupted her search. She waved, and they made it over to their table.

"Guess what?" Rin asked as he took the seat beside her.

"What?" She played the game, knowing he would mention her fight.

"You impressed me big time! Jamaal was a blur of feet, but you... you were powerful! A beautiful power, to be correct." He playfully nudged her with a shoulder. "I see you held out to make an impression." Rin stood to get something to eat.

Leila turned back to Luke's admiration of finally seeing Five-Animals Kung Fu but met Miguel's eyes. The air around him steamed with jealousy. Once he realized she saw, he didn't try to pretend like nothing happened by looking away; instead, he looked at her full-on, not hiding his intentions of gaining her.

Not able to take his gaze or what it meant, she turned back to her food. His eyes lingered. Thankfully, her phone vibrated, and she used it as an escape.

Making her way out of the noisy dining hall, she noticed the caller ID as the station in New York City.

"Hello?"

Leila jerked the phone away because of the roar of her name, whistling, clapping, and hollering on speakerphone.

She pulled her phone back after the other end quieted down. "My ears are bleeding."

Captain Sullivan chuckled. "Sorry, Lei; we had to share the noise during your fight."

"Who's all there?"

Heath spoke next, "Everyone."

"You were fantastic!" DeMarcus added in.

"So was your partner!" another officer yelled.

"But, of course, we knew you would beat those two! You just had to flash your badge at them!"

She laughed. "I considered that."

The praise continued. Leila warned a female officer that Jamaal was already taken. "Thank you, everyone. It's great to hear from you all."

"Bring the belt home!" someone said.

"I'll try my best, but it's only the first day."

Heath butted in, "You got this, Lei. You have fire no one else has."

"Since you have such high expectations, you need to go rest and for the twins in the swamp Wednesday," the captain said.

"They're not gonna be a problem anyway," D said.

"You've seen who we're to fight next?" she asked.

"Oops. We've helped you cheat."

Leila laughed. "I'll pretend like I didn't know."

"Anyway, we'll leave you alone now. Just wanted you to know we're watching," Captain Sullivan said. "And call me to-morrow so we can talk."

Did that mean he found something about Xander? "I will."

The phone grew loud again with everyone yelling encouragements.

"Don't destroy the twins! They're pretty hot!" a male officer yelled over everyone else.

"So, you want me to lose?" Leila asked.

"No! Just don't hurt 'em too bad!"

Captain Sullivan took control again. "Represent New York's Finest well, Lei." They all said farewell, and the phone went dead.

Leila returned the phone to her pocket, basking in the familiar warmth of support from her fellow policemen and women.

"Lei," Jamaal said behind her, and she turned to find him hesitantly approaching.

She smiled, to his relief. "Just support from New York's Finest."

"Good. They showed the matchups for Wednesday—"

"Twin sisters in the swamp."

He stopped, puzzled.

She shrugged. "I would've acted surprised if they didn't tell us."

"Sorry you can't put your acting skills to use. Come on, everyone wants you back inside." They looked through the large windows to see the men at the table watching Luke demonstrate the Snake stance of hers. Jamaal draped an arm around her shoulders to pull her closer for a hug. "Thanks for doing this, Lei."

"I hope you still want to thank me at the end, Jamaal."

"Of course I will—especially when we win."

XXV.

Since the first fights hadn't been terribly hard, Leila and Jamaal headed to the gym with their group. Most contestants—those uninjured—had the same idea.

The massive gym had enough room for its many visitors; it could've fit more comfortably. It was a fighter's dream gym: wrestling mats, three raised boxing rings, body opponent bags, and Chinese training dummies. Above, a track encircled the main floor. Glass windows allowed a view into a weight room filled with treadmills, workout benches, stationary bikes, battle ropes, various machines, and many dumbbell racks—anything that belonged in a Planet Fitness.

A red circle sat in the middle of the Tatami flooring—set before and slightly angled from the boxing rings—for matches. No cameras or platforms were in sight, but they might just be stored away for safety.

"We fight here tomorrow," Miguel said, looking around.

"At least you're in the A/C," Maso said. "Rin and I are in a desert-looking place."

Leila headed over to the group of Chinese training dummies. If smart, the contestants would've watched *all* the fights yesterday like she did to know everyone's technique. Her Five-Animals Kung Fu shouldn't be a secret now; regardless, she would restrain her fighting style to stretching through her forms. She'd attack the dummies in basic moves.

"You have such focus in your fighting, Lei," Rin began close by; she turned to see him watching. "Does anything distract you?"

"I don't like to lose control, so I try not to let anything in."

"How?"

Leila gestured him over, promising to show him the calming techniques Hyun taught her to settle her dark side when its temper grew out-of-hand. She coached him on how to breathe and empty his mind; without realizing, she also instructed him, moving his body in the relaxing forms of the animals she mimicked.

"This is fantastic!" Rin said. "If fighting doesn't pan out—which I highly doubt—and if you weren't already a successful detective, you should be a masseuse. I'd be your most-frequent customer, and not only for the hands," he added with a wink.

She removed her hands off him and hoped her yanking wasn't noticeable.

The voice from yesterday reappeared. *I don't think so.*

What? Leila asked.

Him. Us. It's not going to happen. He should take his flirting somewhere else.

"What are we doing over here?" Miguel asked as he walked up. "Learning how to fight, Rin?" He forced playfulness in his voice, but his big frame was tense and his eyes strained.

He didn't like what he had seen.

The blond Italian straightened. "No. Lei gave me a pleasurable massage."

Miguel's blazing eyes turned on him—she wondered how Rin didn't combust.

Leila jumped in between them before punches were thrown. "Rin asked how I stay focused in fights, and I showed him my calming techniques. Want to learn them too?"

He looked at her—the fire in his eyes died down. "Sure."

Rin spoke up, "Actually, I bet everyone could use those calming techniques." He craned his head to see past the Spaniard's shoulder. "Guys, come on over; Lei's showing some moves we all can use!"

Luke stopped kicking a body opponent bag and eagerly ran over; everyone else followed.

Leila fought to keep her lips from twisting into a scowl. She knew Rin called them over to prevent Miguel from getting 'special treatment' like him. Both men shot daggers at each other, but the Italian's look was smug.

That voice scoffed, disgusted. *Boys.*

To irritate them both, Leila went around giving a hands-on experience to each. Luke absolutely loved 'learning to fight like an animal'. She spent the most time with him, mainly because of his innocence and pure enjoyment… also to piss off the other two.

ONCE EVENING APPROACHED, LEILA STEPPED out on the balcony and called the captain to see what he dug up on Xander. She hadn't felt like dealing with Miguel or Rin any more today, so she stayed in her room; Jamaal went downstairs to play against Luke in some video game.

"Amadeus Vincent Xander, born on December 1st, 1974, to billionaires Victoria and Sebastian Xander," Colin Sullivan began. "He is their only child. Never been married. Graduated from Harvard with a Master's in Business. Clean record.

"Xander Corporations started in 2009 and is still our military's main weapons supplier. He could retire to one of his islands—set for life—but he funds gun safety courses and classes around the nation—overseas too—offers discounts for military and police personnel, and he is a speaker for veterans."

He found basically zip. Xander sounded like what Leila had pictured: a spoiled rich kid who went to one of the best colleges in the U.S. Unlike others of the upper-class, he actually used his earnings and status to help people. Nothing raised a red flag.

Leila hoped the captain didn't hear her huff.

A gut feeling said something was wrong, though. Illegal or questionable dealings—like spying on people—were usually harder to find.

"So... Lei, you wouldn't have asked me to investigate Xander without cause... Want to tell me why?"

No, she didn't. If she told the captain about her unease and suspicions because knowing people's food choices wasn't common knowledge, he'd worry, probably grow upset, and come up with some criminal lawsuit to slap on Xander—pissing off *every* contestant for canceling the tournament.

"I don't have a reason, Captain. Honestly, I don't," Leila said.

"Mmm-hmm," he sounded, full of doubt. "Well, if you have any more of these requests in the future, don't hesitate to call and think of a better excuse."

"Captain, I'm not—"

He interrupted. "Lei, you're keeping something from me. I'm only a police captain, but I don't have to be a rocket scientist to figure that out. I'll let it go because I know you—you'll fill me in on your problem if it becomes too much."

His faith in her had never been shaken; it meant a lot.

"Thanks, Captain."

XXVI.

In the morning, a surprisingly dirty Jeep jostled its passengers, maneuvering through mud puddles, water holes, and ruts from previous tracks on the east side of the island. Consisting of muddy water everywhere, thick foliage of hosanna bushes, and overlapping Cyprus trees with lingering mist in the branches, the swamp had a ghostly appearance. The wind remained stagnant, but the stench of old mud filled Leila and Jamaal's nostrils.

The Jeep finally came into a clearing of shallow water surrounded by thick foliage. A hut built outside the boundary rim held the main televisions, cameras, and the cameramen. The usual cameras placed around the fighting arena stood on wooden platforms and were equipped with waterproof coverings. No audience would gather to watch this fight, preferring firmer ground and cleanliness.

She didn't blame them.

Leila's boots sank in the gumbo of mud as they trudged through the swamp to observe their arena—she wouldn't be using her legs often in the fight. Jamaal had less trouble walking but complained about not being able to see his feet in the stirred-up water and the mud sticking between his toes.

She tried to move quickly, but the mud sucked her boots and wasn't letting them go without a fight. "This fight's going to be challenging." Just as Leila yanked her feet free, the roar of another Jeep caught her attention. The motor died, and a shriek sounded out.

"Seriously!"

Twin sisters dressed as schoolgirls with short plaid skirts, white polos, same-colored ties, and their blonde hair in braided pigtails stepped out of the Jeep. They tried to avoid the mud and water but slipped constantly and turned to tiptoeing.

"I thought when they said swamp it was just some trees and water. Not mud!"

"The mud's gonna leave a stain!"

Since arriving and seeing the challenge of the arena, the heat from the last fight rose in Leila, hoping for an actual fight to test herself. The sight of the girls knocked that urge down— they wouldn't put up much of a struggle. It wasn't surprising they lost Monday, either, dressed in skimpy attire.

Jamaal sloshed his way toward her. "If we throw a clump of mud on them, they'll forfeit."

She chuckled at the possibility of that happening.

"We go live in fifteen minutes!" a cameraman in the safety of the hut called out to them.

"Good." Jamaal sighed. He rotated his shoulders and stretched as some of the crew left the dry hut and trudged through the water and mud to their cameras. "Ready to get out of this."

"Try not to get them too disgusting, Jamaal," Leila asked. "They're cute in their outfits."

"Can't promise that."

The main cameraman clapped to gain everyone's attention and motioned toward a television screen they turned to allow the contestants a view of the opening of the tournament.

With the usual opening, the screen went to Bob in his press box with a digital screen showing brackets behind him.

"Welcome back to Day 2 of the Rulers of the Realms Fighting Tag Tournament on Panordom! Monday, our contestants began by displaying a variety of skills in the first fights of the tournament." The screen behind him widened to show highlights of battles and who fought who today.

"Day 2 is sure to bring more to the table, so let's get to it!" He disappeared to the live footage of a match about to start on a rainy highway where vehicles had stopped behind the fighters. Headlights lit the arena while drivers stood outside in the rain with umbrellas to watch the battle.

"We go live after this fight!" one of the cameramen yelled when another started, and the opponents for the first matchup made their way into the arena, splashing muddy water. The twin facing Jamaal looked disgusted.

Red lights appeared on the cameras, and the official in knee-high boots announced the fight. Jamaal stalked toward the girl; moving away, she nearly lost her balance from the sticky mud.

"Uh-oh. Looks like the Hulen twin is having some trouble moving around," the announcer commented. "The mud *is* hard to maneuver in, so we might not see fantastic moves today."

Finding a firm area of mud, Jamaal took off for the girl. She ducked under his leap, but he wrapped his legs around her neck, bringing her down into the mud with him. She shrieked; Jamaal cut her off by twisting his body around with his legs still secured around her neck and threw her over to land out of bounds.

A whistle blew, but the Hulen twin shook her head—she wouldn't go back in.

"Round One goes to Jamaal Gordon!

"Leila Wells doesn't look too thrilled at her partner." Covered in mud from head to toe, Leila could only see the white of

Jamaal's eyes and his white teeth in a mischievous grin as he approached.

She dodged his attempt at a hug. "At least wipe your face off," she ordered as she headed around him to the arena.

Turning, the clean twin was glancing around her at the mud. "I wonder if these two ladies will play in the mud for us?" The official chuckled at the thought before he announced the fight.

A devilish thought made Leila kick the water toward her opponent, who issued a gasp as the unclean water drenched her.

The commentator laughed at the act, and the Hulen twin looked miserable as the water seeped through her soaked clothes. Her pristine white shirt yellowed, the water outlined her bra and belly button, and her caked-on makeup ran. Other chuckles and laughs joined in.

Since this wouldn't be much of a fight, she'd make her own fun.

Daggers shot at Leila. She smoothly dropped down into Tiger and waited for her opponent to make a move.

With a breath for courage, she ran toward Leila. Leila spun lower with her leg out, sending the Hulen twin flying headfirst into the muddy water.

"Oooo! Talk about embarrassing! The detective is making a fool of the twin!"

She stayed crouched in Tiger as the girl forced herself back up. After wiping the mud off her face, she rushed back toward Leila with a frustrated yell, fists flying. Leila easily blocked and dodged all of the girl's pathetic attempts.

When she tired of playing with the twin, Leila caught a fist. She tried tugging her hand free; unable to, she punched with the other but fell into the same predicament.

"She's got her now!"

Leila pulled the captured arms behind her back, forcing the Hulen twin into her, then brought a knee up into the girl's stomach. She doubled over. Leila lightly pushed her, and the twin fell back in a violent splash. When she wouldn't rise, the official raised a blue flag.

"Round Two goes to Leila Wells! She and Jamaal Gordon advance to the next round!"

The Hulen twin never got up, so the official and a medic hurried out. They raised her where she spluttered, gasping for breath.

Leaving them asking questions, Leila straightened out of Tiger and returned to her now-clean-of-mud-on-his-face partner grinning. "You had to make it interesting."

She tried to wipe the mud off her. "How else are you going to fight in a swamp? We at least didn't destroy them."

Jamaal knew about her promise to an officer. "No, but you made it better." She looked at him to explain. "You turned it into a wet T-shirt contest."

The Jamaican dodged as she tried shoving him into the water. "I wasn't the one who wore a white shirt."

He raised his hands in defense. "Am I complaining? You made quite a few men glad they tuned in today."

"You better watch it; I'll tell Jade."

"That threat won't work; I know how she fights. I can take her."

An idea hit her on getting him back as they headed back to their Jeep: claiming the shower.

His head dropped in defeat. "Just make it quick."

"Oh, trust me, I will. I look disgusting; I'm sure I smell it too."

"Want to put that to the test?"

She looked at him.

"By finding Rin and seeing what he thinks."

Leila successfully pushed him back into the swamp.

LEILA AND JAMAAL SHOWERED QUICKLY, wanting to get rid of the sour swamp smell, and caught Miguel and Alvaro's match against two wrestlers in the main gym. Spectators consisted of contestants who stopped practicing to watch—others didn't, becoming background aesthetics. The wrestlers stood at least a head taller than the Spaniards, and much larger, but were slow and cumbersome, making Miguel and Alvaro look fast as they dodged their attacks.

Miguel easily twisted and dodged the wrestler's moves, and each time he did, he'd punch the man's joints to infuriate him. The wrestler brought his bulky arms around to catch the Spaniard, and Miguel dropped to a crouch. As his arms wrapped around empty air, Miguel supported himself on a hand and smashed his boot into his opponent's nose.

Everyone and the announcer groaned in pain with the wrestler as he stumbled back, hands covering his bleeding nose. "These Spaniards don't play nice!"

Amazingly, the wrestler gained enough bearings to dodge Miguel's fist. Blood flowed from his broken nose and circled his mouth. He tried the same move again, but the Spaniard ducked; rising, he brought his elbow up sharply to strike the wrestler under the chin.

The simple move catapulted the big man into the air. When he finally landed, he was unconscious.

"Round One goes to Miguel Del Toro!" the announcer yelled into his microphone.

As Miguel walked out of the ring for Alvaro, he heard Jamaal's whistle above others applauding. His neck twisted to see who rooted him on. He nodded in greeting to Jamaal but saved a smile and eyes for Leila.

The intensity of his stare had Leila looking down. Jamaal nor anybody else noticed the increase of temperature in the room. His eyes remained on her for a while, and she didn't know if his attention flattered her or if she wanted it gone.

She raised her eyes at the official announcing the fight. Almost before he could skip out of the way, the wrestler charged toward Alvaro. The Spaniard jumped clear but didn't attack; instead, he backed away from him, waiting. The big man tried again but held his arms out to catch the Spaniard. Alvaro avoided him, spun around the man, and leaped upon his back.

The big wrestler bucked wildly to throw off his opponent, but Alvaro's large arms were clasped around his thick neck and legs locked around his waist—he wasn't going anywhere.

Miguel's booming laugh echoed throughout the gym. He shouted something in Spanish to his partner, issuing a smile from Alvaro as he held on.

"Looks like the Matador is trying to tame the bull!" the announcer laughed.

Alvaro's hands never loosened as the man thrashed about and flailed his arms behind him, trying to rip off the Spaniard. Beginning to tire, his eyelids drooped. The ground shook when he dropped to the ground with the Spaniard straddling his back.

"One... two... three..." the official counted, but the wrestler never stirred.

"A sleeping hold gives the second round to Alvaro Munoz! The Spaniards advance again!"

Alvaro passed the medic entering as he left the arena floor. Miguel's immediate walking off puzzled him until he saw his path toward Leila and Jamaal; he followed right after him, pleased to see them in attendance as well.

Miguel's eyes were now an even stronger presence on Leila, but they gratefully slid off to land on Jamaal out of politeness when he stopped at them. "Now we can tell who you are, Ja-maal."

He chuckled. "Please, it just blended in."

Alvaro laughed when he reached them. "No, it made you lighter."

Jamaal looked at Leila. "I've heard mud works wonders on your skin."

She turned on him. "Are you saying I need some?"

"No, of course not. I was just going to share some through my hug, which you denied."

"Nobody in their right mind would've given you a hug."

"Jade would've."

"No, she would've pushed you into the water like I did."

Miguel interrupted their playful banter, "Your fight was quite something. You looked like you enjoyed it." Humor twinkled in his eyes.

She wouldn't deny it, even though not like he meant; she enjoyed taking control of the battle—if it could even be called one. So, she shrugged. "The announcer wondered if we could make it interesting."

"You did that," Alvaro answered with a chuckle.

"If only your shirt would've been white too," Miguel mused but with an obvious glint in his eye.

His heated stare wasn't the only reason she blushed—a heat rose within her, offended and angry that he thought of her body just for pleasure to the eye.

He's a man, she stated.

Then he's not worth your time, that angry voice answered.

That's not what he's doing.

He sees you as nothing but another prize to win and will toss you to the side when he's done.

She picked that up early on: Miguel was a womanizer, enjoying the chase of getting a woman by the force of his eyes. She wasn't such a weak woman.

He's not going to do that.

Of course not; I won't let him.

"Lei?"

Jamaal brought her out of her inner argument to find all three watching her, confusion plain on their faces at her shutting off.

"Just thinking about something. Let's go eat," Leila suggested and turned away to avoid questions. After a puzzled hesitation, the men hurried to catch up.

XXVII.

A glass of red wine in hand, Leila was pleasantly warm snuggled up against David on the couch. The musky tang of the wine on her lips buzzed in her head and body; combined with David's soft rumbling voice as he read, she was being lulled to sleep.

> "No longer mourn for me when I am dead
> Than you shall hear the surly sullen bell
> Give warning to the world that I am fled
> From this vile world, with vilest worms to dwell."

> "Nay, if you read this line, remember not
> The hand that writ it; for I love you so
> That I in your sweet thoughts would be forgot
> If thinking on me should make you woe."

He patted her leg lying across his lap, jolting her back awake. "Keep it together now, I'm not done."

> "O, if, I say, you look upon this verse
> When I, perhaps, compounded am with clay
> Do not so much as my poor name rehearse,
> But let your love even with my life decay,
> Lest the wise world should look into your moan
> And mock you with me after I am gone."

David snapped the collection of Shakespeare's sonnets closed.

She chuckled at his grave expression. "Since when have you grown an interest in literature?"

"Since it relates to what you are to do now."

Leila fiddled with a lock of his brown hair sticking out of place. "What are you talking about?"

He turned to her, eyes grim and remorseful. "You cannot save me, Lei."

A gun fired and a bullet drove through his forehead. David jerked back and the wine glass slipped through her fingers, shattering on the floor and exploding red wine, staining everything with blood as Leila screamed—

"LEILA!"

Her eyes snapped open. She lay in bed shaking from the chilling perspiration clinging to her. The lamp highlighted a wide-awake Jamaal standing over her; he held her shoulders from shaking her awake.

"David finished reading when he was shot; wine went everywhere; he said that I couldn't—" she stammered.

Jamaal interrupted by trying to soothe her, "Shh. Shh. It was a dream; only a dream."

"It couldn't have been! I could feel everything; taste it all."

"But you know that's not how it happened."

Leila looked at him, dumbfounded. "How it happened?" Unfortunately, the memory of David's death slipped under her defenses and hit her like a fist to the heart. She cried out and covered her face to hide her loss of composure.

Jamaal seated on the bed and pulled her to him so Leila could muffle her cries in his chest. He didn't try to speak, soothe her, or even stop her—he just held her, body shuddering from sobs.

When she had calmed down to sniffles, he let her pull back but left an arm around her shoulders. Leila kept her embarrassed face turned away—she had only cried so hard when she learned that David died from Heath.

It remained quiet until Jamaal swallowed. "I know you probably don't want to but tell me what happened. It helps Zaira and Eve to talk about their nightmares, so I don't see why that can't work here."

Leila didn't want to talk. She had to face her own problems.

"Let someone in," David whispered.

She took in a shaking breath. "We were at my apartment on the couch. He read Shakespeare's Sonnet 71; I don't know why because he could never grasp the meanings in poetry."

"What is it about?"

"Shakespeare left behind a note for his lover to read when he is dead. He encourages her to move on."

"Does he want her to forget him?"

She shook her head. "No, not until the world mocks her with their life together."

He shifted. "What did David say about that?"

"He said that is what I must do."

"Did he say anything else?"

Tears stung her eyes. "He said I can't save him before he was shot."

Jamaal released a heavy breath. "Then you couldn't have done anything; you need to stop blaming yourself, Lei. It wasn't your fault."

Her mouth opened to spill her secret, but the fear of admitting it out loud—making it true—sealed her vocal cords. Leila shook her head; she couldn't accept that lie. She didn't cause David's death... Did she?

Leila let Jamaal decide what her headshake meant as she rested her head on his shoulder, ending the conversation.

LEILA AND JAMAAL STAYED UP late talking. Luckily, morning was Thursday, so their inability to go back to sleep wouldn't affect their fighting. She almost stayed in the room to avoid Miguel's gaze; knowing others would be around eased the pressure. Plus, a part of her needed the presence of his eyes. They made her feel again—she had been cold too long.

Their group relaxed around the apartment complex at first, but boredom tugged them to explore the island. Most contestants chose to spend the day in the gym again; others visited the beaches on the east side of the island. They walked the hiking trails through the forest and skirted the beach, talking and corralling Luke when he wandered off.

She forced herself to stay near Rin and participate in conversation, but Leila couldn't escape Miguel's heavy eyes. With his constant attention, she wanted to both return his gaze—for he was easy to look at—and run away.

Walking to dinner, a pair of girls standing near the entrance spotted them—more precisely, Miguel. Both jiggled in their spastic waving.

"Miguel, where have you been hiding?"

"I've missed talking to you!"

His lifted hands kept them from launching their arms around him. "I haven't been hiding." His gaze slid over to Leila. Truthfully, she wasn't jealous—she still had his eyes.

"Liar."

"Is it because you have a new one to look at?" One eyed Leila, sizing her up and down. Leila's defenses rose. She considered herself better.

I'll fix that quick, the voice growled.

"Girls, please…"

Rin boldly draped an arm around Leila's shoulders to guide her into the cafeteria, staking his claim. "I think we'll give you some privacy."

She fell into step, but once they entered, she touched his arm to remove it. But Rin didn't take the discreet hint by sliding in next to her once they sat to eat. Miguel eventually joined them, joining in on the laughter when the men picked at him about the women. His eyes constantly shooting over at Leila told her it had embarrassed him.

With Rin being overbearing and Miguel ceaselessly trying to assure her she still had his attention piled on top of her sleepless night and the haunting of her nightmare, a heat rose within her, irritated at the whole situation. After Rin's intentional bump into her for the fourth time, Leila shot to her feet to avoid punching him. She excused herself for lack of sleep and held Miguel's gaze so he wouldn't think she ran away from jealousy.

Jamaal backed her up with the same complaint. Miguel's eyes lingered on her as she left, further irritating that heat into anger.

I am not a prize to win.
Maybe he can be runner-up.

Her suggestion shut up the anger boiling within.

FRIDAY BROUGHT THEM AGAINST TWO bronzed Australian surfers. They wore only swim trunks as if prepared to leave the battle arena and snag a wave; the arena set on the beach made it a bigger temptation. Leila couldn't avoid looking at their god-coming-out-of-the-water appearance with their defined bodies and tousled blond waves—the same struggle plagued females in the crowd. Some helpful teasing from Jamaal about Rin reacting if he caught her ogling another man helped her kick a foot into those chests to win.

When Friday ended, Bob announced the eliminated. Not surprising, the city thugs and the Hulen twins—among others—never won a match. Her new group of friends survived with no losses.

Nobody had much strength to do anything on their two-day break. Battered and sore, the strain of their muscles, and bruises tugged everyone to their rooms to rest at least for a day.

Jamaal just collapsed onto his bed and fell asleep instantly. Leila didn't bother removing her clothes either, exhausted from the demanding week and lack of sleep the other night. She forced herself to take off her shoes before curling under the covers and grabbing the Morning Glory off the nightstand they shared.

Her eyes didn't have a chance to adjust to the darkness nor did she get to worry about another nightmare before sleep took her.

XXVIII.

Saturday and Sunday refreshed the remaining contestants and pulled them back to battle with more vigor. Leila and Jamaal grew popular on the island; natives, staff, and contestants alike came to watch their fights. At each of their matches—no matter the location or weather—they drew a crowd of spectators. Monday's battle against two Polynesian women provided Leila the opportunity to get Jamaal back for teasing her about Rin.

The women were barely clad in alternating black and white bikinis. She slid up to Jamaal's ear as they waited their turn. "What would Jade say about your thoughts right now?"

He swallowed thickly and glared at her. She laughed as she pushed him out to face the one in black. "Payback," she said.

The women proved difficult in their quickness, and even though their jabs were weak, their repetitive strikes went from annoying to painful as Leila's muscles locked up. They traded out quite a few times to test the girls' endurance and to give the other a break.

As the last girl continued to hover around Leila like an annoying gnat, anger exploded within her. Her body had a mind of its own as she took a fist into her left shoulder, making her left side retract from the hit and pulling her right around. In a fluid motion, Leila dropped to a knee as her fist flew into the girl's exposed left waist.

The snapping of a rib or two was loud; she screamed. Knocked to the ground, the girl clutched her wounded side and continued to cry.

The official rushed over to check her out, waved a medic up, and lifted a blue flag for Leila.

"I think that hit broke some ribs. Jamaal Gordon and Leila Wells advance yet again!" the announcer said.

Leila returned to her feet and felt that heat murmuring in pleasure. *It was good to be released again.*

"Never seen that power before," Jamaal said as he came up beside her.

They watched the girl be placed on a stretcher and wheeled out to the infirmary. "I felt a little bit of it when I helped you the first time."

"What drew it out stronger this time?"

"She got on my nerves."

He laughed. "Remind me not to push your temper."

IN A DUSTY CANYON, THEIR next fight paired them against a man and woman who specialized in Vale Tudo.

Surprisingly, Demi McAllister went out first against Jamaal. Once they got started explained why: she could keep up with the Jamaican's speedy technique from being quick and lithe herself. Demi swept him off his hands but could never keep him down when she pounced—he'd either catapult her over when she jumped onto his raised feet or roll out of the way.

Somehow, she caught one of his kicks; before she pounded his leg, Jamaal shot forward to smack her face. Her grip loosened; he pulled his leg free and jumped off the other one to kick her in the back. Demi crawled to the sidelines to trade out with her partner, and Jamaal did the same.

Leila dropped into Tiger and waited. Corey Abins tried a feint to make her flinch, but she didn't move. He inched closer and closer—his intention clear.

"Leila Wells doesn't make the first move, Abins!" the commentator called to him.

Finally, he kicked at her, making her dip down, but he counted on it by rotating back around with that leg out but lower. She rolled out of the way and jumped up with a kick aimed at his face, but Abins blocked it. Leila came down into Snake and struck him in the stomach three times. On her last strike, she turned her back to him, stomped on his toe then drove an elbow into his chest.

He barely reached the boundaries to trade out in time. Leila moved to Phoenix as Demi came back out, running full blast. She soared into a flying kick which Leila dodged, then danced around her other attacks. As Leila stepped past another one, she flicked her back leg up to throw Demi off, then turning, she slammed a fist into her head. She dropped cold.

"Leila Wells is serious! She wins the first round!"

Jamaal traded to finish Abins; it didn't take long from him already being battered, and once the Jamaican began spinning on his hands and kicked Corey's feet out from under him, it was over. Leila's fight lasted longer because that heat wanted to turn up the intensity by dragging out the fight.

"Temper again?" Jamaal asked as he returned to her out of bounds.

She gave a small smile for confirmation.

"It's getting touchy, isn't it?"

Leila chuckled in a show that his words had no effect, but they did. Her fighting coaxed something dark and angry out of its sleep. She wasn't sure if she wanted it to go back asleep or to stay awake in its fire, providing her strength and power.

SHE WISHED FOR THE ANGER'S presence as she stared at who their opponents happened to be for Friday's fight on the iPad: kickboxers. With their moves reminiscent of Bryan Foster's… Leila wondered if she could face them. But she couldn't back out now; she and Jamaal were good, and it would disappoint him and others. Plus, she had a day to prepare and brace herself.

Leila considered telling Jamaal her problem. His laugh at something foolish Luke did made her decide not to. She would go up against the kickboxers. She had to face her demons.

Or at least someone who reminded her of him.

"Leila, you good?" Miguel's question brought her eyes up. Concern marked his face, and she wondered what had passed over hers.

"Yes; I just had a thought."

His eyebrows scrunched in doubt. "It didn't look pleasant."

Because it wasn't, she wanted to say. "Forget it, Miguel. I'm good."

"You sure?"

She nodded as she stood. "Yep. Jamaal, I'm headed for the room."

Jamaal looked up then got up. "I think I'm ready too."

The others soon joined them for the apartment complex.

"I KNOW. AN UNDEFEATED TEAM against a team with one loss? Yeah; it'll be a good fight, Bob," the announcer replied back to the cameras at something the main announcer said.

Leila tuned out the continued conversation as she looked around the Japanese Dojo. A fairly large crowd had gathered to watch. Her eyes kept returning to their opponents, though. The two white men were average size and dressed like Rin and Maso but with different colored shorts and arm and foot wraps.

"Lei, are you okay?" Jamaal asked beside her.

"When I go fight, I might tag you in."

"Why?" He sounded shocked.

She shook her head. "I'll tell you later."

The announcer finished talking to the viewing audience and turned for the fight as the official motioned for the first opponents. Jamaal headed out to face the man in dark green shorts. They bowed respectfully to each other then moved into their stances.

The official yelled for the fight to begin, and the kickboxer immediately brought his legs up to kick the Jamaican. Jamaal stepped back to avoid the kicks, then dropped to the ground to spin his legs out to trip the kickboxer.

Having his legs knocked out from underneath him, the man crashed to the floor. Jamaal flipped into a handstand and brought both feet down onto his opponent's chest. His breath left him in a painful huff. Jamaal lifted into the handstand to repeat the move, but the kickboxer rolled out of the way.

When Jamaal's feet landed on the empty sumo wrestling mat, the kickboxer brought his fist down into Jamaal's stomach. Everyone now heard Jamaal's breath leaving him, but he recovered much quicker.

The Jamaican smashed his feet against the man's ear and face. The kick knocked the man away from Jamaal; he flipped to his feet, saw his opening, and kicked the man's exposed back. Thrown off his feet, he landed headfirst. He tried to get up to exchange places with his partner, but the countdown expired.

"Quite a fight, but Jamaal Gordon comes out on top!" the announcer said over the crowd's applause.

Leila nodded to Jamaal as they passed, reminding him of what she had said. Her opponent wore purple boxing shorts. They bowed, moved into their stances, then the official announced the fight.

His legs came up in short knee-kicks like his partner; he blurred into Leila's memory of Foster kicking at her. She did the same she did before by pushing down on his legs, throwing him off balance.

As he stumbled, Leila jumped in the air with both legs kicking up. The powerful kicks knocked him back, and she landed in her Tiger stance. The man returned to his feet and ran back at her. Leila froze in recognition at the way he moved—his face transformed into Foster's.

The foreign anger woke her to block the man's flying kick at her face. His leg dropped down; she changed into Dragon, grabbed under his arms, and flipped him over to the side.

When he crashed to the mat, the anger pulled Leila forward to finish him. Instead, she turned to change out with Jamaal—she wasn't as violent as those images in her head. She had even run toward him but halted at the boundaries.

"What's happening? Leila Wells looked to change out with Jamaal, but she's stopped!" the announcer yelled for the cameras.

Jamaal looked at her in puzzlement as she stood there.

I'm not a coward. I'm not weak. The foreign voice returned, angry and ashamed she considered fleeing. Jamaal's warning yell came two seconds after the angry strength sensed her running opponent nearing.

The punch whooshed over her as Leila ducked under the man's arm and spun around. Staying in Dragon, she rammed her palms against his chest almost touching her. As he doubled over, that angry power took over; she fed it full control, wanting to feel the power of triumph.

Her right fist smashed into his face followed by her left to his left shoulder. He stumbled as she drove him back with her fists. Bones snapped and cracked under her hands, but Leila didn't relent. With one last punch to his face, the man fell to the ground unconscious.

The official pushed her back from the fallen man for Leila showed no sign of slowing her onslaught. After he realized her bloodlust was gone, the official dropped down. He checked his pulse, nodded to a medic to approach, then raised a blue flag.

"Leila Wells wins! What power! Jamaal Gordon and Leila Wells advance to the next round!"

Leila looked down at her throbbing hands. Her body hummed with that angry power, and she didn't want to let it go this time.

"Lei, what happened?" Jamaal demanded when he reached her. "You started to tag out but then changed before beating the mess out of him."

She took a shaky breath. "I saw him as Foster."

"What? Why?"

"Because Foster is a kickboxer." Leila looked up at her partner. "What do you mean I changed?"

"You've become more… brutal in your attacks this week, but you have pulled back before causing too much harm. Today, your eyes turned vicious, and you became different. You were terrifying, Leila." Even his voice wavered in fear.

She looked back down at her shaking hands. The power felt good but also scared her. His fear, though, had the blazing fire receding. Leila wouldn't let it go completely but needed to have more control over her temper.

"It feels good, but that's what scares me." She looked at him. "I'm not like that. I shouldn't crave violence."

"Maybe it was your dark side." He draped an arm over her shoulders. "Let's put something on those hands."

XXIX.

Everyone was called to the main arena Friday night. Amadeus Xander greeted them.

"This tournament would not have been possible if not for your participation. We are now at the halfway mark and have reduced our number to some magnificent fighters. I wish to reward you all with a celebration—a relaxing one, of course." He brought forth chuckles and sighs of relief, thinking the celebration required action.

"A party will be held tomorrow evening in the ballroom of your apartment. This is not a mandatory event; I just wish to show my appreciation by furnishing fun. And, yes, those who have been eliminated may attend. Please have an enjoyable weekend. Thank you."

The remaining fighters left the arena energetic about the upcoming party. Leila found it oddly disturbing that Xander knew how to liven up his contestants. Did he want to stretch them too thin where they might snap coming Monday? Especially her?

"What we do until party?" Luke piped up when most of the contestants cleared the lobby to catch up on rest.

"Whatever we wish, Luke," Leila answered.

"What I want?" he asked in general but turned to his partner in question.

"No!" Shamus demanded. "Tomorrow and Sunday are my days off from you. You go do your own thing."

"But, Shamus, what I do?" the Chinese man begged as he chased his quickly retreating partner.

Luke's comic relief took her mind away from suspicion to laugh with the others at the disappearing partners. She blamed the awakening of her dark side for resharpening her awareness of Xander's motive with this tournament—her suspicions had dissipated since the fights pulled her focus away. Now, that heat attempted to force her into tunnel vision, blocking out everything around her.

"I'm gonna hit the courts." Maso announcing his plan as he stretched pulled her even further from her mind. "I'm in dire need of some ball rehab."

"Going to the beach," Jamaal added in with a smile. "The sand's calling my name."

"Maybe gym," Miguel said as he scratched his head.

"Siesta Sunday," Alvaro nudged.

The Spaniard laughed. "That's for sure."

"Lei, what about you?" Rin asked.

She shrugged. "I'll decide in the morning. Sunday I'll be making some phone calls back home."

"I'll be running around the track if you want to join," the boxer invited.

She gave him a small smile that she would think about it but knew she wouldn't join him.

Maso's long yawn showcased the weariness of the entire group. He waved farewell after apologizing for spreading it. "I'm headed to hit the sack. Night."

Rin bid goodnight before joining Maso, and the last four hurried to get in the elevator with them. Rin and Maso got off on the second floor, then the elevator ascended to the third floor for the New Yorkers and Spaniards.

"*Buenas Noches*," Alvaro said before disappearing into their room.

"Goodnight to you, too," Jamaal replied sleepily before heading into the room.

Leila and Miguel were left alone in the hall. She kept her eyes on Jamaal moving toward his bed as the door shut, even though she wanted to look at Miguel's on her. Rising heat warned her of being alone with the Spaniard, but she couldn't leave.

"You've been quiet since the announcement. Are you okay? And don't blow me off like you did before; I knew something bothered you."

Her eyes shot over to him; his eyes reflected concern, wariness, a slight touch of smugness, and challenge. She'd take him up on that. "If you knew, why didn't you say something?"

Triumph now twinkled over the emotions that she had bitten his lure. "Because I could see the decision not to tell everybody. It was a struggle of yours, and you were to handle it."

Her arms crossed. "And how could you see that?"

"I've been watching you."

She would probably regret this, but she wanted to know how she was being received. "What else have you seen?"

Miguel leaned against the wall by her door: legs crossed at the ankles; arms folded across his chest—looking nonchalant. He breathed out a sigh. "You're strong, not only physically, but emotionally. But also guarded, like you're afraid to go out on a limb when I think you need to."

"Being cautious isn't bad."

"No but staying cautious keeps you from taking chances. Life is for the brave."

Leila hoped she looked away quickly enough to prevent him from seeing her reaction to his words: she did so with her time with David and that ended in his death. She craved safety now—reassurance of being in control. "Anything else?"

"Other than you being absolutely gorgeous? No, nothing seems to matter as much."

She tried to keep a smile from lifting the corners of her mouth but failed. "You're not afraid to speak your mind, are you?"

He chuckled. "I've never taken time to beat around the bush—not patient enough. Getting a response is much quicker than if I would've been subtle."

She looked at his twinkling eyes. "Is it the same now?"

"It's taken longer than usual, but I think I'm making better time than Rin."

Leila scoffed. "He's making no time at all."

Miguel grinned, eyes now warming with pleasure. "Good to know."

Someone walking toward them iced the heat rising between them; Leila took a step back out of embarrassment, not knowing she had moved closer to the Spaniard. The trespasser quickened his pace when he reached the two in the hall, feeling his unwanted intrusion on their privacy and Miguel's eyes urging him on. Leila watched the man's stiffened back hurry down the hallway and into a room.

"Rin's advancements seem to annoy you quite a lot," Miguel began as soon as they were alone again.

"He's Italian, they don't give up."

"Neither do Spaniards."

"At least you're not annoying... yet."

"Then what am I?"

She had trouble looking at him. "Flustering."

He smirked. "I can handle that."

Leila wanted the attention off her. "Rin's advancements seem to annoy you as well."

It worked; Miguel's eyebrows lifted. "You've been watching me back?"

"I couldn't help but notice."

"I'm honored you've seen."

"Don't flatter yourself; I'm not the only one to pay attention."

"Jamaal?" A smile confirmed his guess. "He's only noticed because you have; you saw first. And that's something to be happy about."

Her gut twisted under his stare. "It's late; we should go to sleep."

"It's been late." He caught her arm as she turned away. "You're trying to blow me off again by avoiding my question."

"You've asked many questions," Leila stated.

"And you've answered all of them except for the one that began this: what's bothering you?"

She glanced down at the hand on her arm. He took the hint and removed it. She had the thought that he shouldn't have been so considerate of her comfort—her arm felt awfully cold now.

It took her a moment to begin, "It's the party tomorrow night."

He raised an eyebrow for her to elaborate, not satisfied with the short answer.

Leila sighed in defeat and inched closer to whisper, "It's convenient for Xander in throwing something else at us to test our limits. Something about it seems off. Remember, I am a cop, and these feelings have a knack for being right."

"It's just a party. It's a..." He swallowed thickly. "A kindness, on his part."

"But see? You don't trust it either. You have a feeling that this whole thing is a cover-up for something."

"No, I just don't trust Xander; my reason's my own." His eyes flashed at some dark memory.

"This tournament isn't solid; it's shaky, and I don't like it. Everything here is too perfect. And Xander himself... he's shady and reminds me of a snake in the grass. He has a motive for bringing—"

Miguel's hand on her neck halted her breath. "Leila, stop. You're thinking like a cop, looking for things that aren't there. The party tomorrow might be what you need: something to loosen you up and help you relax. Stop this paranoia."

"It's not paranoia," she defended.

"Detective instincts, whatever you want to call it. I just know you weren't brought here to investigate a crime." His jaw worked as if he planned to say something else. "You came here to fight. Do so."

Not only to fight, she thought. "I just feel he's throwing us into a cage and prodding us to his liking. He's waiting for us to break—"

"Us, or you?"

Leila looked up into his eyes, foolishly thinking that he wouldn't catch on. A warning rose in her gut—they were too close. Time to escape. "I don't think I would be this paranoid if I wasn't so tired."

"You're admitting you're paranoid now?"

She scowled at his chuckle. "Whatever you want to call it, I just know I'm tired."

"Then go to sleep." But he didn't release her; instead, he brushed a piece of hair behind an ear. "*Que sueñes con los angelitos.*"

She tried to ignore the touch of his hand, the closeness of their lips, and the deep warmth soaking into his eyes.

Don't react, she ordered herself. So, she raised an eyebrow in question.

Miguel smiled. "May you dream with the angels." He hesitated before kissing her on the jaw.

He released her, and she almost stumbled. "Goodnight, Miguel." Leila retreated and disappeared into her room, struggling not to look back.

After locking the door, Leila leaned against it. She trembled, unsure whether Miguel's bold feelings left her flustered or affronted. Her sudden defense against him had her confused; her hesitancy being so soon after David's death could be a reason. But this was stronger, angrier, and disgusted she would consider Miguel's flirting even a little bit.

A loud and drawn-out snore jolted her back to place. The lamp between her and Jamaal's bed provided the only light. The soft glow highlighted Jamaal's spread-eagled form on top of the covers.

Smothering a chuckle, she pushed herself off the door, moved over to her partner, and pulled the covers over him. He didn't even grumble in his sleep, acknowledging the difference.

Leila's emotions and thoughts running a marathon probably wouldn't allow her to sleep. After getting ready, she slipped into bed and reached for the Morning Glory but stopped. The wrinkles in the blue flower had smoothened, and it looked more alive—like just picked. When she grabbed it, a calmness blanketed over her, making her feel that she found the right path. She switched off the lamp and tucked into bed with the flower close to her chest.

Comforted, she fell asleep.

XXX.

Even though she went to bed plagued by emotions, Leila surprisingly slept well and woke in her usual early routine. She needed someone to talk with about Miguel. After watching Jamaal, she decided not to wake her slumbering partner to bother him with untangling her thoughts and feelings.

Another could help.

She took her shower, dressed, and left Jamaal a note so he wouldn't worry about her disappearance.

Gone out early to think. Meet you at the beach. Lei.

She laid the piece of paper on the nightstand between their beds, placed her blue flower atop it, then quietly stole out of the room, leaving the Jamaican to his peaceful slumber.

The detective walked undisturbed through the still-sleeping apartment since the sun hadn't even begun to rise yet, returned a smile to the receptionists, and felt their gazes following her out of the apartment complex.

Stepping into the dark and dampening chill of the morning helped her shake off her nagging thoughts. Only Tiki lights supplied light; the lack of light comforted Leila—the darkness welcomed her back, hiding her from prying and conniving eyes.

Leila didn't have a destination in mind—as long as she could be alone—and let her feet guide her wherever they wished to. Her feet took her off the lighted paths, toward the lake behind their living quarters.

A wooden bench sat close to the water's edge, and she plopped down, grateful for its seclusion. She bent forward and propped her chin on her folded hands as she tried to think.

After a few minutes of getting nowhere close to unraveling her thoughts on her own, Leila turned to her other option: David. "What do I do about Miguel, David?"

"Whatever you want; you don't need my permission," he replied. *"You're a grown-up woman."*

She chuckled. "I feel like I should."

"Don't feel like you have an obligation to me, Lei."

"You know what's going to happen. Should I waste time only to be hurt?"

"He's not going to hurt you. And you won't be wasting your time."

"Do I need him?"

"Yes."

She wasn't sure if she liked his answer. "Is he him?"

"Do you think so?"

A shadow moving across the lake caught her eye as she searched for an answer. "I… I think it's too soon to decide."

"Don't feel rushed."

"You sure are vague in your answers now. Did death turn you into Socrates?"

David laughed. *"So, I talk like a wise philosopher? I never would've believed you'd compare us!"*

"Will you ever give it to me straight?"

"Would Socrates?" he countered.

With a rueful smile, she dropped her head. Linking them had been a mistake, but she understood his joking reply. No.

Leila pictured him shrugging. *"Sorry, Lei. If I gave you the answer to everything you asked, you wouldn't learn to rely on yourself."*

Gradual lightening in the east revealed the shadow as a leaf adrift on the rippling waters. Afraid of being seen brooding by the rising sun, Leila stood to disappear into the forest beckoning her to enter. Her reflection on the water's surface stopped her retreat.

Her face had regained her true color. For appearance's sake, she seemed happy, but her hazel eyes still held a haunted, empty look. Leila turned away before any memories could overwhelm her and continued toward the forest.

Once the forest shielded her from eyes, she slowed her pace and kept it leisurely, trying to maintain her focus on the topic at hand instead of worrying about a destination. Small songbirds jumping from tree-to-tree guided Leila deeper.

"So, should I show weakness by giving in to him?"

"You wouldn't be asking me what to do if you didn't want to."

She scowled at the trees—he caught her. "But a part of me also doesn't want to. Maybe that's the one I'm leaning toward."

"Stop being so stubborn, Lei. You can fool others but not yourself— and not me."

She laughed. "Sorry, it's a habit of mine."

"Unfortunately."

"I thought you liked that part of me?"

"In certain situations; not when I'm trying to convince you."

"You don't have to convince me on what I'm feeling, David. I'm being drawn toward Miguel, but my hands are on his chest to keep him away. I'm not sure I want to drop those hands yet."

"Don't let my memory keep you from stepping out on a limb. If he makes you feel again, go to him. Feel. You can't anymore with me."

David grew silent, letting her mull over his words and pay attention to her walk through the woods. The rising temperature had no effect on the warmth Leila felt within the silence of the trees—a sense of belonging and accepting; something she thought she *had* in New York City when David lived. With his death, it disappeared as if it never cared for her. As she thought about it, she realized that she never belonged in the city, David did. Because he loved it so did she, but she belonged outside with its quiet and serene nature.

She met a wall of trees preventing entry. Curious, she pushed her way through to an opening and looked about the forest sanctuary. Vacant of overhead trees, the sun shone on the small area. The enclosure had short grass—like someone tended to it—but Leila's eyes drifted up to the single, large willow tree, just like the one overhanging David's grave back in New York City.

Seeing a replica of the tree—minus a headstone—froze her to the spot. Her instincts flickered that this couldn't be natural, and her eyes swept the sanctuary for anything that didn't belong but found nothing.

"Is this a trick?" she whispered.

David took a second to answer. *"No, it's real."*

After regaining her nerve, Leila headed toward the tree. She sat underneath the shadows of the willow, placed her back against its base, and closed her eyes.

"It's unnerving how everything reminds me of you."

"I'm sorry it causes you so much pain."

Leila took a steadying breath. "You warned me it wouldn't be easy, but I didn't expect the tournament to be like… this."

"What do you mean?"

"It seems everything is set up on purpose to remind me of you. This can't all be coincidences."

"Tell me why you think so."

"The steak tasting like those in *Mosely's*. The room Jamaal and I share: Room 308—the fire we went to, and I saved Christie. This willow." She took a breath. "I came believing this tournament would help me escape the pain of our life. But it follows me everywhere; I cannot run from it. And now the problem with Miguel…"

"How is it trouble?" David asked.

She opened her mouth to answer, then shook her head, pulled her legs to her chest, and wrapped her arms around them. "It's not; I'm just being paranoid."

"No, listen to your instincts."

His doubts had already tightened her stomach; his order squeezed it. "Should I be worried, David? Is something actually going on here?" She stopped. "Oh, wait; you can't tell me, can you? I have to figure it out."

"You've got it. Now, tell me what you are thinking."

Keeping information from her didn't make her feel any better, but she complied. "I feel like he's being pressed onto me; not his intentions, but something is doing it. He's placed right next to me making any attempts at evasion impossible. His advancements are pushing me to a cliff, and I know he doesn't mean to. Someone wants me to fall."

"Xander," David guessed.

"Something is off about him. I think he planned this party tonight to put me in a situation that will give the final shove off the cliff. I'm scared about going."

"Go tonight. Don't think if the party has some alternative motive or what it could come by; just go, breathe, and try to enjoy yourself. You need it."

Leila scoffed. "I don't think I can. I wish I was strong like you to block everything out."

"Lei, you've always been the strong one. No one could have possibly gone through everything you have: the death of your parents, everything our job demanded of us—the murders, rapes, and chases. You being severely wounded, my death, and your drive to keep living. Those situations would've broken the weak. You have the ability to block it all out, so it won't get to you; you just rubbed off on me."

"But, David, you have been beside me through all of that. You're still with me; that's the only reason why I can keep going."

"*Yet, you were strong enough to come to this tournament. You decided; I didn't force you.*"

Leila began to argue but stopped when she found it pointless.

"Then what about this new strength? I didn't feel this when you lived, David. It's strong, powerful, dark, and angry… It scares me that I accept it."

"*You've always felt it, just subdued, and I was wrong in trying to get rid of it for it's part of you. Jamaal's right: it's your dark side brought to light because of my death. That is what powers you to keep going…*" He trailed off as if to say more but remained quiet.

Her voice was small. "Should I fight it or welcome it?"

"*It is what brought you back in the hospital and in the ambulance. It wants you to keep living and will fight you to do so. What you should do is up to you. The heat helps you feel alive.*"

She read in between the lines. "But it's temporary until I find him."

David didn't respond.

Leila ducked her head into her legs, trying to decide if she would accept her violent dark side, determine whether Miguel was the one for her, and hold on to David's presence a little while longer.

LEILA WALKED AWAY STILL CONFLICTED when the sun rose for noon. The light blinded her stepping out of the darkness of the forests. After making sure her face was clear of any sign of tears, she headed toward the beach.

The brightness of the hot sandy beach hurt her still-adjusting eyes. When she could see again, the blue waters of the Pacific Ocean glittered in greeting as it stretched on before her.

People were everywhere as Leila looked for Jamaal. Many were in their swimsuits, sunbathing on beach towels or enjoying the coolness of the ocean water. Others played games of beach volleyball or threw around a Frisbee.

Laughter flowing with the crashing waves and screeching seagulls hovering overhead lifted Leila's mood. Everyone enjoyed the weekend, and she didn't see why she should darken it. She soaked up the Vitamin D from the warm sun, inhaled the salty sea air and released it, breathing out her suspicious fumes.

She continued her trek around the beach until she found Jamaal: in swim trunks, no shirt, and covered in sweat from his exertions of playing beach volleyball with other contestants. Leila joined other spectators around the boundaries of the court.

It was an intense game of volleyball as the contestants used their flexibility and speed from fighting to save the ball from going out of bounds and constantly leaped high into the air to spike. No rules allowed any means to hit the ball.

Jamaal was exceptional at the sport; he could easily maneuver in the sand, wasn't afraid to dive headfirst to save his team from losing a point and soared high into the air to spike the ball. His lean form, thoroughly detailed abdomen, and quick movements reminded her of a sleek panther.

With a loud pop from the opponents, the ball sped toward the bounds line. Jamaal wouldn't have been able to reach the ball in time in a normal game but by cartwheeling and pushing off the sand, he got the speed to kick the ball back over the net. Their opponents assumed they had won and couldn't recover their defenses.

The winning team roared in victory and praised Jamaal for saving them and scoring the winning point. After enjoying the win, he caught sight of Leila, finished thanking his team for the game, slipped out of the celebrating people, and headed toward her.

"Hey, Lei," he greeted breathlessly. "Have a good morning?"

"I guess so."

"Were you able to decide on what you had to think about?"

"Not completely but close enough for now."

A staff member gave Jamaal a small towel, and he wiped the perspiration off his body. The Xander employee moved on, handing out towels and water to whoever needed them. "Glad you did. I enjoyed my extra sleep this morning."

Someone calling Jamaal's name making him turn kept him from seeing her face fall at the memory of picking at David because of his love of sleep.

"I knew there was a reason I liked him," David said.

His playful comment lifted her mood. She composed herself before Jamaal turned around.

Leila knew what the person had asked from the sheepish look on his face. "Go, Jamaal. They want you on their team."

"Yeah, but, Lei," he stumbled.

"No, Jamaal. Go," she ordered. "I'll get something to eat and find the others. Enjoy another game."

Hope lifted in his eyes. "You sure?"

"Yes. Go have fun."

Jamaal glanced behind at his teammates calling him to play another game. He gestured at the court. "You want to play?"

Leila denied it quickly. "No, thank you. I don't do volleyball."

"I bet you'd be good at it."

She eyed the female participants in shorts and sports bras. Her physicality would fit in, but the scars would draw attention and questions. "I don't do sports, and I'm not exactly dressed for it. Thanks, though," she ended quickly so he wouldn't continue to beg.

He must've caught her reluctance to play; he accepted it with a nod and headed back to the court.

She watched the beginning of their game then made her way off the beach, ready to eat. Leila passed through the pathways mainly undisturbed but greeted other contestants who walked by. Coming onto the break in the forests leading to the apartments, dining hall, and arena, she was alone when the surrounding woods fell silent.

Hairs rose on the back of her neck. Leila's eyes shot to the darkness of the forests, attune to any sudden sound or movement. Someone or something hid in the shadows, watching her. Fear crept into her body at the thought of the unknown, and her mind began to play tricks on her, making her see forms in the darkness that may or may not have been there.

"Run, Lei!" David shouted.

No matter how foolish she looked, she sprinted out of the forests into the light of the clearing, not wishing to discover what laid in waiting. When she put some distance between her and the forest, Leila looked back at the pathway winding into the trees. Her heart pounded as she searched the shadows for anything following.

But the forest had picked up its normal sounds of cheerful life, and the darkness didn't look as daunting as before. Her wildly beating heart slowed down at not feeling the unknown watching her anymore. Leila hesitantly turned her back on the forests to continue toward the dining hall, not feeling the danger but vowing not to enter the woods alone again.

XXXI.

After lunch, Leila found Shamus and Luke consumed in a video game in one of the apartment's game rooms. They greeted her with two words without ungluing their eyes off the screen. She invited herself to watch the war game they played. Their fingers mashing the buttons with the loud crashing sounds of war—bombing planes, men dying, and rapid gunfire—filled the room.

The testosterone level neared spiking as both men tried to beat the other. Winning the game would declare the better man... In their heads, at least. Leila chuckled. After a long drawn-out battle, Luke became the winner.

Luke jumped up with a celebrating yell while Shamus wallowed in self-pity at losing the game to his young Chinese partner.

"You would think it was the end of the world," Miguel spoke up behind the couch Leila sat in. His voice awoke the memory of his stubble prickling her skin as he kissed her goodnight.

She kept her face on the unmoving screen. "I think it is to them."

Luke turned. "Time for shindig!" He bounced out, still fired up from winning and excited for the party.

They headed up to their rooms to get ready. Leila showered but then stared at her wet reflection, still undecided. She could easily come up with an excuse for feeling bad. David said to go, but she couldn't discard the apprehension of something waiting—and she didn't know if she hummed with excitement or shook in fear.

The door to their room opened and closed as Jamaal ran in. "You ready, Lei?"

She figured she shook from standing there dripping in a towel. "Almost; hang on."

Leila dressed in a mint top and dark denim jeans—she'd put on her heels outside. She added extra makeup on her arms to cover the circular crevices of bullet wounds the shorter sleeve top exposed, unplugged the hair dryer, then hurried out to be replaced by Jamaal.

Jamaal showered quickly as she dried her hair. He dressed simply in jeans and a blue button-up then they headed down to meet the others in the lobby. They traveled together for dinner, then returned to the apartment and one of the ballrooms.

The extravagant room was left with the enormous chandelier, white-clothed round tables near the walls, and its decorations of mirrors over the dance floor and silver designs around the columns. Mirrors multiplied the bright party lights already flashing and rotating, providing the only light in the dark room. Two long tables set up with bartenders serving drinks occupied the corners. The DJ took over the stage with his large speakers blaring an upbeat song, deafening everyone as they entered.

Most of the contestants flocked to the dance floor, already in the mood to start the party and expel the energy they had stored for the night. Some went to the bartenders, needing a drink before or wishing to wait until the party truly heated up.

Jamaal pulled Leila to dance with the already jumping crowd.

"Come on, Lei, dance with me!" Jamaal shouted over the music. He held her hands, urging her to twist and dance.

"I don't feel like it, Jamaal!"

"Come on! Let loose!"

Reluctantly, Leila fell into step with him, swaying and

moving with the music. He suddenly pulled her to him making her laugh, still dancing and spinning in time.

Dancing with Jamaal massaged the tension stiffening her body. When he released her, she didn't need his urging to dance. Soaking in the music, letting the beat control her body and feet, and bouncing off the equally bustling crowd felt liberating. Leila even caught sight of the others joining the large crowd on the dance floor and enjoying themselves.

Nearing the end, the DJ blended the modern song into one that hadn't been heard in a while. The change of music did little to disrupt the dancers—they just adapted to the different tune.

To provide a break, the upbeat music changed to one with a certain dance, and the crowd parted, opening the floor for the brave ones. It came as no surprise to see Luke out in the group; even though he didn't know the dance, he fell into step with those who did.

The song faded out, but the DJ mixed it with another modern song, and the dancing dispersed over the floor again. Luke grabbed Leila and Jamaal and led them back to the others.

Miguel and Alvaro headed toward the tables, Rin and Maso were off dancing, and Shamus had disappeared to one of the bartenders. After gesturing to their staked table the Spaniards headed to, the young Chinese man ran back to dance. With courage, Leila hurried and grabbed a hold of Miguel and Alvaro.

"Don't tell me you aren't enjoying yourselves?"

"Dancing's not me," Alvaro answered; Miguel kept quiet.

"Miguel?" she asked.

"I don't mind it, but not to this." He gestured out to the dance floor at the pulsating crowd moving in time to the hip-hop song.

"Then what will you dance to?"

"More of Hispanic origin, but I doubt the DJ will play something."

"I bet you'll be surprised. He just played a song from the nineties."

"If he does, then I'll dance," Miguel promised.

"But for now, we drink." Shamus appeared with a long neck in one hand and two Coronas in the other.

"*Gracias*," the Spaniards thanked as the man handed them their drinks.

Jamaal looked to his partner for approval, and they headed over to a bartender. After finally getting through the line, Jamaal ordered his island drink from before on the boat, and Leila changed hers to something lighter. Headed back to their table with their drinks, they saw Rin—with another woman—and Maso still enjoying themselves on the dance floor.

Jamaal elbowed her. "Jealous?"

She laughed. "Not one bit."

The drinks and music relaxed the group into plain conversation, along with listening to Luke's recounts of a dance before he ran back off. Surprising Leila, Rin never showed to whisk her off to the dance floor.

Coming had proven to be a good choice. Her suspicions began to drag her down, but now she felt better. She was actually having fun.

Leila and Jamaal returned to the dance floor quite a few times.

"Thank you, Jamaal," she said in between a quieter part of the song they danced to. He held her close with one hand holding hers as if they planned for a slow song but danced with the fast beat.

"No need to." He hugged her tighter as they finished out their dance.

The time flew by; people began heading to their rooms after exhausting their energy dancing. One of the last songs the DJ played was a suave Hispanic song.

Leila turned to Miguel. "You promised."

He sighed as he stood. "*Sí*, I did." He held out his hand for her, but she looked at his hand then up to him, puzzled.

"You can't Tango alone."

She finally took his hand, and he led her to the dance floor. Turning to face her, Miguel put his hand on the small of her back, pulled her to him, and offered his hand for her to hold just as she and Jamaal had done but not at all this intimately. The heat rising around them—for there was no space between them—was smothering.

"I don't have a clue how to Tango," Leila began with a blush.

Miguel grinned. "It's just in your hips."

He began with a few intertwining steps along with the beat of the song. After she mastered the transitioning footwork, Miguel picked up the speed, and then Leila had trouble. It wasn't the smoothest Tango, but they enjoyed performing the dance. They constantly laughed at Leila's attempts, but she did well when he twirled her away then twirled her back.

It was an intimate dance with her hardly ever leaving his chest; his hip constantly brushed hers, catching a spark at every touch. When the song faded, they were pressed up against the other with faces far closer than before.

Miguel's heart pounding in his chest competed against her own. A hand of his traced down her jaw, fluttering her eyes closed. His breath mingling with hers slowed as he leaned in. She lifted to meet his kiss.

Is he the one?

The icy question snapped like a whip, jerking her from his lips. Miguel let her step away but kept a hand firm around hers.

Trying not to look hurt and puzzled, he raised her hand and kissed it.

She took her hand back, and they returned to the others at the table with space between them.

"We're calling it a night," Miguel said.

The Spaniards bid goodnight to everyone. Miguel's questioning eyes lingered on her, but Leila refrained from returning his hot stare. Giving up, he joined Alvaro in going to their room. The others decided to call it a night as well and followed the Spaniards' lead.

Leila eagerly dressed for bed, feeling itchy and uncomfortable in her party clothes. After checking her phone for any messages, she turned it off and curled underneath her covers as Jamaal came out of their bathroom dressed for bed.

Jamaal seated on the edge of his bed facing her; Leila knew she couldn't avoid him. Her eyes slowly came up to meet his, steeling for a confrontation. "You've been quiet since you danced with Miguel."

Her silence encouraged him to continue. "What happened? You two seem to have a spark between you."

"I don't know." Releasing a long breath eased her into talking. "There is something heated between us. I know Miguel has feelings for me, and I think I hold the same for him, but something pulled me away from him after our dance."

"Did he do something?"

"No, it was me. A doubt of him not being the one jerked me back. I think this is all too soon."

Jamaal sighed as he leaned forward on his legs. "I don't know what to tell you, Lei. Miguel seems like an alright guy, but if you feel he's not the one you're meant for, then he's not. Don't second-guess your instincts over your thoughts."

Leila pulled the covers up higher as she thought about his advice.

He leaned back, chuckled, then stood to crawl into bed.

"What are you laughing about?" she asked.

"Rin being thrilled that he still has a shot at you."

She grabbed a pillow and chucked it at him, withdrawing more laughter from him and some even from her. "Rin never once asked me to dance tonight; he actually danced with another woman."

"Offended?"

"No, hopeful. Maybe he's forgotten about me."

He tossed the pillow back. "I doubt that."

Leila tucked the pillow back into her collection. "Thanks, Jamaal."

He grinned before turning off the light. "No problem."

Even though Jamaal was right about trusting her gut and not her thoughts or wants, the warmth of Miguel's kiss lingered on her hand; she wondered what his lips would've felt like on hers.

XXXII.

After reaching complete blankness in a deep sleep, she began to shake—one that shook her bones. Knowing the signs of a nightmare, she braced for it, but a heat rose up within her and pushed back, scaring it away. With the danger gone and comforted by the heat watching over her now, she drifted into sleep's warm embrace.

Like smoke coming in through the crack under a door, it reappeared. This nightmare was determined. Once again, though, the heat scared it away. Recognizing the heat—the body of flame from her dream in the hospital—she fell deeper into sleep.

Then a presence gently nudged in, full of love, warmth, and concern; she attached to it immediately. David. The body of flame disappeared as she turned her attention to him—she didn't need any other protection.

"*Leila.*" His whisper trickled down in a flowing stream, warming every tendon, nerve, bone, and muscle as it traveled to her heart—banishing the pain of losing him. She had gained him again.

"*Leila,*" he said louder and not so distant, like he was right beside her.

"*Leila,*" David said again but something seemed different to his voice, a distant concern and urgency.

"*Lei, wake up,*" he ordered. Even though his presence surrounded her, she sensed something ˉdarker seeping in—the nightmare found a back door.

"*WAKE UP!*"

Leila's eyes shot open, terror seizing her at not knowing what David feared.

Silver light shined through a space in the curtains; air currents fluttered the sheer layer. Staring long enough, she made out the shadows of furniture in the room. A dark lump identified Jamaal to her left; it was quiet except for his soft snores.

David woke her for a reason, but nothing seemed amiss. Even the air held the calmness of the night. She waited a moment longer but gave up and rolled onto her back, hoping she could quickly return to her dreams with David being so close. He had been a jokester in life; maybe he was in death, too. Her body sagged back into the mattress.

Not even a few minutes passed before the nightmare returned, painfully shaking her from the inside out. But it wasn't the normal signs—seeming to be *outside* of her and as the same cold fear from earlier when the forest fell silent around her. This wasn't a bad dream.

Hair rose as something loomed over her. Her eyes shot open, and her scream pierced the silence.

The body of a mangled wolf with sickly glowing eyes hovered above her. Long claws dangled off its arms. Dark fur, possibly gray or black. Inky smoke coming out of the end of its body took the place of legs—only the torso of a wolf floated above her.

When it realized she was awake, the mild curiosity in the creature's golden eyes changed to a savage, wild animal preparing to attack. Its lips pulled back, baring massive rows of white canine teeth. A low, menacing growl emerged from its throat.

Leila's hands flailed above her to knock the creature away. Her hands passed through its suddenly transparent body, and the effort threw her out of bed.

"LEI!" Jamaal cried, startled, and pulled awake by her scream. He switched on the lamp on the nightstand; with the light, Leila could see better in her fight to loosen herself from the entanglement of bed sheets.

"Lei, what's wrong?" He leaped out of his bed to assist. "Did you have another dream?"

Free of the sheets, she jumped up and spun around to look for the ghost-wolf, but it was gone. Her eyes scanned every shadow created by the lamp. Nothing hid in the shadows, and even the curtains hadn't been moved aside. She went to the window anyway to check the lock and balcony.

"Did you see someone?" Jamaal asked.

It hadn't been tampered with, and the patio furniture looked undisturbed—no one broke in to mess with her.

"No."

"Then what?"

"There was a, ummm…" she struggled to explain. "A ghost-like wolf thing was above me." It sounded ridiculous, but she saw it.

Silence. "It may have been a bad dream, Lei."

Leila turned to him. "No. I know it wasn't a dream. It was there."

"Then maybe a hallucination?"

"No," she answered but began to question herself. "Well… I don't know anymore." Doubt crept in. Maybe it hadn't happened—there was no evidence of the ghost-wolf. But David woke her in urgency, the body of flame appeared to protect her, and she felt the fear.

David, can you tell me what that was? she asked.

He answered quickly. *"I can't. You must figure it out."*

A loud banging caused them to jump and spin around. Someone stood at the door.

Jamaal chuckled at his own jitteriness and moved to answer. Leila couldn't breathe—her heart had jumped out of her chest. Once her heart resumed pounding, it hurt so much she sat on her bed and kneaded a hand into her chest, trying to massage it back into a normal beat.

"Is everything alright? We heard a scream." The accented voice belonged to a concerned Miguel at the door.

"I think so. Lei thought she saw something," Jamaal said.

"Leila, are you okay?" She looked up to Miguel and Alvaro in the lighted hallway, shirtless and bleary-eyed.

She nodded. "I will be. Sorry to wake you."

Jamaal thanked them for making sure they were fine. Alvaro nodded before bidding them goodnight again and headed back to his room. Miguel lingered in the doorway watching Leila. After she forced a reassuring smile, he bid them night as well before disappearing.

"I'm sorry, Jamaal," she began after he shut the door and headed back to help her place her sheets back on the bed.

"No need to apologize, Lei. I'm just... worried."

With a sigh, Leila sat back on her bed. "I am too. First, my dreams, and now my doubts getting to me. This has been so hard." Her voice broke at the end, and she looked off to hide the moisture in her eyes.

He sat beside her. "I can only imagine, but then I'm sure I wouldn't be even close to imagining what it's like. All of this has to be happening for a reason, right?"

"I guess that's one way of looking at it."

"It's the only way. You're being prepared for something much bigger."

"*You will rise when the time comes*," David whispered, warming her coldest wound. She massaged it without thinking.

"He spoke to you?" Jamaal asked.

She nodded. "He agrees."

"Then why aren't you comforted by that?"

She turned to him. "I'm changing. I feel it, and you have seen it too—that angrier side, the dark side. I felt it again protecting me. What I'm scared of is who will I be when I land? Me, or it?"

"You, of course."

"But am I who I'm supposed to be? I'm starting to think I'm not. David can't tell me—it'd be 'predicting the future'."

Jamaal pulled her into him. "There's no way the outcome of this could be bad or you wouldn't have been urged to come. It might take a little while or something else will show you how it helped."

Leila remained quiet, imagining possible outcomes but could only see the flame-engulfed body consuming her and taking her place.

XXXIII.

She couldn't sleep the rest of the night, seeing the ghost-wolf every time she closed her eyes. Leila kept her back turned to Jamaal and pretended to sleep. As she waited for the sun to light up the curtains for Sunday, she had plenty of time to reminisce. Her sturdy declaration that the ghost-wolf had been real became weaker as her thoughts withdrew—all her doubts and suspicions were transformed into a horribly mangled wolf.

Why a wolf, though? She found no reason for that specific animal.

When light outlined the curtains, Leila threw back her covers and hurried to take a shower. The warm water would wash away the fear clinging to her, and she'd wipe away any signs of restlessness before Jamaal saw that she didn't sleep.

After his shower, Jamaal decided to leave while he spoke on the phone, and so Leila had the room to herself.

She called the captain's personal cell first and listened to his praise about her miraculous fighting the entire station watched in the squad room every day. They were all confident she and Jamaal would win it all.

Ending the conversation with the captain, she tried to reach Hyun.

"Hey, Lei."

"You answered this time," she said.

He chuckled. "I couldn't answer before. Anyway, you make me proud every day on TV."

"Glad I can do so, but I figured you would want to talk my ear off about the entire tournament."

"Oh, I haven't gotten there yet. But for common courtesy, I had to say how good you are compared to the other contestants."

Hyun launched into detailing her fights, what he observed, and what he thought she should improve on. He switched to some of her upcoming opponents' fights so she could be prepared. Leila assured him she monitored her field—knowing he would stress awareness. He loved it.

The Hawaiian brothers—Haloani and Kaiapo Ikaika—concerned them both. None of their opponents have gotten a solid hit. Really aggressive. Many losers left matches with broken bones.

"This Kālu Ku'ialua they use," she began. "Explain it."

Hyun sighed. "Hawaiian martial arts specializing in bone breaking, joint locks, throws, and pressure point manipulation. It's brutal to watch.

"Maso Bonucci and Rinieri Anton face them tomorrow."

Leila mentally reminded herself to warn the guys. "I'll tell them."

"And the ones you fight tomorrow—the Germans—fight using a form of Sambo. The best comparison is Shinirokugo-ken. Raidon used it to put me out of commission."

"Do I sense a bitter memory coming through this phone?"

Hyun chuckled. "Maybe just a little bit; he was the one who beat me out of the trophy."

"Should Jamaal and I be worried?"

"No. They will put up a fight, but they aren't close to the expert level of Raidon."

"Are you hinting that we couldn't stand against him?" she challenged.

"Of course not."

"Then are you saying that we're better than you?"

"Watch it, Lei," he warned, but a smile softened his tone.

Leila laughed at his defensiveness. "But what do you think?"

Hyun took a moment. "Jamaal would be a challenge with his speed... but I think I could take him. You, on the other hand, would annihilate me. Before this tournament, I could definitely beat you—I did quite a few times."

She frowned. "You don't have to remind me."

"Oh, just reminding myself. But with you becoming stronger, more violent, and driven to win, I would put up a sorry fight. You're plain-out intimidating now."

Leila didn't respond at first; Hyun could see through the television she was changing. "That's good to know—puts a notch in our belt."

"But remember, this is you fighting me after twenty years of being at the top of my game *and* Raidon breaking my leg," he added.

She laughed again. "I'll let you blame that."

"Anyway, back to this tournament: if the brackets go the way I have predicted, you and Jamaal will face two Africans on Thursday. They'll be a match for Jamaal since they fight nearly the same, but you shouldn't have any trouble—you know how Jamaal fights, so you have an idea about their fighting styles."

"Thanks for the heads-up."

He paused to change the subject. "How's everything going off screen?"

Leila sighed. "Troubling."

"Uh-oh. How so?"

Her cheeks flushed at telling this to Hyun. "There's one who's been coming on pretty strong, and honestly, I'm not offended. He's given me something to hold on to, which has only been fighting until now. But as I want to draw closer, another part of me holds me back, angered that I'm trying to move on. I don't know what to do."

The other end remained silent until Hyun released a long sigh. "I pushed you toward this tournament because I thought it would help, but I feared you'd face this kind of situation... Who is it?"

"One of the Spaniards: Miguel Del Toro."

"Hmmm." She couldn't tell if he approved or not, and he didn't explain. "Does he know about David?"

"I don't think he does."

"If he knows, maybe he'll understand your hesitation."

She thought about it. "Perhaps. At least his advancements have halted another's…"

"You have *another* suitor?"

Leila almost lost control laughing at his disbelief. "He is *not* a suitor. This one I have been rebuffing, politely."

"Alright, who is this other stud?"

Why did I mention this? "Rinieri Anton."

"Hmmm." This time was definitely disapproval. "Miguel looks better."

She shook her head. "You're not making this any better."

"Then I'll leave you to your suitor ordeal since I can't give good advice—that's Nuan's station. But I will tell you to go discuss... everything with Miguel. Keep winning, Lei."

"I'll try. Bye, Hyun."

The call shut off, and Leila wondered how best to approach Miguel when a door shut in the hallway, and a shadow passed by her door, from the direction of the Spaniards' room.

Leila threw her phone on her bed as she hurried to the door and wrenched it open.

Miguel just pressed a button at the elevator.

"Miguel, wait!" she called as she closed the door behind her and hurried down the hall. The Spaniard turned and watched her approach.

She stopped before him as the elevator doors opened. "Can we talk?"

Miguel studied her for a second before gesturing toward the empty elevator. "Sure."

Leila stepped in with the Spaniard but neither spoke as the elevator made its way down after stopping on the second floor to pick up other contestants. After dropping off everyone on the first floor, it shut and raced back up to attain more passengers.

"Where to?" Miguel asked.

"Somewhere private," she said.

"How about the lake?"

Leila only nodded and headed through the cheerful lobby. As she passed, contestants saw the gloomy cloud hanging over her and stepped clear, not wanting her unease to kill their laughter. She didn't notice the glances her way, too occupied on going over what to say to Miguel and how best to approach it.

They headed around the apartment complex toward the sparkling waters of the lake and found it vacant. Ignoring the bench, Leila walked to the water's edge and stared down at her nervous reflection; she practically saw the machines grinding in her head. Miguel hung back from her. She appreciated his distance but also wanted his arms around her for comfort.

"You seem uneasy," Miguel began after a long silence.

Leila took a shaky breath. "Because I am. I don't know where to begin."

He took a few steps closer. "Just say whatever's on your mind."

"I'm sorry for last night," she blurted—eager to begin—as she turned to face him.

"It was nothing—" he began.

She interrupted. "No, it was—especially to you." His eyes showed her rejection still stung. "You wouldn't understand my actions unless I explain."

She paused to steady herself with a breath. "You already know I'm a detective in New York City. But you don't know that my partner, David Neal, Jr.—my boyfriend—was killed in front of me by Bryan Foster. I also died, but the paramedics revived me; David had no chance.

"We were out celebrating David's birthday when we got the call. We were together for five years." Emotions turned her face away, not wanting Miguel to see how exposed she was.

After composing herself, she turned to the silent Spaniard. She braced herself to tell him the rest: her fault with David's death, the discovery of the engagement ring, her connection still with David, and his order to find the one she was meant for, but the pity, sorrow, and recognition in Miguel's eyes ceased the words in her throat. For some reason, she didn't want to expose all.

"That is the reason for my actions last night. I was—am— confused about my feelings. I do care for you, I'm... I just don't know what to do."

Miguel breathed out and averted his eyes to the ground as his hands slipped into his pockets. He didn't respond for the longest; the silence wasn't awkward. "Maybe I should have been more subtle."

Leila smiled at his playful attitude. "No, it's not your fault; it's mine. If you had been subtle, I probably wouldn't have noticed, too tangled in this confusion of thoughts."

His eyes shot up at her, twinkling in humor. "That sack of crazy cats in your head won't scare me off, you know. I'll give you some space but not out of arm's length."

"I wouldn't want to run you off."

"I'm glad that you don't."

"But I am sorry that I'm this way, Miguel. I'm sorry for not moving on."

He moved closer to her after a sigh. "Leila, I understand your reasons, but mostly, I understand your pain and struggle to let go. Maybe not in the same way, though."

Miguel stopped beside her. "My reasons for coming here are, in ways, like yours. I wished to escape the pain of losing someone as well, but I can't, no matter how hard I try. She's on my mind, always."

A pang of jealousy hit Leila. She admonished herself for it; she didn't know who 'she' was.

He leaned down and picked up a few pebbles. "My sister was murdered," he said bitterly as he skipped a rock across the placid waters. "We planned to meet for lunch in our hometown of Roda de Isábena: a quiet little place visited only by locals for its white cathedral with a rose window and a café."

He skipped another rock. "The day seemed perfect—no clouds in the sky; the sun's rays were absorbed by Isabella's midnight hair, pulled in a side bun. She wore a white dress. Only a few feet from the café I could see a waiter leading her to our table outside. Fighter jets appeared overhead, dropping bombs; everything exploded, throwing me into one of the buildings behind me, knocking me out.

"When I finally came to, I heard gunfire. The café was reduced to smoldering rubble and parachute troopers shot at who they could see. I panicked; I knocked one of the troopers down, took his gun, killed him, and killed the others. I should've helped those trapped under debris or screaming in pain, but I could only think of Isabella. It took me seconds searching through the debris to find her, her white dress splotched with blood."

Miguel didn't speak again for a while. His jaw had tightened, and the sorrow in his eyes meant he dealt with the picture of his dead sister again. "Those jets and the men I killed wore Xander's logo." He tossed the last stone, and it dropped into the lake with a splash. "I am here to enact revenge for the death of my sister and all those others."

Her insides murmured in approval at his drive for revenge. *Foster...*

Leila shook off the desire to do the same. She was a cop and wasn't going to dirty her honor by adopting criminal acts. Instead, she focused on Miguel's reaction to Amadeus Xander the first night; now she understood his look of murder.

"You believe Xander ordered the attack."

"Yes," he answered.

"Do you have any proof he was involved?"

"Other than the planes, no," was his abrupt reply as he looked across the lake. "Because of your suspicions of the tournament, I've asked others' reasons for coming here, and they all have a disaster in common. Then came the invites, and they're trying to win the money for their bankrupt towns or villages or their sick and dying relatives." Miguel turned to look at her. "You can't tell me that this is all coincidence."

"I'm a cop. I don't believe in coincidences." But fear set in—his statement confirmed her suspicions that everything was connected. She should've done the work asking questions instead of him; being concerned with her own problems was a poor excuse. He seemed to be the detective instead of her, acting on her suspicions. Something else to be ashamed of.

"Miguel, has anything here reminded you of Isabella?"

"No." His brow furrowed in concern. "Has something reminded you of David?"

"Everything," she said.

Realization hit him. "That's why you think Xander has something out for you. But why? Do you think he ordered David's death?"

She shook her head tentatively. "I don't know. I'm scared to find out."

They fell quiet, both feeling dark intentions pressing down on them.

"It's time for me to be a cop. I need to settle these suspicions."

"Your paranoia was right."

"Detective instincts," she corrected.

He chuckled. "Whatever you wish to call it."

She turned to him, bracing for an argument. "Now, this detective will tell you something you don't want to hear. I know you long to avenge your sister's death, but—"

Miguel turned on her to interrupt, "Don't you want to avenge David's murder? That's what cops do; they get the bad guys."

"I can't do it through revenge. Even though I hate Bryan Foster, I can't go down to his level and slander my reputation. As a cop, I took an oath not to set out for personal gain. I have to let justice take control."

"Justice," he spat. "What good will justice do for David? What good has it done? You need to quit being patient and take justice into your own hands. Don't let the thought of how others will portray you stop you from doing what needs to be done. Every cop has a bit of criminal in them—let it become dirty with revenge. You can clean yourself up later."

She found herself warmed again by his suggestion but shook her head. "I can't. That's not me."

"Then what about your dark side? That's part of you."

She shook her head again but less adamantly. "This isn't about me."

"Not until you listen to your instincts that it is."

Leila couldn't say anything. He just increased her worry and decreased her refusal to admit it. She hurriedly went back to the subject. "We can't do anything until we know nothing else is going on—something much bigger than our troubles."

He turned his head away with the angry snort of a bull. After giving him a moment to think it over, Leila placed a hand on Miguel's folded arms. "Promise me you won't lose your head and head straight for Xander, Miguel. We need to know all that he is guilty of beforehand, instead of me scraping up a reason for releasing you on him."

That brought a smile to his hardened lips. More time passed before he released frustrated air in defeat and nodded.

"Thank you." She began to remove her hand from his arm, but a hand shot out from the folded arms and snagged it.

"I'm sorry for your loss, Leila."

"I feel for yours as well, Miguel."

She allowed him to keep her hand as they watched the shadows from the setting sun extend over the waters, hinting at them only scratching the surface as the mastermind danced out of reach.

XXXIV.

Monday had the remaining contestants more eager to continue the tournament, being so close to crowning the champions. Leila told Rin and Maso what Hyun said about their opponents the prior evening. The iPads didn't store past fights, so they couldn't study how the Hawaiian brothers fought.

The team of Germans waited for them in a construction yard. As large as Miguel and Alvaro, the fighting technique the blond men specialized in—Sambo—consisted of grappling and throws they learned in basic training to become German soldiers.

Jamaal won his match by taking advantage of the landscape: staying entirely on his hands, his legs spun like fan blades and stirred up gravel-mixed dirt to strike his opponent. So not only could the German not stay on his feet, but most of the time, he was blind.

Leila's turn proved more difficult. She could barely get a strike in before he trapped her in a throw or a grapple, but she managed to slip out before he could inflict any serious damage.

Her dark side kept nudging for a release. When he stumbled back after a hit to his face, she let the heat burst through. In the form of the Phoenix, she jumped at him and kicked upward with both feet; landing, she twisted around with her leg up to kick him across his turned back, then after switching to her other foot, she extended her leg straight into his back, sending him flying to the ground.

After the count of ten seconds, Leila was declared the winner, and the unconscious man wheeled off to the infirmary.

Hurrying over to the command post, they caught the end of Rin and Maso's fight. The black kickboxer had already been defeated by Kaiapo Ikaika; now, Rin faced Haloani and was annihilated. He couldn't keep up with the swift Hawaiian.

Leila didn't get to study the Kālu Ku'ialua expert before the battle finished. He jabbed Rin in the crook of his elbows, and the boxer's hands never rose again. The Italian tried charging headlong or kicking, but Haloani locked one knee, and he dropped. Unable to fight, Rin called forfeit.

THE MAJORITY OF TUESDAY LEILA spent confirming Miguel's information by talking with contestants. He was right, but she noticed the fighters more driven to win had larger issues than those who had been eliminated but remained on the island.

The next concern to address: if anything seemed centered on them—like how everything was arranged to remind Leila of David. Nothing did.

So, only she had the problem. Not comforting in the slightest.

She couldn't scour Panordom for evidence in one day and *without* drawing attention to herself. If any paper trail existed, Xander wouldn't have left it for easy access with a detective on his island, so Leila compromised her longing to search by asking his staff.

The questions were innocent, but every now and then, she'd ask about Xander or wonder how they prepared a meal for someone's food allergies without asking. All repeated what

Leila already knew about the multi-billionaire and guessed that some notification came from those contestants.

Xander's staff lied—they had an idea on how contestants' personal information had been obtained, but they weren't telling Leila.

She had no way of forcing the truth out of them. She didn't have jurisdiction here and possessed no proof of criminal wrongdoings. Only suspicions, still.

LEILA SEARCHED THE OVER-250-POUND men of nothing but muscle for any show of weakness that Wednesday. They were quite solid on their feet and had no sign of injury or sore spot.

"Hyun said to go after their legs," she whispered to Jamaal.

"What about you?" he asked.

She continued to watch them, knowing the men would lengthen the fight. Their exposed muscled and tattooed torsos meant to intimidate by advertising their massive strengths. Leila and Jamaal were considerably leaner than the ex-MMA fighters and only a hair quicker. They could win by avoiding hits, likely being knocked out cold.

Leila looked at him. "I'm to do the same."

Past his shoulder, she saw Miguel and Alvaro in the crowd. They both smiled and nodded in encouragement, but now Leila had the presence of Miguel's eyes pressing down on her. His eyes lingering on her already made her want to both flaunt in her moves and squirm in displeasure.

It was a glorious day to visit the park today, the evening sun casting long shadows. A slight breeze. Vibrant green grass. Birds singing in the trees. Free entertainment fixing to begin with their match.

The official stepped into the ring, encouraging Jamaal and his opponent to join him. They performed their greetings, jumped into their stances, and rushed into battle as soon as the fight began.

Punch. Throw. Thud as an attack landed. Cartwheel. Grunt. Kick. Dodge.

Leila paced her edge of the boundaries as Jamaal and his opponent traded hit after hit—Jamaal somehow avoided the man's extreme power behind his fists.

Jamaal dropped to his back to dodge a punch and twisted his legs and torso around, sweeping the man off his feet. He crashed hard to the ground, and the two thrashed and grappled as they rolled.

They broke free and as he scrambled back to his feet, Jamaal bent back on his hands then brought both feet crashing into the man's back and head. He dropped onto his chest, facedown, and didn't move again.

"Round One goes to Jamaal Gordon! What an intense fight!" the announcer yelled after a blue flag lifted.

The Jamaican came back to Leila wincing and walking gingerly. "They're going to be sore tomorrow." He looked down at his battered feet.

"Get in the Jacuzzi tonight, that'll help." She moved past him to face her opponent.

Leila bowed and moved down into Panther; he just held his fists up in front of his face as he bounced on his feet. The flags dropped, and he rushed at her with a flying kick. She rolled out of the way and lashed out at his legs when he landed. But he was quick; he jumped over her arms, turned in midair, and brought a fist down to smash into her back.

A hand helped her lean back, and his fist grazed her stomach. Her free hand smashed into his nose, reeling him to his knees in pain. Keeping her weight supported on her left hand,

Leila flung herself around, striking her legs into the man's face. He fell back as she completed the rotation.

"Leila Wells is dominating this fight!"

The announcer presumed too soon. The man miraculously rolled back to his knees, grabbed Leila's left arm, and yanked back around, twisting as he went. She screamed in agony—the knives stabbed her elbow again.

He let go to fling her across the arena. She wanted to curl in on her side and cradle her arm. The sudden flood of anger and heat saved her from being knocked into unconsciousness: the power tugged her to roll away from the man's dropping hammer of a fist and kick up into his stomach.

"Trade out, Lei," David urged.

His voice cleared her thoughts of taking advantage of the man's loss of air and beating him under her fists. "JAMAAL!" she cried as she scrambled up to her feet, clutching her hurt arm, and ran for the bounds.

Jamaal came in just as she exited. His moves were more violent themselves, angry that this man inflicted pain on his partner. She held her arm tightly to her, panting against the excruciating pain, watching Jamaal finish the fight.

When the ex-MMA fighter fell, and a flag rose for Jamaal, her knees buckled, and she collapsed, bending her torso, and trying to regain air. Leila knew her arm hadn't been rebroken, but he twisted the tender areas, feeling like it had just happened. And the memory of that event kept crashing in on her.

Hands touched her as someone dropped down. "Leila, is it broken?" Miguel asked.

Leila shook her head but didn't open her eyes. "No, he just twisted what has been."

"Let me check." He gently tugged her wounded arm free of the protective one and traced from her wrist to forearm, elbow and up before following its way back down; after finishing its task, his hand wrapped around hers. He must have nodded to the other two crowded around her that it wasn't broken for heavy breaths were expelled.

"We still need to check and make sure it's not splintered," Miguel stated. She could stand on her own, but Jamaal helped her up, Miguel kept a hand around hers, and a hand of Alvaro's patted reassuringly on her back. Miguel wrapped an arm around her, holding her to him as the four of them headed for the infirmary.

"THERE'S NO SIGN OF FRACTURING, but from the way I heard of your fight, it came very close to breaking... Well, re-breaking from the looks of it," the doctor said as the four fighters observed the X-Ray scan of Leila's arm.

Leila didn't need his confirmation that her arm wasn't broken. Yes, the severe twisting of it nearly caused her to black out from the pain. The memory of it snapping the first time along with the replay of David's death did more damage. She had done well not to fall back into that dark memory—now she broke that streak.

The doctor prescribed some pain pills, assured the others she would be able to fight Friday, and left. Leila remained staring at her left arm resting on her lap, feeling three sets of eyes turning on her and not wanting to meet them.

Miguel cleared his throat, causing her to cringe at the questions soon to come. "It wasn't just the pain of your arm, was it?"

"No."

"When were you hurt?"

Her voice dropped into a whisper, "The night David was killed."

Fortunately, they understood the real reason for her pain—it cowered within her answer. They didn't press her to elaborate.

The secluded examining table remained silent for a while, then Alvaro broke it cautiously. "How bad?"

"I was shot six times, and my arm broken in two places, as you saw on the X-Ray."

Jamaal sighed. "Well, it looks like neither of us will get much sleep tonight."

His playful poke at lightening the mood pulled up her smile. "Sorry I inconvenience your sleep, Jamaal."

He chuckled. "I don't mind pulling an all-nighter."

"Tomorrow you might not feel the same."

"What are you talking about?" Alvaro interrupted.

Jamaal turned to him. "I stay up with Lei to help with her… memories. I'm not leaving her alone to go through all of that by herself."

"Even though I would prefer it," Leila muttered.

"If you don't get any sleep, I don't think I should."

"None of us should."

Leila turned to Miguel grinning.

XXXV.

At the knocks, Jamaal went to the door and opened to admit Miguel and Alvaro. "We brought chips and salsa."

The Jamaican laughed.

"You brought food? Where did you get it?" Leila asked as they walked in with a container of dip and a bag of tortilla chips.

Miguel shrugged. "The cafeteria; I'm sure they won't notice."

"I'm not running to the room if I get hungry," Alvaro said as he dragged a couch out of the lounging room. After positioning it where the bathroom was still accessible—only by squeezing past his long couch—he tossed the pillow he brought at one end, then threw himself on it. He stretched his long frame, then fell back into the cushions with a sigh. Miguel watched his partner getting comfortable.

He asked him a question in Spanish. Alvaro shrugged; he motioned toward the floor. Miguel barked back in Spanish as he turned.

He shooed Leila over with his hands. "Scoot; I'm not sleeping on the ground."

With a scowl directed at the wickedly grinning Alvaro, she scooted closer to the edge by the nightstand. Miguel dropped a knee on the bed then turned as he fell on his back.

After filling paper bowls with salsa, Jamaal performed a balancing act to serve them.

"You should work for a circus," Miguel suggested.

Jamaal grimaced. "I'm not a fan of clowns." He took a seat on his bed.

Miguel turned to Leila. "How's your arm?" He didn't wait for her answer—his eyes already winced at the dark bruise covering the inside of her elbow.

"Not bad." She twisted it for proof.

"Doesn't look that way."

"It's fine." She turned away from their closeness to watch Alvaro turning on his couch to prop his legs on Jamaal's bed, then he opened the bag of chips and commenced eating.

Miguel grabbed one of the pillows behind him and chucked it at his partner. Alvaro had enough control that he didn't jerk and spill the chips. "You have to share."

He scowled. "I don't hear anyone asking for them."

"You'll bite if we do."

The Spaniard made a show of folding the chip bag and tossing it to Jamaal, grumbling all the while in Spanish.

Miguel jerked his hand at him. "I need my pillow."

Alvaro picked it up, added it behind him, and ended by folding his arms.

His partner laughed. "You're such a child."

"Since when were you an adult?"

"For a while now."

Alvaro made a sound in his throat. "I can't tell a difference."

Miguel turned to her. "So, how are we getting this sleepover started?"

"Earlier it sounded like you planned to babysit me," Leila said as she accepted the chips from Jamaal.

Jamaal ate a chip full of salsa. "But before didn't include food."

The night consisted of trading the bag of chips, and conversations avoiding the reasons why they were drawn to the tournament and delving more into Leila's injuries and nightmares. But apprehension made the air heavy. A punch was coming—one impossible to dodge, though, since it would come from the man stretched on the bed beside her. Miguel wouldn't let her escape, so she had to take this one. She hoped it wouldn't cause her too much pain.

Gradually, the bag of chips depleted, along with their conversations and energy. Jamaal and Alvaro fell asleep almost simultaneously, seeming to have been in a collaboration of giving Leila and Miguel time to talk.

They were now lying down and facing each other, close enough for Leila to discern a scar underneath the stubble running down to disappear under his shirt. She traced the puckered line.

"I've never seen this before."

He grabbed her hand before she pulled it off his collarbone. The beats of his heart and his warmth felt good. "My third Matador fight: the bull caught me under the chin. I learned not to lower my defenses once a bull passed—it wasn't done yet."

"Did you ever get hurt again?"

"Minor; nothing as serious."

She wanted to keep the focus off her if possible. "What about Alvaro?"

Miguel chuckled. "That one has gotten more hurt getting drunk and fighting for a señorita already taken."

"And?"

"He always wins the fight, but never gets the girl."

Unlike you. That angry voice rose up, surprising Leila at its disgusted view of Miguel at what he left out, but she filled in. He probably fought some to win their girl or fended off those from what he had.

If he's as gallant as you picture him, why doesn't he fight more for you?

Because I'm not his, she said.

Nor will you ever be.

Miguel stayed quiet watching her deal with an internal discussion, but it gave him an opening to prepare the confrontation she knew was coming. Cursing herself for giving him this chance, Leila got ready.

"Do you want to talk about it?"

It was her injury linked to David's death and her emotions trailing behind the pain. Physical and mental. Leila considered opening to him—especially with this being her second opportunity—but the thought of his reaction to her confession held her back again. She didn't think he could truly understand her guilt. "Not really."

He rubbed her arm. "I hate you had to go through that."

"I wouldn't be here if I hadn't."

His eyes sparkled. "So, there is a reason you're here."

"It has to be."

But not what you think it is.

Why can't it?

Unease settled in her stomach at the disagreement within her of going to Miguel and not. She tried to shake it off by shifting focus, "Jamaal says it has to be."

"But you're not sure…"

She met his eyes. "How can I? It's easier for those who haven't experienced what we have to see light past the darkness. We can't see anything."

"Those on the outside can help us *not* fall back once we've emerged. The ones like you and I help guide each other through the darkness."

She looked away. *How can one help the other if both are lost in the darkness?*

You can't, that voice answered. *He's making you stumble with him, thinking you are helping. You have to find your own light.*

Miguel speaking brought her out of her head, "You pull away much more now in what looks like an argument with yourself, and you never look pleased with the other answer."

She had also put some distance between them. "I haven't found something we agree on yet."

"Am I one of the topics?"

Leila couldn't look at him, but embarrassment crept up her neck. "Yes."

"Well, I must be doing something right since I'm thought of."

His eyes glittered, and she found herself sharing his light and airy aura. "Don't get too excited. You're not the only topic in my head."

"I don't have to worry about Rin, do I?"

"No. If I think about him, it's a brief thought that annoys me like a gnat who refuses to go away."

"I'm sure I can make him stop." Miguel's eyes lost their cheerful light.

"No; no need in that." She didn't want Rin hurt over his annoying but harmless flirting.

Are you just a piece of meat he feels ownership over that he has to fight over like wolves? Is that all you are to him?

She tried to smooth over the tension in both of their bodies by chuckling. "Besides, his persistence has driven you to be the same. You're not playing games like most men do."

The lightness came back into his eyes. "I don't play games when I see something I want."

He kissed her forehead and pulled her in closer. Her head fit under his neck, and she basked in being curled into him. Miguel's hard body maintained a comfortable heat like a set space heater, his scent soaked into her brain, and the gradual slowing of his breath and heart brought hers down as well.

THE HEAT WITHIN HER WOULDN'T cool down—it kept burning in a steady fire. That combating the heat outside of her body made her shift in discomfort. Once her face lifted to cooler air, Leila awoke in alarm.

Miguel held her close to his chest, both arms around her like a cage. She was curled into him, cramped in a little ball. Anger followed by shame washed over her at sleeping next to him. The heat inside and outside suffocated her.

By his even and heavy breathing, he was lost in deep sleep, so she tried to worm out of his arms without waking him. She feared her movement would cause him to pull her back in tighter, but Miguel unlatched his arms and rolled onto his back. Leila quickly got up, slipped by an equally unconscious Alvaro sprawled on the couch, and shut the bathroom door behind her.

The heat from within already started to tone down with her urgency to get out of Miguel's arms, but she hoped a cool shower would get rid of all of it.

XXXVI.

L eila wrapped her elbow for extra support and to hide the ugly bruise from her opponents. She repeated Hyun's warning to Shamus and Luke about the Hawaiian natives; the two men went into the match confident while she and Jamaal headed toward the beach to face off against the two Africans with Rin and Maso tagging along.

Miguel's fight right after hers today wouldn't let him attend hers, and she was glad of it. That heat made her feel ill at every thought of the Spaniard; she feared what she would do at the sight of him. Leila didn't want to ram a fist into his face like she felt drawn to do. At least, she didn't think *all* of her wanted to. Sleeping so close to him had thrown her back off balance, and she needed time to right herself again before something else threw her off the scales completely.

Their opponents wore native warrior clothing with darker tattoos across their dark-skinned muscular bodies, man-made necklaces of animal bones and stones, and strips of brown leather for bottoms. Ceremonial war paint on their faces enhanced their third world look.

Because of Hyun's prediction, she and Jamaal paid close attention to these African brothers' previous fights.

"If I can't get a move on them, we'll trade out," Jamaal said as they waited. "They'll be no match for you."

The large crowd around them erupted in applause at the sight of the commentator. "After three long weeks of fighting, we have grown fond of a few fighters who have proven their worth; I'm talking about a certain Jamaican and one of New York's Finest.

"Today shall be interesting for the crowd favorites, Jamaal Gordon and Leila Wells, face off against the two Africans, Washun and Olemnsk Tureg. Both teams have strengths in the Capoeira fighting style, and there is also the worry about Leila Wells fighting with an injury she obtained at Wednesday's match. Will our undefeated team keep their title?"

Done pepping the crowd for the fight, Jamaal and Washun stepped up; the official joined them, and with the roar of the crowds, he began the fight.

The African attacked, and Jamaal matched the punches with his own. Soon, it became a synchronized dance with hand flips, spinning on their hands and legs propelling around like a whirlwind while the other ducked, dodged, and blocked.

After repetitive attempts and failing to gain ground, Jamaal signaled Leila he was withdrawing. He leaped out of bounds as Leila entered and immediately moved into Crane, waiting for her opponent to attack.

Washun charged, then dove right in front of her to begin a series of cartwheels and flips. Recognizing the move as one of Jamaal's, she jumped over his sweeping leg, blocked his mid-hit, and like the sharp wings of a crane, backhanded him in the face, chest, then spun around him to drive her elbow into his back in 'Crane's Wing'.

As he struggled in a daze, she loosened the restraint of her broiling dark side. Careful not to use her left arm other than for balance, she struck him relentlessly—his body lurched from one extreme to be sent sprawling to the other.

To end him, she flipped him over her knee to land on his chest. When Washun finally got to his hands and knees, his countdown had expired.

"Her injury doesn't seem to be a factor. Leila Wells wins Round One!"

Leila turned to see if Jamaal wished to return, but he denied. "He'll fight just the same. I won't get anywhere, like before."

Turning back to face her next opponent, the weight of someone staring made her scan the cheering crowd for the owner of the eyes—it wasn't the familiar lingering of Miguel or Rin, but a stark disposition. She found one not cheering.

He stuck out because of his complete lack of enthusiasm and black motorcycle gear. Leila didn't have to look down at the snakeskin boots to identify him. His green eyes were locked on her just as hers was frozen on him—disbelief at the shock of his appearance made her question a hallucination.

Once his mocking smirk slid into his eyes, the heat simmering like warm coals exploded. Ignoring the warning in her heart and of her coldest wound, she jolted toward Foster to avenge David's death, prepared to rip out his throat.

Pain suddenly pierced her side, throwing off her run as she recoiled from the hit. Leila turned back—not realizing the official had begun the fight—to have her vision blinded from a strike to the face. Tears rose to her eyes as Leila fell to the sand.

The crowd and commentator gasped, but her partner sounded above all.

"LEI!" Jamaal yelled in warning.

Her sixth sense warned her of Olemnsk coming to finish her. She rolled to the side as her opponent came down with a fist; when the man's hand collided with the empty sand, Leila kicked him in his stomach.

The African stumbled back, clutching his stomach as Leila jumped to her feet. Her face was hot from being kicked, and she tasted the rust of blood as some dripped down her lip. Pain answered every breath, but at least her ribs were only bruised, not broken.

Enraged at seeing Foster and being attacked fueled her anger even more. She didn't hold herself back; her dark side took over, and through the Phoenix, she released a relentless onslaught. As soon as Olemnsk dropped unconscious, Leila scanned the crowd for Foster, ignoring the official backing her away from her downed opponent, announcing that she won, or of the crowd's joy at her close comeback. He was not where she first saw him, so she patrolled the bounds, making the crowd shy back because of the severity of her face.

Jamaal ran up to her. "Lei, are you okay? What happened?"

"Foster's here," she answered, not bothering to stop her search of the crowd.

Fear froze the Jamaican. A second passed for him to recover, and he looked for the murderer with wide eyes. "I can't find him."

"I saw him; he's here somewhere."

Out of the corner of her eye, she saw Rin and Maso hurrying up to them, concern plain on their faces and in their voices. Behind them a medic approached but cautiously, sensing how on edge she was.

Leila ignored the help and Rin and Maso's encouragement to do so, but Jamaal accepted. "Lei, we need to get you checked out. I doubt he hung around after the fight."

Furious that she had missed her chance to kill him, she wanted to go track him down, but Jamaal tugged her away. He suggested the Italians wait for them at the cafeteria so Leila could have a chance to cool off. But on the walk to the infirmary, the angry flame that usually faded after a fight increased in its dangerous boil at every thought of Foster. Off the balancing scales she went.

A nurse led them past a team being checked for a sprained ankle to another examining table. The nurse closed the curtains for privacy as Leila eased onto the table and Jamaal pulled up a chair.

"Sorry, Lei," he began.

"For what?"

"For not being skilled enough to go back into the ring; if I had, we wouldn't be here again."

"Jamaal, neither today nor Wednesday was your fault. Olemnsk seized an opportunity I opened for him to take; I shouldn't have left myself open," she stated.

"Why didn't you trade out like before?"

"I had too much fury; I had to let it out."

He breathed out long and heavy. "I'm also sorry for that. I would never have thought Foster would follow you here."

"To remind me of the pain he's caused. It's not like I need help remembering," Leila trailed off bitterly.

Jamaal studied her for a long moment. "Are you sure it was him?"

She looked at him; he wouldn't say it out loud, but he doubted Foster had actually been there—a hallucination, just like the ghost-wolf. Her anger rose in defensiveness.

"I not only saw him, Jamaal, but I felt him there gloating."

His eyes dropped to the floor, ashamed he suggested such a thing. "I still can't see why he showed up. Does he want to taunt you into going after him? Why would he do that?"

She couldn't answer for the longest, struggling not to voice her troubling thoughts. *He wants me to seek revenge, and he's just making it easier for me to follow that path.* She found herself gleeful at the thought.

But she tried to shake it off. "I don't know."

The entrance of the same doctor as Wednesday ended their debate. "I'm not too happy to see you again. How's the arm?" He checked her face, but the hit had only broken skin, causing her lip to bleed.

He checked her ribs for any breaks, confirming her suspicion of only bruising, and checked up on her arm. The doctor told her to finish out her previous pain medication and left to attend another patient.

As Leila and Jamaal left, the call of their names brought them over to Shamus and Luke. The red-headed man sat in a chair, and Luke rested on the examining table, holding his limp left arm. Their slumped postures and bruised and battered forms showcased their defeat.

"Did you get hurt?" Shamus asked.

Leila brushed it off, "We're fine. What happened to you?"

"The Hawaiians," Shamus answered with remorse.

"Moved in blur," Luke piped up. "Hit with snake hands, like you, Leila." He held up his right hand to demonstrate but winced at the pull of his arm and lowered it.

"That's Kālu Ku'ialua; they go after the pressure points in your strongest area like I said."

The two wounded men looked at her, Shamus better at hiding his surprise at her snapping. He instead scrutinized her. "Are you okay, Leila?"

"Perfect, other than being struck and missing a chance."

Their faces twisted into even more puzzlement, but she stopped him before Shamus could ask her to explain—she wasted time she could be using to search for Foster. "Sorry, I'm just not up to talking."

Jamaal hoped for the best on Luke's arm behind her, then he jogged up to catch Leila leaving.

XXXVII.

L uke's arm being sprained was the only good news. Bad news came that evening with Shamus and Luke's *and* Rin and Maso's elimination. They remained on the island, though, as encouragement for the New Yorkers and Spaniards.

Even though the sight of Bryan Foster shook her terribly, Leila's focus never wavered—the angry heat that had exploded increased her fury, and she released it Saturday and Sunday mornings in the gym when no one was awake. His visit sparked the desire of taking revenge, and she kept an eye out for Foster everywhere she went.

Nothing cooled her dark side now.

Her withdrawal affected Jamaal, but he didn't approach her about it until Sunday night.

"Alright, what's going on? I know Foster's visit disturbed you—it definitely got me—but you're not acting like it bothered you. It's like his visit made you realize you *have* to seek revenge. I thought you were avoiding that temptation."

She settled back into her headboard. "I'm not set on revenge, but I'm preparing myself to do something about it. The heat my dark side provides makes me feel whole again—the only thing to do so. I'm sorry for withdrawing, but I'm not about to let it go."

Jamaal sighed as he crawled into bed. "I'm just worried you'll become too attached."

"I'm sure I can let go... when the time comes."

She seemed to assure Jamaal, but Leila didn't feel too sure that she told the truth.

CHAMPIONSHIP WEEK BEGAN WITH THEM back in the arena. Leila and Jamaal stood alongside six other teams on the raised mat arranged based on their winning records. The couple who specialized in Vale Tudo—Demi McAllister and Corey Abins—had survived since their loss to her and Jamaal in the second week. Corey sported a taped-up broken nose.

For even battles, perhaps one team would get a BYE. She hoped it wouldn't be her and Jamaal—she needed to lessen more of her fury. Obliterating dummies in the gym for two days hadn't been enough.

But with their perfect score, they'd probably get the BYE.

"Welcome to Championship week!" Bob began. The chubby announcer stood to the side of Leila and Jamaal, slightly in front to be separate from the quarterfinalists. "I wanted us to get here, then I didn't because the tournament would end." He laughed at himself. "Oh well.

"Our tournament is coming to a close after three and a half long weeks of fighting, but it is only because of all of our brave and courageous contestants!" He clapped enthusiastically, encouraging everyone to join.

"Now, the arrangement for today's fight is different than those previous. I bet the fighters have guessed at what's to happen," he said, looking at those lined on the mat.

Bob turned to face the audience and cameras. "We have the seven best teams here, but only six can fight today. So, to keep things even, the team boasting the best record earns a BYE. And there is only one team who has such."

With a dramatic sweep of his arm, the cameras turned to them in the ring. "Congratulations to Jamaal Gordon and Leila Wells, hefting the undefeated record of 9-0!" The arena exploded in applause, whistling, and cheering.

She forced a smile and waved, but inside frustration boiled. Now she had to wait two more days to release her anger.

The cameras returned to Bob. "Our remaining six teams fight in three battles, all randomly chosen beforehand. And to keep our New Yorkers from gaining an advantage by watching their opponents, they will be isolated from the arena."

Leila's eyebrow rose. That was a surprise. Maybe she could return to the gym, beat out her rage at waiting.

"So, we must bid *adieu* to Leila and Jamaal," he said. The announcer smiled sadly as he gestured for them to leave. People yelled their farewells, and Miguel caught her eye, nodding.

Her wish wasn't granted. She and Jamaal were taken to a secluded back room in the arena. Every now and then they could hear the roars and cheering of the crowds.

In the lounging room, Jamaal laid out on one of the couches and fell asleep, appreciating this break. Leila sat on her couch for a little while until her stored-up energy and anger forced her to pace. Thoughts hounded her.

Her suspicions had been raised even before the tournament began, but now they were through the roof with the semi-finals arrangement.

How could they have known Jamaal and I would remain undefeated?

The tournament was rigged from the start, that other voice said. *Your fights overall were easy and only grew slightly tougher later on to avoid suspicion and to deepen our relationship.*

Our *relationship? So, who, or what, are you to me?*

Your dark side.

She looked down at her hands. A part of her—something she couldn't deny.

Alright, back to the tournament being rigged. Why? Why would Jamaal and I need this BYE?

You expressed frustration at it.

Leila stopped, realizing what her dark side talked about: keeping her anger in for two more days. Doing so ensured her dark side would be powerful.

But why would her dark side be important?

That, I do not know, nor do I care. You try to remain humble, when we deserve the spotlight.

A staff member retrieved them when the quarterfinals concluded. Bob watched their approach with a smile; only three teams stood on the mat with him: the Hawaiians, some Japanese women dressed futuristically—one had a shock of electric-blue hair and the other's was dyed bright pink—and the smirking team of Miguel and Alvaro.

Amadeus Xander remained vacant to Leila's growing unease.

"When we first began the Rulers of the Realms Fighting Tag Tournament, sixty tag teams from all over the world came to prove that they were the best fighters, but now, we are down to four teams. Allow me to introduce our semifinalists!"

He turned to the fighters. "From Tokyo, Japan: Utada Jukina and Kairi Han!" The Japanese women bowed to the audience's applause. Utada would be an interesting challenge to Leila—she also used Five-Animals Kung Fu.

"From Honolulu, Hawaii: Haloani and Kaiapo Ikaika!" The Hawaiian natives bowed, both shirtless with tribal tattoos wrapping around their upper arms and dressed only in grass skirts.

"Our Matadors from Roda de Isábena, Spain: Miguel Del Toro and Alvaro Munoz!" Both Spaniards smirked and gave small waves.

"And our undefeated team, from New York City, New York: Jamaal Gordon and Leila Wells!" The two of them waved as the arena grew loud—clearly the favorites.

Bob turned back to address the audience. "Our first semifinals begin Wednesday with the Spaniards against the Hawaiians followed by the New Yorkers versus the Japanese! Whatever the outcomes, those teams will compete Friday in the finals. Then we crown our Rulers of the Realms! Who do you think it will be?" He offered the microphone to the audience for predictions shouted in an indiscernible tangle.

As the arena continued to proclaim the winners, Bob spoke to the cameras, reminding viewers to tune in two days from now for the semifinal matches.

EXCITEMENT ABOUT THE SEMIFINALS PREVENTED the entire island from retiring to their rooms, but Leila didn't feel like staying up and celebrating. Even though she tried to order Jamaal to stay and visit with the others, he went up with her, saying that he wasn't leaving her alone for a second. As they reached their room, the Spaniards caught up with them.

"Good luck on your match Wednesday," Miguel began as they stopped before them.

"You too," Leila replied.

Alvaro waved it away. "No, no. No need in that. We won't win."

Miguel grinned at their shocked faces. "We stand no chance against the Hawaiians—they're too quick for us."

Leila frowned. "I am a cop; I know when someone is lying."

Both Spaniards chuckled. Miguel presented his wrists. "You got us. Are you going to arrest us?"

"No, I don't have my handcuffs, and I want you to fight."

253

"Oh, we're fighting; we just know we won't win. But we'll give them a hard fight like the Spaniards we are."

"Like the *mad* Spaniards we are," Alvaro corrected.

Miguel's face lit in laughter, and he replied in quick Spanish to his partner. Then he turned back to Leila and Jamaal. "We'll make them sore for you to beat." The Spaniards grinned mischievously.

"Don't throw in the towel; don't do it for us," she pleaded.

Alvaro's eyebrows furrowed at the saying; Miguel turned to explain. "She means don't give up before we start." He looked back at her. "We're not giving up; we just know to admit defeat when there's no hope of victory."

"We want you to win," Alvaro said, finally explaining their reason for throwing the match.

She felt smug and pleased at the same time. "Knew there was a reason."

Jamaal struggled to speak. "I guess I'm trying to say that I wish you wouldn't."

"There's no changing our minds; we came to fight, not win."

"And get answers." Miguel looked at Leila meaningfully.

The detective nodded. "I understand."

"Well, I don't," Jamaal huffed.

Both Spaniards gave a grim smile. "I'll leave it to you to explain," Miguel said.

"*Que duerman bien,*" Alvaro said.

"Sleep well," Miguel translated before turning and heading back down the hall to join the others downstairs.

Jamaal turned to her after they were in their room. "Care to explain?"

Leila sat on her bed, and after a long sigh, explained the reason for the Spaniards competing in the tournament.

Jamaal's mouth hung agape, speechless, when she finished. "It's hard to believe it's all coincidences: David's death, Isabella's death, the debt many competitors' villages and towns are in; it's too similar not to be connected, and that's scary. Nothing is ever as it seems, is it?"

"No, everything seems to have an alternative motive."

"Have you dealt with something like this?"

She shook her head. "Not as monumental as this, or as confusing… or as personal."

"How do you think David's death ties into all of this?"

"The same as everyone else: being enticed into this tournament. Other than that, I have no idea."

Jamaal's eyes widened as he made the connections she had already made. "We have been so oblivious all this time. What does Xander want? What could he possibly gain?"

"I hate that I can't figure it out."

They fell quiet as both racked their brains for a plausible reason but came up empty. Leila headed for the bathroom to get ready for bed knowing if she kept beating her brain for an answer, it wouldn't spit out one from being pressured like a stuck vending machine.

When she came out, Jamaal hadn't come to that conclusion—he still straddled the corner of his bed, his forehead scrunched in concentration.

"Let it rest, Jamaal. Overthinking never works. We don't have any evidence, only our suspicions."

His eyes followed her to her bed. "Is that what cops do on a case: let things settle until an answer pops up?"

"It never happens immediately and without evidence, but, yes, sometimes we have to take a step back and hope the criminal makes a mistake. It takes time and patience. But mainly we start with some scraps of evidence and work to get more."

"Xander looks too meticulous to be sloppy and make a mistake, though."

"Unless it's not done as a mistake."

Jamaal looked at her in disbelief. "You think he would intentionally mess up?"

Leila shrugged as she grabbed the Morning Glory and slid under her covers. "It happens. Some criminals want to be caught to show what they can do."

He groaned in frustration and pressed his palms against his eyes. "I don't think I can take much more! My mind is simple: food, sleep, family, fighting. I can't think like a cop." Shaking his head, he moved into the bathroom.

While he was in the bathroom, her eyes slipped down to the blue flower in her hand. Wrinkles now took dominance on the smooth petals and the flower drooped. With a frown at its sudden decline, Leila placed it back on the nightstand—she would worsen its condition by sleeping with it.

"Sorry for overloading you with these thoughts, Jamaal," Leila apologized when he reemerged.

He waved it away. "If you can handle all those thoughts, suspicions, and your nightmares, I'm sure I can handle some measly brainteasers. I wish I had your ability to hold that much in."

She gave him a small smile over her covers. "It takes restraint. Thanks, though."

Sleep long avoided her—Jamaal too, for he tossed and turned, his mind refusing to rest. Leila asked David to put him to ease, and eventually, she didn't hear him moving anymore. Even if she did ask for help to go to sleep herself, she wouldn't be able to—for nights on end, she had gotten so little sleep from a constant heat pulsing within, urging her closer to the lighthouse.

XXXVIII.

"Now for our semifinalists!"

Volume neared ear-bursting as the semifinalists filed out to join Bob up on the fighting mat. Their excitement for the fights increased Leila's hunger to be released again.

Bob greeted them all with a smile, then turned to readdress his audience and the rolling cameras. "Today begins the semifinals!" He chuckled as the arena roared again. "I may be the most excited for these fights—I almost can't talk. I don't know what I'm going to do about Friday.

"Don't need to get ahead of myself. So, beginning the first of the two matches is Miguel Del Toro and Alvaro Munoz against the Ikaika brothers! Best of luck!"

Bob gave each team an encouraging handshake before following the Japanese women off the mat. Leila and Jamaal headed over to the Spaniards.

"Good luck—even though you don't want it," Leila said.

"Oh, we'll have fun," Alvaro commented, looking over at the Hawaiian natives in their grass skirts, eyes twinkling.

"Just be careful."

Miguel grinned. "We'll try."

They stepped off but remained close to the raised fighting arena above them. Changing routine, Alvaro stepped out first to face against the Hawaiian brother Haloani, moving into his casual stance with his fists up as the native crouched down menacingly. He chuckled—Ikaika's intimidation wouldn't work on him—as the official stepped onto the mat.

The roars of the crowds increased with the raising of the red and blue flags, then stalled as the official held off the anticipation. After a few agonizing seconds, the official brought the flags down, and the arena exploded.

The opponents circled each other, looking for a weakness. Alvaro lurched forward, causing Haloani to dance nimbly away, appearing to be frightened by the big Spaniard. He grinned and lunged for the man again; Haloani dodged but brought up a sharp hand—looking like the snake Luke had described—and jabbed the Spaniard in his extended elbow.

Alvaro yelled in pain as his arm fell to his side.

"Haloani struck the Spaniard in a pressure point! That arm is useless now!" Bob said.

He considered his useless arm before dodging Haloani's next attempt of striking another pressure point. Miguel yelled something in Spanish at him over the roars of the crowds; Alvaro answered curtly.

The Island native lunged, his sharp hand seeking Alvaro's shoulder. The Spaniard dodged, smashed his fist into the insides of Haloani's arm, and then his elbow met his chin. He reeled back, senses knocked out and tears blinding.

"Amazing hits by Alvaro Munoz! He may have just saved this fight."

Appearing to still be struggling, Alvaro took his opening and threw his whole body into the punch. Haloani ducked, and the Spaniard punched empty air.

It seemed to happen in slow motion: Alvaro looked down in astonishment while Haloani's hands shot out and stabbed the big man in the outside of his knees. He released an agonizing howl as his knees gave out, and he crumpled down on his back.

"Oh no! Alvaro Munoz is down! I may have spoken too soon," Bob said with disappointment from his press box.

Alvaro tried to return to his feet, but his legs remained unresponsive. Propping up on his right elbow, he continually attempted to push himself up only to fall back down. Smirking—knowing he had won—the Ikaika brother advanced to finish the big Spaniard off. The cocky Hawaiian leaped to land on the downed Spaniard.

Falling back and grimacing, Alvaro lifted his legs, catching Haloani by surprise and catapulting him over. He landed in a loud thud—almost out of bounds.

Everyone moaned; even Bob rooted for the Spaniard.

"So close!"

Haloani Ikaika jumped back up and found the big Spaniard returning to his shaky feet with the encouraging roar of the crowd.

"The Spaniard won't give up!"

Alvaro stayed hunched over, his entire weight on unstable legs, but his fiery eyes never left the cautiously advancing Hawaiian. His eyes taunted the Ikaika brother to attack.

With a shrill battle cry, Haloani did. Even unsteady, Alvaro defended every attack, and because of his perseverance, he hit his opponent. Somehow, Haloani slipped around one of the Spaniard's attempts and came up behind him. Moving in a blur, Haloani's hands struck Alvaro in the back. No sounds came from Alvaro's mouth—his face only contoured in anguish as he crashed to the floor.

The official rushed in to keep Haloani Ikaika back and began the countdown. Alvaro attempted several times to get up, but his exhausted and battered body wouldn't let him. Looking to the bounds, he lay too far away to trade out with Miguel. Drained of energy, he allowed the countdown to end. The official raised a red flag for the Hawaiian's victory.

"Quite a fight to the finish! Round One goes to Haloani Ikaika!" Bob said over the applause in the arena.

Miguel went out to help his partner up but waved for help, needing another to get Alvaro off. One on each side, they helped him up to useless legs and dragged him off to a bench. Alvaro collapsed onto it, and the medic checked him out. After a quick couple of questions, Miguel returned to the fighting mat to face the last brother.

The arena grew deafeningly loud again as the opponents took their stances and the official took his place with raised flags. The flags dropped, and the opponents jumped into action: a blur of punches, kicks, catches, and throws. Miguel would throw the Hawaiian off him, but Kaiapo would quickly return and strike the big man in his pressure points.

"These two are unbelievable! I don't think any one of them has the upper hand!"

They broke away from each other; both battered, bruised, and out of breath. Kaiapo broke the unspoken hiatus by twisting to the side and shoving a hand into the back of Miguel's shoulder. To thank him for locking up his shoulder, Miguel spun with his fist down low, aimed at the man's stomach.

Having the breath knocked out, he remained hunched over Miguel's arm. As Miguel retracted his arm, the Ikaika brother grabbed the big man's arm and with a few quick jabs and pulls, he locked the joints in his arm.

With a yell of rage and pain, Miguel flung Kaiapo across the fighting mat.

"Oh no. It looks like Miguel Del Toro's arm is useless as well."

Once he regained his footing, Kaiapo raced back. Miguel braced for impact. At the last moment, Kaiapo dove to Miguel's side with legs out to trip him up; Miguel jumped to avoid tripping. Kaiapo Ikaika adjusted, spun to a crouch, and his snake hands shot out to the pressure points on the Spaniard's legs, locking the joints in his knees.

Miguel crumpled, and quickly rolled over, but unlike his partner, he jumped back to his feet and threw a punch to meet the Hawaiian native moving to end him. When Kaiapo ducked to dodge the attack, Miguel changed tactic by kicking the brother under his chin.

Everyone cheered when the Hawaiian landed hard. "Nice surprise hit!"

Miguel struggled to keep his balance. It took just a second for the rising Ikaika brother to see it.

Kaiapo soared through the air and ducked into a roll right in front of the Spaniard. He stumbled back on unsteady legs to gain distance. The Hawaiian shot up with sharp hands and drove them into Miguel's neck and chin.

The blow knocked the big man into the air. Crashing to the ground a few feet away, he tumbled even farther like a lifeless rag doll and ended up on his back, eyes closed—immobile.

Gasps sounded throughout the arena and from Bob in his press box.

"MIGUEL!" Leila cried. A few seconds passed before the official raised a red flag for Kaiapo, notifying all that the Ikaika brothers advanced to the finals, and she ran up on stage.

Jamaal, a medic, and a limping Alvaro followed her. Leila called out his name again as she dropped down beside the immobile form. He was so pale.

A groan rumbled out of the Spaniard's throat. "Not so loud."

Leila breathed in relief and grabbed his hand. "You told me you weren't going to get hurt."

Miguel's brown eyes flickered open. "That wasn't a promise." He grinned. "Although, it assured me that you do have some concern for my health."

She scowled, and Alvaro chuckled behind her. "You made me believe you were too confident in yourself to need reassurance."

"Well, everyone needs reminding."

Jamaal and a medic helped the Spaniard up, but Leila ducked under an arm to help him down. The medic asked him different questions about being lightheaded, but Miguel brushed him off that he felt fine. His face drawn in pain meant he was more nauseous than he would admit.

"You can admit that you're in pain," Leila began. "You don't have to be strong for me."

Miguel looked at her with amusement. "What makes you think I'm in pain?"

"I'm observant."

"But confessing's not manly, is it?"

"It can be."

"Not to this man."

She and Jamaal helped the big Matador down the steps and to a bench where the medic checked him over.

"We beat 'em up for you," Alvaro commented with a smile. "They'll be stiff now."

"Now, get to the finals," Miguel added.

"*Buena Suerte*," Alvaro wished.

"Good luck," Miguel translated, then he grimaced as the medic touched something sore.

Leila frowned at his pain. "Sorry."

He waved her apology away. "I'm not. Went down like Spaniards and made sure they felt us. Now, go beat the Japanese girls."

His gaze held hers until she turned to follow Jamaal up the steps to the fighting mat. The Japanese women waited on the stage in their futuristic-looking clothes—or for a techno-type rave.

"Now, Utada Jukina and Kairi Han against Jamaal Gordon and Leila Wells in the second of our semifinals!" Bob said through the speakers. The rest of what he said could barely be heard from the arena being revamped, "Whoever is pronounced the winner of this fight will advance to the finals against the Ikaika brothers! Best of luck to our last battle of the day! Make it a good one!"

Pleasing Leila, Kairi Han—with her neck-length pink hair smoothed back—faced Jamaal as the official took his place. The first match had only increased the crowd's hunger for another spectacular fight. The official didn't try to hold off anymore and brought the flags down swiftly.

Serious about winning, they launched into it, not showing off intricate moves. Her technique being a combination of Ninjutsu and Taekwondo allowed her to keep up with Jamaal's quick Capoeira. She would block his legs. He would block her arms.

Jamaal went into one of his flurries of kicks, impossible to stay standing under the onslaught of his legs. But she did. Han somehow ducked under a leg, then miraculously caught the next kick.

In three chops, she dropped Jamaal to the floor, grimacing in pain. He fought through it to roll out of the way of her follow-up and jumped back up.

"That was something! No one's been able to catch him!"

He motioned to Leila that he wasn't hurt before diving in front of Han and letting Capoeira loose. Staying on his hands the whole time his legs whirled in the air, striking Kairi, and not giving her time to recover before another leg struck her in the head.

She managed to slip out for a breather; Jamaal transitioned from his hands to his feet and with all power directed in his legs, he shot out—a headbutt right into her rib cage.

All the air huffed out of her. Knocked a few feet away, she rolled to a stop on her back. The official began the countdown, and she tried to get back up, but she hadn't regained her breath and kept falling.

Bob's praise at Jamaal's victory couldn't be heard over the arena at the raising of the blue flag. Jamaal gave Leila an encouraging smile as they passed each other.

Through with admiring Utada Jukina's blue hair—which looked like she stuck a finger in a light socket—the New York City detective took her beginning stance. The Japanese woman smirked, then moved into the stance of Dragon. Leila smirked back and also dropped into Dragon.

"This will be a fight to see for they both use Five-Animals Kung Fu!"

The official announced the fight, and the Japanese woman lashed out in the moves of Dragon. Leila blocked her attacks and retaliated with Tiger. Utada wasn't to be outmatched; she changed to Tiger as well and counterattacked.

Both women fought equally, but neither could gain an edge over the other. Switching the five styles of Animals Kung Fu brought no advantage. Even though Leila used the Phoenix stance and Utada didn't, she matched it with Dragon. The routine continued as they stepped away from each other, then engaged fiercely again, but to no avail—they knew every move the other performed.

"I don't know what's going to happen now, folks! I think one of them will either have to trade out or change up their game plan!" Bob determined after their repetitious attempts to defeat the other.

The two opponents took a break by circling the other. Leila thought about changing out with Jamaal, but the dormant heat flared to life.

You will not trade out. We are stronger than this woman.

Needing an advantage, she stepped back and let her dark side take her place. *Then prove it.*

The release felt good, like stretching in the morning, reawakening all her muscles. Leila kept a foot in the door, not giving full control to her dark side and allowing it to shut her out.

Uncertainty flashed across Utada's face at the change in Leila, being grounded in her challenge and the hollowing of her eyes. Ignoring the caution, she picked up her attack. Leila read her opponent's plan in her eyes.

She dodged the fake punch, caught the actual kick, and flung her around in a throw.

The arena roared at the sudden change of the fight.

"I think we're now in business!"

Utada angrily returned to her feet; her dark side made Leila taunt her to retry. Utada tried, but Leila blocked and deflected every move, and through the Phoenix, she battered her enough to where she grew stiffer in her attacks.

In a sudden smack against her face, the Japanese woman stumbled back to establish distance, but Leila's dark side wouldn't allow it. In a leap, she closed the gap and continued to destroy her opponent, giving her no break.

"New York's Finest has become hungry and ruthless for the win!"

"*Pull back, Lei,*" David warned.

Leila snapped out of the hypnosis her dark side put her under. Not being held up by punches, the unconscious Utada fell forward, making Leila hop out of the way as she collapsed.

If made of glass, the arena would have shattered from the deafening explosion at Leila's victory. She couldn't hear Bob praising her win. The official and Kairi Han came on stage to check out her immobile partner.

Hands on her waist lifting her up in a spin shocked her back into fighting mode. Her violent struggle made the hands drop her quickly; Leila whipped around to find Jamaal apologetic and hands up to slow her.

"It's me, sorry."

She breathed out her tension and tried to let go of that heat, but it clung on. The one fight hadn't been enough of a release. "No, my bad. Haven't cooled down yet."

He made a show of going in for a hug. "But you did it! We're in the finals!"

The Japanese women disappeared for the infirmary; Bob practically bounced onto the stage to replace them, joined by the Hawaiians. Leila and Jamaal lined up on the other side.

It took a few moments for the arena to quiet down to a level where Bob could be heard. "Wow! What a morning this has been! Never could I have imagined fights like that! May I introduce our finalists!"

He turned to the Hawaiians. "Haloani and Kaiapo Ikaika from Honolulu, Hawaii!" Then he presented the Jamaican and the detective. "And Jamaal Gordon and Leila Wells representing New York City!" The arena erupted with more cheers.

"I am excited to see what Friday will bring based on what we saw today! Whoever wins, I will be honored to crown them the Rulers of the Realms!"

Bob leaned toward the cameras to remind the viewers about what time to watch the finals, and the arena bursting with excitement again for the final match became background noise. Leila didn't even try to smile as big as Jamaal for the cameras before they ended the broadcast. That heat throbbed in time with her heart, seeping into her body and mind, making her realize that she was nothing without it; making her understand this tournament never mattered.

Finding out her strength and potential did.

And Foster.

XXXIX.

Forcing a smile all the way from the arena to the dining hall made the muscles in Leila's mouth stiff. She and Jamaal had to take the onslaught of everyone on the island coming to congratulate them on making it to the finals as they fought to reach the cafeteria.

Jamaal sat before her, massaging his jaw, after finally getting their meal. Those who missed sharing their congratulations sought them out now since they weren't moving targets. The New Yorkers painfully returned the thanks with smiles.

Leila grew annoyed with the constant interruptions. Even though she appreciated the praise, her temper prickled dangerously.

Having given out their praise, the ex-contestants turned their attention to getting their own food and gave Leila and Jamaal a break to eat. But not for long since Rin, Maso, Luke, and Shamus joined them at the table. She contemplated abandoning her food as Rin sat beside her and gave her a long congratulatory hug.

"Congrats, guys!" Luke exclaimed.

"Very well played," Maso added.

"Made New York proud," Shamus said with a grin.

"Now, you just have to win Friday," Rin said.

Miguel was missing, along with Alvaro, of course. Leila thanked everyone for her partner who had a mouthful. "Where are Miguel and Alvaro?"

Rin answered with resentment dragging his voice down. "They took Miguel to the infirmary to make sure his arm's not broken."

"We'll go check up on them."

"Not until I'm done eating," Jamaal said around a fork of pasta.

"I wouldn't drag you away from your food."

He smiled his thanks without stopping eating.

"Maybe Miguel's arm like mine," Luke hoped as he held up his bruised arm. "Sprain only."

The men at the table joined in on a conversation about Luke's arm, but Rin turned to her. "So, what's your plan for the Hawaiians?"

Leila began to answer, but Jamaal beat her to it. "Move quick enough to stay away from their hands. Ready, Lei." Knowing she wanted to get away from Rin, he stood without waiting for Rin to respond to put up his empty tray.

She seized the opportunity to leave. "We'll give you a heads-up on Miguel's arm." Leila eagerly dumped her tray and joined Jamaal on his way out, feeling Rin's somber eyes following her.

"RIN STILL SEEMS TO HAVE a soft spot for you," Jamaal said as they headed toward the infirmary.

Leila sighed. "Unfortunately."

"What made you not like him?"

"The extreme attentiveness, pursuing, and him not seeing I don't like that might be the reason."

"It wasn't the face?"

She laughed. "No, not really. He's attractive, but he came on too strong too fast."

"What about Miguel? What made him different?"

She shot him a glance. "Really? We're going to talk about my attractions?"

Jamaal shrugged. Leila didn't answer immediately, not really knowing what to say and thanking the occasional ex-contestant congratulating them. But Jamaal had become like Hyun—someone she could talk freely to.

A heavy sigh announced her willingness to talk. "I honestly don't know. Nothing about him bugs me but neither does anything attract me... well, other than his heat."

"Heat?" Jamaal sounded confused and wary.

"No, I mean his heat as... He makes me..." She huffed in frustration. "I don't know how to explain."

"Let's see if I can help by ruling things out: it's not strictly the heat coming off his body, right?"

"No."

"We're getting less sexual; good."

"Good for me, or for you?"

"For me. Back to eliminating options: is it his face?"

Leila turned her red face away. "No, that's not only it."

"But that's part of it?"

She wouldn't answer that. "Next question, Dr. Phil."

He scoffed. "I'm no Dr. Phil. I couldn't help people with their problems; I can't help my own."

"You're attempting to now."

"Trying and succeeding are two different things. I'm not really helping though, am I?" With her silence taken as a no, he continued, "How about this: can you tell me why you doubt he's the one destined for you?"

She took a good while to think about it, and they stopped within sight of the infirmary so they could finish. Leila finally shook her head. "I can't. I just think that he's not the one even though part of me wishes he was."

Jamaal thought for a bit as well. "I think you're thinking too much about the future. Go on your instincts and feel."

"Do you know how foreign that is to me? I've always thought things through."

"Well, maybe Miguel can help you jump without looking."

Leila fell silent again and looked at the infirmary housing the wounded Spaniard causing so many conflicting emotions and thoughts.

"I think I'm scared that if I do jump, I won't be able to climb back up to David." She hurried to intercept Jamaal. "I know David wants me to, but I can't let go of him yet. That's the reason for my doubt: Miguel hasn't replaced David, and I won't be able to jump from holding on; I'll be left dangling over the edge trying to claw my way back up."

"Maybe you don't have to completely forget David; he'll always be a part of you, just you'll latch onto another."

He took a breath. "I love Jade enough that if she had a past lover, I wouldn't want her to forget. He took care of her and kept her heart warm and steady for me. He was a part of her, just as David is for you. I wouldn't want to break that bond; it might destroy her."

"*He will,*" David whispered.

A hand massaged her warming coldest wound, sending re-assurance through her. Jamaal noticed. "David said he will."

The Islander smiled. "Then, you shouldn't worry any-more."

The conversation ceased, and they picked up their walk toward the infirmary doors. As she thought about David's an-swer, the warming reassurance dropped in temperature.

That he will understand or force me to forget?

NEARLY ALL THE WHITE SHEETS separating the examining tables were pulled back to show vacancy, and the finalists headed toward the closed one. Spanish grew louder as they drew closer.

Conversation halted when the fabric shuddered from Jamaal's taps. "Everyone decent?" he asked with amusement lacing his voice.

"No," Alvaro answered and laughed when something hit him.

"We're good," Miguel answered.

With a grin, Jamaal pulled the curtain back so they could enter. Alvaro balanced on his chair's back two legs with his booted feet propped up on the examining table that Miguel perched on, one foot hiked up on a step pulled out, the other almost touching the floor. He looked well except for the perspiration on his forehead, his face being pale and drawn in pain, and his left arm in a sling. Both were bruised and looked exhausted but presented a smile at their entrance.

"Broken," Miguel answered as he followed their eyes to his arm.

"How bad?" Leila asked, uncomfortable at his pain.

"Not too badly, I guess. I have to wear the sling for a month."

"Sit and stay a bit," Alvaro suggested.

"They can't with your feet blocking their seat," Miguel growled and knocked his partner's feet off the examining table. Alvaro's chair popped as the front legs hit the floor; he scowled.

Chuckling, Miguel waved them in.

Leila sat beside him, and Jamaal grabbed a chair, straddling it backward. Jamaal broke the silence. "So, it broke when the Hawaiian grabbed your arm?"

"Guess so. Either that or when I hit the ground."

"It didn't hurt?" Leila asked.

"Not for long. When he hit a pressure point, it was only a sharp pain like a stab of a knife, and everything down from there went numb; I couldn't feel it."

"Same here," Alvaro added in. He moved his arm and legs as an example. "Everything moves fine now, but I'm still stiff."

"After some meds," his partner corrected.

Alvaro's eyes narrowed, and he barked at his partner in Spanish, pulling a laugh from Miguel at his comment.

"So, any suggestions you can give us?" Jamaal brought the conversation back to include the non-bilingual partners.

"Don't get hit," Alvaro suggested with a grin.

Miguel shot him a look before turning back to the New Yorkers. "If they can hit you, it'll be focused on your weakest strength. Both of our legs are strong but they're the most vulnerable."

"They'll go after my arms," Jamaal stated. "I nearly can't do anything without support."

Miguel looked at Leila. "I can only think of your arm as the obvious choice."

Leila's bullet wounds reflected back to her like a warning—they consisted mainly in her torso with one in her leg, and all close to a pressure point. But if they… A hand unconsciously drifted up to the coldest wound by her heart. Miguel and Alvaro watched curiously.

"My most painful wound," she explained.

"Your heart?" Alvaro asked in bewilderment. "You seem to have a strong heart to me."

Leila smiled grimly. "Remember when I told you I was shot? The worst is nearest to my heart."

"It still bothers you now?" Miguel asked.

She sounded in approval but wouldn't let him know that it was also a connection with David.

Miguel cleared his throat in unease. "I highly doubt they watch New York news or read the paper, so you don't have to worry about it."

"Just worry about your arm, the rest of your body, the pressure points, and winning." Alvaro tried to cheer them up with a smile, but it didn't reach his eyes. The news had troubled the Spaniards.

"Oh, congrats on the win," Miguel said. "We saw the Japanese's bruises."

Miguel's attempt at changing the subject didn't work, for Jamaal still worked on the puzzle of what they talked about. He almost jolted out of his seat when the realization hit him. "Lei, no; we can't fight Friday."

"Why not, Jamaal?"

"Because you can die!"

His statement didn't bother her. The lingering heat comforted her; it would protect her... always. "So can you. We could've died plenty of times this tournament if we had been stricken in the heart—anybody could've. A single hit to the heart rarely causes death; it must be powerful, direct, and timed right. There's no reason to get scared now."

Miguel grabbed her hand. "But it causes great pain; we don't want to see you hurt anymore."

She looked at him. "You're going to prevent me from fighting just because I might get hurt? Fear of getting hurt or dying doesn't keep you or Alvaro from being Matadors, does it?"

It took him a moment to answer. "It's not the same."

"How is it not?"

"Because the bull is directed at you."

She pulled her hand out of his. "No, I'm fighting. I never run."

"How can you be so calm about this?" Jamaal pulled her attention back to him.

"I'm a cop; I've faced death many times before this, and I've always come out. Even with that one time death actually had me, I still escaped."

"Lei, I'm not sure about this. Money's not as important as your life."

"I will be fine, trust me. We both will."

He continued to shake his head, mumbling his disagreements the whole time.

Leila leaned toward him. "I know the realization of facing death is scary. But defeating it is exhilarating—you feel it every time we win a match. It'll be the same Friday, only more intense because the stakes are higher—"

"STOP!" Jamaal jumped to his feet. "What is going on with you, Lei? It's like you're trying to convince me that I enjoy risking my life. I don't think of it that way; I see fighting as a way to prove myself. You enjoy the thrill of almost dying again, don't you? I see it now: it gives you a high."

She grew defensive from him nailing the truth. "What do you expect me to do?"

"Do as David says! Stop allowing your dark side to convert you toward what it wants."

"We both want the same thing."

"Detective Leila Wells doesn't want to seek revenge!"

Her anger flashed dangerously. "Maybe she does."

Taking a moment, Jamaal rubbed his face and released a breath, calming himself. "Lei, this isn't you speaking. You know you don't enjoy risking your life. You know you have friends to return to; you aren't that careless and selfish."

Miguel laying his hand on hers jolted her. "Please, don't do this. Don't let pride stop you from running."

It was her turn to jump to her feet. "Pride has nothing to do with it! I have to fight to see who I am. I died that night along with my identity, and the heat from within brought me back. Fighting has rekindled it; it gives me life, warmth, and purpose. I'm not letting it go. I don't need anybody but myself."

Leila didn't wait for responses; she whipped around like a flame and blazed out, her soul burning to let that dark side out.

XL.

The fight hadn't started but knowing one of the teams would soon be crowned had exhilaration spiking in the arena.

Leila felt odd; not sickly, nervous, or even guilt at the wall between her and Jamaal. Apprehension sent spasms of chills up and down her back, but fear's icy fingers caressed her neck. Just like with her and David, something awaited her and Jamaal.

Her eyes darted around, looking for warning signs, and she locked onto the Hawaiians. Knowledge twinkled in their eyes. She restrained from massaging her wound every time they observed her, knowing it was just intimidation.

Just paranoid.

Heat pulsed within, reminding her there was nothing to worry about and coaxing out that deep, influencing voice of her dark side: *Rely on me; let me protect you.*

Jamaal tried to break the wall by leaning over. "I don't like the way they're looking at you, Lei."

He could feel the premonition. "They're just trying to frighten us. Don't worry."

With a frown, he straightened back up as the cameras went live and Bob began his introduction.

"Welcome back to the last day of the Rulers of the Realms Fighting Tag Tournament! This has been an exciting and intense four weeks, but our original one-hundred and twenty contestants have dwindled down to just four fighting partners. Allow me to introduce our finalists one last time!"

The round announcer stepped aside to allow the cameras a view of the two teams. "From Honolulu, Hawaii: Haloani and Kaiapo Ikaika, and from New York City, New York, the Jamaican: Jamaal Gordon and one of New York's Finest: Leila Wells!

"With a good luck wish for both of our teams, and the hope that no one will be seriously injured, let the match begin!" The chubby announcer made a hasty retreat as, somehow, the arena grew even louder.

Jamaal headed out to face his opponent as the official made his way onto the stage. She thought to attempt breaking the wall down too—they didn't need division now in the most important fight.

"Jamaal." He slightly turned his head. It stung some that he maintained the cold shoulder. "Good luck."

He dipped his head before turning, the wall still between them. She walked out of bounds as her dark side bristled. *At least we tried. Looks like someone needs to remove their pride.*

No, it's not his fault. It's mine.

He's just afraid of death staring him in the face. We're not.

Not for him, for me.

The voice and the heat receded, annoyed at her denial.

Jamaal and the Hawaiian bowed, then took their own stances: Haloani crouching down menacingly and Jamaal in his never-ending dance. The official lifted the red and blue flags, extending the agonizing wait before dropping them in a quick swoosh.

Predictably Jamaal ran straight toward his opponent, but Haloani Ikaika didn't wait. They met in the middle with Jamaal's legs kicking up and the Hawaiian's hands already sharp like snakes, flying toward the black man's pressure points. Jamaal avoided the hazardous hands but being so busy dodging

Haloani's attacks, he couldn't get in a good hit. Leila could tell the Hawaiian moved slower.

Maybe Miguel and Alvaro did hurt them enough to give us a chance.

Jamaal spun down to perform a back handspring and kicked the man in the stomach. Haloani recovered quickly and moved in to return the favor to Jamaal who landed on his chest. The quick Jamaican rolled out of the way to avoid the Hawaiian's attack. He jumped up and hit his opponent with three consecutive punches in the stomach and face.

"Jamaal Gordon is doing excellent at evading Ikaika!" Bob said gleefully.

Haloani dropped, and Jamaal stepped back as the official hurried to intervene. But the Ikaika brother used the injury as a ruse to drop Jamaal's defenses. His hands struck out like striking snakes into the Jamaican's thighs.

Jamaal cried out as he tumbled back. Haloani jumped on top of him and struck his arms, hard.

With an immense amount of strength, Jamaal knocked his opponent off.

"Jamaal?" Leila asked.

He ignored her as she paced the boundaries, looking for a way in. "Jamaal, don't be a fool!"

He shook out his arms a few times and rushed to meet Haloani coming for him. They were a blur as they fought, trying to take advantage of openings. Jamaal had predicted right—his only chance of winning was his legs, but he needed his numb arms to support him.

The Hawaiian knocked Jamaal back down and forced him to crawl to get away from his next attack. Leila continued to call, urging him to trade out.

"Something is up with Jamaal Gordon. He doesn't seem to have it together right now," Bob said.

Like fanning a fire, being ignored inflamed her dark side. "You're going to lose! Trade out!"

"I've got this!" he yelled back.

He spun his legs around, tripping Haloani coming up behind him. As Haloani rose, Jamaal's torso twisted as his hands splayed on the ground to lift him into a handstand. Leila held her breath, hoping his arms would hold.

His arms shook from the strain of holding up his body. His legs rotated like helicopter blades and repeatedly struck the stunned Hawaiian.

As Haloani struggled to regain his senses, Jamaal's arms gave out. He crashed to the floor but jumped up and charged his opponent. The Ikaika brother raised his arms to defend as Jamaal jumped, pulled his legs into himself, and then shot out in a powerful double kick, breaking through his defense and into his chest.

The Hawaiian flew backward. He rolled over to his knees, brought up a leg, and stood... for a second before toppling over. He continued to rise and fall back down. Haloani couldn't remain up long enough before the countdown expired.

"Haloani Ikaika falls! Round One goes to Jamaal Gordon!"

Leila ran out to her fallen partner, eyes closed in exhaustion and breathing hard. Before she could ask if he was okay, Jamaal spoke.

"I'm sorry."

She kneeled beside him. "Why?"

"I should've traded out, but I wanted to prove that I could do it."

"No, I shouldn't have—"

"No, I had to face death." He looked at her. "I see why you need to do the same."

She helped him up. "And you won. Do you feel okay?"

"I think so." He winced as he stretched his back. "Just some bruises." He tested his afflicted arms next. "They didn't stay numb long."

"Miguel and Alvaro must have knocked their strength out. Maybe they're not as strong now."

"It didn't hurt as bad as I thought it would."

The official urged Jamaal off.

"Lei—"

She stopped his worry about her fighting, "I will be fine; I'll have no more trouble than you."

"This may be it, folks! Jamaal Gordon and Leila Wells are halfway there, but Kaiapo Ikaika could throw a halt on things by getting a runoff! I'm ready to see some fireworks! Best of luck, finalists!" Bob yelled over the noise of the audience.

Leila bowed and dropped into her beginning stance, never taking her eyes off the Hawaiian. And neither did he. As the official raised the red and blue flags off to the side, Kaiapo grinned like a wolf seeing his prey already wounded.

Warnings rang off in her head, and even her coldest wound throbbed in unison—he *did* know about her heart being her weakness. That angry heat tried to push the caution aside, but she wanted to be conservative in her attacks.

The flags dropped, Kaiapo Ikaika ran straight at her, and she waited. When he came close enough, Leila dropped into Tiger and spun with her leg out to trip him, knowing he would jump over. When he landed behind her, she leaned back into a handstand, wrapped her legs around his neck, and flung him back across the ring.

The arena erupted at the new and powerful move.

"Leila Wells has been holding out on us! That was something!"

Her opponent glared as he returned to his feet, angry that she had tricked him. With an equal venomous grin, Leila moved into Snake, mocking his own. The Ikaika brother's eyes narrowed in contempt before charging, which she did in return. They met with both of their hands dancing around each other, looking like snakes answering their masters' beckoning for a show.

Their sharp hands sought openings to slip into and strike. As one of Leila's hands got close to stabbing his side, one of Kaiapo's would get close to her leg. Blocking his move, he blocked hers. Her dark side rose, irritated at this teasing, insisting on more aggression. Being pulled two ways made it harder to focus.

His right hand somehow found a loophole and slipped through to stab her in the left shoulder. Leila yelled out as her arm stiffened. She brought up a knee to break up their entanglement. As he bent over to regain his breath, she vainly shook feeling into her arm.

Bob gasped. "Leila was hit in her left shoulder!"

Her arm tingled back to life like it had fallen asleep and blocked Kaiapo's lunge for her. His hands shot out at her remarkably fast, but she prevented his attacks. Fear seized her when his hand slipped through another opening and came dangerously close to her heart.

She swatted it away, but his other hand jarred her in the side. Leila rammed her shoulder into his chest, and that desperate attempt made him stumble back.

Her dark side stirred within, begging to be released, but she blocked out offense to focus on defense as he returned hungrier to hit her heart. After she swatted away more of his attempts, Leila kicked him in the shins to leap clear.

"Kaiapo is after something, but the New Yorker won't give it to him!"

Leila's lungs screamed for air from her sides being repeatedly jabbed. Her legs shook underneath her—she wasn't sure if they could hold her weight much longer. Her vain attempts to defeat the Hawaiian left her stiff and bruised. She had barely inflicted any damage on him.

Kaiapo raced toward her. He changed course by sliding by her side to jump up behind her. She spun around to block his stabbing hand into her back and continued to evade his attempts at striking her heart but received hits in other places.

Instead of his right hand heading toward her heart like she expected, his hand slammed into her nose. Her vision brightened and tears stung. She stumbled back, trying to put space between them as she recovered from the breach. Her sight cleared, but her reactions were delayed not to catch Kaiapo's sharp hand jabbing her heart and retreating.

The pain was fierce. He snatched away her breath, and she couldn't get her lungs to inhale the much-needed air. Nothing responded and everything shut down. He drove a serrated knife into her chest and didn't care what organs he slashed by ripping it out.

Leila stood stunned for a moment, her body reeling from the shock until her knees buckled and she crashed to the floor, nearly bursting them open. The pressure weighing down on her chest prevented her from drawing breath, and she fell forward. She needed to pass out, but that heat tugged at her.

A lash of fire suddenly blew off the pressure. *Rely on me.*

Her tight chest gulped in air, choking her from the flood of oxygen. Her blinding vision dimmed, and she could start to make out forms. Presences hovered near her, and there were sounds.

"Wait! Wait a minute! She's moving!" stopped the worried whisperings of the audience.

Leila lay on her chest. Right beside her face was Jamaal, bent down and eye level with her. She could now feel his hand on her back, slightly shaking in hopes of rousing her. His face had paled in fear.

"Lei! Lei, get up! Please! Let me know you're okay!"

The heat not only took away the pain in her chest but also aches in her muscles or numbness in her limbs. It mixed with a soothing balm as its liquid flowed through her, restoring and renewing her—David.

"Lei, I'm here. Get up," David whispered. His voice awoke her whole body. Strength, energy, and adrenaline surged through her veins. Arms groggily obeyed by bringing a hand up to flatten on the fighting mat, followed by the other. Her arms shook underneath her efforts of rising, but she locked her elbows and stayed on all-fours.

Jamaal's hand remained on her back. "Lei, are you okay?"

The official asked her the same, hesitating to call a medic.

Leila took a moment before nodding. "I will be. Give me a second."

The man rose to wave a moment longer for her.

"Come on, Lei. I'm right here. Let me help you," David's voice appeared again.

His spirit surged through her veins, reenergizing her muscles. After rousing her, the heat intensified into anger toward Kaiapo—her dark side craved to pulverize him. David's gentle murmurings cooled the inferno and turned her focus to standing; she pushed herself up and staggered to her feet.

"Leila Wells is back on her feet! It's not over yet, folks!" Bob said.

"Want me to finish for you?" Jamaal asked, concern still making him hold on to her.

"No; I'm finishing it."

"Are you sure?"

Heat flared as she caught Kaiapo's smug glance her way. "Yes."

Jamaal hesitated a bit longer—making sure she could stand on her own when he released her—before walking off.

Her rising restored the crowd's hype, and it increased, even more, when the official motioned that it was a Tie: one point for Leila, one point for Kaiapo. No more second chances.

As the official raised the flags for the third and final time, Leila felt drawn to move into her favorite stance: balancing on her right leg, her left coming up, and her arms out beside her for balance and looking like wings—the Phoenix.

The flags fell, the arena exploded, and Kaiapo moved. A revived-Leila—like coming in fresh to the fight—danced away in the nimble Phoenix to avoid the Hawaiian's attacks. He grew visibly frustrated at how easily she evaded him.

"*Look at his legs,*" David whispered.

Leila glanced down at Kaiapo's tanned, muscled legs. Even though he ran and moved smoothly, he refrained from quick footwork and leaned more on his right leg than his left. Her simmering anger purred in pleasure.

"*His weakest strength is his legs.*"

Kaiapo saw the realization in her eyes that she found a way to defeat him; he shifted his weight but swallowed his unease and raced toward her.

"*This is it. Jump!*"

Leila moved into Panther, blocked the Ikaika brother's punch, grabbed ahold of his broad shoulders, and bounced over his head like playing Leapfrog. He couldn't turn fast enough before Leila spun and jabbed the outsides of his knees in Snake.

Kaiapo yelled as his knees buckled, but as he fell, Leila leaped up to land on his shoulders then leaned backward, bending the man as she curved. Her hands steadied her on the mat, stayed in the handstand, and kept her legs around the Hawaiian only to let go halfway down, flinging him across the arena. His heavy body collided with the floor and tumbled farther away.

Leila spun around on one knee, ready to jump back into action and saw Kaiapo struggling to his feet.

"Unbelievable! This is a survival of the strongest!"

"*You have to finish him, Lei. He's not going to forfeit,*" David encouraged.

David backed off and unleashed her dark side struggling to be freed. Leila sprinted toward the slowly standing man, burning for his destruction.

His brother barked out a warning, but Kaiapo looked up too late to defend himself. When she came close enough, she jumped. Feeling like a gust of wind lifted her to fly on wings, she grabbed the bewildered man's shoulders; the momentum kept Leila going frontward as she flipped over the Hawaiian. Rage fueling her strength lifted Kaiapo over her and hurled him farther across the ring.

She moved back into Phoenix as he crashed to the mat with shuddering force and rolled to the bounds. His brother called out to him to trade out since he lay right at his feet—he just needed to touch his hand to tag out—but Kaiapo remained motionless. The official raised a blue flag for Leila's victory, and the arena erupted.

"Leila Wells won! Leila Wells won! The New Yorkers are the Rulers of the Realms!" Bob screamed.

Her anger faded as soon as she breathed out and dropped out of the Phoenix, but the heat—belonging to her dark side—remained a constant presence. She turned to the sound of someone running to her.

All coldness from the argument in the infirmary and fear from her being hurt were gone as Jamaal smothered her with a hug. "You won! You won!"

"*We* won," she corrected over the celebrating audience and loud music.

His smile widened as he kissed her on the cheek and hugged her closer. Only the spirit of David supported her, but it soon left her; Jamaal felt her losing grip around his neck—he steadied her and kept a hold on her just in case.

They turned at the sight of the chubby announcer hopping onto the fighting mat followed by Amadeus Xander holding the champion belt. Just the sight of him reawakened the burning anger within Leila, and she straightened her spine in defensiveness—anger gained from speaking with Miguel about his sister's death, the odd trouble throughout everyone's life, and the musings of all the connections with Jamaal.

What is his plan with this show of a tournament?

A fleeting look of glee from Amadeus sent a tingle down her spine—he wasn't just excited they had won. Pieces were falling into place.

The look disappeared, and he flashed his freshly whitened straight teeth. He offered a strong hand.

"Congratulations to both of you. You deserve it," Xander said. When he grabbed Leila's hand, she felt an unnecessary squeeze—he forced himself to commend her and didn't want to touch her from the quick release of her hand like he had been burned. Her police senses picked up odd gratitude and disdain toward her.

Bob waving for the music and audience to quiet down pulled her away from her scrutiny.

"Quite a tournament this has been, and this is the first one! I'm shaking with happiness! After four long weeks of seeing extravagant fighting—and I have been waiting eagerly to announce this—we finally have our winners!" Bob turned with a flourish to the victors accompanied by loud applause and cheering from the arena.

"Congratulations to our victors: Jamaal Gordon and Leila Wells from New York City!" As they bowed, confetti exploded and rained multi-colors upon their heads. Amadeus Xander handed them the champion belt, and Leila and Jamaal raised the belt over their heads.

"Yes! Yes! We have our winners, but we have something a little extra to award our Rulers of the Realms if they accept! Our gracious host has the details!"

The arena quieted down to hear the surprise as the announcer handed over the microphone.

"We have one extra match just for our victors. The match will be at sundown against the Changeling. Can't give too much detail or it wouldn't be a surprise anymore. But I will tell you of the reward: two rounds, and with a victory, you receive an extra million dollars each!"

The arena roared in approval; Leila and Jamaal exchanged a look.

Xander raised a hand to calm the arena. "I must tell you: this Changeling will not only test you physically but mentally as well. You must be strong in mind and heart to face the Changeling. Not just anyone who can fight can do this. You must look into yourself before you make a decision."

Something within her trembled with the idea of another challenge.

"Lei?"

Jamaal's eagerness to prove himself the best physically and mentally shone in his eyes, but uncertainty and hesitation also flickered within. He left the choice open for her to decide.

"The rest of the day is yours to rest and prepare. We will even provide any medical assistance you require." Xander paused. "So, what will it be victors? Prove yourselves to be the best physically and mentally and go home with four million dollars, or call it quits?"

Leila considered the desire in Jamaal's eyes a bit longer before looking long at the man in the expensive black suit, hoping to uncover his motive for springing this fight on them. The prize money was incentive enough to get another fight out of anybody, but the challenge adhered to her dark side. This surprise looked like Xander counted on it. Unlike before, she couldn't find anything in his gray eyes, only the fact that he *was* guarding something.

She looked at the chubby announcer, the cameras with the viewers at home, and finally the entire arena—all waiting for her answer.

Refusing would be admitting defeat; I do not give up, that voice stated.

She locked eyes with Xander.

"We accept."

XLI.

"There they are!"

A wall of ex-contestants congratulating them on their win halted Leila and Jamaal's entrance at the dining hall doors. Being whisked off the stage and sent straight to the infirmary as soon as she announced they would fight delayed congratulations. It seemed everyone decided to ambush them when they came to eat.

Thanking the proper person for their congratulations or responding to the voice complimenting their fight became impossible. The ex-contestants made a path for them toward the buffet, but it was slow wading through the mass of people. After receiving their food, people still pressing on them to say their praises kept Leila and Jamaal from going to their usual table.

"Everybody move!" a deep voice boomed out, followed by a higher-pitched, accented voice belonging to a Chinese man.

"Yeah! Move, people!"

The crowd parted like the Red Sea, revealing a straight path to their usual table. Luke Zheng stood on the table arching over heads, blocking his sight of Leila and Jamaal. He vigorously motioned them over, and they hurried so his bouncing wouldn't break the table.

When they got closer, Luke jiggled in expectation of jumping. Jamaal's tray clattered on the table just as the Chinese man launched off the table to be caught. Leila stumbled away to safety as Luke wrapped himself around the Jamaican and hung on like a monkey.

Unfortunately, she bumped into Rin as she escaped. "I promise I won't attack you."

Jamaal grinned as she placed her tray down. She refrained from a scowl and stepped into the boxer's hug, expecting a tight squeeze but his arms remained soft around her.

"I'm okay, Rin, I don't feel any pain."

Before he could bring her back in for a better hug, hands grabbed her waist. She tensed in alarm, but the attacker only spun her around.

"They must have fed you meds," Alvaro's voice rumbled by her ear.

Not that I took them. The arrival of David and her dark side to save her erased the pain, so she threw the pills away behind the doctor's back.

Letting her back down, he wrapped an arm around her shoulders for a more proper hug. "Congrats, Leila."

"*Gracias*, Alvaro."

When he released her from his hug, she didn't have time to look for Miguel before the others swarmed her, all wanting to give a congratulatory hug.

"Proud of you, Leila; kept on fighting to the end," Maso praised.

Shamus was next. "Quite a dramatic finish."

Leila eyed him. "Was that you yelling?"

"Luke couldn't see you."

The Chinese man opened his arms, and a large grin signified that he wanted a hug now. Leila ducked into Luke's arms.

"Fight bravely, like Bruce Lee!"

"Fought," Shamus corrected.

Luke glared at his partner. "Mine English fine, Shamus!"

Shamus began to correct him again but shook his head and raised his hands in defeat. "I give up. You English fine, Luke."

The Chinese man beamed.

"Lei doesn't get a hug like me? Does that mean I'm special?" Jamaal piped up behind them.

"Course it do!" Luke replied and ran into the black man again, nearly knocking him down. The others turned to congratulate Jamaal now and allowed Leila to find the absent Miguel. He sat at the table, watching her. As she approached, he came to his feet.

"Congrats, Leila," Miguel said as he hugged her with one arm, but she wrapped hers snugly around his waist.

"Thanks." She leaned further into him, breathing in his husky scent, and enjoying the warmth and comfort he provided.

He held her closer. It wasn't just a congratulatory hug. "Thought I would have to throw Rin off you."

"Alvaro saved me; I thought it was you."

"Disappointed?"

"Slightly."

"I regret it wasn't me." His breath heated her neck when he angled his head to whisper, "Are you okay? Your heart good?"

That power twitched irritatingly at Miguel's touch and caused Leila to step back, puzzled at this sense of defensiveness. "I'm good. The pain quickly vanished; I only felt it for a moment."

Only the furrowing of his brow showed her sudden change of affection had an effect. "When you were hit I—"

"Freaked out," Alvaro finished. Miguel frowned at his partner. "I held him back from flying down the stairs, jumping over the railing, and going to you."

Leila turned back to Miguel. "That worried about me?"

The concern remained in his eyes. "Extremely."

His openness of confession nearly drew her back into his arms. Her dark side's irritation held her back.

"I can't see how they knew." Alvaro speaking helped erase the heat rising between the two.

Leila shrugged like it didn't matter. "They must have been in the infirmary when we came to see you and overheard us talking."

"Whoops."

"We put you in danger," Miguel apologized.

She waved it away. "They just cheated."

"They *did* cheat," Alvaro trailed off.

"Alvaro, it doesn't matter. We defeated them anyway."

"With nothing but skill," Jamaal spoke up. "Shows you how confident they were in themselves."

Them reverting to sneaking around to find the easy win didn't add up. There was no one else in the infirmary, and no one came in later. Someone else told them, without having to eavesdrop. Her gut squirmed.

"Leila, you look uncomfortable. Are you sure you're okay?" Miguel started to place a hand on her back and pull her into him.

She nodded. "I'm fine; I'm just getting really hungry."

"Now, we're on the same page," Jamaal said as he sat at his tray.

Everyone joined him; Leila found her spot already staked out beside Rin. After a few bites, the questionings began on what it felt like to win, then they geared toward what the Changeling battle would be like.

"It wouldn't surprise me if it's some robot Xander wants to try out," Leila mused.

"Or it's superhuman, like Mutant off *X-Men*. Or, or, modified human with powers! Or, some creature or alien!" Luke suggested.

Shamus shook his head. "You watch too much Sci-Fi stuff."

The Chinese man turned on him. "It could happen! It all possible! And it not stuff!"

"Stuff that could happen in *Star Trek*, *Star Wars*, or even *I Am Legend*."

"First, *I Am Legend* happen maybe, and *Star Wars* could be in galaxy we know not about!" Luke defended.

"*I Am Legend* could really happen," Maso sincerely added.

Shamus turned on the black kickboxer. "You believe that junk?"

"Well, not *Star Trek*, but a biological attack could happen."

"See?" Luke said victoriously.

"You can't tell me there are Jedi!"

"Might be!"

"Really? Prove it. Read my mind." Shamus placed his elbow on the table and his chin in his open hand.

"Fine. I try!" Luke copied the white man, focusing hard.

They stared at each other for a while.

"You think I stupid," Luke said after the silence.

Shamus laughed. "That's not hard to figure out."

"Another."

"Guess what number I'm thinking." Shamus held up four fingers behind his back for everyone to see.

Jamaal leaned back and held up four fingers behind Shamus for Luke to see.

"Four," he answered smugly.

"What?" Shamus gaped and whipped around to catch Jamaal straightening back up like he didn't do anything—proclaiming his guilt.

"Jamaal, you cheat!" He threw a French fry at the laughing Jamaican, ducking around Maso to avoid fire.

"Don't use up your energy now," Leila suggested.

Jamaal emerged around Maso to answer. "I can't prepare for something I don't know about." He got hit in the process by one of Shamus' missiles.

"Well, we know it's going to be a fight," Shamus said.

"But mainly mentally," Rin stated, then turned to Leila. "How do you prepare for that?"

"You don't," Alvaro said.

Miguel looked right at her. "You must know who you are to have confidence that you won't run."

"Is that what's involved with being a Matador?" Maso asked.

"Bulls?" Luke asked, looking at the Spaniards to settle his interest.

Alvaro tried to explain, but his struggles faded into background noise since Miguel's eyes never left hers, almost like he telepathically asked a question.

Do you know who you are yet? Are you ready for what you will find?

She broke eye contact, not wanting him to see her lack of confidence in herself. The pressure of his gaze lessened as he turned his attention to helping Alvaro explain in terms Luke would understand.

"But what do you think?" Rin began again, only addressing her. "Will you go to the gym to practice so you don't lose your focus?"

"No, I'm going to treat this as a normal fight; I can't overthink it. You never know what's exactly coming." Plus, if this fight focused on her dark side like she began to think, she needed to be rested.

"So, what are you going to do?"

"Get some sleep so I'm not dwelling on it," Leila stated.

"That sounds like a plan to me," Jamaal cut in.

XLII.

Unease kept Leila from resting like she hoped. At first, she couldn't stay comfortable since her soft bed became a rock, then her thoughts wouldn't stop running. Jamaal had no problem though, as soon as his head hit the pillow, he was out.

She lay in bed, listening to Jamaal's light breathing and trying not to let her mind wander toward the coming night's unknown events. The men's playful jabs at the future fight did nothing to settle her; they unintentionally made it worse. Leila knew it like a heavy rock in her stomach: there was more to this fight. What had they gotten themselves into by accepting? An image of the transparent ghost-wolf drifted through her mind.

It was just a dream.

She hid under the covers, hoping the warm sheets would shield her from that chilling memory, but it still crept in. Irritation exploded within, making her throw off the sheets and sit up, angry that she waited instead of facing it head-on.

Facing what?

Your fear, it answered.

Her eyes shot over to the Morning Glory resting in a glass of water. *Him?*

He's not your fear.

Her heart stopped. She shook off that terror by denying it. "No, I'm not. He said I wasn't," she whispered.

Did he?

She blocked out that trembling doubt by pulling out the flower. With it in her hand, Leila calmed down and the inside voice disappeared. On closer inspection, the blue flower had more wrinkles than when she put it in the water. 'This will help you keep your promise,' Hyun had said.

Am I not doing right?

"You promised to let me go by loving another," David reminded.

Leila stood and headed for the balcony. *I'm starting to think I can't.*

"You've never been one to back out of a challenge, Lei. You always strive to survive against all opposition. You've relished in it."

Only because you did. She brushed aside the layers of curtains holding out the light, opened the balcony door, and slipped outside.

"You know that's not true. A part of you enjoys it."

Which part, David? I'm so conflicted now, I don't know who I ever was. The cooling air of the evening made her shiver, and she curled up in one of the lounging chairs, watching the colors of the changing sky.

David took a while to answer, but when he did, it was a regretful whisper, *"Your dark side."*

So, everything—the love of our job, everything you loved, my love of you—wasn't real? Because just a part of me loved it? She clenched the poor flower. *I refuse to believe that.*

"It wasn't fake, only your dark side made you fall in love with what I did. What it wanted wasn't so farfetched; you wanted to experience its pleasure in adrenaline but in your own way—by loving me. You know you didn't enjoy our job as much as I did; some days, you forced yourself to go along with it."

She blurted out loud, "Then why didn't I leave if I didn't love it?"

"Because you were good at it. You were a cop because I was; you stayed, sustaining the need of release of your dark side to stay near me.

"Now that I'm dead, that side has turned angry and vengeful, and it scares you. You've attempted to tear yourself away but are at odds with it again—that is why you are conflicted. You believe that you aren't what this dark side is changing you into. You are at war between heading toward revenge like it wants or toward the promises you made to me."

"I believe I'm not? So, does that mean I am? I'm just making it harder on myself thinking I'm a better person by fighting against it?"

"Not exactly. This is your dark side; this is a part of you. You must decide how much of it is."

The opening of a door pulled her away from David's words to see Miguel. She forced a twitch of her lips when he noticed her.

"You okay?"

"I'm good. Just... thinking." A touch of emotion quivered in her voice.

The Spaniard frowned, went to the edge of his balcony, grabbed a hold of the railing and even with the use of only one arm, he threw himself over to land on Leila's balcony.

Leila jumped up. "Miguel!" She didn't think he could have jumped that far.

He chuckled. "Those Matador skills coming out in me."

"Warn me before you go hopping across balconies next time."

"Will do." He gently grabbed an arm. "Now, are you sure you're okay?"

She was aware of his hand on her arm and the closeness of their bodies. Heat rose between them again as his hand trailed down her arm, raising goosebumps in its path, and his breathing became heavier, thicker. No one could douse their magnetism this time.

Leila could scarcely breathe. "No. Yes, well... I don't know."

"Tell me why."

"It's you; you make it hard to think."

His lips actually brushed hers as he spoke, sending tingles down her spine, "Do you need to think?"

"I'm not so sure anymore. I second-guess everything now. I just want to feel again."

"Then feel." Miguel didn't say more, nor did he let her try. His lips latched onto hers with such fervor she wanted to melt into him, never again forced into the cold, empty world—forever lost in his burning soul.

He crushed her against him; his burning desire trembled through his hard body as the kiss became urgent, sporadic. Rough stubble rubbed against her hand as she pulled his face closer. Passion brought forth a low growl as he pinned her against the wall, lips trailing from her mouth to her throat and up her neck. She could only run her fingers through his thick hair, keeping him close.

Enough about what her dark side wanted and didn't want, enough about her promises to David. She needed this; she needed him to make her feel.

His kisses slowed into a steadier speed, less lust-driven and shallow. She remained curled around him, legs wrapped around his waist and his hands rubbing her back, content near his neck and in his warmth. Giving in didn't hurt at all.

"I think I've been looking for someone like you," he breathed into her hair.

The warmth disappeared at his words compared to what David had said about not looking but waiting. All the heat and desire belonged to him, not her. He wasn't the one she's meant for. Just like David.

"Leila?"

She slid out of his arms and moved away.

"Leila, what's wrong?"

"This isn't right."

A hand grabbed onto her shoulder in a desperate reach to pull her back. "How can you say that?"

She slipped out from under his hand by dropping down to a lounging chair, her face hidden in her hands. "It just isn't."

Miguel hesitated at this sudden flip before walking over and lowering his big frame on the rest of the chair. "What do you mean? It feels right to me. You can't deny that pull we have to each other."

"I'm not denying it. But that heat is all you; I don't feel it myself."

His silence meant her words stung. She needed to explain. "I do care for you, Miguel. But there is also a part pulling me away. I think I just want to stop going on alone. I need someone with me that understands; that's not fair to you."

"I don't understand everything, do I?"

It took her a moment to admit it, "No. I can't bring myself to reveal everything just yet."

Because he's not the one.

Silence fell between them and gave her the chance to notice the Morning Glory. Strange that the water had finally taken for the flower now stood straighter, seemed firmer, and had retaken its vibrancy. Just like after the night in the hallway with Miguel.

By showing her she was on the right path—by lowering her walls and loving another—the flower did what Hyun said it would.

Miguel found his voice again. "Maybe I pushed too far this time."

"No, I don't think you did."

He turned to her. "How did this help any? Other than throwing you into a bigger spiral of confusion and making me want to have you even more?"

"You showed me that I can't rush anything just because I'm tired of holding back or that I'm in the heat of the moment," Leila said. "I still don't know who I am, but I'm closer than before by knowing I must focus on what I need, not what I want."

Miguel turned away, hiding his hurt at her words again.

"I'm sorry I can't decide yet. It seems I always rise to fall."

He remained quiet for a long time. "Isn't that one of the animals you mimic in your fighting?"

His sudden change of topic brought her to look at him. "What?"

"Don't you mimic a phoenix in your fighting?"

She nodded, not understanding what he was getting at.

"Out of the ashes the phoenix rises; a phoenix must die to be reborn. You're a phoenix. You find strength in destruction."

Leila just looked at the Spaniard, not realizing the significance of her favorite stance, but now noting how well it fit.

A light bulb turned on in his head. "You remind me of what the phoenix represents: renewal, a new life. The time came when you couldn't stay the way you were; you had to move out of your routine. And maybe, your new life isn't in New York, it's waiting for you somewhere else."

Leila tried to brush it off, not wanting to believe it. "You're sounding like Luke."

"He speaks of fantasy, but what I'm speaking of is symbolic—a phoenix must die to come back stronger. I personally believe that the creatures of myth were based on a person who stood out, just like you do.

"David dying killed you spiritually, but your anger—the Phoenix—brought you out of those ashes. That anger is toward Foster and keeps you alive to seek revenge. The Phoenix gives you a purpose again and supplies the feelings you lost with David's death."

"But what about your anger toward Xander?"

He shook his head. "Isabella's death did not destroy me; it only made me want revenge. I'm not set on taking down Xander—I'm not even sure if he is truly to blame. My anger can get wild, and I don't think before acting. Unless he stumbles—then I will move in for the kill."

"Now you're sounding like my Tiger stance."

They fell quiet again, letting her reflect on what he had pointed out. Her dark side must have always been this Phoenix—where her temper originated, and why her outbursts blistered. The Phoenix must've been the voice in her head pulling her away from Miguel and directing her to hone her anger. It scared her, but she leaned toward it more and more; it helped her more than anything. Perhaps she needed it to fulfill her promise to David.

She sighed. "I was scared about leaving, making that first step of moving on, but now, I'm afraid of returning home—returning to my past to have it overwhelm me. I'm tired of being torn in two, but I don't want to lose who I think I am by giving in to the Phoenix just so I can feel. I'm not set on revenge, it is." She looked down at her hands. "At least... I think I'm not."

"Leila." He turned her to face him. "Give in to the Phoenix for its anger gives you the strength to keep going. Ease yourself of some burden, stop thinking, and let it control you; let yourself feel again."

"What if it makes me too hard? What if I withdraw too far?"

A hand cupped her face. "If it keeps you safe, then so be it. We must make sacrifices."

"A quest for revenge always ends in destruction," Leila stated. "Why should I go through it? Haven't I been through enough?"

"Because you want to go through those flames, and you know you will come out of it."

XLIII.

Either the coolness of the dim hallway or her nerves caused butterflies to awake in her stomach and raised goosebumps on her arms and neck. She rubbed her arms to warm them—she had never felt this uneasy before. Glancing at Jamaal beside her, his eyes shot around in apprehension of something awaiting them in the dark.

It seemed the Phoenix paced within her, annoyed at this waiting game and longing to spread its wings. Her talk with Miguel and his encouragement for her to do so had the Phoenix eager for her to finally give in.

The round announcer making his way down the hallway from the direction of the arena floor caught their attention.

"Congratulations again," Bob greeted with a cheerful smile, but it didn't reach his eyes. His shifting gaze and slumped posture—like he expected something to pop out of nowhere—had Leila freezing—if he was nervous, something was definitely up. Her instincts were proven right... again.

He spoke again, "I'm here to tell you about the change in the arena so it won't be a surprise. You will have access to the entire ground floor of the arena; there are no bounds, and our decorators renovated for this battle. The biggest change, however, is that the arena will be silent. The audience will be there cheering you on, but you won't hear them. We have surrounded the entire floor with walls, keeping the loudness of the arena out so you focus on the fight before you—they can see in, but you cannot see out."

We're on display?

"As a reminder, both of you will have one chance at defeating the Changeling—no tag outs. You won't have an official announcement if you win your round, but you'll know when your battle is over."

Bob smiled, and this time it actually did reach his eyes. "My best wishes to both of you. I'm confident that you'll persevere. I have faith in you, along with the rest of the island.

"A staff member will lead you to the ground floor when we are ready. Good luck." He shook their hands before heading back the way he came.

Their breathing and the occasional shuffling of feet echoing from some distance provided the only noise in the hallway. Bob's departure took the calming sense of normalcy he had brought, and the dampening apprehension settled on them again.

"Why do I feel like this fight isn't just a fight?" Jamaal broke the silence and turned to look at her.

"Bob didn't seem like his usual thrilled self; he looked... wary," she said.

"I'm embarrassed to say this, but I don't want to go out there. Is it too late to back out?" he asked with a humorless chuckle, more of a nervous huff of air.

She placed a comforting hand on his taut back. "Don't worry; this is just another match." Her encouragement fell flat—she didn't even believe her own lie.

"If I feel something wrong, you definitely have to suspect something being used to listening to your instincts. What are you feeling about this?"

Echoing footfalls coming from the arena saved her from answering—a staff member with a black headset hurried toward them.

He stopped halfway, vigorously motioned for them to follow, then turned and headed back without waiting for a response. They followed him down the hallway, hurrying to ease the nerves threatening to overtake their bodies and sending them bolting the other way.

The staff member waved at them to stop when they reached the entrance into the darkened and silent arena and placed a hand on the headset to speak with whoever was on the other end.

Leila looked up at the black man, finding his eyes shifty. Hoping he couldn't feel the same fear in her tensed body, she wrapped her arms around his neck. "Good luck, Jamaal."

The tension in his neck and shoulders relaxed as his hands came around her to return the hug. "Good luck to you too, Lei."

"Courage, Jamaal; it's just a fight."

He turned his attention back before him as the staff member turned and motioned them in.

"Good luck," the staff member whispered as they passed.

We need reassurance that this is merely a fight.

They walked into the unrecognizable arena: everything black with hues of red and violet, and numerous tall candelabras providing the much-needed light on the dark floor. Sheer, dark curtains—more draped down from the ceiling—hid the one-way walls.

But the silence was unnerving—so used to the roars and cheers of the onlookers and the watching cameras' red lights. Even though they knew they weren't, the atmosphere made them feel alone.

The partnership made their cautious venture onto the main floor, eyes ceaselessly searching for their opponent. Once far enough—to where they deemed the middle—they stopped and waited for the Changeling to reveal itself.

Something caught Leila's eye at the supposed boundaries; she touched Jamaal's arm and gestured at the suspicious area. It was dark... and surrounded in black smoke. As their eyes strained to make out the advancing obscure figure, cold fear crawled up her neck—the same she had felt in the woods and when the ghost-wolf thing woke her. Leila's coldest wound warmed in warning as unnatural golden yellow eyes froze every nerve in her body.

"Jamaal," she breathed. "It's the ghost-wolf."

The mangled wolf with its lower torso in billowing black smoke emerged into the candlelight. In full view, it looked even more hideous than when she found it hovering over her. Its humped shape blended in with the dark tones around it, making its size small and big. Only its sickly eyes kept its shape anchored; they were disturbing to look into... Leila found it impossible to look away.

As she stared, her iced fingers constricted in a tight snake-like grip around Jamaal's forearm. Her doubts shattered like someone took a hammer to a block of ice—she *hadn't* imagined the creature. It didn't comfort her. Jamaal's muscles turned rock hard in shock like electricity had jolted through his body at the sight of the wolf.

"It's... real."

The ghost-wolf hovered at its end of the fighting arena, watching the two frozen humans—not advancing toward them anymore or trying to cower back.

"It's waiting," Leila said.

Jamaal swallowed, seeming to shake free from the fear paralyzing them and loosened her vice-like hands around his arm. "This is what we fight then; this is the Changeling."

"But, Jamaal, how are we to fight it? It's transparent."

He locked gazes. "Then we weren't meant to leave victorious. This is a fight we can't win." Leila gaped at his back as he cautiously stepped out to face the creature.

The Changeling cocking its head as it sized him up halted Jamaal's venture. The two opponents stared at each other, the ghost-wolf patient and Jamaal unsure of whether to move into his stance on the offensive or stay on his toes ready to spring in defense.

All of a sudden, the Changeling shook violently like having a seizure. Jamaal backed up at the change of the wolf, not knowing what was happening but prepared for an attack.

It didn't charge Jamaal like Leila expected. Instead, it continued to shake as it solidified with black smoke curling up around its body. The Jamaican glanced back at his partner; she shook her head in the same puzzlement.

When he and Leila looked back, a woman stood in the wolf's place—a dark-skinned woman dressed in sparkling green Samba shorts and a bikini top with matching feathers attached to her back. The same woman in the pictures back in New York City sparring in Capoeira with Jamaal: Jade Gordon.

Jamaal staggered back. The Jamaican took a few steadying breaths as he stared at his wife.

"Jade?" he asked in disbelief.

Her eyes blinked open, green eyes matching the light color of the jade necklace around her neck. She flashed him a dazzling smile and opened her arms invitingly.

Jamaal released a heavy breath and headed toward his wife.

His movement woke Leila out of the stupor she fell in at the sight of the woman. She couldn't have been there; she was back in New York City.

"Jamaal!" Her yell stopped him halfway. "Jamaal! That can't be Jade! She's back in New York. You know this!"

He hesitated. "Lei, that's my wife. Look at her."

Jade smiled at him. "Who's behind you, Jamaal? I can't see." She tried to peer around him.

"Lei, that's Jade's voice." Jamaal picked back up his advance toward her.

"No, Jamaal! That's not! You know Jade! She wouldn't leave little Eve and Zaira back home!"

That halted Jamaal. He looked back at his partner then turned to Jade suspiciously. "She's right. Where are Eve and Zaira?"

Jade staggered back. "Jamaal, what is this suspicion? You thought I would leave our daughters alone? I asked a friend to watch over them; I couldn't afford to buy them a ticket too. Now, can you please come give your wife a hug? I've missed you so much." She opened her arms again.

Leila could see her partner giving in. *This is a trick.*

"*This is the test of your heart,*" David whispered.

"Jamaal! This is our mental test! That may be Jade to your eyes, but that is not her physically. That's an imposter! That's the wolf! The Changeling!"

It struck a chord. He remembered why he was there. "Jade?"

She smiled. Her eyes changed, flickering from light green to yellow and back quickly.

Jamaal took a step back. "That's not you."

Jade's smile faltered, and she looked devastated. "What? What do you mean, Jamaal?"

He continued to retreat. "My wife is back home. You are not my Jade."

"How dare you talk to me like that! I'm your wife! I'm right here!"

"No, no you're not."

"This is unlike you, Jamaal. What has brought on this change?" Her eyes lit up. "This tournament. I knew it! I knew something wasn't right about it! And you still wouldn't listen to me."

Jamaal's head dropped in shame. "I know, I just didn't want to ruin this chance of—"

"Of what? Chasing a dream?"

"Of providing for you and the girls! I've tried so hard—"

Jade laughed mockingly. "You've done your best? Well, it was never good enough! Do you know how many nights I didn't eat so you and the girls could have supper? You stay in your own little world, thinking everything's okay."

Her hands went to her hips as she planted her feet. "You can't do anything on your own, can you? Someone has to guide you by the hand, and that woman is your newest guide."

"She's not," Jamaal said weakly.

"No? Nothing improved until after she showed up. Your sudden attachment to her has gotten me thinking: am I not good enough for you? Does she make you feel like a man, and you're more driven to impress her?"

"No, that's not—"

She interrupted again. "Or is it that you don't want her to excel past you because she threatens your manhood? You have to keep up with her, so her fame won't reveal your insecurities?"

"No."

"Then, what is it?"

"I can't disappoint you!" Jamaal yelled. His shoulders slumped under embarrassment. "I don't want to fail. I've been nothing but a letdown. I can't let you down again after this lifting your spirits. Lei's not as important as you and the girls."

She scoffed. "Sounds like another excuse."

It took a while like he replayed her words, but his head lifted at her sneer. "Jade's never blamed me for anything before. In fights, something may have been my fault, but she doesn't rub it in my face."

Jade's eyes narrowed, yellow flickering in them again.

His back grew straighter as he continued to talk, "My wife isn't boastful. She ends a fight before we can say something we regret. She has never talked down to me. That is why you are not her."

"I am Ja—"

"You are a fake!" Jamaal took off running toward her. A grin swiped across her lips before she met one of his moves with her own.

Anger and frustration took over the Jamaican's body; he moved swifter but stiffer. The fake Jade blocked every move he performed and then tried to similarly counter which Jamaal recognized and dodged. It looked to have been a practiced routine they performed when sparring with one another in Jamaica.

Leila watched helplessly from the sidelines as the two Jamaicans tried to take advantage over the other but knowing the other's moves made it impossible. The Gordons finally broke away from each other and stood panting, glaring at each other.

"Jamaal," the fake Jade began as she straightened. "I'm sorry. Let's stop this," she pleaded, appearing meek and sincere.

"Don't give in," Leila encouraged.

The Changeling's yellow eyes flashed over Jade's kind green ones. "She's with you!"

"And she's here to stay!" The synchronized Capoeira began again, and still, neither could get the upper hand. The Jamaican woman toyed with him.

Jamaal's intensity skyrocketed when he realized it. His frustration brought out vicious moves Leila hadn't seen before; neither had the fake Jade.

The woman began giving ground under the unfamiliar moves. He struck her repeatedly, endlessly, and since she was unable to block or dodge his moves, she begged for him to stop. Her pleads infuriated him more.

"Jamaal, please! I love you!" she cried out after a series of consecutive hits.

"You're not her!" He slapped her across the face.

Her head snapped to the side, but she whipped back around and glared at him through yellow eyes. If looks could kill, both would have dropped dead.

Green eyes reappeared as she reached up for her husband's face, but Jamaal lashed out at her. He slapped her hand away, curled his hands into fists and drove them into her stomach. Jamaal ignored her cries as her mouth popped open in shock and pain, jumped into the air, and thrust his feet into her chest to send the woman flying backward.

Tumbling for a distance, she ended up lying in a crumpled heap. After a moment, her head came up weakly.

"Jamaal," she called his name, full of betrayal and more than just physical pain. Jamaal started forward, believing once again it was her.

"Jamaal, no," Leila warned.

He stared at his supposed wife before turning to Leila. Fighting his wife etched emotional pain on his face more than anything, horrified at what he did.

Jamaal sighed heavily. "I know, Lei. That is not my Jade."

A terrible screech snapped them around to the woman posing to be Jade Gordon convulsing. She slowly became transparent; her female features melted away, contorting back into the wolf.

Soon, the fake Jade disappeared entirely to be replaced by the mangled wolf hovering where she used to lie.

XLIV.

The wolf remained motionless, watching them with its sick eyes. "I think it's my turn," she said.

Jamaal looked at her, but Leila kept her gaze locked on the wolf, not wanting her fear to be seen. He moved out of the way but brushed her shoulder with a comforting hand. She forced her legs to carry her before the Changeling.

Recognition flashed across the creature's eyes as it focused in on its newest opponent. Once it set its eyes on her, there was no escape, and Leila found herself hypnotized by the strange eyes. The recognition suddenly blazed with anger and a low growl vibrated through sharp, bared teeth.

She expected it to charge, but the ghost-wolf's large head sank down to its chest, and it shook like it had earlier before changing into Jade.

Fear overtook her body. Every muscle and nerve had frozen; she couldn't avert her eyes from the monster going through another transformation. Leila was terrified of whom it would change into. The Phoenix tried to avert her focus, to thaw her, but failed.

Foster. Foster. Change into Bryan Foster. I can fight him, she mentally begged.

The ghost-wolf continued to tremble, becoming more solid as the black smoke billowing out of its lower torso curled around the top half of its body. Growing so dense, Leila couldn't see through the smokescreen as the creature continued its transformation.

Panic shot through her body and took every sane thought from her mind. Her legs were locked into place, ready to spring, but she couldn't move her body. She stared helplessly ahead, dreading who would be standing in the smoke when it cleared.

Foster. Foster. Foster.

A foot materializing out of the black smoke halted her breath, made the presence of the Phoenix trying to keep her together disappear like it never existed, and stopped the spinning world. It wasn't a snakeskin boot but plain black. The smoke began to clear, but she couldn't bring herself to look up at the face.

Her eyes followed the dark denim jeans up from the boot to the belt, but the sight of the man's hands stopped her. Leila could feel the calluses and the gentleness of his hands as they caressed her face. She closed her eyes to shut off the memory of everything they had done together. Leila felt faint. She couldn't see his face. Not now, not here; not as her opponent.

"Lei?"

His voice knocked the breath out of her chest. Her heart pounded, and every fiber of her being wanted to forget everything and run into his safe, warm arms. But she knew if she looked at him, she would lose it: her emotions, her control, everything.

"Lei, what's wrong?" Concern floated toward her. His voice was so warming but luring.

"No," she whimpered as she shook her head.

Footsteps thudded as he approached her—oh how she could see him walking toward her! Leila continued to mumble as she stepped back and shut her eyes tighter. Maybe if she could deny his presence, it wouldn't be real. The Phoenix reappeared, tugging her farther away.

"Lei, why won't you look at me?" He almost loomed over her.

"Lei!" Jamaal broke the dream/nightmare she had created. "Don't open your eyes; don't look at him!"

"Who was that?"

It grew harder to keep her eyes closed—he sounded just like him. "You're not real. You're not here, just like Jade."

"…Jade?"

She could picture the comical confusion on his face just as it coated his voice. The Phoenix screamed in protest, but she craved to see him again, to know he wasn't an imagination. Just one peek…

An eye opened, but the other popped open when he took her breath.

He stood at the exact place where the ghost-wolf disappeared into the black smoke—she'd only imagined him advancing toward her. His presence took place of the Phoenix. His face—his body—was whole and exact, before that fateful night when he was taken from her. When he died.

Her lungs screamed; she had been holding her breath, and she choked for air.

Leila took a big swallow. "David."

The brown-haired man flashed the smile she missed so dearly. Then he chuckled and healed everything in that moment. The wounds in her heart disappeared. Her shattered soul fused back together. All scars—mental, emotional, and physical— were no more. He stood there before her. He never left her alone, just as he had said.

"Lei."

Saying her name brought the tears back Leila thought had dried up. She gasped for air again as she covered her face. The Phoenix broiled within, infuriated that she gave in and replaced it so easily when she knew better.

"Lei, are you okay?" David asked, heavy with concern and love.

She took up shaking her head again. Even as much as she needed him again, she tamped that desire back down. The Phoenix murmured in agreement. "You don't know how much I need you back; it would end all of this, but you can't be here."

"Why do you say that?"

Leila removed her hands to shout at his confused face, "Because you died! You're dead, David!"

David Neal looked at her like she lost it then he stepped toward her. "Lei, I'm not dead; I feel very much alive. I'm right here."

She stumbled back as emotions overwhelmed her body. "I can't do this. I can't." Leila shook her head, hoping to make her dead boyfriend disappear.

Yes, we can; he's not needed anymore, the Phoenix tried to convince her.

"No, no I do need him. He can fill that hole; you can't." Her denial pushed the Phoenix out some.

"Lei, I'm so confused," David Neal said through a nervous chuckle as he continued toward her.

"Leila! Lei! Look at me!" She turned to Jamaal, sorrow creasing his face.

"Remember, that's not him. That's the Changeling. Just like Jade. That may be David to your eyes, but you know he died. He's in your heart. Listen to the true David."

Her coldest wound heated up.

"I did... die." She turned to David, looking around in bewilderment.

Leila nodded. Like Jamaal did with Jade, she had to see through the trickery.

"Yes, David. You died at the hands of Bryan Foster... I went to your funeral." Her voice broke as more tears flowed down her face.

He looked down at his upturned hands. "No, no I wasn't."

"You were, David. I still have all the wounds to prove it. I was in that bank too."

David's head lifted, and his brown eyes widened as her words wrung a bell. "You were in there too."

Leila shut her eyes to block the video replaying his death. "I died too that night, but the paramedics brought me back."

Hardness came into his eyes. It surprised Leila—he never looked at her like that. "I died, yes, I understand that, but you have it wrong."

Fear pulled itself up her spine with freezing fingers. "No, no I don't have anything wrong."

"Yes, you do. Bryan Foster didn't kill me."

Her heart stopped as bullets punctured her lungs at the realization of what he tried to say. Color drained from her face, leaving her weak and shaky.

"No." Her plead came out in a small whisper.

His eyes narrowed. "You killed me."

"No, Foster did." Leila couldn't tell if she tried to convince him or her. She had held on to the doubt that she was to blame—she *truly* dealt the killing blow.

David stabbed at her with an accusing finger. "You shot him, making him shoot me a final time. He's not the guilty one; you are, Leila Wells."

Her knees buckled, and she dropped. "I didn't pull the trigger..." Her voice quivered.

"Who comforted you with those words? You held the gun just as much as Foster did."

For the longest, she stared at the ground, unseeing and not blinking. What else could she say? Only the truth, just as he had laid it out. Her face lifted to see his contempt. "I am so sorry. I wish I would've stayed dead with you."

David looked down at her, disgust plainly written across his face. He shook his head. "There is no apology."

His words shattered her fragile heart piecing itself back together. She couldn't remove her gaze off her lover's scorn; she couldn't breathe, and the tears had even stopped. He was right—she was scum for blaming another when she shared guilt. David's blood stained her hands just as it colored Foster's.

There was no point going on if David couldn't forgive her; no one mattered now. David advanced on her, still spitting out poison, "Everyone upholds you as being strong and brave, but you're nothing but a coward and a weakling for not being able to accept the blame. You've held back the truth, too scared of the looks directed at you. What do people think of you now that your true nature has emerged?"

Something sparked within her. "True nature?"

David replied, but she didn't hear, noticing a pulsating heat in time with her heart. It pulsed like a lighthouse in the inky darkness of night, giving hope of rescue to the hopeless.

Leila shut out the noise and focused on keeping her head above the numbing waters, turning her attention to the beacon. She clawed her way toward it, hypnotized by its light and warmth like a moth to the flame. It beckoned her onward, and she pushed herself harder against the waves trying to beat her down.

A gentle murmur warmed her even more and gave her the strength to keep struggling against the doubts and insecurities she couldn't face. She needed something to protect her frail soul from everything wanting to tear her down; something to take the heat and wouldn't crack under the pressure, instead, it would be fuel. Her dark side—the Phoenix—and it provided the light steering her to the safety of its wings. It waited on the shore.

"*Lei, relent to the Phoenix; let it shield you.*" David's voice drifted through the dark sky and gave her the courage to exit the sea and crawl up onto the shore, collapsing in submission.

Her restraint on her dark side—the temper and heat of anger she tried to keep in check—exploded, and power rushed through her veins in a flood. She had fought against it so long, not wanting to release David in self-realization that she didn't need him to go on. Belief in herself was all she needed. Leila curled into the heat, having it envelop her and the Phoenix's flaming wings folded around her.

Its hot anger surged into her, and she opened her eyes to the imposter David still glaring at her and approaching with hatred blazing in his eyes. The way he moved toward her mirrored a predator stalking its prey.

But his appearance didn't faze her; the Phoenix actually smirked.

"Thank you."

The fake David jolted to a stop, wariness now reflecting in his eyes alongside the anger at the change he saw in her. "For what?"

"For freeing my true nature." The Phoenix ordered her legs to lift her back up so she wouldn't be seen cowering before him.

"A nature of cowardice?"

"Of strength and power."

The imposter sneered. "Trying to deny the truth again, Lei?"

"Don't call me Lei!" she snapped, furnished by the Phoenix's touchy flame. "You are not what David was."

His eyes narrowed like she was still in denial. "I am David."

318

"No, David Neal died. I attended his funeral. I visit his grave every day back in New York City."

"I died because you killed me."

She shook her head and advanced on him. "That's why you're not David; he doesn't blame me for his death. He made a choice to go into the bank too. I have beaten myself down with guilt for his death, but I have been holding in my anger and not directing it toward the only one to blame: Bryan Foster."

As she talked, her confidence grew in the truth of her words, encouraged by what David had been trying to tell her all this time. Holding on to her supposed guilt over his death became her way of holding on to him.

The fake David gave ground under her anger, and that sign of fear fueled the Phoenix. "You caused Foster to raise his arm; you are to blame!" he said.

"David Neal was taken from me for a reason. He was meant to die to push me to discover who I am."

She stopped in front of him, her face inches from his. David's brown eyes disappeared into the yellow eyes of the Changeling, glaring in murderous intensity at her.

Something snapped.

David's arm struck out, but the Phoenix blocked it. His other arm came right after, but she deflected it too. They soon became entangled in each other, deflecting hits and kicks, but never did their eyes break off from one another.

"I am not the one who killed David. I have accepted his death and my own fate without him," she declared.

His eyes flashed, and his lips pulled back in a snarl; now the ravenous animal had reemerged.

She kept going, seeing her sturdy declarations affected the creature. "I am the Phoenix. I had to die to come back stronger."

The fake David chuckled—not the warming rumble of his voice but mocking. "Can you rise from those ashes?"

"I already have."

Leila kneed him to make him stumble back. Before David could react, she jumped to his side and lifted, shooting both legs out, throwing him off his feet and farther away from her.

She returned to her feet, furnished by the angry Phoenix and her belief in herself, to find a dazed David kneeling with one knee up and leaning against it as he tried to clear his head. The Phoenix enjoyed his defeated posture and yanked her forward to finish him off. She sprinted toward her fake boyfriend, put a foot on his raised leg, and propelled herself into the air.

Leila flew like a gust of wind lifted her. David watched her flight in bewilderment. As gravity took control, she twisted her body to kick the man down in the shoulder, and the other foot collided with his head. His head whipped around from the powerful hits, and his body followed.

The fake David tumbled away until he finally lay in a motionless heap. She landed and moved into the Phoenix, looking over at the body of her dead boyfriend. His body began to shimmer and transform back into the ghost-wolf... or so she thought. He lifted his head and struck her with such distress that she faltered out of her stance with a gasp like punched in the stomach.

A hand slid out from under him and reached for her. "Lei."

The Phoenix had been stricken by the look as well, so, without it supplying her power, Leila sank to the floor. A hand of hers started out for his, but then it dropped beside her; she shook her head. "David's dead."

Overwhelming sorrow and failure trickled into the yellow eyes. Defeat overtook it, and David's body shimmered again until he faded away. The Changeling was gone.

She stared at the vacant spot, knowing she should react to the re-death of her boyfriend, but she felt nothing—the Phoenix had wrapped its wings around her heart and pulled it in tight to its chest so nothing could ever penetrate and hurt her again.

"Lei?"

She turned—forgetting that she wasn't alone—to a worried Jamaal cautiously approaching, poised to run toward her.

"Jamaal." Leila just said his name in acknowledgment, not as a whimper or a sign of desperation; she didn't need comforting.

But he did. He looked more shaken by their fight with the Changeling than she did. Jamaal ran out to her, dropped down and clung to her like he needed something firm to steady him before he lost it.

She took a breath to speak; Leila knew she was grounded and wasn't in danger of drifting into the blank waters again, but Jamaal needed to know that. "I didn't get to say goodbye again."

His arms constricted more around her. "Final goodbyes are seldom heard."

A sudden boom echoed out like something large unlatching itself. Startled, Jamaal jerked, but Leila mildly looked up from the spot where the Changeling disappeared to the blackened curtains receding.

As soon as the walls lifted an inch off the floor, noise struck them—the long-awaited roars of the arena applauding their drawn out and difficult victory. Their struggle hadn't been private; it had been watched by everyone in the arena and filmed for those through television.

Leila immediately rose so they wouldn't be perceived as now admitting defeat by staying on their knees; Jamaal followed. Her submission to the Phoenix made Leila secure in a strong foundation, and with the truth of David's death now embraced, she felt liberated. Jamaal beside her seemed shaken by his confrontation with Jade and at what he had done. He didn't find the test of the heart as uplifting.

When the walls lifted high enough, the arena lights blinded the partnership—accustomed to the darkness of their secluded fight, it actually hurt. Their vision soon cleared and saw the standing ovation all around them: the ex-contestants up in the arena seats along with staff members on the ground floor.

An unintelligible chant rippled through the audience and when everyone joined in to make crashing waves of voices in unison, Leila and Jamaal understood what the masses said.

"Panther! Phoenix! Panther! Phoenix!"

Two figures made their way to the Jamaican and the detective, the chubbier one trying to shuffle his feet faster to reach them. The other—much taller and leaner—continued his easy pace, not in any show of excitement like his announcer.

Bob's face was red from whooping and hollering. He shuffled straight to them and threw his chubby arms around them both, squeezing them into him and against one another. His hug was both enthusiastic and full of relief that they had persevered.

"CONGRATULATIONS!" he yelled when he finally released them. "What a remarkable and extraordinary fight!"

Bob moved out of the way so Amadeus Xander could give a congratulatory handshake, still with no sign of being thrilled they had won. Leila noticed once again a strange glee sparkling in his gray eyes, and it didn't fade away—he wasn't excited, like Bob. He was pleased, and it prickled Leila's unease.

"Congratulations," he said coolly. "You fought well."

I think I did to your gain though. She returned his forced gesture of friendliness.

Bob tried to quiet the audience continuing the chant, but he gave up and decided to yell over them—he did have a microphone.

"What a four weeks of fighting we've had!" The audience roared in agreement.

"When we started, quite a few of our contestants stood out as the best contestants for their skills, strength, and power. But unity was the most important factor, so those numbers dwindled to the most remarkable group outlasting everyone, and they have proven that they are the best fighters! They cannot be defeated! They are indestructible! Here are our Rulers of the Realms: Jamaal Gordon and Leila Wells who have persevered yet again—our fighting Panther and everlasting Phoenix!"

Bob turned and showcased the victors. Leila pasted on a smile for appearances as she grabbed Jamaal's hand and bowed to the roars of the arena. When they straightened and finished waving to the delight of the crowd, the multi-billionaire held the microphone. Jamaal didn't release his death grip on her hand, still needing her to keep him grounded.

"I am honored to have discovered such a strong partnership and to have you participate in this tournament; it is only fitting the title of Rulers of the Realms and the Strongest of Hearts is yours. My greatest gratitude goes to you two by representing what this tournament means: True Heart. Thank you." He bowed in gratitude, but Leila didn't feel the meaning it meant to have—it was only for show.

Xander straightened and turned to his audience. "Thank you as well for coming to my island and competing with sportsmanship. Without your participation, this wouldn't have been possible."

He moved over to stand beside Leila and Jamaal, draping an arm over her shoulders as he faced his audience and the cameras. She held back the Phoenix's desire to throw off his arm.

"But all good things must end. It is with great sadness that I declare the Rulers of the Realms Fighting Tag Tournament officially over. Yet, I plan to host another tournament three years from now, and I hope to see all of your faces back to persevere again, so we may crown the next Rulers of the Realms!"

The arena fell along with Xander by ending with roars of anticipation for the next tournament. The always-watching cameras finally removed their gazes off the team; Jamaal released a heavy sigh of relief as the constant pressure of being watched disappeared. He was glad that it was finally over.

Leila knew it wouldn't be. The tournament ended, but their fame just began, along with Leila's admittance to the Phoenix's quest for revenge. She—more than Jamaal from being in the police force—would have even more eyes on her. Nothing would end until Foster was dead.

XLV.

Along with the guys, it seemed the entire island came to congratulate their victory. Leila didn't feel the praise; it wasn't touching her because she didn't want it... or at least, the Phoenix didn't. To satisfy everyone, her thanks came through a twitch of lips for a smile and stiff returns of hugs—none more so than toward Miguel.

She didn't lean into him, comforted into releasing her tension and breathing in the scent of him like before. It felt like they had never shared a kiss or harbored feelings toward one another. In the way he held her close to him, he expected her to break down. Leila bristled because the Phoenix did at how he thought of her as weak.

The Phoenix threw up a wall to protect her even further, shutting her heart away from ghosts of emotions tricking her into pain, and blocking Miguel. Her stiffening and turning to ice made him step away in puzzlement. The defensiveness of the Phoenix in her eyes warned him to stay back, and he did only out of surprise.

Leila responded politely to the call from the police station congratulating hers and Jamaal's victory, but the captain, Heath, and DeMarcus forced enthusiasm—they weren't too sure what to think about her fight with the Changeling. A hesitant conversation awaited her at J.F.K.

Now on the Xander ferry, they headed home. Leaving Jamaal to sleep, she slipped into the bathroom and extended her shower since his fight with the Changeling left him drained. He was abnormally quiet too these past two days.

As she dressed, the foggy mirror continued to draw her toward it, wanting to show off the form that had emerged because of the tournament. Leila wiped a clear streak for her to see.

Her body looked like its old self again—if only better with taut muscles and more defined abs. But not nearly the same because of the discolored circular scars marring her skin. The ones in her arms and at her waist had blended more into healing, but the one nearest her heart would always remain.

Her gaze lifted to her hazel eyes. During the tournament—and her fling with Miguel—life shined through the emptiness in her eyes. Now, a blunt hardness blocked off the light: the Phoenix's hollow and determined eyes reflected back at her. It emerged to take on the hateful world while her soul remained shielded behind it. Nothing would get past its watchful gaze or slip through its impenetrable wall that protected Leila.

"He will," David whispered.

His voice lessened the intensity in her eyes. *How?* she asked.

"Through his experience with his dark side. He will help you control it."

Do I have to control it? It gives me strength.

"Eventually, you will need to. Right now, you must learn to rely on yourself, so it is necessary. But if you feed it too much power, it can be an uncontrollable evil—as is revenge."

Leila threw on a shirt and dried her hair as she thought about his words, both chilling her with the realization that she could lose herself in her drive of revenge and thrilling her with that same idea.

This is a tall wall to scale.

"No, he won't get over it and leave it intact, so the Phoenix's temper will block him off again. He's going to tear that wall down and help you out of the rubble."

Finished dressing, she turned toward the door. *It'll take more than three marches around my wall of Jericho to make it fall.*

"Yes, but once he starts chiseling, it'll all come down."

He must have the best chiseling tool known to man.

"He does, it's his own aching heart."

Uneasy with the thought of anybody slipping under the Phoenix's ever-watchful gaze and protection had the walls closing in tighter. She walked back into the room and found Jamaal propping himself up by his elbows, blinking the sleep out of his eyes.

"We're both exhausted, but you still get up early."

"It's a habit of mine; I can't help it."

He shook his head in disbelief as he threw off the covers, stretched, and disappeared into the bathroom, yawning the whole way.

His slumped shoulders and him dragging his feet expressed his tiredness, but the defeated air around him seemed like he lost instead of won the tournament. He was exhausted, but she could jump right back into fighting. Finally gaining submission, the Phoenix longed to show more of its strength as Leila rested. She now considered the tournament had been invigorating and empowering.

Her eyes caught sight of two envelopes on the coffee table: their earnings from winning the tournament.

Bob disapproved of her asking for all the money to be written out for Jamaal. He actually looked affronted and touched, but he puffed up like a blowfish in preparation of arguing all at the same time. After some bartering, they came to a compromise, with Xander writing three million dollars for Jamaal and the last million written for the New York Police Department—she couldn't take any with thoughts of it being blood money. David's death pushed her into the tournament, and it felt like she was being paid a recompense.

Jamaal showered quickly, and his reemergence brought her out of suspicions of the multi-billionaire. Before she could look him over to see if the realization of them winning had conquered his gloom, a waiter brought breakfast, then vanished.

They ate in silence for a while until Jamaal broke it. "Was it even worth it?"

Leila looked up to his trembling eyes, wishing for an answer but scared of it. "You don't think so?"

"Do you?"

"Do you regret coming to this tournament… or just the Changeling?"

"I… I don't regret…" He looked down at his plate of half-eaten scrambled eggs and bacon. After he couldn't find the right words in his food, he released a heavy sigh. "I don't know."

"Jamaal, tell me what you're feeling."

"I don't want you to think of me as… cowardly or weak."

"You think I would? The only one I can think so lowly of is myself. Now, talk to me."

The Jamaican kept his eyes on his plate and after a while, it came out in a rush. "I just don't know if it was worth me fighting the Changeling or not. It was better for you because you seem more rooted, more confident, and more determined in yourself. Fighting David—the Changeling—empowered you; well, it did to the Phoenix. But it helped you too; you turned to yourself for help instead of David's memory. With me… I feel like I murdered my mother and grandmother, along with my wife. It did nothing to help me. So, was it worth it… for me?"

Leila couldn't answer immediately. He had confirmed what she began to think: his heart wasn't in fighting anymore, but he needed to decide that for himself after some time passed.

"I don't know what to tell you, Jamaal. My fight was just facing my fear and admitting my doubt. Maybe you'll realize the reason for your fight down the road."

He nodded but wasn't entirely in agreement with her. The partners grew silent as they refocused on finishing their breakfast, but neither could; both wrapped up in troubling thoughts.

Putting everything into perspective worried her as well: if someone else saw how beneficial the fight was to her and how degrading it was to him, it confirmed her suspicion of the fight being arranged... but only for her benefit. How did Xander know she needed a final push to give in to her dark side? Why did she need to? The Phoenix bristled at the multitude of thoughts directed at Xander's schemes involving only her. It started to usher her further under its wings so it could face his intentions without hurting her.

"So, what's going to happen to the belt?" Jamaal asked after abandoning his plate. Lost in ruling out possibilities of her role with Xander, Leila didn't hear, so he touched her knee to gain her attention and repeated his question.

Her gaze drifted back to the envelopes where the large golden belt also lay. "Maybe you can take it to Jamaica."

"Jamaica?" he repeated blankly.

"With the thre—the money you won." Finally snapping to, she caught herself before revealing the secret too soon.

Reminding him why he wanted to win the tournament cured his gloominess; Jamaal's face brightened, and his slumped posture straightened. "That's right! We have enough to go back!"

With his mind drifting off to happier thoughts of going home, Leila tried to do the same, but knowing her share would go to the station and returning to New York City wasn't appealing to her, her mind went back to thinking like before.

He brought her back again. "What are you going to do with your share, Lei?"

She scrunched her forehead for a show of concentration. "I don't know yet."

"Well, we can put the belt in Hyun's gym."

His suggestion caught her by surprise, and she blinked at him. "Why his?"

"Why not a gym? We're fighters, and we won it in a fighting tournament. It's where it belongs."

Where do I belong?

Wherever Foster will look, the Phoenix answered, but the question still bothered her.

Cheerful now, he patted her knee as he stood. "Come on, Phoenix, Rin said something about a farewell party today. I'm sure he wants you there... along with another," he added in with a wink.

Luckily, he had turned so he couldn't see the Phoenix flash in her eyes at the playful jab at her attraction to Miguel. She pushed back her anger—it shouldn't be directed at Jamaal or the Spaniard.

He turned to see why she hadn't risen yet; she quickly rose. "Lead the way, Panther," she matched his joking tone to soothe him.

Jamaal turned back to open the door with a grin, and she forced herself to follow, hoping she could control the Phoenix at Miguel.

XLVI.

Fewer people attended this party, for some had left the island earlier. Luke tried to keep Leila and Jamaal captive in their circle, but ex-contestants continued to pull them away for pictures and more congratulations. Leila fought to keep a smile plastered on her lips. It brought relief, though, for she continually avoided an approach of Miguel, asking why she had acted as she did. But she couldn't escape his questioning gaze pressing down on her.

"Grab them before someone else can," Maso ordered the group after they returned with a dark blue camera in his hands.

He got someone to take the picture as they gathered in: Alvaro, Miguel, Shamus, and Maso got behind the four in the front. Rin made sure to get beside Leila and brazenly draped as arm across her shoulders. The Italian's touch irritated the Phoenix, and Leila struggled against the rising heat to punch him; Miguel inching closer in preparation of doing the deed made it nearly impossible to maintain control.

They took a few retakes because Luke made faces, but Leila used it to mask her features since the Phoenix didn't care who saw her temper. Maybe Miguel would feel the heat and be warded off...

Everyone felt the heat of the Phoenix from them skirting around her, unsure of what was going on and unwilling to find out. But he ignored it. The Spaniard grabbed her shoulder and pulled her to the side after they finished taking pictures; it took an immense effort not to throw off his hand.

"What is going on? You're avoiding me; why?" he whispered; hurt weighed down his voice.

The Phoenix glared. "This is what you told me to do. Is it not to your liking?"

"This is the Phoenix?"

"What did you expect? Something you could control by saying the right words, like you usually do to ensnare women?"

Miguel winced. "Is that why you think I said that? In the beginning, yes, I viewed you as another beautiful woman, but that was before I got to know you and realized you understood my pain. I've never cared about someone like you, and neither have I had a connection."

"There was never a connection."

He couldn't reply for the longest. "So, I meant nothing to you?"

She started to walk off. "Of course you did, but not anything that mattered."

He turned her back to him roughly, desperately. "Don't turn away from me yet. We just began to heal each other; I need you to finish it."

She peeled his hand off her arm. "It's time for us to heal ourselves." This time, he didn't stop her from returning to the group.

Leila's return without Miguel brought a long and awkward silence. Rin tried to cover it up. "So, what's everybody's plan when you get home? We're headed back into the ring." He gestured between him and Maso.

Luke hung his head. "Back to work."

"It can't be that bad." Jamaal attempted to lighten his mood. They didn't need the peppiest of the group to also fall under Leila's gloomy cloud.

Shamus laughed. "It is when your entire family runs a Chinese restaurant, and they stick you in the back doing dishes. They don't trust him to do anything since a Fortune cookie incident."

Luke's lips poked out in a pout for his partner bringing it up. No matter how much the others begged, Shamus wouldn't explain—either out of politeness or enjoyment at toying with them.

"I'm headed back to work, too," Leila began. "I've been away from the force too long."

"What criminal would want to challenge a Ruler of the Realms?" Shamus asked.

Alvaro chuckled. "A stupid one."

Bryan Foster would. The thought of a future confrontation thrilled the Phoenix, and Leila.

"Why back to work for? You have money now." Luke speaking pulled her back.

"It's my life; it's what I do best."

Maso looked at her incredulously. "If you consider your expertise in fighting lower than your job as a detective, I don't see how there are any criminals in New York City!"

The men continued talking about her skills in fighting compared to her fame in the police department, but it faded into the background as the captain's voice overshadowed them: 'This life was yours *and* David's. Now you need to ask yourself if you can do this job alone.'

The horn blowing outside brought Leila out of her thoughts to see Lima on the horizon. A crew member guided everyone onto the deck to take a group shot of the contestants. Those with their own cameras handed theirs to the crew members, then they piled into the picture.

They were organized according to rank in the tournament: Leila and Jamaal kneeling in the front as the winners, Haloani and Kaiapo Ikaika squatting beside them as the finalists; Miguel and Alvaro stood behind them as the sole semifinalists since the Japanese women were on the other ship headed back toward Tokyo; the rest of the contestants bunched behind them.

The crew members took the multitude of pictures and finished as the South American harbor came into view. Everyone dispersed to their rooms for their luggage.

"You think you'll return?" Jamaal asked when they returned to their rooms.

"Without you? Doubtful."

"I think you should. Find someone who'll match your fighting level and won't drag you down with lack of surveillance skills or slow thinking."

"Jamaal, I am no more of a fighter than you are. I just use a dark side in my fighting. What I need is more restriction."

"Restriction or control?"

She zipped up her duffel bag before responding. "A little of both, I think."

"You'll figure it out."

Once again, she couldn't respond in a timely fashion. "Before I hurt another."

It was needed, the Phoenix said.

"Another?" Jamaal asked as he opened the door and the Spaniards walked past. Alvaro gave a small wave, but Miguel didn't acknowledge them, he just kept his furrowed eyes forward. "Oh."

Leila appreciated his cold shoulder, but she still felt a stab at his denial—she had grown too accustomed to him looking at her out of the corner of his eye. The Phoenix helped her brush off that longing.

Crew members waved in farewell as the surge of passengers disembarked. Noise from the docks welcomed their return along with individual calls of names and applause for their victories.

Once off the gangplank, contestants hurried into the embrace of loved ones: men and women to their lovers, children running up to their mothers or fathers, friends greeting friends with smiles, hugs, handshakes, or slaps of backs for congratulations, and even parents waiting for their grown children.

Those who didn't have someone waiting snagged a taxi and headed to the airport without any delay. Leila and Jamaal reached the airport in no time and set out for their terminal—all return trips paid for by Xander—joined soon by Shamus and Luke.

A flight attendant came on the speaker to announce first-class to board. The hurried arrival of Maso, Rin, and Alvaro pulled them out of line.

"We want to see you off." Rin gave everyone a handshake, but he saved a hug for Leila.

"Will I see you in three years?" he asked only her.

"I don't know. I guess I have to see."

"You see us again!" Luke piped up, overhearing Rin's question. The Italian nodded for him, but Leila not being set on coming back disappointed him.

Rin released her to give Maso and the one Spaniard a goodbye hug. "He's sulking," Alvaro whispered when she hugged him.

The Phoenix felt smug but not Leila, not entirely. "I hope it's not only me."

"It's also going home without vengeance."

Now pointing it out, she felt the same: fearing the defeated return to hollow memories of a past life.

"I understand."

"I know you are ending things, but don't forget about us."

"I don't think I could."

His deep grin understood more than her words. "You're not alone, Leila, but come to Spain if you feel it. We don't have to include him."

"That sounds impossible, but I don't see myself heading overseas anytime soon."

"Just know. *Adios*, Leila."

After a final hug, he straightened and addressed those leaving, "*Buen Viaje*."

Everyone waited for him to explain, and after looking around, realization hit him. "My translator's not here. Safe travel."

The group of New Yorkers waved a final time to the Italians and Spaniard before they disappeared into the terminal.

Leila and Jamaal found their seats in the first-class section. Shamus and Luke were placed behind them—Luke sitting by the window so he could watch the runway fly past as they took off.

"We're headed home." Jamaal longed to be back.

"Home," she repeated; a place she missed, feared, and now knew could never hold warmth and a sense of belonging for her. It would never be her home again.

XLVII.

The plane skidded down the slick runway when they landed at J.F.K. International Airport. Rain was gone, but the clouds remained murky and gray, threatening to unleash their load again.

"Daddy!" a unison of familiar squeals sounded out when they came into sight of the lobby. Two little black girls ran toward the woman and three men. Jamaal threw his duffel bag on the floor, dropped to his knees, and flung open his arms so his daughters could pummel into his chest.

"I. Have. Missed. You. So. Much." After every word, he alternated between kissing Zaira and Eve, pulling forth giggles and return kisses from both.

The real Jade Gordon hovered behind her children, being patient but wanting to throw herself at her husband like them.

Jamaal stood and cut off whatever she began to say by seizing her face and kissing her hard. Her eyes popped open in shock, but she melted into the kiss and returned it just as feverishly.

"My Jade," he murmured when he finally broke away from her, tracing the curves of her face. "My Jade. Am I lacking?"

Either the way he said it or the look in his eyes alarmed her. She kissed him instead of delving into what caused him to say that. "Never in my eyes. Others may think so, but that means so am I. We're a team; we always will be."

Leila turned from the Jamaican family to give them privacy to her own familiar faces: David's parents, Heath, DeMarcus, the captain, Hyun and Nuan. She didn't hurry like Jamaal by throwing her bags on the floor but took her time, making sure her mask—shielding her emotions—was secure before meeting those familiar eyes full of pity, worry, and questions she couldn't answer.

The first was Captain Sullivan. Even though his eyes were cloudy with questions and murky with sadness at seeing what she went through, he placed on a genuine smile and opened his arms. "There's our New York's Finest."

Heath scoffed as she moved into the captain's arms and received an extra-long squeeze. "And what are we?" He motioned between him and DeMarcus.

"New York's Most Complaining."

DeMarcus scowled as his partner defended himself. "It's his fault!" Heath pointed at the black man. "Now with Lei back, I don't have to deal with him any longer."

The accused turned to his accuser. "It's the opposite, and I'm equally glad Lei's back so she can pull you away to leave me to my station."

"Your station?"

Heath and DeMarcus continued to fuss at each other. Leila looked at the captain. "Sounds like I've been missed."

Captain Sullivan chuckled. "More than you know. You're the only one who can handle their leashes. And *my* station will be much quieter and organized with you back." He made sure to loudly announce his ownership so the two arguing could hear.

With the Phoenix's temper, I might just scramble us into a tangle we can't unwind.

The two partners quit bickering long enough to give her a hug and a few congratulatory words on her win.

But Heath strained her hold on the Phoenix. "Umm, Lei, can I ask you about—"

"Not now." He mumbled something as she briskly walked away toward Hyun and Nuan. Already, the Phoenix's defensiveness walled her in, not allowing her to hurt herself with going over her fight with David again.

The grinning Hyun in his traditional relaxed attire and stance—shirt, jeans over cowboy boots, and his black ponytail—and Nuan smiling in a simple blouse, black pants, and flats pushed the rising wall back down, so Leila could emerge and truly embrace her friends with feeling.

Even though they whispered congratulations, they spoke more through their long and tight squeezes. They hated what she went through, but she needed it. Leila absorbed that thought like a desert longing for water: she needed to experience a self-reflection; she had become too numb and required an awakening.

What they hadn't seen yet, and what she didn't know, was if she pushed that self-reflection too far. David said that she needed the Phoenix, but had she awoken a slumbering beast that could spiral out of control?

"We have something to tell you," Nuan began after they broke their hug.

"But not until you are done greeting everyone," Hyun finished with a knowing look at the Asian woman.

She turned to David's parents. They both opened their arms like inviting a child home, their eyes warm and cushiony. "We are so proud of you, Lei," Julianne Neal began.

David Sr. pulled her out of his arms to cup her face. "And so is David." At the mention of his son's name, the Phoenix threw up the wall around Leila again. Concern crossed into the father's face seeing the change in her eyes and feeling the stiffening of her body.

He obviously wanted to question the sudden wall in her eyes but pulled her back into him. The tighter hug told Leila that seeing the price of her moving on scared him.

She could only nod—worried what the Phoenix might slip through her mouth—and turned to find Shamus and Luke speaking with her fellow partners, and Jamaal with his arm around Jade's waist speaking with the captain. His daughters were intertwined around his legs but peeking around them at Leila; seeing her now free, they ran toward her.

Eve reached her first with her arms out, expecting to be lifted. Leila pulled her up for a tight squeeze as Zaira wrapped her arms around her thighs, only her head reaching her waist.

"Are you okay, Miss Lei?" Eve innocently asked.

Leila hoped the girls didn't feel her jolt. "Why do you ask that?"

"Because you didn't look happy after your last match, and you still don't look happy now, even though you're home."

"I'm fine." She pulled the girl in for another hug, hoping it would reassure her.

"That was a mean trick they did!" Zaira declared as she ducked her head into Leila's thigh.

"I know, but just a trick."

"Like in a magic show?"

Leila couldn't answer, so she nodded.

"What kind?"

"One to trick your heart."

Zaira frowned. "I don't like that one; I like it when things disappear."

I do too.

"Alright, girls, I want to give Lei a hug," Jade said as she moved toward them. Eve clambered down as her sister released Leila's leg, freeing her to accept their mother's hug.

"Thank you for watching after Jamaal; I'm grateful that you were there to bring him back."

"He helped me too."

"But not as much as you did," Jamaal stated as he came up beside his wife.

She pulled Jamaal out of his sea at his struggle against the Changeling, but he just helped her maroon herself on an island, shrouded from view by the Phoenix's wings.

Leila couldn't respond, so she turned to Hyun and Nuan. "Now can you tell me what I don't know?"

Nuan glanced at Hyun, and after a smile of approval, she held out her left hand. A chilling apprehension stung Leila before she ever caught sight of the single set, flawless diamond engagement ring.

She masked the light dimming in her eyes by turning her attention solely to the ring. "You proposed without telling me?"

Hyun shrugged. "I wasn't able to bring it up."

"I knew he had something planned because he never babbles on around me," Nuan began.

As she pretended to admire Nuan's ring, Leila rubbed her own ring finger, feeling the ghostly presence of David's ring. She had tried it on a few times but never told them David planned to propose. Nuan lowering her hand for the little girls straining to see gave her more time to shake it off completely.

Leila scoffed. "Aren't you fortunate."

"Watch it, Lei," he warned. "You may have won the tournament, but you won't stand a chance without Jamaal if you went against me."

"You want to bet?"

The Phoenix flashed in her eyes at the challenge and Hyun unfortunately saw. He brushed it off but gave her a quick questioning look. "Never mind; I've grown too soft from being out of the competitions."

"Blame that," the Phoenix said victoriously.

The engaged couple blinked in disbelief at the boldness of Leila's change; Nuan ended the shock before it could become awkward. "We need to get going soon; I don't want to be caught in the rain."

Shamus and Luke tagged along. The group made their way through the airport with a few people recognizing them and asking for either an autograph or a picture.

Leila and Jamaal waited with them for a cab while their friends and family headed to the parking lots for their vehicles.

"Keep yourselves out of trouble or I'll be paying you a visit," Leila warned, then hugged the two Brooklynites.

"Does that mean you'll get us off the hook?" Shamus hoped.

"Depends on the crime."

"Might be only time to see you; you might be real busy," Luke butted in as their cab pulled up.

"We'll see."

"Bring a smile!" Luke said through his own. He avoided her eyes shooting to him by hugging Jamaal then slipping into the taxi.

"Leila," Shamus began as he came up to her after speaking with Jamaal. The Phoenix turned, expecting him to say something as well from his hesitant air.

He gave a brief smile and rubbed her arm. "Hope to see you again someday." Shamus ducked into the backseat; the door shut, and the yellow car sped off toward Brooklyn.

I don't need any pity, the Phoenix declared. Insulted air radiated off her skin and maintained the heavy silence between her and Jamaal. The Gordons' white sedan pulling up to the curb punctured the Phoenix's bubble around Leila so she could be cordial by saying goodbye.

"Jamaal, don't refuse it when you get home," Leila said when they broke out of their hug.

His brow furrowed. "Refuse what?"

She opened the passenger door for him. "You'll see."

The puzzlement turned to a disappointing frown. "Bye, Lei." He gave her another hug but then cupped her face so she would look at him. "Take care... and stay you."

She couldn't hold his gaze for long and couldn't say that she would; she nodded instead. Jamaal took in a breath to speak but let it go and got in the car. Leila shut the door after the girls and Jade said their goodbyes, then watched the car head toward the city.

David's parents drove up to take her home.

Julianne gushing about her fights and how they were so proud of her covered up the tension in the car—of the complete dominance of the Phoenix over Leila's curt answers and the parents wanting to ask her about the fight with their dead son. With the conversation mainly one-sided, she focused on the city outside the window. Everything was familiar: the sounds, the buildings, streets; but she felt no sense of homecoming—all dull, uninteresting. New York City had just become another city.

After spending an extra fifteen minutes in normal New York traffic, Leila entered her apartment with David's parents. She didn't need Julianne's explanation to know she kept her place dust-free during her time away.

"Is there anything that you may need? A run to the store?" Julianne began when she re-emerged after disposing of her duffel bag in her bedroom.

"No, I'll do it later. I just want to—"

"Be home," Julianne added in for her with a smile.

Not how she would've put it. Leila didn't need to spend more time with them before she got acquainted with the Phoenix. Being around anyone wouldn't be a good idea. "Yes."

"Well then, I guess we'll go," she suggested and hugged Leila in farewell. "I'm glad you're back."

David Sr. didn't move, and she readied herself. "Lei, why was David, or what appeared to be David, there?"

She couldn't keep hoping to brush off the subject like she did with Heath; they had a right to know about their son. With Julianne's downcast eyes and silence, she wished to know too.

But she didn't know herself, and how to word it to them. The conflict worked in her hesitation and across her face.

"I… I don't know, Mr. David. I've come to see it as a reflection; a chance to face my fears on my involvement with his death. But how… I don't have the slightest clue."

They remained silent for a while. "So, is that…?"

"Yes, that is how it really happened. I thought I had killed him, but I couldn't tell anyone because I couldn't bear the thought of rejection." The Phoenix rose to protect her. "Now that you know the truth, if you do want to disown me, I won't be devastated; I'm stronger now, I can take it."

She couldn't remove her stare off the wall behind them to tell if anger or shock kept them silent.

"How could we possibly…" Julianne began and pulled Leila's eyes over to her. Tears brimmed in her green eyes, and she shook her head. "Always thinking of others before yourself." She hugged Leila again, but Leila actually returned the hug, relieved at her acceptance. She looked over at David Sr. to find his eyes watery.

"Leila, you are like a daughter to us. How could we possibly disown you when we need you?" He came forward to hug her as well, enveloping them both.

It was ridiculous that she even considered the possibility for a second.

"Now, no more thinking like that, okay?" Julianne fussed when they pulled back.

"I'll try."

"You know to call us for anything."

"I do."

David Sr. stepped up when his wife stepped back. He touched her face tenderly, then kissed her on the jaw. Julianne touched him to go, and with a final look at her, the two left.

Leila let out a big sigh of relief. The Phoenix had prepared for unnecessary scenarios. Her dark side only focused on the negative, not allowing a sliver of hope that could so easily be snuffed out and hurt her.

She remained in the living room, not moving and trying not to talk herself out of the decision she made on the flight back. Her phone ringing in her pocket pulled her out of her stupor to find Jamaal on the ID.

He found out.

"You can't take it back," she beat him to talk. "Xander's not going to sign another."

"Lei, it's too much! You don't have a fair share!" Jamaal defended.

"To me it is."

"You didn't keep any for yourself, did you?"

Her silence confirmed his suspicion.

"Who are you giving it to?"

There was no point in lying. "I'm giving it to the police station."

Jamaal remained quiet for a moment. "Why will you never take something?"

"Others deserve it more than I do."

"I think you do deserve it."

She wasn't going to say why she wouldn't, because then he would demand his money go back too. "I got what I needed. And I planned this if we won."

"I… we can't take all of this."

"You are, and you're taking your family to Jamaica like you planned."

"But Lei—"

His persistence to argue irked the Phoenix, and her voice came out harsher than she wanted, "No. You're taking it all and going to Jamaica; you need some time away to think. There's no more discussing this."

Jamaal didn't respond for the longest, and she thought she had frustrated him to where he hung up. "And you don't need time away to think?"

"I've had my chance, now it's yours. I've kept myself away long enough."

"But now it seems like you're distancing yourself more, like you're cutting all ties!"

"Jamaal—"

He cut her off. "You've come back as someone else, and you're pushing away those that want to help you."

"That's not what I'm doing. I've been hiding and supported by others for too long; now I have to stand on my own."

"You promised me you wouldn't become too attached. It's sounding like you are because the Lei I know wouldn't let something take her place."

"The Leila you knew was timid and fragile; that is not me!" the Phoenix snapped.

He didn't argue back. She pushed her dark side down to feel the guilt. "Jamaal, I'm sorry…"

"That wasn't her, but neither is this. Hold on to who you are, Lei." The line went dead.

She looked at the black screen where Jamaal's grinning face disappeared. Part of her didn't feel guilty—it was necessary for her to focus on herself for once. But she didn't have to shove him away; that was the Phoenix's plan and how easy she gave control over to it worried her.

Speaking of necessities—her eyes drifted to a picture of her and David then to the window, still overcast but not raining. Leila couldn't hold it off any longer.

She grabbed her car keys and left.

XLVIII.

L eila parked before looking over at the willow tree and the headstone beneath it. Grabbing an umbrella in case it decided to rain, she opened the car door and headed up the hill.

She stopped at the receded bump, hoping her conversation with David would go better than the one with Jamaal. What she came to do nearly sent her running, but the Phoenix banished that idea of flight—it would have its say.

"I can already see this might be a problem," Leila began.

David speaking eased the Phoenix's presence, "*It will if you give it too much control.*"

"It seems that it already is."

"*Only because you haven't fully given in to it; you're still trying to hold on to who you were.*"

She sat down beside him. "So, what it said through me to Jamaal is true?"

"*Yes, and no. You're not who you were before, and you're not who you are now. It will fight you to go for revenge; it will convince you that is the only path. Nobody becomes who they are until they find balance with their dark sides.*"

"How am I to find balance if I can't find equal ground?"

"*Him.*"

He didn't say any more, letting her think unhindered since the Phoenix backed off, waiting for her to do it.

She let out a long breath. "Then I can't go on like this, David. As much as I crave your voice, I'm not moving on; I'm still holding onto you. I have to pull away and do this on my own if I'm to focus on my promise."

She could imagine a sad smile. "*I know. I could only provide comfort as you looked inside and saved yourself. That is all I can do. You see now that I'm not needed.*"

"So, are you leaving me now… completely?"

"*No, I never will until you let me go. I won't be a constant presence, but I'm not gone. I'll step in if the Phoenix becomes too much. Call on me, and I'll be there.*"

Something light touched her hand and before she could look, another touch landed on her head.

"*It's starting to rain.*"

Leila reached for the umbrella she brought but stopped.

"Can we do something together?"

"*How could I say no?*"

"Remember that day in the park when the captain forced a break on us?"

"*I do.*"

"Remember me suggesting we lay in the rain?"

"*I think this is considered a drizzle, not rain.*"

She smiled with him as the slight mist picked up to hard droplets. "It's raining now."

"*Good.*"

Leila lay down, parallel with David six feet under. The rain increased to a downpour, but it didn't matter that she became soaked.

"*Lei, I want you to know that I couldn't let you go either.*"

Her intake wavered, but she let it go smoothly, soothing her emotions. Now she was grateful for the Phoenix's composure. "I know."

David didn't speak anymore. Water poured down her face, indiscernible as the rain or her tears.

If you loved this book, please leave a review on Amazon and Goodreads—it helps me and potential readers!

Thanks again!

TURN THE NEXT PAGE FOR A SNEAK PEEK

Read a little bit of the sequel
to ASCENSION OF THE PHOENIX!

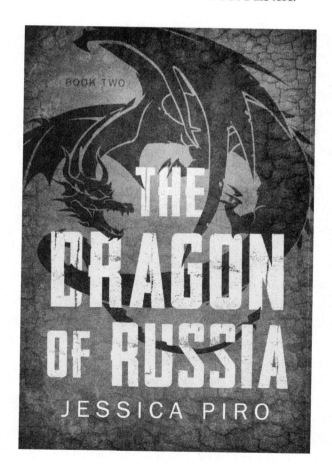

I.

I could live here.

Few sights could compare to the warm, welcoming palette of Michigan in summer. No clouds had marred the sun shining on the trees during her two-day stay, and now it sparkled on the clear waters of the lake outside her window; everything advertised warmth, comfort, tranquility, and a sense of settling down.

No, not until Foster is dead, the Phoenix declared. *New York City draws him, not a boring place like this. We will wait there for his return.*

The Phoenix was right. Leila couldn't get distracted. But... her eyes returned to the lake. What if she left uninteresting and routine New York City for a place like this? She could forget revenge, forget Foster and David, and hide in this wilderness. Didn't she deserve happiness too?

We won't find happiness until he's dead. You know this.

A light groan followed by the sliding of a shoe on the wood floor sounded behind her. She didn't turn, not wanting to lose sight of the scenery despite the Phoenix's attempts to dilute its beauty. If she opened the screen door, she'd be free.

Why can't I run? Wouldn't it be easier?

After what we've been through and devoted, you want to give it up? No, your regret and guilt would kill us.

But I'd be safe. No one would ever get hurt again trying to protect me. Leila placed her hand on the rough wood framing the screen window, preparing to push.

Don't be naïve! Foster wouldn't stop because you did. He would hurt everyone you left behind because we weren't there to protect them. Because you only thought of yourself. Because you were cowardly.

"Wha—" someone said behind her.

She pulled her hand off the door. *Fine, I get it. I can't run. I can't stop.* For the first time, clouds passed over the sun, and Michigan darkened. It wasn't as inviting or promising of a care-free future.

"Detective Wells?"

She still didn't bother to turn, but the Phoenix became her voice as it did so often now. "I honestly thought you were smarter than to run from me."

He grunted, and the chair creaked as he struggled against his handcuffs. "I thought you couldn't come here."

"I can't unless I'm invited." She propped against the cabin wall, still refusing to look at him. "I was going to let you go—let the ones that call themselves 'detectives' claim you, but they were having trouble. In two days, I tracked you here to your cabin."

"Then you're done. You got me."

"Technically, yes. I'm taking you back to New York for the trial of murdering Howard Stanen, and that would be it—I did my job."

She let the apprehension grow by trailing off. "But…?"

"Howard Stanen tried to redeem himself by turning you in—he had good intentions. Since you know who I am, you know I go beyond what I am called to do and make it a personal priority to see things through.

"I know your supply comes from here and that you are one of the leaders. You are going to tell me where to find the drug labs, I will relay the locations over to the detectives, they and the rest of the nation will be rid of one less drug cartel, and we will return to New York where I will go on about my business and you will go to prison."

Astonished that she had everything planned like a vacation agenda kept him speechless until the ridiculousness of it all brought out his laughter. "Turn on my guys? Are you serious? You've grown too used to getting your way. The famed Phoenix can't scare me!"

She let him enjoy his laughter for a while. "What about death?"

It disappeared. "What?"

"Aren't you afraid of dying? Most people are."

"Are you threatening me?"

Leila finally turned to face Emilio Delgado-Valdez, originally from Puerto Rico and now a U.S. citizen, cuffed to the wooden chair she had found in his abandoned-cabin-getaway. The Phoenix gloated at his blanching. "I'm promising you."

"You-you can't do that... You're a cop!"

"You think that will stop me?"

"It should!"

"I'm not the Detective Leila Wells from before, am I?"

Valdez tried to stare her down, but the Phoenix overwhelmed him into backing off. After weighing his options, his shoulders slumped in defeat—there wasn't a doubt in his mind now. "It doesn't matter. I'm dead either way."

"It matters because I'm sure they won't be so merciful in their killing tactics." His face turned white, confirming what Leila figured the drug lords would do to him when caught. "Or you could live in cushy witness protection, and they'll be here in prison. It's just, you will always be watching your back.

"I prefer an eye-for-an-eye, but you can convince me otherwise." Leila folded her arms and leaned against the wall. "So, what will it be?"

"I'll never snitch."

"You sure? There's nothing I can do to change your mind?"

"We all die in the end."

"Brave words." She pushed off the wall and walked toward him. "But hollow."

His eyes widened at the sight of her gloved hands. "Why are you wearing gloves?"

She kneeled beside him. "To keep my fingerprints off the syringe you shot up with to overdose on heroin. Why else?" She tied his arm off and grabbed the waiting syringe on the floor.

"I wouldn't overdose!"

"Tell me a junkie, like yourself, wouldn't. Picture it: the walls closing in about you as you trapped yourself, me breathing down your neck, and the reminder of the drug cartel coming for your head if one of them gets caught. You have a way out; why not escape it all with one last high? That is what I will tell them. Now, convince me it won't work."

His bottom lip quivered as she pulled up the syringe, removed the cap, and tapped it to test the needle. "No one will believe you."

"And who would believe a drug dealing-murdering-junkie over a renowned detective with no incriminating evidence?"

Valdez couldn't argue. She patted his arm to ready the vein, then looked at him. "Last chance."

His mouth flopped like a fish, speechless. His eyes remained glued to the syringe holding his death.

She gave him longer to recover but then lowered the needle when he still didn't speak.

Order *The Dragon of Russia*!

WANT MORE?

Was Jamaal a favorite of yours? Want a little bit more of him?
Check out the companion short story, *The Panther's Pride*.

*Available only as an ebook!

ACKNOWLEDGMENTS

Without our unfathomable God, *none* of us would be alive to read, and I wouldn't have this ability to tell stories. So, He deserves praise above all others.

Now, down to Earth, there are some fellow humans who have helped me along this writing journey, and with *Ascension of the Phoenix* in particular. Huge thanks to Mark Gardner for giving me countless marketing advice. (I suggest checking out his books, reader.) To Fay Lane for designing my book covers. To my editor, Paul Martin with Dominion Editorial, for catching my comma misuse and correcting ALL the capitalization errors (I'm so embarrassed I did that. Sorry!). My beta readers and more fellow authors, Simon Hillman and Michael Holiday, your suggestions tightened my story from its fragile beginning. Everyone on the Keep Calm and Write On Discord chat—y'all have helped tremendously.

Savanah Allen, thank you SO MUCH! You've stuck with Leila since the beginning, you've helped proofread (Five-Animals Fung Fu), and you've always been supportive. I hope I can keep you as a #1 fan!

Mom and Dad, never have y'all told me I couldn't do something, and my love of books stems from both of you. Dadoo (John) and Jacob, thanks for making light of this hard writing process. (And don't worry, y'all weren't side characters killed… in this book.) Mawmaw Mae and Pawpaw John, thank y'all for being with me, too, and always asking about updates—and when I would get rich.

To my church family. So many of y'all have been supportive. Especially Ms. Sandy Lowintritt who this book is dedicated to—because of your enthusiasm for my writing.

Even though they're no longer around, thanks to the websites *Authonomy.com* and *WriteOn.com*, and all the users on there. Without these sites, I wouldn't have gotten the courage to release my book babies into the world and grown thicker skin to take criticism—good or bad. Thanks also goes to *Wattpad.com* for further growing my author journey.

And finally, to you the reader. I wrote this story mainly for you to enjoy. Without readers, authors wouldn't exist.

ABOUT THE AUTHOR

Jessica Piro is the author of The Phoenix Trilogy, which has won multiple accolades, writes in multiple genres, and is in a wheelchair with Type 1 Diabetes. Her work caters to young adults, new adults, and adults.

She graduated from the University of Louisiana at Monroe in 2015 with a Bachelor of Arts in English and a minor in History. She lives in Northeast Louisiana with her parents and two brothers.

You can find her on X (formerly Twitter) @AuthorPiro or Instagram @authorpiro. For updates on upcoming books, or even access to FREE works, visit jessicapiro.com.

Made in the USA
Columbia, SC
28 July 2024

39441732R00202